PRAISE FOR CANDACE

"If you need an infusion of ~~~~~~~~~~~~ t the prescription!"

+++**IRENE HANNON,** best ~~~~~~ ~~~~~ ~~ ~~~ ~~ es of Quantico series

"Talk about fiction first aid! *Nobody* writes a prescription for heart-pounding medical drama/romance like Candace Calvert. A gritty glimpse into the heart and soul of Mercy ER and its men and women in the trenches, *Code Triage* is an adrenaline high with professional realism ripped from today's headlines and enough romantic tension to spike your pulse. An ER (exciting read!) experience you will never forget. . . . I *loved* it!"

+++**JULIE LESSMAN,** award-winning author of the Daughters of Boston series

"In *Code Triage* . . . Candace Calvert paints medical scenes that ring with authenticity and drama, while giving us a glimpse into the lives and hearts of the people behind the stethoscope. This is great writing that's full of faith and hope."

+++**RICHARD L. MABRY, MD,** author of *Code Blue*

"Candace Calvert has proven she knows her stuff on the ER stage. Excellent writing, appealing characters, and an honest portrayal of human emotions—this book is a great read, and I predict a huge reader-ship for the author."

+++**HANNAH ALEXANDER,** author of *A Killing Frost* and the Hideaway series

"*Disaster Status* grabs the reader from its opening pages to its rivet-ing end. Compelling characters keep you turning the pages to see what happens next."

+++**MARGARET DALEY,** author of *Forsaken Canyon* and *Together for the Holidays*

"Candace Calvert succeeded in thrilling me, chilling me, and filling me with awe and respect for ER trauma."

+++**DIANN MILLS,** author of *Breach of Trust* and *Sworn to Protect*

"The story flows well and keeps the reader's attention. . . . Characters find not only psychological healing, but also spiritual renewal."

+++*CHRISTIAN RETAILING*

"This is such an action-packed, heartfelt, really gripping story. I just couldn't put it down."

+++**NORA ST. LAURENT,** Novel Reviews

"Good-bye, *ER*. Hello, *Critical Care*! Candace Calvert delivers a wonderful medical romance that peeks inside the doors of an ER to discover a cast of real-life characters who learn to love and live and discover God's truths, all in the high-stress world of medicine."

+++**SUSAN MAY WARREN,** award-winning author of *Happily Ever After* and *Nothing but Trouble*

"I've always said if I weren't an author, I'd be in the medical field, so it's no wonder I ate up Candace Calvert's *Critical Care*. I lived and breathed the problems and struggles in the ER along with the characters. Terrific story and terrific writing."

+++**COLLEEN COBLE,** author of *Cry in the Night* and *Lonestar Secrets*

"Finally, a reason to turn off *ER* and *Grey's Anatomy*. Here is a realistic medical drama with heart. Candace Calvert gets it right with page-turning prose, a heartwarming love story, and hope."

+++**HARRY KRAUS, MD,** best-selling author of *Salty Like Blood* and *Could I Have This Dance?*

Code Triage

CANDACE CALVERT

TYNDALE HOUSE PUBLISHERS, INC.

CAROL STREAM, ILLINOIS

Visit Tyndale's exciting Web site at www.tyndale.com.

Visit Candace Calvert's Web site at www.candacecalvert.com.

TYNDALE and Tyndale's quill logo are registered trademarks of Tyndale House Publishers, Inc.

Code Triage

Designed by Mark Anthony Lane II

Edited by Sarah Mason

Published in association with the literary agency of Natasha Kern Literary Agency, Inc., P.O. Box 1069, White Salmon, WA 98672.

Library of Congress Cataloging-in-Publication Data

Calvert, Candace, date.
  Code triage / Candace Calvert.
    p. cm. — (Mercy hospital ; no. 3)
    ISBN 978-1-4143-2545-3 (pbk.)
    1. Women physicians--Fiction. I. Title.
  PS3603.A4463C63 2010
  813'.6—dc22   2010004052

Printed in the United States of America

16 15 14 13 12 11 10
 7   6   5   4   3   2   1

For Andy,
my real-life hero and husband—
you made me believe in happily ever after.

ACKNOWLEDGMENTS

Heartfelt appreciation to:

Literary agent Natasha Kern, for all that you do and for who you are—a blessing, truly.

The incredible Tyndale House publishing team, including editors Karen Watson, Jan Stob, Stephanie Broene, and especially Sarah Mason—your suggestions were invaluable.

Critique partner Nancy Herriman—talented and loyal first reader, dear friend.

Kendall County Sheriff Roger Duncan and Lieutenant Louis R. Martinez—for graciously answering general questions regarding law enforcement procedures.

Daughter-in-law Wendy MacKinnon, DVM, and Abigail Dimock, DVM, for reading equine scenes—your generous help was much appreciated. Any inaccuracies are mine.

Fellow nursing, medical, fire, rescue, law enforcement, and chaplaincy personnel—this story means to honor you.

St. Helena's Church, Community of Hope, and Bible study sisters—you're great!

My family, especially sister-in-law Jean Bramble—for your encouragement and for inspiring hero Nick Stathos's Greek lemon soup.

And in memory of a bay mare named Winter Winds—you gallop on in my heart. Forever.

Give thanks to the God of heaven.
His love endures forever.

—PSALM 136:26

CHAPTER ONE

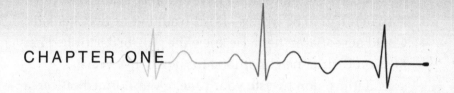

Don't drop that baby; don't—

Heart pounding, Officer Nick Stathos slammed the door of his car and sprinted toward the police perimeter, gaze riveted on the panicky young mother at the window of the second-story apartment. She clutched her infant against her baggy navy scrubs and leaned farther out to stare at the scene below: police officers, neighbors in pajamas and robes, patrol cars, a fire truck and ambulance. Lights sliced red-white-blue through the grayness of the late September morning. She craned her head backward, and her eyes, mascara-streaked and desperate, followed the San Francisco PD helicopter hovering above the shabby, converted pink Victorian. Nick hoped that methamphetamines, once Kristi Johnson's drug of choice, weren't at the root of today's drama. She'd been allowed to keep her kids after a previous skirmish, and he knew how rare the mercy of a second chance was. He'd been praying for one in his marriage for the better part of a year.

He jogged forward through a gathering crowd of reporters, flashed his badge at the first in a line of officers, then slowed to a walk. The mother lifted the baby to her shoulder and disappeared from view, then returned to lean over the windowsill again. The baby's legs dangled limply as she fought with the tattered curtain, and Nick winced at a childhood memory of eggs dropped from a highway overpass. A baby's skull wouldn't have a chance against concrete. Dispatch had to be wrong—Kristi wouldn't neglect her kids. Could never harm them. He knew the girl; he'd patrolled her Mission District neighborhood for nearly five years.

"Stathos, don't waste your time." A uniformed officer, a paunchy veteran he recognized from the Tenderloin station, stepped forward, raising his voice over the dull *thwoop-thwoop* of chopper blades. He exhaled around a toothpick clenched between his teeth, breath reeking of coffee, cigarettes, and bacon. "SWAT's on the way." He glanced up at the window and shook his head. "911 call from a four-year-old, and now Mom—one Kristina Marie Johnson, twenty-two years old—is refusing to let us do a welfare check. Landlord informed us she has a gun in there. Says the boyfriend deals meth."

"Gun?" Nick growled low in his throat. "Let me guess: same landlord who's been trying to evict her? Think he could have a reason to lie?" He watched the window. "There's no gun. The boyfriend's under a restraining order and long gone. I'll talk to her."

"She's not talking; that's the trouble." The officer crossed his arms. "Her kid told dispatch she and the baby were left alone all night. That they were 'real sick.' You should hear the tape; it'll rip your heart out. Said she'd been 'singing to Jesus' all night to keep from being scared. Begged for someone to find her mommy. Then Mom shows up a few minutes before we get here and won't let us in. Child Crisis is on the way. The medics need to check those kids."

"So I'll talk to her." Nick pushed past him.

"You can't fix this one, Stathos. Give it up."

Nick looked back over his shoulder. "You don't know me very well. I don't give up." His jaw tensed. "Ever."

The officer shook his head, eyes skimming over Nick's jeans and hooded USF sweatshirt. "Think you'd come up with a better way to spend a free Friday, but go ahead and knock yourself out. Colton's in charge. Fill him in, and—"

They both looked up as Kristi Johnson shouted.

"Officer Nick! Don't let them take my babies! Tell them I'm clean now. You know I am. Tell them I would never . . ." She shut her eyes and groaned. "This is all a mistake. My girlfriend sleeps over while I work nights at the nursing home. She comes over after her swing shift. Always gets here fifteen minutes after I leave." Her brows drew together. "They're only alone for fifteen minutes; that's all, I swear. I had them tucked into bed, but I guess she didn't show up last night. I didn't know!" She shifted the baby in her arms and his legs swung again, floppy as a home-sewn doll's.

Nick stepped forward and cupped his hands around his mouth. "All they want is to make sure your kids are okay, Kristi."

"They are. Abby got scared. It gave her a headache and a sick tummy. That's all. She's okay." She glanced over her shoulder. "She's my little trouper. Aren't you, sweetheart?" She stared down at Nick, her eyes pleading. "Can't you tell them to go away? I'm here now. This won't happen again. Please don't let them put my kids in foster care."

Foster care. His gut twisted. "How about we let the medics have a look?"

Kristi glanced out toward the street. "Is one of those social workers down there? from Child Crisis?"

"No," he hedged, hoping they'd hold off a few more minutes—and praying it wasn't Samantha Gordon who'd been dispatched. *Not today.* The farther he stayed from her, the better. The clock was ticking, and if he had any hope of saving his marriage, he couldn't risk having Sam in the picture. Even professionally. He shoved the thought—and an all-too-familiar stab of guilt—aside. "Let the medics have a look, okay?"

"No." Kristi's eyes darted back and forth. "You. You come up. Only you. I know I can trust you."

He turned to Colton, answered murmured questions and agreed to orders, then took the offered radio. He glanced back up at the window. "I gave these officers my word you don't have a gun."

"I swear on my baby's life. You know me. I'm just trying to keep my kids, hold on to a job, pay the bills . . . save my family." A tear slid down her face. "Please . . ."

"Okay." Nick nodded. "I'm coming up."

He took the creaky stairs two at time, feeling the bulk of his off-duty weapon in the holster at his waist and breathing in the familiar smell of the old building. All of them the same: cooking oils, garbage, cat urine, mildewed carpet, soggy newsprint. The cloying stink of poverty, struggle, and hopelessness. He'd breathed it and worked in it—fought against it—from the day he was sworn in. For a large part of his life, in truth; he'd be thirty-nine next month and was no stranger to hard knocks. He had no idea if he'd ever really change things for these people. But just as he'd said a few minutes ago, he wasn't giving up. He knew what it was like to grow up without parents, a real home. If there was any way to keep Kristi Johnson from losing her kids, he was going to give it a try.

He reached the second-floor landing and saw her peeking through the barely cracked door.

"Nick, are you . . . ?"

"Alone," he confirmed, hearing what sounded like retching in the apartment beyond. "What's going on in there?"

"It's Abby." Kristi stuck her head out and peered up and down the hallway before she opened the door. "She's throwing up again. A flu bug, I guess. I wanted to give her some 7UP, but with all those people down there, hassling me . . ."

Nick stepped in, glancing first into Kristi's red-rimmed eyes—*pupils look normal, not dilated*—then scanning the room: portable crib, sofa bed heaped with toys and a piled-high laundry basket, a flashlight on the pillow next to a stuffed pony and a storybook. The little girl sat in a beanbag chair on the floor, hair in pigtails, eyes closed, face flushed pink . . . and lips so cherry red that he wondered if she'd been playing with her mother's makeup. She wore a fleece robe and a knit cap and had already dozed off, still holding a vomit-splattered saucepan in her lap. The baby lay quietly in the crib.

Cold in here. Nick shivered, despite his sweatshirt. The room couldn't be more than fifty degrees. He glanced around again. No lights. No TV. "Your power's off?"

Kristi hugged her arms around herself. "Yes, but only for a couple of days. I got my first check from the care home last night, and I'm planning to go down there and pay my bill, get the electricity turned back on. The rent had to be first. My pain-in-the-neck landlord doesn't cut me any slack." She moved toward the window, gazing down. "Things have been tight since I broke it off with Kurt, but I'm making it work. I told Abby we just have to pretend we're camping. That it's an adventure." She tried to smile. "Bundle up in extra clothes, play shadow puppet shows with the flashlight, sing songs, sit close to our little stove, and—" She turned to look at Nick, her eyes wide. "I see her. That social worker, the blonde. Miss Gordon."

Sam. Nick's stomach sank.

"She's the one from before. She wanted to take the kids then, because of Kurt." Kristi plucked at his sleeve, her eyes pleading. "Don't tell her about the power, please. I'll have it on by noon. Like it never happened. I promise." She jumped as Nick's radio crackled.

He turned his back to her and lowered his voice. "I'm in," he told Colton. "So far, so good. Give me a few minutes." He turned back as Abby began to cry.

"My head hurts, Mommy." She moaned, then retched, her shoulders shaking. Kristi hurried to hold the saucepan, crouching in the narrow space between the beanbag chair, the porta crib, and . . . Nick's gaze fell on the round metal object on floor beside them. A sickening sense of dread washed over him. Did Kristi say *stove*? *Camp stove?* His mind flashed to the image of her at the window holding the baby, his little legs dangling limp as a doll's.

"Wait," he said, crossing toward her. "Have you been running a camp stove in here? Is that propane?"

"Mm-hmm." She nodded, stroking her daughter' cheek.

"Kurt left it behind. It was his father's. But don't worry; Abby knows it gets hot, don't you, honey? She's real careful not to touch it."

"Turn it off!" Nick ordered. "And pull Abby up; get her over here in the fresh air while I . . ."

He dropped the radio on the bed and scooped up the baby, his anxiety increasing as the infant's arms and legs drooped, flaccid and still. *Please, Lord, don't let . . .* Cradling the boy in the crook of his arm, he moved toward the open window and popped open the chest snaps on the fleece sleep suit. He watched the baby's chest for movement, searched for signs of respirations while holding his own breath for an endless moment. *Cherry red lips like his sister's . . . Carbon monoxide?* Nick slid a sleeve away and felt for a brachial pulse—it was there. But the breathing was too slow, weak.

Kristi tugged at the sleeve of his sweatshirt. "What are you doing? What's wrong with Finn?"

"Pick up my radio, Kristi." He kept his voice steady as an aimed weapon. "Hold the button down. Tell them to send up the medics. Don't argue with me." He held her terrified gaze for an instant longer, insisting she trust him one last time. "Do it. Now." He exhaled. "Tell them your baby's barely breathing."

"Oh no—"

"Do it," Nick ordered again, pointing toward the radio.

He raised the baby in the crook of his elbow, bent low, and covered the tiny nose and lips with his mouth, his brain scrambling to recall CPR protocols. *Short breaths. Puff your cheeks; careful, careful . . . Twenty times per minute.* He gently filled the fragile lungs, saw the small chest rise. He did it again and then over again. He'd do it until the medics got there, and then he'd keep at it as long as they needed him to. He'd do it; he had to. Inhale; exhale; raise the little chest, one breath at a time, over and over. *Hang on, Finn. I won't give up on you.*

+++

Dr. Leigh Stathos brushed back a strand of dark hair and nodded to the nurse readying the gastric lavage tube—rigid, transparent plastic, thick as a snake. She looked down at her patient. "We're going to wash out your stomach. Remove what's left of the pills and then inject a charcoal slurry to absorb the rest."

"Can't we wait until . . ." The woman's eyes, red and tear-swollen, darted toward the door of Golden Gate Mercy ER's code room. Sirens wailed in the distance. "My husband—is he here?"

Leigh glanced at the young assistant chaplain on the other side of the gurney.

Riley Hale shook her head, streaked blonde hair brushing the shoulders of her gabardine suit jacket. She cradled a hand under her dark arm sling and gazed down at the patient. "I'm so very sorry, Mrs. Baldwin," she said, her Texas cadence stretching the words like pulled taffy. "I left messages, but unfortunately your husband hasn't responded."

"And we can't wait," Leigh added firmly, checking the vital sign display on the monitor mounted above the gurney. "Acetaminophen is liver toxic. We don't know how many were left in that bottle, and in combination with the other pills and the alcohol you ingested . . ."

The woman clutched the sleeve of Leigh's white coat, fingers sinking into her forearm. Her eyes searched Leigh's face, chin shuddering. "Please, you have to understand. I've never done anything like this," she insisted, her voice thickened by the drugs, breath pungent with alcohol. "I don't drink. Ever. But I haven't slept since my husband left me two weeks ago. I can't eat. I can't work. I can't . . ." Her voice dissolved into a wrenching moan. Tears splashed down her face. "We said *vows*. He made promises before God. Twenty-three years. Two children. We're a family. He can't be with that woman." She trembled, her eyes riveted to Leigh's. "You have to understand."

I do. Leigh took a breath, pushing memories down, then extricated herself from the woman's grasp. "Please cooperate. If you swallow the stomach tube willingly, the process will be easier." Her heart tugged at the painful vulnerability in her patient's expression. "But regardless, we're doing this procedure now. Even if it means restraining your arms and holding you down. We have to."

Leigh watched her patient's eyes for a moment and knew, with familiar and painful certainty, that this ugly, uncomfortable procedure was nothing compared to what this poor soul had already suffered. And would continue to endure over the sad months ahead. *I've been there—I've been you.* She squeezed the woman's hand gently. "We want to help you. Help us do that."

She stepped away from the bed so that the nurse could raise the head of the gurney and explain the procedure. Then watched as she applied lubricant to the end of the tube, slid a bite block inside the patient's lips, inserted the tube, and checked its placement. The nurse released the clamp on the attached tubing to start the flow of liquid from the distended bag hanging above the gurney. Into the stomach from the bag and back out into a collection container near the floor— one liter, two, or more, whatever it took to wash out the pill fragments, to save this woman's life.

Riley Hale moved close, took hold of the patient's hand, and murmured words of encouragement. The woman was cooperating; that was good. That made it easier. But . . .

Leigh saw her patient's eyes move expectantly again to the exam room door. Hoping for a glimpse of her husband. Praying, perhaps, that the promises of love and fidelity made before God would be restored. Leigh knew how that felt. And she knew, too, that though this shattered woman had chosen to cooperate with having her stomach pumped, swallowing the truth was much, much harder. *Even with vows . . . nothing lasts forever.*

She glanced at the large clock on the code room wall, designed to accurately time resuscitations, ticking second by second during a fight for life. She sighed, thinking of her own timetable, her own life. So much to do now that she was back in San Francisco full-time. Finish clearing out the house, turn it over to the leasing company, schedule job interviews, make sure her sister was settled in a new apartment . . . and following through with her counseling appointments. Then Leigh could move on with her life. Give up—quit once and for all—the painful struggle she'd endured for nearly a year. One more week—*October 3, and we're over, Nick. I need this to be over.*

She repeated her orders to the nurse, gave Riley an appreciative smile, and strode across the ER's main room toward the doctors' desk. She glanced at the large assignment board, then around at the circular arrangement of patient rooms, frowning. Half of the patients were "campers," waiting endlessly for admission to rooms upstairs. All too common these days, but nonetheless frustrating. A large part of the reason she'd gone into emergency medicine was the fast patient turnover. Many of her friends were internists, family practice specialists, or pediatricians with office walls full of fading patient photos. They loved it that way, wanted the long-term relationships—and accepted the turmoil and grief that often came with that—but that's not what Leigh signed on for.

She liked it fast, furious, fully caffeinated, and adrenaline-pounding. And as uncomplicated as possible. "Treat them and street them." The old ER mantra. Not that she didn't care—of course she did, and she wanted to help, use her skills to save lives. But she needed to walk away when her shift was over and leave it all there. That's what felt best; that's what worked for her. She needed that cushion to keep the job, the people, from getting too close. For anything more, there were chaplains like Riley. And when Leigh wanted companionship, uncomplicated, pain-free, no strings, she went to the stables and flung her arms around the neck of her horse.

"Dr. Stathos?"

Leigh glanced toward a nurse at the door of an empty patient exam room. "Yes?"

"Looks like we've got a heads-up on patients coming our way." She beckoned, pulling the red stethoscope from around her neck. "Come take a look at the news."

Leigh walked into the room, and the nurse turned up the

volume on the small patient TV mounted on the wall. "I'm pretty sure they said they'd be coming to Golden Gate. Possible carbon monoxide poisoning."

Leigh watched as the reporter, a familiar woman from a local channel, spoke into the camera. ". . . initially relayed to 911 operators in a heart-wrenching call from a four-year-old girl. Thought to be a case of child abandonment, but officers discovered—oh, wait, folks." Her face disappeared for an instant, then returned. She nodded eagerly. "In fact, I've just located the officer who first discovered this medical emergency. SFPD patrol officer Nick Stathos."

Leigh's breath caught. The camera panned over a group of uniformed officers, a woman in a steel gray blazer with spiky blonde hair, and focused in on . . . *Nick*. His face filled the TV screen. Black hair mussed, shadow of beard growth, and the oh-so-familiar dark-lashed eyes.

"Is it true," the reporter asked, extending her microphone, "that you were the one who started CPR on the baby?"

"I did some mouth-to-mouth, that's all. Until the medics got there."

"And," the reporter continued, "you were off duty, but you responded to the call anyway? Put yourself on the line for this family, even when you weren't required—"

"This is my patrol area," Nick interjected, dark brows drawing together as if he couldn't quite fathom her question. "It's like my own neighborhood. I know these people. Of course I'd help them. It's what I do."

And who you are, Nick. Always. Leigh swallowed against a raw lump that should have healed months ago. She couldn't watch this. If the ambulance brought the family here, fine, she'd deal with it. Nick was off duty, so he'd likely not accompany them. He'd promised to give her space, and he'd kept that promise so far. She hadn't seen more than a passing glimpse of him since she and her sister moved back into the house the first part of August. Leigh turned to leave the room just as the reporter asked another question.

"Officer Stathos, is it true that the SWAT team was on its way here because the mother refused to allow officers and paramedics in? that there may have been weapons in that apartment? and you volunteered to go in despite that danger?"

Leigh left the room—she didn't need to hear Nick's answer. She'd heard versions of it over and over during the three years they'd been married. Of course he'd taken the risk. He always did. Because . . . *"It's what I do."* And it was one of the reasons— a pair of soul-killing reasons—she had to end their marriage.

+++

Sam glanced at Nick's older-model black BMW, parked next to a trio of Vespa scooters. "Okay if I ride with you to Golden Gate Mercy? That way, Carla can have the city car." Her eyes—icy blue-violet in the morning light—met his, and he knew she was forcing the casual expression.

He'd made it clear long ago that their brief affair last November had been a mistake, and they'd managed to settle into a casual, if awkward, friendship. She was his best friend's sister and they still shared grief over his death, but there could be nothing more. These past two months he'd done his best to avoid her altogether. He knew it hurt her, but with Leigh back at the house, he wouldn't let anything jeopardize the chance that they could save their marriage.

"Riding with me isn't a good idea," he said, after glancing toward the paramedic crew loading Kristi and Abby— both already on oxygen—into their rig. Lights flashing, the ambulance with the baby pulled away from the curb, its siren giving a warm-up yelp.

"But you're going to the ER, right?" Sam dragged her fingers through her new short hairdo, and for a moment her expression reminded him so much of her brother, Toby, his best friend, that his heart stalled. "You promised that mother . . . um . . ."

"Kristi Johnson," he said, supplying the name and trying not to think that Sam's report to Child Crisis would be a deciding factor in the family's future. "Yeah, she trusts me."

"Of course." Sam's expression lost all casualness. For an instant she looked vulnerable, soft. Hopeful, maybe. "You're that kind of guy." She shifted the clipboard in her arms, and the tough-girl look returned. "So, catch a ride?"

Nick met her gaze fully. "Leigh's working."

Sam hesitated, letting the receding siren fill the quiet between them. Then she sighed. "I'll have Carla drop me off."

"Good—thanks." He started walking back to his car, then heard her speak again.

"Nick?"

He turned his head. "Yeah?"

"I'm going there. That's my job. And this was bound to happen sooner or later. Your work, mine, hers—they all intersect, you know?"

"I know," he said or tried to. His heart had climbed into his throat, and his breath came in short puffs . . . almost the same way as when he'd been trying to save Kristi Johnson's baby.

Because despite a sheaf of legal papers, he refused to believe there would be a divorce. That Leigh would really end it. He'd barely had a glimpse of her in the past six months—she'd commuted back and forth from her sister's treatment center in Sausalito, working just enough shifts to stay on staff at the hospital. And now, when there was so little time to change his wife's mind, he finally had a chance to see her beautiful face again. The same morning she'd finally meet Samantha Gordon—the reason she'd given up on their marriage.

+++

Leigh set down her coffee cup and punched the button on the base station radio. "Golden Gate Mercy, Dr. Stathos, go ahead."

"Ten-four, Dr. Stathos. This is Medic Seven, paramedic Kenny Walsh. Coming in Code 3 to your location with an eleven-month male in respiratory distress. Possible carbon monoxide poisoning. Monitor shows sinus tach. Respirations assisted via bag valve mask with 100 percent oxygen at 20 breaths per minute. Pulse ox: 99 percent. Skin very pink. Baby lethargic. Weak cry. We're attempting an IV line."

Leigh nodded. "Copy that, Medic Seven. What's your ETA?"

"Three minutes. Be aware: there are two more victims coming your way."

More victims . . . It was going to be a busy morning, but she'd get through it. If there was one thing Leigh had learned in her life, it was that nothing—good or bad—lasted forever.

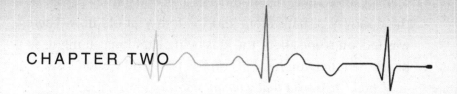

CHAPTER TWO

"No sweeter sound," Leigh said, raising her voice over the infant's vigorous cries as the EMTs wheeled the gurney into the ER exam room. The pair of respiratory therapists standing beside the intubation setup were thinking the same thing, no doubt: *Keep screaming, babe, and we don't slide a nasty tube down your throat.* She turned to the medic. "I like this better than your report en route."

The paramedic, a redhead with a square jaw and sunburned nose, nodded. "This little man doesn't like needles, for sure. I tried a brachial vein—it blew. Sorry. But I think the high-flow oxygen assist was bringing him around anyway. I hear some wheezes on the right. There was emesis on his nightclothes, so I'm wondering if he aspirated. The sister was vomiting too."

Leigh lifted her stethoscope from around her neck as she checked the medics' portable monitor: sinus rhythm at 128, pulse ox 100 percent. She looked down at the baby. Eyes tracking normally, strong cry, vigorous movement of extremities. Skin—face, chest, limbs—*cherry red.* "So why are we thinking carbon monoxide? What was the exposure?"

"That crummy apartment was closed down tight with

newspapers around the windows to keep out the drafts. While an old propane camp stove was cranked up full blast. For at least two days, I hear. Baby's crib was right next to it." The paramedic glanced over his shoulder as a second gurney passed by the doorway. "That's Mom and the four-year-old now. There was talk on scene about the kids being left alone all night, so be warned that you have PD on the way. And Child Crisis."

Child Crisis. Not that woman, not . . .

"I can handle it," Leigh said quickly, refusing to start down that old path of nerve-racking paranoia, confusing nightmares, searing anger. It was over now. Ended, same as her marriage would soon be. Pointless to waste energy on ugly confrontations that wouldn't happen.

The medics moved the baby to the hospital gurney, and the nurse connected him to their monitoring equipment. Leigh pressed her stethoscope to the baby's chest, listening to his lungs top, bottom, front, and back. The paramedic was right, a slight expiratory wheeze right upper lobe. But no grunts, no retraction of sternum or ribs. She looked up. "Rescue breathing was started by a first responder?" The TV image of Nick's face intruded and she pushed it away.

"Right. Off-duty PD officer. He said the patient was limp and the respirations were barely visible. A little better when I got up to the apartment, like—" he consulted his run sheet— "about twelve spontaneous breaths per minute initially. Heart rate 98. The officer said he felt a strong pulse, so he didn't start compressions. I saw him doing the rescue breathing; competent job."

Leigh nodded. Nick gave everything his best. *Except our marriage.*

"But then—" the paramedic glanced toward the door again—"if you want to hear it firsthand, I could probably find that cop for you. He's following us in."

Nick's coming? Leigh squeezed her eyes shut for an instant, then turned to instruct the respiratory therapists. "Let's keep him on humidified high flow for now. Restrain his hands if he tries to pull the mask off. Let me know if his respiratory rate drops. I'll need some blood gases." She signaled to the nurse. "Get lab here—I'll want a carboxyhemoglobin along with a blood count and metabolic panel. Chest X-ray as soon as we can. Bag him for a urine, and let's put that IV line in." She draped her stethoscope around her neck and checked the monitor again. "I'm going to take a peek at Mom and the other child, and then I'll be right back. I've got a call out to the peds intensivist. Call me if you need me."

The paramedic caught her as she turned to leave. "Dr. Stathos, what about that police officer? You need him?"

"No. I don't."

+++

Nick parked his Z4 in a space assigned to emergency vehicles after getting an okay signal from Cappy Thomas, Golden Gate Mercy's longtime security guard. The tall, gray-haired African American limped toward him, and Nick was reminded of Leigh's concern about the hospital's security team. Their average age was late sixties, at best. Helpful and congenial, all of them, but she often felt that paging security for "Mr. Strong," the hospital code for a violent and unruly patient, seemed at odds with reality. Though Cappy was still muscular for his age, he'd had recent cardiac bypass surgery and a knee replacement. Tackling a belligerent patient or visitor was the last thing he should be doing.

Nick smiled at Cappy. "Hey, friend. How're you doing?"

"Can't complain." The guard's engaging grin widened. "And if I did, who'd listen?" He raised his hand and scratched his brow with a key, one of a heavy cluster strung on a ring decorated with plasticized family photos. His age-lined eyes studied Nick's for a moment, his concern palpable. "Long time no see, Officer Stathos. When Dr. Stathos came back to the city, the Mrs. and I were hoping it meant good news."

Nick shook his head. "She came back to help her sister for a while," he explained, touched by the man's kindness. Whether Leigh knew it or not—or even wanted it—her hospital staff was as much a family as the people in his workaday world. "But tell your wife I appreciate her thoughts."

Cappy clapped him on the arm. "Prayers too. That woman's praying for all of us. Best thing I ever did was marry her."

"That's great. You're one lucky man, Cappy." Nick raised his hand, and the guard's knuckles bumped his. He glanced toward the emergency entrance, at the paramedics busy reloading their gear. "I promised I'd check on some folks. The mother and kids who just came in Code 3."

"Right." Cappy nodded. "That social worker told me you'd be coming. Miss Gordon said to tell you she'd meet you in the ER."

+++

"Doctor—" Kristi Johnson's translucent green mask fogged as she tried to speak—"can I take this oxygen off now?" She watched with an anxious expression as Leigh examined her daughter on the adjacent gurney.

Leigh pulled her stethoscope from her ears and nodded at the nurse. "Let's switch Kristi to a cannula at two liters." She smiled at Abby. "But we'll have the princess keep the special mask for a little bit longer, okay, sweetie?" The child, her cheeks still flushed, nodded bravely and hugged her stuffed pony close. Leigh touched the toy's dingy yarn mane. "And maybe later I'll show you a picture of my horse. His name is Frisco."

"Is Finn okay?" The mother glanced toward the exam room door, tears shimmering in her eyes. "I was only using the stove for a few days, just until . . ." She bit her lip. "Is he breathing better?"

"Yes." Leigh raised her palm and signaled the mother to wait for a moment as she finished listening to Abby's lungs: *Clear, all fields.* She glanced at the monitor: BP 88 over 60, heart rate 92, respirations 22, pulse ox 100 percent. So far so good. She pulled her stethoscope away and draped it around her neck, then walked back to Kristi. The nurse finished adjusting the nasal prongs and left the exam room.

"Finn's breathing completely on his own now," Leigh reassured her, "so that's much better. But I need to see his chest X-ray and his lab tests. Especially his carboxyhemoglobin levels." She saw Kristi's brows draw together and searched for a way to explain the situation; this woman was a new nurse's aide and had some basic medical training. "The problem with carbon monoxide gas is that it binds with our bodies' red blood cells much more easily than oxygen does. Since red blood cells' job is to carry oxygen to body tissues, if they're carrying carbon monoxide instead, the body tissues can be starved of oxygen. And there's danger of damage to vital organs like the heart and brain."

"But I didn't smell any gas."

"That's what makes it so difficult. Carbon monoxide is colorless, odorless; can't taste it; isn't even irritating to breathe. It can be produced by woodstoves, furnaces, motor vehicle exhaust, and camp stoves. Especially if they're used in contained spaces. That's why it's important to have a CO detector as well as a smoke alarm." Leigh glanced at Abby. "The symptoms of exposure are mild at first—headache, flu-like symptoms, nausea."

"That's what I thought. That she had a little flu bug, and if I kept her warm and gave her some 7UP to settle her stomach, she'd be okay." A tear splashed down Kristi's cheek. "I'm so sorry. I try hard to take good care of my babies." Her eyes widened and she turned her head toward the exam room doorway. "Is that woman from Child Crisis here?"

Leigh tensed and she told herself again that she was being ridiculous. The city had a least a dozen Child Crisis workers. "I don't know."

Kristi twisted a fold of the sheet across her lap. "I saw her from the window when Officer Nick came up." Her chin quivered and tears brimmed again. "What if he hadn't been there? What if—" She stopped short, her gaze on the doorway.

"But I was there. And I'm here now." Nick's eyes met Leigh's. "If that's okay with Dr. Stathos."

"I . . ." She struggled against a foolish wave of dizziness, told herself that his sudden appearance shouldn't affect her like that anymore. The ER was her territory. She was in charge, could deny him access. She could ask Cappy Thomas to restrict anybody but medical personnel. *And then he couldn't look at me like that, and . . .* "I'm finished here." She turned to Kristi. "Do you want to visit with him?"

"Oh yes, please."

"Well, then, fine." Leigh picked up her clipboard, willing her hands to stay steady. "I'll order your labs and X-rays. And see how things are going with your son."

She walked toward the doorway, glanced down as Nick stepped out of the way, hated it that her pulse quickened. *Two more steps and I'm out of here.* She brushed by him, and he caught her elbow.

"Leigh, may I talk with you?"

+++

Nick released her arm reluctantly, the first time he'd touched her in more than nine months. Since she packed her things, loaded her horse into the trailer, and took off to Pacific Point without a word. And now her eyes, brown like his own, filled with wariness. "Just for a minute?"

"Well . . ." Leigh glanced toward the nurses' desk, where a middle-aged man was engaged in earnest conversation with the clerk.

Nick's gut tensed as Sam walked past the desk, head down and searching her briefcase. He had no choice but to warn Leigh. She'd recognize Sam's name.

"I'm busy," Leigh said finally. "Is this regarding the baby you rescued?"

"Yes," he said, after glancing quickly toward the desk again. "Can we go somewhere?" *Home?*

"Okay, step over here. But I only have a minute."

Leigh walked toward the doorway of an empty patient exam room and he followed, watching the way she walked. Back straight as when she sat in her saddle, graceful but strong, her dark hair, caught back in a ponytail today, swinging with her movement. The ache to grasp her arm again, stop her from walking away—from leaving him—was almost unbearable. One week was all he had left. And now Sam was here.

She stopped inside the room. "I saw you on the news clip. And the paramedic already reported that you started rescue breathing on the baby. Was there something else you wanted to tell me?"

That I love you; I'm sorry—and I can't stand this. He cleared his throat and let his gaze linger on the curve of her jaw a few seconds longer. "Only that the propane heater was running off and on for two days. She didn't want anyone to know, but her power was turned off for nonpayment. She's taken on a second job to help pay expenses—working nights at a nursing home—and had an arrangement with a friend who slept over and watched the kids."

Leigh glanced out the doorway, toward sounds at the desk. The man's voice had escalated. She turned back to Nick. "But I heard that the daughter called 911. That she and the baby were alone."

Nick scraped his fingers across his mouth. "The friend didn't show and Kristi didn't get word. She arrived home, and right after, her building was surrounded by police . . . and Child Crisis." He kept himself from looking to see if Sam had returned, though from the noise it was clear there was some sort of problem out there. He had to get this said. "Kristi's worried that her kids will be taken away; she's been questioned before. By the same Child Crisis investigator who's here today." This time he did look; no sign of Sam, but Cappy Thomas was talking to the man at the desk, who'd begun pacing back and forth. Clearly agitated.

"So you're warning me that anything I reveal to this Child Crisis investigator—" Leigh stopped as Nick took hold of her arm. Her expression was wary. "What?"

His heart pounded in his ears. "You need to know something."

A barrage of curses exploded outside the door; then there was a flurry of voices—Cappy's, a nurse's, the clerk's—before the man shouted again: "I want to see my wife! Let me . . . see . . . my . . . wife!"

Nick bolted through the doorway with Leigh following. Then he walked forward slowly, addressing the agitated man. "Is there a problem, sir?" He kept his voice modulated, casual, doing his best to sound concerned and not authoritative; hands in plain sight, palms extended in a nonthreatening manner. *Settle down, buddy.* "Can I help?"

The man crossed his arms, glared at the ward clerk, then looked past Nick to pin his gaze on Leigh. "Are you the doctor who's treating my wife?"

Leigh took a step closer to the man, and Nick moved to stay between them.

"And your wife is . . . ?" she prompted.

"Linda," the man said, a play of emotions twisting his features. "Linda Baldwin. I got a message from a chaplain. She said my wife was brought in here by ambulance." His hands balled into fists and he cursed again. "I'm telling you, no one's going to stop me from seeing her. Not a doctor and not some rent-a-cop security guy. I'll take this place apart if I have to!"

Nick widened his stance but kept his voice calm. "Mr. Baldwin, I see that you're worried about your wife. I can understand that, trust me. I worry about mine." Leigh shifted beside him. "But let's take this down a notch."

"And who are you to tell me . . . ?"

Nick met his eyes directly. "I'm a police officer, Mr. Baldwin. Nick Stathos, San Francisco PD. And if you'll cooperate, I'll be glad to help you get the information you need. Deal?" He watched the man's eyes, saw his anger recede visibly. Whether out of fear of police intervention or relief, Nick wasn't sure. But he'd take it.

"Okay. Okay." The man turned his attention back to Leigh. "Can you tell me what's going on?"

"Yes. I'm Dr. Stathos, and I'm treating Linda." Leigh beckoned. "Step this way, would you?" He followed her as she walked away from the desk, and Nick did the same, at a distance. But close enough that he could protect Leigh and overhear what she was saying.

"Your wife's in stable condition, Mr. Baldwin. I'll take you in to see her. But I want to explain something first. She's given me permission to talk with you about her treatment, or I couldn't do that because of confidentiality. You understand that?"

"Right. But what's wrong with her?"

"I've had to pump her stomach. She took what could have been a lethal overdose of several medications, complicated by the fact that she's consumed alcohol."

"Alcohol?" Mr. Baldwin pressed his fingers to his forehead. "Linda doesn't drink."

Leigh glanced toward Nick. She faced Mr. Baldwin, crossed her arms, and sighed. "She tells me she's been despondent. Can't sleep or eat or work—doesn't know how she'll live anymore—because you left her for another woman."

Ah . . . no. Nick stepped back to lean against the corridor wall, guilt making his stomach churn. Then saw Sam watching him from the nurses' desk.

CHAPTER THREE

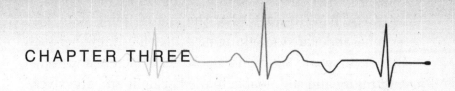

Leigh squinted into the noon sunshine, closing her eyes and wondering if the San Francisco Bay air smelled different than the breeze at Pacific Point. Same ocean. Couple of hours south by car. A safe cushion of space from heartbreak and loss. *From Nick, my broken marriage . . . and the miscarriage he knows nothing about.* Yes. Better air there. Safer. Even when it was threatened by that pesticide scare. She shuddered at the memory, then turned to Riley, seated beside her on a bench outside the ER. "Did we finish off Mrs. Cappy's health nut cookies?" she asked, setting her knitting aside.

"One left. Split it?" The assistant chaplain, eyes as blue as her native Texas sky, fumbled one-handed with the ziplock bag sitting between them.

"Need help with that?"

"Nope, I've . . . got it. Voilà!" She lifted the pecan-sprinkled cookie like it was a trophy. "Think the occupational therapist would count cookie snagging with my nondominant arm as progress?" She rolled her eyes. "No, I'd probably have to grab that big pencil and actually write, *cookie, cookie, cookie.*" She held out the treat and Leigh snapped it in half for her.

"Ziplock therapy looks pretty impressive to me." Leigh

smiled, thinking once again how much she'd come to like this nurse–turned–assistant chaplain. Riley had only been at the hospital for about three months, but Leigh had already come to respect her dedication, compassion, and spunk. It had to be hard to leave what she knew—home state, profession—and start something new after life threw her such a cruel curveball. Six months post neck fracture and spinal cord injury and still unable to use her right arm effectively. Time wasn't on Riley's side anymore.

She hadn't given many details about her accident and Leigh hadn't asked. She didn't pry, either, about any personal situations she'd left in Houston. Or how she managed to end up with a job as a chaplain's assistant two thousand miles away. Leigh wasn't sure there had ever been an assistant chaplain assigned to the ER until Riley. But it was hard not to notice the impeccable styling of the clothes she wore. That, combined with the fact that Leigh had seen the Hale name listed prominently on the endowment plaques in the lobbies of several Mercy Hospitals, implied that this injured nurse had a privileged background. Her family had pull.

Leigh pointed to the sling on her other arm. "How's it going, by the way? With your right arm?"

Riley sighed. "If I believed that doom-and-gloom neurosurgeon, I'd give up physical therapy and any hope of returning to ER nursing." She bit into her cookie and smiled around it. "Good thing my hope comes from a far more reliable source."

Leigh nodded, glad Riley wasn't one to press her convictions regarding faith. Even if she'd started conducting her own version of the hospital ministry started by Pacific Mercy nurse—and Leigh's friend—Erin Quinn. Called "Faith QD," after old medical terminology for "every day," the fellowship invited staff to meet in the chapel fifteen minutes before their shifts, praying for patients, asking for God's guidance during their workdays. Didn't affect Leigh. Although she'd recently begun to speak to God in sporadic grumpy monologues, she'd given up on actual prayer this past year. It was pretty obvious that God had cut her loose.

"You're still going to physical therapy?"

"Twice a week. But I've set things up so I can do the exercises at home too. Every night, for at least an hour. I'm not giving up."

Nick's words surfaced, the vow he'd repeated so often this past year: *"I won't give up on us, Leigh."* She glanced toward the ambulance bay; he was still around here somewhere. She'd probably have to ask him to leave. She picked up her knitting—baby caps for an international charity—and turned back to Riley. "You sound like Linda Baldwin's husband; he wasn't going to give up on seeing his wife. That was quite a scene. Glad he wasn't armed. I'm not up for a Code Silver."

Riley grimaced. "And I'm glad your husband was there to defuse the situation. He was calm and rational." Her eyes met Leigh's. "That must have been tough for you."

"Yes, well . . ." Leigh glanced away. She wasn't sure if the chaplain's concern was about Nick's being here or the fact that he'd intervened in a situation far too close to her own. The hospital world was a small one; Leigh's pending divorce wasn't a secret. Nor, likely, were the reasons behind it. After her swift exit from San Francisco last December, people had to be wondering. And talking. The expectation of privacy was about as guaranteed as covering your backside in one of those hospital gowns. But the fact was that Leigh wasn't at all like Linda Baldwin. She was moving on, moving away.

She worked a few stitches, then looked back up at Riley. "All I'm thinking about now is finding a supplement that will put a little weight back on my horse, discovering a magic potion to keep the rest of the leaves from falling off my dwarf citrus tree, and—" she sighed—"getting my sister solidly on her feet after all the problems she's gone through these past months."

Leigh saw the empathy in her friend's eyes and reminded herself that anything she said would remain confidential— chaplain or not. It was the kind of person Riley was. "The drinking was only a symptom. Getting her into a counseling program and convincing her to start the mood-stabilizing medication is what's really made a difference. I'm so grateful that the hospital granted a leave of absence. Between inpatient and outpatient treatment, it was over four months, and I wasn't sure they'd hold her job in the lab, but—"

Riley nudged Leigh. "There she is."

Leigh shaded her eyes and looked. It was Caroline. Hard to miss in the bright purple scrubs assigned to the phlebotomists. And because she was—had been since the day she was born—so astoundingly beautiful. As tall, willowy, and angular as Leigh was petite and curvy; broad forehead, wide-set gray eyes, and cheekbones that belonged on a New York fashion runway. Exactly what their mother had pushed for so ruthlessly. Caro had been as troubled as she was beautiful for as long as Leigh could remember. It worsened in the months that Leigh was living in Pacific Point.

"I'm glad you don't have to make that commute anymore, and that you're both back at your house," Riley added. "It's good you came home to help her, Leigh."

"Nick came and got me." Her chest constricted at the memory of Nick in the chapel at Pacific Mercy Hospital. She'd thought he'd come to talk her out of the divorce and had been ready to tell him to go away, to stop trying to change her mind. And then he'd explained about her twenty-three-year-old half sister. The DUI, her night in jail. He'd taken her home to the house—*"our house"*—and had one of her nurse friends stay with her. His plan was to get her into a respected treatment facility in Sausalito and finally have an evaluation for her increasing bouts of depression and mood swings. He'd been deeply concerned. And completely right. *She's better because of him, not me.*

"Nick's always thought of her as his sister. Always stuck by her. And . . ." Leigh's eyes moved back to where Caro stood, leaning against the brick wall of the hospital. Her voice dropped to a whisper. "He still is."

Nick walked out of the ER doors and joined her sister.

+++

"Hi." Nick stopped a few feet from where Caroline leaned against the building. The last time he'd seen his sister-in-law, she'd been in pretty bad shape emotionally. Not that he would have expected much else after she'd spent the night in jail for hitting a parked car while under the influence of alcohol and leaving the scene. And then being released into the custody of the brother-in-law who'd betrayed her sister. He'd talked to her a few times on the phone during her stay in

Sausalito. Knew that Leigh was trying to get her interested in going back to college, maybe even pursuing a nursing career, but . . . "Long time, no see," he said tentatively.

"Yes, well—" Caroline met his gaze—"not my fault you're living somewhere else."

He hid his flinch. *Nice shot, little sister.* There was no bulletproof vest for this situation. He hadn't known what to expect from her—she'd always been capricious, moody—but what he saw now, despite the medication, looked like hurt wrapped in anger. Not that he didn't deserve it.

"No, it isn't your fault. It's mine." He studied her face for a moment, thin as always, small shadows under her dove gray eyes. She'd been through a lot, he could tell, and it took all he had not to put his arms around her, tell her if she needed anything, he'd be there for her. But hugging his sister-in-law wasn't an option anymore. He'd hurt her, too. "I was here on a call, saw you . . . thought I'd ask how things were going."

"How things are with me or with Leigh?" She didn't wait for his answer. "She's out at the stables more than she's home. But when she's there, she's packing—boxes all over the house, job applications spread out on the breakfast bar. We've only been here a couple of months and already Leigh wants to leave so badly she can taste it." Caroline watched his eyes for a moment, then took aim again. "You'd better come rescue that precious lemon tree of yours. She's killing it."

The lemon tree. Our honeymoon in Capri. He resisted the urge to look toward where Leigh sat on the bench, imagining how she'd react when he told her that the Child Crisis investigator standing in her ER was the woman he'd taken to bed in a grief-induced blur of confusion, anger, and pain after Toby was killed. It wasn't going to be easy. But leaving Leigh to discover Sam's identity on her own wasn't an option. He glanced at Caroline as she spoke again.

"You were going to use the lemons for that Greek soup," she said, her expression softening. "That one you always made . . . You know, with the eggs and rice."

"Avgolemono," he said, memories hitting him full in the heart. The kitchen in their old Victorian fixer, always in stages of remodel. Black granite counters, stainless steel, Leigh standing barefoot on the hardwood floor watching him as he cooked, teasing him about being a macho SFPD cop with a whisk in his holster. He'd offer her a sip of the creamy soup from a wooden spoon. She'd murmur with passionate approval, then move into his arms, lifting her face for a kiss. Her lips would taste of lemons, and . . .

He was surprised to see sudden tears in his sister-in-law's eyes.

"I believed in you two," she said, her voice thick with emotion. "For the first time, I'd started to think that it was all possible. Love, marriage, family . . ."

Oh, Lord, please . . .

"Caroline." He reached for her arm, seeing the pain behind her anger. "Listen to me. I wanted that too. I still do."

She yanked her arm away and stared at him. "I thought you did, Nick. I tried to believe it. But how can that ever happen with *her* around?" She looked over her shoulder toward the ER. "She was there when I drew that baby's blood. I read her name badge: Samantha Gordon." Caroline glanced toward Leigh. "This isn't going to work. She's leaving us both."

+++

"Finn has pneumonia?" Kristi tightened her arms around her daughter, asleep in her arms with oxygen prongs in her nostrils. "How did that happen? He hasn't had a cold, not even the sniffles."

Leigh glanced at Riley, grateful as always for her presence. "He'd been vomiting during the night," she explained as gently as she could, but she saw the immediate guilt in the young mother's eyes. *When he was left all alone.* "And the X-rays reveal that he breathed some of that in, causing what we call aspiration pneumonia. Normally a baby of his age would be able to protect his airway—spit the vomit out—but the gas fumes made him too drowsy to do that."

Kristi closed her eyes for a moment. "Will I be giving him medicines at home, then? antibiotics? I've done that before when he had an ear infection. It's not a problem. He's really good about taking them." She blinked at Leigh, the look in her tired eyes not nearly as hopeful as her words.

"No. We'll need to keep Finn at Golden Gate Mercy. He'll get the antibiotics intravenously, and he'll stay on oxygen. I've consulted with a specialist, a pediatric intensive care physician who is very qualified. He'll be overseeing things." She exhaled slowly. "Unfortunately, apart from the pneumonia, the blood tests show that the carbon monoxide exposure was enough to pose problems. Borderline in terms of numbers, but still worrisome."

"No, oh . . . no." Kristi's eyes widened, the color draining from her face.

"His vital signs are good," Leigh assured her quickly. "But we won't know for several days—perhaps weeks—if there will be any actual damage to his organs. In order to be safe, his treatment will need to be aggressive and start immediately. The specialist will explain his plans to you this afternoon." She smiled. "He's not only an excellent doctor; he's very, very kind and caring. Your baby will be in good hands, Kristi."

"And Abby?" she asked, tears welling. "Is she okay?"

"Yes. Both you and your daughter had normal carboxy-hemoglobin levels and your chest X-rays are good." Leigh's heart tugged as a tear slid down Kristi's face and splashed onto the stuffed pony in her daughter's arms. "But we'll want to keep you both in the hospital a day or two for observation."

Riley nodded. "We think we'll be able to have you all in the same room. And I'd be happy to get you a phone or make some calls for you. Family, pastor?"

"No. No family. And I'm new at my church." Kristi lifted her chin as if willing them to understand. "I've been trying so hard to make a fresh start. To take care of my children. That's why I took the extra job on nights; that's why I wasn't there last night when . . ." Her words dissolved into a painful moan. "Is Child Crisis going to take my children away?" She glanced toward the door, her body trembling. "Where's Officer Nick? Maybe he'll talk to her. He knows me; he knows how hard I've been trying. I haven't seen my ex in months. There's no drug deals going on in our apartment. Please get Officer Nick. He's the only one I trust." Tears gathered again. "This can't be happening."

"I'll get him," Leigh said as Riley bent low to comfort the young mother. Leigh had trusted Nick too, but it hadn't worked out. And if she hadn't had the miscarriage, she could have been a single mother herself. Or would a baby have changed things? She'd never know now. "I'll get him for you," she said again over the lonely and heartbreaking sound of Kristi Johnson's crying.

+++

"You mean someone broke in there?" Nick asked, leaning against the door of his car and holding the cell phone to his ear. "Did you check with the landlord? I wouldn't put it past him to cause problems."

"Someone tossed it, big-time," Colton said. "Busted the medicine cabinet clean off its hinges, cleaned it out, went through her closet and then threw her underwear all over the floor. Even emptied her refrigerator. Doubt the landlord would tear things up. He doesn't want to spend a dime more than he has to on that building. The only thing keeping those moldy walls up is a million cockroaches holding hands."

"Was the door forced open?"

"No. Landlord swears he locked it, but then he doesn't look like Mr. Responsible to me. Anyway, that young lady's not going to be happy when she goes back there. Her kids okay?"

"I'm not sure yet," Nick said, thinking that he'd bet the landlord wouldn't object if he went into the apartment, put things back in order. He caught a glimpse of Leigh heading past the visitors' gazebo and toward him. His throat tightened. "Doctor's coming now. I'll check with you later,

Colton. Thanks for the heads-up." He closed the phone and slid it into his pocket as she arrived beside him. She looked worn-out.

"Cappy said you were out here," she said, managing somehow not to look him directly in the eyes. "He was busy, so I thought I'd come out here myself." She shook her head, and a strand of her hair snagged across her lips. He stopped himself from reaching out to brush it away. "My patient's asking for you," she said, swiping at the errant strands. "Kristi Johnson. Her baby's blood shows the effects of the exposure, so we're keeping him. She and her daughter will be staying for at least tonight."

Nick frowned. "It's serious, then, for Finn?"

"Could be. Brain damage is a big concern. I didn't mention it to her, but the peds team is thinking about hyperbaric treatment. At any rate, they'll be aggressive." She sighed. "Why on earth don't they require carbon monoxide monitors in these old buildings? But then she shouldn't have been using a camp stove. And should have called to be sure her babysitter arrived, not blindly trust . . ." Her words trailed off as she met Nick's eyes for a brief second, then looked away.

Like you shouldn't have trusted me?

"Anyway," Leigh said, glancing at her watch, "she's worried about the Child Crisis investigation. Apparently she's had some trouble before, related to the children's father. A drug problem, it sounded like. She said you know the situation, and maybe you could put in a word for her. She's very insistent on talking with you."

"I'll talk to her. But while I'm here, I wondered if we could sit down and talk about some things." He watched her eyes, told himself to take a breath and keep going. "I know I promised to stay away, but we've never talked, really talked." His chest constricted at the expression on her face. *Leigh, don't . . .*

"No. I've told you before, there's no reason to talk. Even if there was, I don't have time. I shouldn't even be out here." She glanced toward the ER entrance. "I need to get Mrs. Baldwin hooked up with psych services and send the Johnson baby upstairs to peds. Then I've got to try to find a minute to speak with that Child Crisis—" She stopped as he caught her arm.

"You need to know something. I need to tell you . . ." He saw the wariness in her beautiful eyes, knew she was about to protest again. "It's not about the divorce. It's about that investigator." He fought the memory of the moment he'd told Leigh about the affair. The hurt on her face and pain in her voice: *"Who is she? What's her name? Oh, God . . . who is she?"*

"The investigator is Sam," he said, suddenly as dizzy as the moment he heard that Toby—Sam's brother—was dead. "Samantha Gordon." He watched the color drain from Leigh's face, her pupils widen. "I'm sorry, Leigh. But it's like she said: this was bound to happen someday because our work—mine, hers, yours—they intersect." His eyes searched hers, willing her to understand that it wasn't personal. It was work, nothing more. "She's as uncomfortable with this as you are."

"Uncomfortable?" The color returned to Leigh's cheeks. She crossed her arms, her body trembling. *"Uncomfortable* is what you say about a hangnail or a splinter. Or a stupid pebble in your shoe." She flinched back as he tried to touch her again. "Don't. Don't touch me, Nick; don't try to talk to me. And don't use that calm, rational, police officer voice to tell me that *your* lover is standing in *my* ER, and that she's as *uncomfortable* as I am."

"Leigh, wait."

"Leave me . . . alone!"

+++

Leigh whirled away, white coat flying and heart pounding so loudly in her ears that if a Code 3 ambulance raced in with sirens wailing, she'd never have heard it. She kept moving, jogging past the gazebo, gulping in air to clear the nausea, to push the frightening snarl of anger and humiliation away. And to get away from Nick. Because if she weakened and started to cry, or if she began pounding her fists on his chest and screaming—things she hadn't done, depths she wouldn't allow herself to sink to all these long, miserable months—he might think she wasn't over him. That she wasn't ready to move on, move away.

She took another deep breath, slowed to a walk, and squared her shoulders. Kept her eyes on the doors to the ER and calmly tried to recall the only photo she'd seen of Samantha Gordon. Online, in an old San Francisco County newsletter, an employee picnic. A fuzzy black-and-white shot of her playing beach volleyball: wavy blonde hair, big sunglasses, square jaw, compact body, muscular calves . . . nothing memorable. Except that she'd taken Nick. That was unforgettable. And left Leigh slogging through a depression as dark, thick, and visceral as a gastric bleed before it threw her into a lethal backdraft of searing anger that frightened her soul-deep. Made her stop praying, stuff her clothes in a suitcase, load her horse in a trailer, and run. But now, nine months later, she was better; she could handle it. "Uncomfortable" or not.

Leigh crossed the last few yards of parking lot and pushed the coded buttons to open the ambulance bay doors, stepping back as they whooshed open, and walked into her ER. She heard the familiar beeps and whirs of monitoring equipment, the far-off whine of a cast cutter, smelled the scents of iodine and surgical soap and someone's breakfast of day-old pizza. The same, always.

She was a physician who'd taken an oath to heal, and there were patients to see and medical decisions to be made. She was a seasoned professional who had handled plenty of tough things before. Difficult people. This was her turf, same as Nick's Mission District neighborhoods were his. She breathed in through her nose, exhaled slowly, and forced a smile as she passed Cappy Thomas in the hallway. *Nothing different about today.*

Except that in a hospital where she'd saved dozens of lives, she was about to face the one person that she'd killed over and over in her nightmares.

CHAPTER FOUR

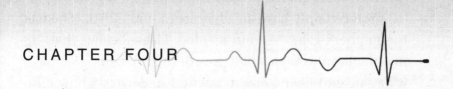

Sam pulled a sheaf of papers from her briefcase, scanned the top few pages, and then glanced up at Kristi Johnson. "I see that you've been busy since we last met. You've been working, attended Narcotics Anonymous support meetings, taken some church-sponsored parenting classes?"

"Everything I promised. All of it. You can ask Officer Nick if you don't believe me." Kristi peered over the top of her sleeping daughter's head. She lifted her chin and tightened her arms protectively around her child.

Sam wasn't surprised by the look in the young mother's eyes; she'd seen it with parents countless times before—defensive, frightened, hostile sometimes. It came with the territory. In her years with Child Crisis, she'd received threatening phone calls, had her county car vandalized, and been called every vile name in the book. Didn't matter. Didn't scare her. Sam's job was to protect children, the way she wished someone had protected her when she was Abby Johnson's age. Bottom line: she did whatever she had to do to get results. At everything. Professional and personal.

"I did talk with Officer Stathos." Sam thought of him,

his fierce determination to protect his city, his "people," so much like SFPD's motto: *Gold in peace, iron in war*. Nick Stathos, same as Sam, had seen too much war in his life; he deserved some golden peace. So did she.

"You certainly have an advocate in him, Kristi." She met the mother's gaze. "And in me, too. Please believe that. It's my intention to keep children with their parents. As long as it's a safe and loving environment. I understand how difficult it is to raise a child alone. I'm a single mother too." She reached into a side pocket of her briefcase and produced a snapshot, brushing her fingertip across its surface. The worn image of a chubby two-year-old wearing her uncle's police hat. "This is my Elisa."

She handed it to Kristi, the same way she'd done with countless other mothers before. Except that these days, these past months since Toby's death, she thought of Nick whenever she did that. Of Nick taking Elisa from her arms at the funeral when Sam's knees gave way and she sank down beside Toby's flag-draped casket, her sobs mixing with the sad drone of bagpipes. And those other times, in the painful gray aftermath, when she sat, numb, in her brother's lonely house and Nick kept her company. He put aside his own grief to make Elisa giggle, carried her on his shoulders, bought her a balloon at the zoo. *Then awakened beside me in bed.*

But now, his guilt, his distance, the pain in his eyes . . . She glanced toward the doorway, at staff in scrubs in the distance. And at the female doctor in a white coat. *She's divorcing him. I can wait another week.*

"She's cute," Kristi said, the wariness in her eyes receding slightly. "When Abby was that age, her daddy took us to Disneyland, and . . ." She glanced down.

Sam lifted a page of her report, the rustling sound deafening in the awkward silence. "The restraining order is still in effect against Kurt Denton."

"I haven't seen him. I swear."

Sam pulled her fingers through her hair, still surprised at the feel of the short tufts. "Having him in your home, around the children, is not an option. Having him deal methamphetamines out of that apartment, bringing strangers of all kinds into contact with those children—" she fought a shudder, ugly, shadowy memories of her own childhood trying to intrude again—"*cannot* happen. If I have even the smallest suspicion that it is—"

"It's not!" Kristie blurted, causing Abby to open her eyes and whimper. She shushed her gently. "I swear. And I'm clean; test me. Go ahead. Test me."

Sam smiled grimly. "They already did. And you are." She spread her hands on top of the papers. "You've had no contact with Kurt Denton?"

Kristi kissed her daughter's temple, then tucked the stuffed pony under the gurney sheet. "No. He's gone. I don't even know where." She raised her eyes to Sam's again. "I'm trying, Miss Gordon. I'm trying every day, with everything I have, to make this work. To be a good mother, and . . ." Her voice broke, tears welling. "Last night was a horrible mistake. My girlfriend was supposed to be there. She called me just before you came, to explain. She was sick and left a message on my cell phone, but I didn't get it. Because I ran out of minutes. I don't have a credit card, and . . ."

"You had to heat your apartment with a camp stove," Sam added. It wasn't the first time she'd heard something like that. It wouldn't be the last. But excuses didn't cut it.

"I have the money now." Kristi lifted her chin. "My girlfriend's coming to get my check. She'll have my power turned back on. And buy me a phone card. This won't happen again."

"It can't, Kristi. And even with your recent good efforts—your work record, the clean drug tests, parenting classes—I can't promise what Child Crisis will decide. Your son remains in danger. And I still have to talk with Dr. Stathos."

Kristi's eyes darted toward the doorway and Sam turned. Nick leaned against the doorframe, black hair tousled, beard growth even more prominent, faint shadows under his eyes.

"Excuse me," he said, summoning a small smile for Kristi. His gaze returned to Sam, and she was struck again by the pain in his eyes—and something that looked impossibly like fear. It made her want to run to him, hold him, offer the comfort he'd given her so many months ago. It made her want . . . *so much more.* He nodded. "I'm leaving, I guess."

She guessed that his wife had asked him to.

"Unless you need me for anything?" He raised his brows.

Don't ask that. "No." She glanced at the young mother. "I've told Kristi that we talked. Temporary decisions will be made when she's ready for discharge. And she knows that I still need to talk with Dr. Stathos regarding her son." She could feel Nick's tension even before she turned to look at him.

"Well . . . okay." His lips pressed together for a moment. "I'll check with you later, then."

"Good."

As she watched him walk away, Kristi spoke. "My doctor's last name is Stathos. Is she his wife?"

"Yes," Sam said, watching the white coat in the distance. *Until next Friday.*

+++

Riley, stomach rumbling, waited impatiently for the hospital elevator and then smiled when the doors opened to reveal Caroline Evers. She hadn't had many opportunities to talk with Leigh's half sister. Although, seeing the lab tech's sullen expression, she wasn't entirely sure they'd find enough conversation to fill the short ride to the basement.

"Hi," she said, stepping onto the otherwise-vacant car. "Are you headed down to the cafeteria too?"

"Already ate." Caroline's eyes, darkly lashed in contrast to her hair, were the color of gathering storm clouds. And empty somehow, sad. Riley thought of the few things Leigh had relayed about her sister's stay at the treatment facility and their recent move back to Leigh's home. A house now full of packing boxes. A lot of change in such a short time. *I know how that feels.*

"I brought food from home," Caroline added, her expression softening a bit. "Trust me, Nick Stathos lives to feed people. And still buys like he's doing it for his restaurant. He stuffed that freezer with meals." She glanced away, but not before Riley saw the sadness in her eyes. "Before he moved out."

"I met him today." Riley kept her voice casual. "He helped us out in the ER. Belligerent visitor. Your brother-in-law's quite a mediator."

"Good thing, I guess." Caroline's lovely mouth twisted into a pained grimace. "I'm sure you heard about the situation he's falling into today."

Riley kept silent. Listening was her job these days.

Caroline gathered her long hair into one hand at the back of her head. "How'd you like to *mediate* between your wife and your mistress in the middle of a jam-packed emergency department?" She shook her head. "I wouldn't know who to place bets on, my big sister or that sorry home wrecker, Samantha Gordon."

The Child Crisis investigator?

"Besides—" the empty look returned to Caroline's eyes— "it looks like I'm going to have to give up on them. Whatever happens, happens." She stepped through the doors, then glanced back at Riley. "Aren't you coming?"

"I . . . forgot something," Riley hedged. "I'd better go back."

She leaned against the elevator wall, watching the doors close over one last glimpse of Leigh's sister. She wondered if there was even a small chance she could convince her to come to a Faith QD meeting one morning before her shift. That young woman needed to fill her emptiness with something solid.

She started to push the floor button with her left hand, then frowned and edged closer, pulling her right index finger from the sling and pushing it against the button. No sensation, dull as a block of wood. Once the skilled hand of a working trauma nurse, now a teacher's pointer against a blackboard. Riley sucked in her breath, pushed harder, and the button lit.

The elevator opened on the first floor and she stepped forward, nearly bumping into a young man hurrying aboard. Slight in build, shoulder-length brown hair, patch of a beard below his lower lip. Dressed in navy blue scrubs and a shiny gold 49ers jacket. His face was dotted with perspiration. "Oops, sorry 'bout that," he said after stepping out of her way. "I'm . . . late." He offered her a hasty, apologetic smile. Then sniffed and rubbed a jacket cuff across his nose. "I'm new here."

"Not a problem," she said, reaching out to hold the door as she exited. She smiled. "And welcome to Golden Gate Mercy. It's a good place to work."

"Yeah. Um . . . can you tell me which floor is pediatrics?"

"Sure," she said. "Second floor, north."

"Thanks."

Riley headed down the corridor toward the ER, ignoring her growling stomach. If Leigh needed her, even just to sit quietly by, she'd be there. It wasn't trauma nursing. But it was what she had to offer right now. And she needed to feel useful again.

+++

Nick slid his key into the lock, heard the click of the dead bolt, then turned to peer down the Richmond District block—*our block*. Rows of mismatched homes, mostly Victorians, some lovingly restored with fresh paint the colors of sherbets, leaded-glass windows, shingled turrets; some with sagging porches and peeling paint; most with wrought-iron entry doors. Trees rising from sidewalks; shrubs in planters hugged close to foundations; window boxes filled with purple bougainvillea, butter yellow chrysanthemums, and trailing orange nasturtiums. He cocked his head, taking in the timeless blend of sounds that was the voice of this neighborhood: shouts of children at play, pigeons on the wires overhead, honks, and the distant hum of buses moving along the crisscross tangle of electrical lines. Farther out . . . gulls, foghorns, and the faint whoosh of the ocean.

He drew in a breath of crisp, sea-scented air and peered farther down the steep slope of cracked asphalt where—when the fog rolled away—there was a barest glimpse of the majestic Golden Gate Bridge. Rising from its piers in the bay between huge towers, a breath-catching span of vermilion suspended over the ocean with scalloped cables like . . . frosting on a wedding cake. He remembered Leigh's words: *"We don't need a wedding cake, Nick. We have the Golden Gate . . . every morning and every night."* And now she was at the hospital with Sam, while he was cleaning his things out of their house. He turned as a familiar voice called out to him.

"Nicky, darling, is that you?"

He waved to the elderly woman on the paint-layered pink porch next door—flowered housecoat, gray braids looped over the top of her head, red-framed glasses. She extended a large piece of broccoli toward a birdcage.

"Antoinette! What's the word from Cha Cha this morning?"

She glanced at the gray cockatiel, a grin lighting her face. "Same thing he's been saying for fourteen years: 'Forever and ever. Forever and ever.'"

Nick grinned back. Then remembered Leigh straining to

understand the bird that first time, when they'd been invited for tea. She'd been certain Cha Cha was squawking, "Never, never." His smile faded. He should have seen the writing on the wall back then. He glanced at the lowered shades of his neighbors' house. "And how is Harry?" he asked gently.

Antoinette's shoulders sagged beneath her housecoat. "Good days and not-so-good ones. He needs the oxygen most of the time now. But he knows my name and still loves his tapioca. I fix the instant now; found it for a dollar thirty-nine at the Safeway." Her sparse brows drew close behind the red frames. "I worry about having something on the stove. Hot pans, you understand." She shrugged. "We're managing. Signed on for the long haul, Mr. McNealy and I. Forever and ever."

One week.

"It's so good to see you there. I'm still praying that . . ." She sighed.

"Thank you." Nick's throat tightened. "I'm here to pack up a few more things. While Leigh and Caroline are at work. That's the arrangement."

His neighbor's face scrunched into a rare frown and she crossed her arms, making the broccoli look like a switch in the hand of an angry schoolmarm. "And it's a lousy one, if you don't mind my saying so."

He wanted to hug her. "I don't mind. And you keep saying those prayers, Antoinette."

"I never quit, darling."

He opened the door, stepped into the foyer, and saw the lemon tree. And the yellowed leaves on the tile floor beside it.

Caroline was right. Leigh was letting it die.

Leigh glanced out the exam room door toward the nurses' station and released the breath she'd been holding. She refused to succumb to anxiety that already felt too much like waiting for the other shoe to drop. There had been no further sign of the Child Crisis investigator she'd spotted from a distance at Kristi Johnson's bedside. And right now the only people at the desk were the ward clerk, Cappy, a housekeeper, and Riley. *Maybe she got the information she needed from the chart; maybe she left. Gone . . . to be with Nick.*

"I'll be giving you some steroids in addition to the diphenhydramine," she said, studying her patient's rash-splotched face. "That's the Benadryl. Same antihistamine you've used in capsule form for your allergies, but we injected it through the IV this time." She watched as the woman's eyelids drooped. "It's what's making you feel sleepy now, Mrs. Wong."

Her patient, a forty-two-year-old teacher, scratched at her neck, then peered up at Leigh. "Will I be able to go home?"

"Yes, I think so. After we watch you for another hour or so to make sure those hives are gone and no wheezes crop up." She smiled. "And if you promise to stay away from strawberries. Fresh, frozen, dried, or juiced—they are not your friend. It's a common allergy; my sister reacted to strawberries when she was just a baby." Leigh saw her patient's eyes droop again and thought of baby Caro's miserable hives, the way she'd scratched and scratched. And how Leigh, at age fourteen, was the one to administer the Benadryl liquid and trim her sister's tiny fingernails to prevent her from scratching herself raw. Because their mother wasn't there, as usual. And because her stepfather couldn't cope . . . after his wife left him to hunt for husband number three.

Leigh stepped back to allow the nurse to inject the steroid into the IV port and checked the clock on the exam room wall. Almost two. Another couple of hours and she'd be able to get away—stop by the house to change into her riding breeches, grab an apple and some carrots for Frisco, and drive out to Golden Gate National Park. The stables were her escape, her refuge, more and more these days. Away from lists, packing boxes, a rapidly emptying house still filled with too many memories. Some of them painful, barely healing. She pressed her palm low against her scrub top, unable to stop the thought. And the confusing mix of feelings that always came with it. *I was almost a mother. Would it have changed things with Nick? Should I have told him?*

"I'm finished, Dr. Stathos," the nurse said, stepping away from the bedside. "And her latest set of vital signs is up on the monitor."

"Great. Thank you." Leigh scanned the display and lifted her stethoscope from around her neck. "One more listen and I'll let you rest," she told her patient. She pressed the plastic disc to the woman's chest, asked her to inhale and exhale, and then repeated the sequence on her back. "Very good," she assured her. "And your hives are fading nicely."

Mrs. Wong's sparse brows scrunched. "It could have been worse, couldn't it? There was a little boy at our school who took a bite of someone's peanut butter cookie and died. They tried and tried but couldn't save him."

"It happens, unfortunately. That's why we hear so many warnings these days about peanut allergies and why doctors write prescriptions for EpiPens. That's injectable adrenaline, to stop the allergic reaction and support the vital body systems."

"Did I get that medicine?"

"No. You didn't need it. Your reaction has been limited to the skin—hives and itching. The more serious allergic reactions involve rapid swelling of the face, lips, and airway—with wheezing, a sudden drop in blood pressure, and loss of consciousness. It's called anaphylactic shock, and a true emergency. We see it most often after bee stings or with some food allergies like peanut butter and shellfish. Many times as a side effect of medications. Antibiotics can be a real problem." Leigh patted her patient's shoulder. "But don't worry; your strawberry reaction isn't going in that direction. We'll give you a prescription, as well as plenty of written information on allergies. Meanwhile, rest a bit. The nurses will check on you, and I'll come back and see you later. I have a few other patients to finish with."

Leigh crossed to the desk and checked with the ward clerk regarding the admissions. Mrs. Baldwin had gone upstairs, with her husband accompanying her. Kristi Johnson's baby was in a pediatrics room that would accommodate his sister as well as his mother. They were expected to be transferred up there within twenty minutes.

Leigh peered down the corridor. "And Child Crisis? Did that investigator ask to talk with me?"

Riley spoke up. "I haven't seen her since she finished talking with Kristi. Not sure if she's still here. I'll check around, if you like."

"No," Leigh said, seeing compassion in Riley's eyes. *Does*

she know? "That's fine. I think I'm going to grab my knitting and a cup of coffee and take them outside. Relax for a couple of minutes." She saw Riley nod and was certain she did know. For some reason it helped. "If anyone needs me, you know where I'll be."

She filled her coffee cup—a ceramic mug with a handle shaped like the hindquarters and tail of a bay horse—and carried it outside. For once, the parking lot was clear of ambulance and rescue vehicles. Just one young employee, wearing a 49ers jacket over his scrubs, getting into his car. Leigh settled onto a bench and took a sip of the coffee, thinking once again how convenient it was to live so close to the hospital. She wouldn't have to fight the notorious San Francisco rush-hour traffic. Just drive home, get dressed for the stable, leave this stressful day behind. She closed her eyes and listened to the comforting blend of sounds: traffic on Geary Boulevard, gulls calling overhead, the electronic click and whoosh of the ER doors opening, and—

"Dr. Stathos?"

Leigh's eyes snapped open and her heart climbed to her throat.

"I'm Samantha Gordon."

CHAPTER FIVE

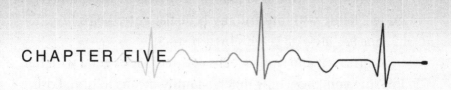

Leigh stared at her husband's lover.

Samantha Gordon's lilac blue eyes were unblinking, her expression composed. "For what it's worth, I'm sorry."

Leigh breathed through her nose, fighting an alarming wave of nausea. Was this really the shadowy apparition who crowded so many ugly, angry nightmares? Her gaze moved over the woman's face. Sharp, narrow. Too much makeup, short hair . . . *Nick likes long hair. Why, why . . . ?*

"Sorry?" Leigh rose to her feet, finding satisfaction in the fact that despite her modest height, she still topped the Child Crisis investigator by at least two inches. "You're sorry? Now that's . . . a word."

Sam chewed her gum for moment. "I don't expect you to believe me."

Leigh's heart thudded in her ears, shouting escape as insistently as Frisco's hoofbeats against a clay trail. "What exactly *do* you expect from . . . this?"

Sam glanced away and sighed, her breath a humid waft of cinnamon. She ran her fingers through her hair and met Leigh's gaze again. "I expect that we—all of us; you, me, Nick—can be adults." For the first time, her expression showed a hint of vulnerability. "And I expect that things will get easier for Nick soon. So he can move on with his life. My brother's death hit him hard. And coming so soon after your separation . . ." She nodded, the softness in her expression gone. "Being with me and my little daughter helps him."

She has a child? Leigh's breath stuck.

Sam saw it and smiled. "Elisa's three. Nick's good with her. I'm sure you know how much a family means to him. Losing his mother the way he did, being raised in foster care—"

"Don't." Leigh raised her palm. "Don't you *dare.*" The nausea swirled again. "Don't stand there and presume to explain my husband to me." She realized with horror that she'd started to tremble.

Sam took a step backward but kept her gaze leveled at Leigh. "All I'm saying is that I understand where he's coming from. We're very much alike. And I want you to know that I think you're doing the right thing. With the divorce. It's hard on Nick right now; he's confused. But that won't last forever. It never does."

Leigh bit into her lower lip, grateful for the wail of a siren in the distance.

"Looks like you've got more work to do," Sam said, her voice completely matter-of-fact. As if their entire conversation had been that way. "So do I." She patted her briefcase. "I have all the information I need on Kristi Johnson; anything else I'll get from her admitting physician. I'll be visiting regularly during the baby's hospitalization." The frosty eyes captured Leigh's. "And I'm sure we'll see each other again." She turned and walked away.

How Leigh made it back into the ER—punched the lock

code, put one foot in front of the other along the length of the corridor to the nurses' station—she had no clue. When she got there, Riley glanced up with questions in her eyes but said nothing. Leigh caught the charge nurse's attention. "What's the ambulance?"

The nurse glanced at the ward clerk's computer screen. "Transfer from a nursing home. Needs a catheter change."

Leigh scanned the dry-erase assignment board. "Anything I need to do urgently in the next few minutes?"

"No, we're fine, and your relief doc's here early."

"Good." Leigh hugged her white coat around her and faked a smile. She met Riley's eyes for a risky instant. "I'm going to run to the physicians' library for a minute, and then I'll be back."

She made it there on the same autopilot that got her away from the bench in the parking lot. The same way she'd navigated so many days this past year. She crossed the thickly carpeted and dimly lit room, grateful that it was unoccupied. Leigh breathed in the smell of leather and newsprint, trying to dispel the scent of cinnamon gum and the knifing jab of Sam's words. And mostly trying to stop the childhood memory that had played and replayed for as long as she could remember. But it came anyway.

She'd been barely twelve, and school let out early. She walked home, let herself in with the key she'd daubed with bright pink nail polish. Tried to think which of her favorite shows would be on TV—*The Cosby Show*, *Growing Pains*? She'd get her homework done early and still have time to look at her latest horse magazine, then surprise her father with his favorite snack, peanut butter and salami on Ritz crackers with a cold Dr Pepper. She'd have it all ready, meet him at the door with a bear hug and the silly joke she'd been practicing all day. It would be hours before her mother got home from her new job. Leigh would help her dad forget how her mother picked on him, ran him down about being "only a plumber." Leigh would make him laugh again.

She took the stairs two at a time humming that new hit song "Somewhere Out There." She loved how romantic it was, two people wishing on the same star, love seeing them through; she secretly loved everything to do with romance. It made her hope that someday she'd have that too: a handsome husband and her very own happily ever after.

She bounded down the hallway past her parents' open bedroom door and heard a deep, unfamiliar male voice, followed by her mother's tinkling laughter. She backed up, peered through the doorway. And almost threw up.

"Pull yourself together, Leigh!" her mother had hissed after sending the man—her new employer, Alton Evers—to the bathroom and wrapping herself in a flowered bedsheet. With her lipstick smeared and eyes narrowed, she'd grabbed hold of her daughter's trembling chin, insisting that she stop crying, stop wailing about her father. Things were over between them. Leigh was smart enough to know that.

"You're twelve years old now," her mother said, breath bitter with alcohol, "and it's high time you stopped believing in fairy tales. Nothing . . . nothing lasts forever!" She'd glanced over her bare shoulder toward the sound of the running shower, then calmly instructed Leigh about etiquette, as if they were pulling on tidy white gloves to attend their church's annual mother-daughter tea.

"Mr. Evers and his wife will be joining us for dinner. He's an important man, so everything must go well. We'll eat in the dining room, the way we do on holidays. You'll sit at the table and smile pretty; you'll pass the gravy and you'll cope. You'll keep on as if none of this happened. Do you understand?"

She didn't understand but helped her father put the leaf in their big mahogany dining table, laid out the linen napkins and silverware—forks to the left, spoons and knives to the right. And she coped, though her hands were trembling so badly she scratched the surface of the table, leaving a mark that forever reminded her of that awful day. Then, not quite five years later, she watched her mother leave her baby half sister's father for the next man. And the next. Each time she remembered her mother's words: *"Nothing lasts forever."* Leigh supposed it was part of the reason she'd stalled when Nick proposed marriage and why she hadn't been completely surprised about Sam Gordon. On some level, Leigh had been expecting it all along.

She hugged her arms around herself. Then why, *oh why*, was she having such a hard time with this now? Why did seeing that woman standing there today make her feel so . . . *Oh, please no.* Leigh clapped her hand over her mouth and raced toward the restroom as her stomach, empty since Mrs. Thomas's home-baked cookies, finally refused to cope.

Afterward, she washed her face, rinsed her mouth, and walked back to the ER to finish her shift.

+++

Nick set the packing box down and knelt beside the lemon tree, gingerly touching a fingertip to one of the yellowed leaves. It separated from the stem and dropped onto the pile of others, withered and dying, on the hardwood floor. He thought of seeing Leigh at the hospital, how he'd briefly taken hold of her arm—seen her, touched her, after so long—and how it had ended with her running away when he warned her about Sam. Had he really expected anything else? Had he been foolish to ever believe that she wanted their marriage—wanted him? He glanced toward the adjacent dining room, his throat constricting. No table. Never had been. Never would be, now.

In the two years since they bought the home, he'd taken Leigh shopping at least a dozen times. Everywhere. From the 45,000-square-foot Limn showroom in Mission Bay, to that Moroccan place Tazi Designs, to dusty, dark antique stores, then IKEA, and finally, in desperation, driving to addresses he'd found on craigslist. To see tables outgrown and replaced. Some with scratches, layers of wax, teething marks—the rich patina of families. Each time they came home empty-handed, having discussions that sounded like a ridiculous porridge scene from "The Three Bears." With Leigh, like Goldilocks, shaking her head: "Too dark, too heavy, too much glass, not comfortable, just . . . not . . . right." It became an issue somehow. *Another* issue. He hadn't wanted that to happen; he'd simply wanted a table. Her horse had two stalls, for pete's sake. Couldn't he have a dining room table?

Nick lifted the fallen leaf and ran his thumb over the surface. The truth was he'd wanted far more than a table and chairs. He wanted what he'd always believed came with that table, what he'd missed in his patchwork life of foster care: family, permanence, a home with a solid center. A place to join hands for a blessing at dinner, a spot to linger over afterward with coffee. A place where, someday, he'd help his children with their homework. He glanced at the empty room: bay window, waxed hardwood floor, a framed watercolor they'd bought in Capri, the vintage crystal chandelier with its chain tied up like a hanging victim so it wouldn't bump them in the head when they passed by. Because it belonged over a table, and there wasn't one.

Leigh said she'd know the right table when she saw it, asked him over and over what the rush was. They weren't formal people, and their few guests always stood in the kitchen to watch Nick cook; their schedules were hectic and they rarely had time to linger at the table; they had the breakfast bar. They'd find a table . . . in time.

He was nearly thirty-nine years old. And time had run out.

He picked up his packing box and stood, looking down at the dying lemon tree. If he took it, rescued it, he was sure Leigh would consider it an accusation. That Nick didn't trust her with a plant. Criticism . . . from a man who couldn't be trusted to keep his marriage vows. Best to avoid that ugly irony. And best to finally try to accept the truth. It never was about choosing a table. Leigh regretted choosing him.

+++

"For coffee then? After your basketball game?" Sam leaned against the kitchen counter and watched Elisa play with LEGOs on the floor near the dining room table. A small, round oak table prepared for three, with flowers, the new set of brightly colored stoneware, and a plastic booster seat. Her brother's table, now hers. And maybe someday . . .

"Thanks, but I can't," Nick said, his voice breathless. In

the background there was the echoing thump of balls dribbled against a hardwood floor—the SFPD youth program.
"I said I'd help one of the boys with his math, and . . . I
can't."

*Because you haven't accepted the fact that you need me. But
you will.* Sam traced a finger across the folded *San Francisco
Chronicle* she'd placed on the breakfast bar beside the bottle
of merlot and two glasses. "Sure," she said, keeping her tone
casual, "I understand. I'm not trying to put pressure on you.
It's just that Elisa made you something. Macaroni pasted
onto paper. It's supposed to be a butterfly. She used to give
all her art projects to Toby, and . . . she misses you."

There was an awkward silence punctuated by distant
thumping and boyish shouts.

"Nick?"

"After I left the hospital today . . ." His voice suddenly
sounded less like he was breathless from playing hoops and
more like he was choking. She knew why. "Did you talk with
Leigh?"

She pressed her lips together and glanced toward the dining room table. She'd never see him sitting there until he
gave up on his marriage. And giving up wasn't something
Nick Stathos did well; but then neither did she. "Yes," she
answered lightly, as if meeting his wife was as benign as sitting with Kristi Johnson and her little daughter. "Though it
turned out I was able to get most of the information I needed
from the hospital charts."

"How did she react?" The basketballs thumped like a spray
of bullets.

"React?"

"You know," he said, rare impatience creeping into his voice, "to meeting you. C'mon, Sam. You know what I'm asking."

She exhaled slowly. "Like a professional. Nothing other than that. We talked about the case; I let her know I'd be around . . . the hospital, I mean. It was businesslike and basically cordial. Nothing more, nothing less." She traced her finger down the bottle of wine and measured her words carefully. "It's obvious that she's moved on, Nick."

She couldn't hear him breathing, and for a minute she thought he'd disconnected.

"I'd better get back in the game."

"Right. We'll keep the macaroni butterfly for next time."

She disconnected from the call before he could tell her that there wouldn't be a next time. She uncorked the wine and poured herself a glass. Then reminded herself that Leigh Stathos had made things clear all along. She wanted the marriage over with. She'd insisted on a separation long before the tragedy of Toby's death brought Nick . . . *here to me, for those few precious days.*

If Leigh had wanted Nick, she'd have taken him back. He'd tried so hard. Sam took a long swallow of the wine, remembering his gut-wrenching remorse. He'd told Leigh the truth immediately afterward, begged her forgiveness, asked the police chaplain to intervene when she wouldn't accept his pleas. He'd slept in his car outside their house for days, left messages, sent texts. And kept it up. All but ripped out his heart and left it thumping on that Victorian's painted doorstep. And his wife's response? A threat of a restraining order if he didn't leave her alone. Telling him she'd complain to his superiors, essentially ruin his career. Cold, heartless. Still, he'd probably have persisted and risked his badge if the chaplain hadn't intervened again. Just days before she packed up and left the city without a word.

Sam watched Elisa add a yellow block to her LEGO castle, light from the modest chandelier splashing over her curls. She wondered what it would be like to have a man pursue her with such single-minded fervor as Nick did Leigh. To be wanted that much. Elisa's father would never have done that, even if he hadn't been married. Sam shook her head. Despite all the education, the privileged upbringing, and that starched white coat, Leigh Stathos was a stupid fool. And Sam had never been more grateful for anything. The doctor may have been shocked at their meeting today, angry as the devil, but she was nothing more than a wimpy quitter. Sam saw it in her eyes: she didn't have the guts to keep trying. Even for a man like Nick.

She picked up her wineglass and walked to the foyer to flip the porch light on in case Nick changed his mind and came by. His visits had been infrequent over the past year: brief stops to see Elisa, fix a faucet—nothing else. He'd made it clear he couldn't offer more. But Sam wasn't giving up. He had to be tired of the pullout bed at the police chaplain's cramped apartment. Nick was a man who wanted a home, and at one time her brother's house had been as much a home to him as the one he'd shared with Leigh. She'd taken over this lease knowing that—counting on it. What she and Nick had together, even for a few grief-shrouded days, had to mean something to him. He'd be back. She'd do whatever it took to make that happen.

Sam set her wineglass on the dining room table before joining Elisa on the floor. She tousled her daughter's silky curls and smiled. "Mommy will help you finish the castle. Then we'll sit at the table and make a macaroni butterfly for our handsome prince."

+++

Kurt Denton slouched down in his car when the porch light went on, grateful he'd parked beside the bushes. The Child Crisis investigator wouldn't be able to see him, and even if she did, she wouldn't know who he was. He was being paranoid, jumpy again. He hated the feeling; being high—flying, invincible as Superman—was so much better. And right now that know-it-all, controlling *witch* made him want to . . . He sniffed, rubbing his nose across the back of his hand. His pulse hammered in his ears as a grim smile stretched his scab-dry lips.

It would take like thirty seconds to sprint across that investigator's lawn, pound down her door, and show her what a real "crisis" was. She'd never know what hit her. And she deserved it for convincing Kristi to take out the restraining order and keep him from seeing his kids. He hadn't seen them in months. Not without hiding behind bushes and buildings. Sneaking around like vermin.

He swore, thinking of how he'd watched the apartment these last weeks, seen Kristi leaving for the night shift, her scrawny, clueless girlfriend coming in to babysit. And then last Sunday—his teeth clamped together so fast, he snared his tongue and tasted blood—he'd seen Kristi coming out of a church, smiling and talking with a guy. That jerk with a smile like a toothpaste commercial, wearing a sport coat and carrying a Bible. Looking down at Kristi like she was somebody special. Like she'd moved on, moved up, gotten her whole pathetic life figured out, now that Kurt wasn't in the picture anymore. He laughed out loud. Until yesterday, that is, when she'd screwed up royally and the cops came down on her like the loser she was. He'd seen the news. She was being investigated again. Stupid, stupid girl. But still . . . *My girl. My kids.* Nobody was going to change that. Or keep him away. No court, no Child Crisis investigator, no old geezer of a guard in some hospital.

He looked down at his scrubs, the ones he'd taken from Kristi's closet before trashing the place. Good thing she wore them baggy; they almost fit him. It had been easy to slip into Golden Gate Mercy. He'd gotten to the pediatrics floor without a problem, slick as snot. And he'd been close enough to see his kids in that room. Not close enough to violate the restraining order, but near enough to see the look in Kristi's eyes when she caught a glimpse of him. She'd seemed confused, uncertain—he looked different: hair, beard, and weight too, probably—and then he'd seen what he'd wanted: a small flicker of fear.

She should be afraid. They all should. No one was going to make him give up and go away. He was a man. And even if those kids didn't have his name, they were his family.

He sniffed, rubbed at his nose, and then fumbled in the folds of the 49ers jacket on the seat beside him. Until he found the gun.

He squinted at the porch light once more, then started the car's engine and drove away.

CHAPTER SIX

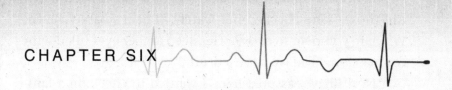

Riley reached for the stairway doorknob and hesitated, fighting a crippling wave of fear that she'd prayed would stay behind in Texas. *Stop this. Open the door. It's safe now.* She peered up and down the hospital corridor, still dimly lit at this early hour, then turned back to the door. She twisted the knob. No one was following her. No one wanted to hurt her. No one would—

"Riley!"

She jumped, gasping, and turned toward the voice.

"Oh, sorry." Gilda Watson, the heavyset hospital operator, chuckled and shook her head, sending her short dreadlocks bouncing. "For a plus-size woman, I'm afraid I have a knack for sneaking up on a person. Didn't mean to scare you, darlin'."

Riley pulled her hand from her chest, willing her breathing to return to normal. She smoothed the strap on her sling and dredged up a smile. "Oh, you didn't, really. I feel so silly for jumping like that." *And remembering lying at the bottom of parking garage stairs with a broken neck.*

Gilda glanced toward the far wall. "Elevators down again? Or are you getting some exercise?"

"Yes," Riley said, "exercise, I mean. Or penance. Cappy's wife brought pecan cookies yesterday. And the cafeteria made banana nut bread."

Gilda held up a fleshy palm. "Say no more. Been there. Ate those." She checked her watch. "But it's barely seven. Why are you here so early?" Her deep amber eyes filled with compassion. "Did we have a death?"

"No," Riley reassured her. "I wanted to check on a family that's been admitted up on peds. A mother and her two children. They had a rough time yesterday."

"And you thought you'd try and make it easier for them. You're a blessing, Riley. I mean that. I was just telling the new girl down in PBX that God knew what he was doing when he sent you here from Texas."

Riley felt her face flush. "Now what am I supposed to say to that?"

Gilda laughed. "Amen?"

"Well, thank you," Riley said, watching as the woman started back down the hallway. "See you at Faith QD?"

"'Faith every day.' Wouldn't start my shift without it," the operator called over her shoulder. "I'll be there. Count on it, darlin'."

Riley reached for the stairway door, then let her hand drop. It was trembling. She'd do this stair hike tomorrow—or the next day. And pray there wasn't a fire or other elevator-disabling event in the meantime. *I'll get it, Lord. Someday . . .*

She walked across the hallway to the elevators, reached into her sling, snagged her index finger, and forced it against the Up button. She waited for the car to come, thinking about Gilda's warm words of encouragement. About God sending her here from Texas. It was kind, but it was so far from the truth. God hadn't sent Riley. Fear had. She'd fled to San Francisco like the devil was chasing her . . . because it was true. *Someone tried to kill me. How do I get past that?*

When she arrived at Kristi's room, she paused outside the doorway to say a brief prayer like she always did, as her training in lay chaplaincy had taught her. To ask for God's presence and to remind her that her job wasn't to fix or judge, but only to listen. A challenging change from the days when she walked into a patient's room with a syringe, an IV bottle, or an Ace wrap. Awkward at first, like one of those childhood dreams where she'd showed up at school in her underwear or for a test she hadn't studied for. But in time she'd found that though God hadn't necessarily sent her to San Francisco, he'd followed her. And equipped her. She was grateful. Now if he could only get her to walk a flight of stairs by herself.

"Hi." Kristi reached to turn down the TV.

Riley smiled, then looked at the children—the baby in his crib complete with monitoring equipment and Abby dozing in her youth bed, holding her stuffed pony. "How are you feeling this morning?"

"Okay." Kristi smiled back at her after glancing at the doorway. "Are you alone?"

"Yes," Riley assured her. And surmised by the fatigue etched on the young mother's face that, though her children were resting, she hadn't yet slept well. "Would you like a brief visit?" She patted her name tag. "We met in the ER. I'm Riley Hale, with chaplain services."

"I remember." Kristi's voice dropped to just above a whisper. "And I would. I would like to talk with you. It's confidential, right? You don't report to Miss Gordon with Child Crisis?"

"Confidential," Riley said gently. "Though I'm required to act in the event you expressed any intent of self-harm or told me about something that might endanger someone else. That's for safety, of course."

"Sure," the young mother said quickly, "I understand." She swallowed and glanced toward her sleeping children. "All I want is for my kids to be well, and to keep them." Her eyes shimmered with sudden tears. "I'm afraid they'll be taken away from me."

Riley pulled a chair close. "Have you heard news regarding that?"

"Not exactly, but . . ." Kristi began picking at the woven hospital blanket. "Miss Gordon is the one who talked me into getting that restraining order against my ex, Kurt."

"Restraining order?"

"About three months ago. He was really, really furious about it. Kurt has an evil temper. And he hates it when he isn't in control."

"He's hurt you? the children?"

"Not the kids—never the kids. And he only pushed me a few times."

Pushed. Oh, Lord . . . Riley struggled against the remembered scent of dirty concrete, car exhaust, and the feel of her body colliding with cement steps, one after the other.

She took a breath. "Were you injured?"

"Not really," the mother said quickly. "And it was only a few times, when he was feeling jumpy because of the drugs." She groaned. "Drugs were the problem. And the biggest reason

Miss Gordon wanted the restraining order. She was sure he was dealing out of our apartment, and the kids would be exposed to strangers." Kristi leaned forward, her eyes intense. "I wouldn't let that happen. Ever. And I'm clean now, I swear. I'm paying my bills and taking church parenting classes."

"And Kurt? He's obeying the restraining order?"

"Uh . . . uh, sure," Kristi said, glancing away from Riley's gaze and toward her daughter's bed. "I told Miss Gordon that. I told Officer Nick, too." Her eyes connected with Riley's again. "I want my children. I need a new chance. I'll jump through every hoop it takes to get that."

Riley reached out and touched Kristi's hand. "I believe you."

Kristi's breath shuddered as it escaped. "And I don't want to be afraid anymore, you know?"

Riley nodded, unable to speak. *I know.*

+++

"Whoops, wrong pew, little guy. Who are—*what* are you?" Leigh peered through the wooden slats of the stall next to Frisco's, trying to get a good look at its occupant in the waning light. The animal's being there was an obvious mistake. She paid a hefty sum monthly to keep this stall empty, for a safe cushion of space around her high-strung thoroughbred. Leigh climbed onto the lowest board of the gate and gazed over the top into the twelve-foot square enclosure freshly bedded with pine shavings. Her brows rose as she took in the diminutive body, tiny hooves, and big fuzzy ears. A miniature donkey?

The animal raised his muzzle to stare at Leigh, and she

gasped softly. His left eye was bloodied and the eyelid too flat, as if the globe had been punctured. The fur around it was matted with what appeared to be a fluorescent green . . . *paint?* His right eye, dark as a coffee bean and fringed with almost-fanciful lashes, regarded her kindly. She reached over the gate and extended her palm, then stroked his velvet-soft nose. Her gaze traveled over the rest of his thin body, her eyes widening as she took in his raggedy coat, clipped bare in spots. What on earth?

"My girls are calling him Tag." The stable owner, Patrice Owen, arrived beside Leigh. "And I see someone's put him in your extra stall by accident. I'm sorry; I'll have him moved." She shook her head and sighed. "Poor little guy. He's a rescue animal. Came in this afternoon."

"Is that paint all over him?"

Patrice nodded. "Spray paint, gang 'tagging.' And profanity." She frowned. "You don't want to know what it said. One of the girls spent two hours trying to clip it all away. This animal was left tied to a post behind an apartment complex. No food, no water."

"And his eye?"

"Pellet gun, the vet thinks. He'll be blind on that side."

Leigh's stomach churned. She glanced at Frisco, sleek, shiny, and picking with his usual disinterest at a flake of alfalfa. She was surprised he wasn't anxious, agitated at having another animal close enough to touch noses. *Uh-oh, touching noses?* She glanced at the scruffy donkey and grimaced. "He's been wormed?"

Patrice caught her expression. "Yes, and we gave him his shots." She lifted a small halter from its peg on the gate.

"But you're right; Tag should be kept apart from the others for a while. I'll move him myself." Her lips pursed. "Though it's a shame—I think he and Frisco could be good for each other."

Leigh decided not to answer. She knew Patrice felt she was too protective of Frisco, that her philosophy ran more toward "Let a horse be a horse." And a kid a kid. Patrice Owen and her husband, Gary, were foster parents for troubled children. Their Golden Gate Stables offered equine therapy, a program that put horses and kids together. Leigh was familiar with the concept, based on growing evidence that offering children experience with an animal that was nonjudgmental and gave unconditional affection provided both physical and emotional therapy. And it seemed to be working here. On any given day, Leigh was certain to find children in wheelchairs or with walkers, braces, and riding helmets; kids with autism and muscular dystrophy. And sometimes fearful and anxious little victims of abuse and neglect, all about to be paired with a gentle and patient horse "therapist." The sign posted over the Golden Gate Stables entry quoted Winston Churchill: "There is something about the outside of a horse that is good for the inside of a man." Leigh had no doubt about that. It was the only thing saving her sanity right now. She'd never been more relieved to have a day off.

Patrice opened Tag's stall. "C'mon, little buddy; let's find you a new spot to camp."

Leigh watched her lead the donkey under the stable's walkway lights, noticing anew his clipped and spray-painted coat. Tag—the nickname fit. She had no doubt this abused animal would soon be the newest Freud in what Patrice thought of as a large, extended family. Exactly the way Nick felt about his patrol neighborhood, his youth basketball team, and . . .

Don't; it's over.

Leigh drew in a deep breath of air sweetly pungent with the scents of molasses-laced oats, pine shavings, alfalfa, old leather, and musky horseflesh. She reminded herself that she was here for self-prescribed therapy, designed to erase the stresses of her last shift. Overdoses, asphyxiated children . . . Sam Gordon. It would take more than a few deep breaths to erase that woman. But Leigh would do it, and before long she'd load Frisco into the trailer again and move on to a new job in a different city. And a stable more suited to her horse's needs. They'd never belonged here anyway, a "hot-house horse" and a woman with rapidly raveling family ties, in a barn that was set up to bring abandoned animals and wounded people together.

Leigh stepped back quickly, prepared to dodge a nip as Frisco thrust his elegant head over the top of the stall gate. With surprise, she watched her big thoroughbred crane his neck to peer down the walkway. A deep whinny rumbled upward from his chest to rattle his nostrils. Tag's squeaky bray answered.

+++

"Pizza, Nick? I saved you some. But I think most of it's stuck to the box lid. High-speed delivery. San Francisco hills." Buzz rolled his eyes and swiped a beefy paw over his crew cut. "When Sally's not around to remind me about decent nutrition, I pretty much decompensate to my sad bachelor ways."

Nick smiled at the police chaplain sitting in a recliner across from where he sat on the green plaid sofa, which had also been his bed for nearly two months. Since he moved out of the house to accommodate Leigh and Caroline. Both Buzz and his fiancée had been more than gracious with their time and concern. "Trust me, I had more than enough cheese-coated cardboard after last night's game. I tried to talk the boys into grilled chicken, but . . . they're kids."

"And I'm lazy." Buzz Chumbley glanced at the pizza box on the kitchen counter, his expression laden with guilt.

Nick laughed. "You're busy, and you're generous. You know how much I appreciate your letting me stay here while things are winding up. Or down, not sure which. Less than a week and I'll be single myself."

Buzz's gaze met Nick's and he leaned forward slightly—his listening posture. This chaplain knew the whole ugly story. And never judged. "How are you doing with that?"

"Not so good." Nick amended it quickly at the chaplain's expression. "Don't worry; I'm not doing anything to risk my badge. Or to make Leigh uncomfortable." He winced at his choice of word, the same stupid one he'd used yesterday morning. And gotten an explosive reaction to.

"But . . ." Buzz nodded slightly.

"Sam was dispatched on a neglect case yesterday morning. The children were taken to Golden Gate Mercy." He shook his head. "Leigh was the physician on duty. They finally met."

"Oh, I see. How did that go?"

"I wasn't there. Sam called me at the game last night, said there was no problem with the meeting. That it was 'businesslike' and obvious that Leigh has moved on."

"Do you believe that?"

Nick frowned. "You mean Sam's version of the meeting, or that Leigh is moving on with her life?"

"Both."

"I think Sam would say anything to encourage me to give up on my marriage. And I think my selfish, inexcusable actions have hurt two women. I don't believe that Leigh blew off her meeting with Sam like it was nothing. But . . ."

"But what?"

"I do finally see that my marriage is ending. I didn't want to believe it. Didn't want to give up—I'm not somebody who gives up." He stared at his friend, making sure he understood. "And it sickens me to know I was weak enough, stupid enough, to let our separation, Toby's death, and a few glasses of wine convince me that it was okay to break my marriage vows. How could I have done that?"

Buzz sighed. "Because you're human, Nick. And we're all flawed. That's where grace comes in."

"I know; I've been down on my knees, grateful for that. And somehow, I kept thinking that I'd convince Leigh. I thought if I apologized enough, prayed enough, and tried hard enough . . . that if God forgives me, she could too. And she wouldn't give up on our marriage. I let myself hope that because she agreed to come back for her sister, live in our house, we'd start talking. And now . . ."

Buzz waited, his very silence compassionate.

Nick tried to swallow past a huge lump in his throat. "I'm starting to realize that maybe she gave up on our marriage a long time ago. Before Toby. Before Sam. I'm the one who pushed to get married. The same way I pressured her about having children, about—" a sharp laugh tore free—"about buying a dining room table. I don't think she wanted any of that. And now I think all our arguments about those things—about my job, the time she spent at the stable, and the loss we took on the restaurant—maybe those weren't the real problems. Maybe . . ." For some reason he thought of the lemon tree dying in their hallway. He glanced away for a moment, clearing his throat, then managed to meet the chaplain's eyes again. "I'm not sure Leigh ever wanted to marry me in the first place."

CHAPTER SEVEN

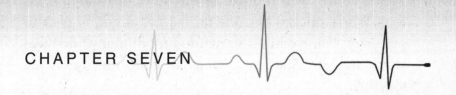

"Well, I guess Nick was right about one thing, anyway." Caro paused in the dining room doorway and crossed her arms. "You finally brought your horse into the house."

"It's a saddle, for heaven's sake. And my bridle." Leigh glanced up from where she knelt, sopping sea sponge in hand, and tried to deny the reaction she still felt at hearing her husband's name. On October 3 the divorce was official and things would settle down. Meanwhile . . . She drew in a breath scented by damp leather and Murphy Oil Soap. "Since the den's full of boxes, I thought I may as well pull the saddle rack in here. Plenty of room."

Her sister looked toward the darkened bay window, then up at the chandelier with its chain tied short to keep it safely out of the way. Prisms darted over her face like fireflies—impossible in California. "You got that right—plenty of room," she agreed, wearing the smirk she'd perfected by age six. "Enough for a horse. Match point to Niko."

Niko. *Niko's . . . Nick's place.* The irony struck anew: she'd fallen in love with the owner of a Greek restaurant and woken up married to a cop in a bulletproof vest. Leigh let the sponge drop into the shiny, commercial stainless-steel mixing bowl she was using as a scrub bucket. Then stood, her calves sore from her hour's ride. Frisco had been a handful tonight—and ever since they'd moved back from Pacific Point. Even though he was still noticeably off his feed. Worry pricked her. She turned her attention back to her sister. "Did you find something for dinner while I was at the stables?" She felt a twinge of guilt; they rarely ate together.

"Yes, I'm good." Caro twisted a section of her long hair and let it drop back against the sweater she'd pulled on over her workout clothes. "I just made coffee. Black, strong—the way you like it." She smiled, rare warmth flooding into her gray eyes. "Want some?"

"I . . ." Leigh fought a rush of emotion, wanting to run to Caro, fold her into a bear hug. How long since she'd done that—pulled her baby sister close? Not since that day at the treatment center when she'd broken down, finally accepted the need for medication. It had been tough for her and such a brave step in the right direction. "Coffee sounds great."

Caro led the way to the kitchen, opened the glass-front cabinet, and pulled down two black mugs. She filled them with coffee and handed one to Leigh, then leaned back against the dark granite counter. "So I've gotta ask," she said. "How was your demon horse tonight? Ready to become a therapist for handicapped kids?"

The single dimple appeared beside Caro's mouth, a beautiful genetic mark that never failed to remind Leigh of her half sister's handsome father, high-powered CEO Alton Evers. And that ugly conversation with their mother. *"He's an important man. . . . We'll eat in the dining room. . . . You'll cope. . . ."* Leigh never sat in a dining room again without thinking of it. She studied her sister's face for a moment, wondering what memories Caro had of their meals together. She was glad they were having their coffee in the kitchen.

Leigh took a sip—Nick's aromatic arabica blend—and laughed at her sister's question. "Therapy horse? Hardly. Never in a million years will Frisco be a part of Patrice Owen's barn 'family.' He'll always be the loner in a corner stall, with the 'Caution: this horse bites' sign on his gate. I ought to have it tattooed on his neck." She blew on her coffee and rolled her eyes. "Although tonight . . ." She shook her head, remembering. "There's a new rescue animal out there. A shaggy miniature donkey they call Tag. Sad story—he was abused by gangbangers. Shot in the eye with a pellet gun and tagged all over with paint graffiti."

"Oh no." Caro pressed her hand to her chest. "Is he going to be okay?"

"Yes." *He is, you are, I am . . . we'll all be okay. I promise.* "He still has one good eye, and he's getting good food now. The vet was out to worm him and give him his immunizations." Leigh grimaced. "The stable hands accidentally put Tag in my extra stall next to Frisco. He could have been there for hours, and I'm trying not to imagine what sort of bugs he might have been carrying."

Caro snorted, setting her coffee down. "You sound like our snooty mother, when you told her you were marrying Nick. Remember what she asked you?" She put her hands on her hips and narrowed her eyes, mimicking. "'But who are *his people*, Leigh?'" Caro frowned. "It was bad enough that she handed you that baloney about how a doctor shouldn't marry 'beneath her status.' But her reaction to Nick's mother being a runaway, not knowing who his father was, and being raised in foster care, after she dumped you with my father, then took off . . . ." Her bitter words faded as her eyes met Leigh's. "Anyway. They moved that poor donkey out of your stall?"

"Yes." Leigh set her coffee down, fighting a shiver. She should have changed out of her riding clothes; they were still damp from hosing Frisco off after their gallop. "He's two stalls away now. And already has one little girl in love with him. You remember the Owens' foster child Maria? the six-year-old?"

Caro nodded, lifting her cup again. "The little girl with cigarette burns on her arms. The one who's mute."

"Right. Hasn't said a word in more than six months, apparently. Not since Child Crisis removed her from her home, after a boyfriend beat her mother to death. No physical reason she can't talk. Just won't." Leigh's heart tugged. "Maria spent more than two hours sitting with Tag tonight, brushing him. Feeding him carrots."

Caro smiled. "And she didn't even care who his 'people' were?"

"No." Leigh's throat tightened, thinking of the silent little girl standing on her tiptoes to brush the donkey. "I think maybe Maria wants to *be* Tag's 'people.'"

Caro raised her brows, watching Leigh over her coffee cup.

Leigh shrugged. "And, weirdly enough, I think Frisco likes him too, because he—"

They both turned toward the sound of someone knocking. Before they could get there, the door opened and their neighbor Antoinette McNealy stepped in, eyes wide behind her red-framed glasses.

"I'm so sorry to bother you, but I need help. I'm afraid Harry's wandered off."

+++

Nick stood in front of Frisco's darkened stall, wondering how he'd ended up here; he was no fan of horses. Quite to the contrary. He had no patience with, or interest in, all that horse ownership entailed. And this horse had been a thorn in his side for years. But he'd been at the cemetery visiting Toby's grave, and Golden Gate Stables was on his way back home. *No. Not home—Buzz's apartment.*

Sometime in the next few weeks he'd have to find a real place to live. *Real.* For a fleeting instant he felt a lonely wave of déjà vu. From way back when he'd wonder about his next foster home; those days he felt like Disney's Pinocchio, wishing on a star to find a family and finally be a "real boy." It had been a longing, combined with fear and uncertainty, that very often put an ugly, defensive chip on his scrawny shoulder. But it was a lifetime ago, and things had turned out fine in the long run. More than fine. He'd learned a valuable lesson in the process: that family wasn't always the one you're born into. Sometimes God brought people together according to his own plan.

Nick turned at a sound in the dimly lit walkway.

A little girl about six or seven years old, with dark braids and a sandwich bag filled with carrots, stopped at a stall two spaces down. He smiled, and she stared back, her dark eyes huge and luminous.

"Is that your horse?" he asked gently, wondering if she belonged to one of the people he'd seen at the entrance to the barn.

She watched him in solemn silence.

"He's lucky to have a friend with a bag of carrots."

Her brows drew together for a moment; then she approached the stall, reaching into her sack. Shy, probably, and he didn't want to scare her. Especially since he didn't even know why he was here in the first place. *I don't belong here.*

He studied Leigh's horse, standing with his face toward a corner of the stall. There was a blue plaid blanket buckled over his back and chest, and his lower legs were encased in blue fleece wraps, neatly and carefully applied. His mane had been secured with rubber bands into what Nick had learned were "training braids," a procedure that apparently encouraged this animal's unruly hair to fall to the "proper" side. Nick shook his head, wondering if his wife considered him unruly, his broken vows a training failure. Or if she thought he'd failed her all along. When the restaurant floundered and he'd been drawn to law enforcement. When he'd wanted to buy the fixer Victorian instead of a glass-and-steel condo. Or that humiliating time he'd angrily admitted to being jealous of a "blasted horse" because she spent more time with Frisco than with him.

"Hello. May I help you with something?" A middle-aged woman stepped close and smiled.

"No, I'm . . . This is my wife's horse."

"You're Frisco's dad?" She laughed, eyes crinkling, at the immediate reaction on his face. "I'm sorry. We're kind of a crazy, big family out here. You're Leigh's husband, then."

Till Friday. "Yes," he said, embarrassed he'd come. "I'm Nick."

"And I'm Patrice Owen," she said, offering a warm handshake. "My husband, Gary, and I own *Golden Gate Stables.*" She pointed to the signs Leigh had posted on Frisco's gate. "I should have guessed who you were. That's your number listed under emergency contacts."

He squinted, looking from the large bite-warning sign to the smaller laminated card beneath. It included his first name and his cell number, below Leigh's. She'd forgotten to take it off. Or maybe his responsibility as an emergency contact would end when his marriage did.

"It's still current?" Patrice asked.

"Yes," he answered, deciding against inflicting too much information on this kind woman.

"Good," she said. "I hope we don't need to call you. Leigh's a careful rider. And this young man—" she peered over the gate at the big horse—"is a healthy sort. Even if his appetite's been a bit quirky lately. We'll be keeping an eye on Frisco. Don't worry."

He had no intention of telling her that he wouldn't worry about this beast. Ever.

"Well, it's good to meet you, Nick. I look forward to seeing more of you. But now it's time for Maria to have a bath." She beckoned to the little girl with the dark braids. "Something tells me we're going to have some donkey hair to brush off her clothes first; won't be the first time in this family. And

Lord knows, not by a long shot the worst thing we've dealt with. But we hang in there. We always do."

Nick's throat tightened without warning. "I'm sure you do."

Patrice took a few steps and gestured to the child again.

The little girl trotted up the walkway, stopping beside Nick. She reached into the sack, took out several small carrots, and handed them to him. Her lips curved into the faintest trace of a smile.

"Thank you, Maria," he whispered as she trotted off.

He stared from the carrots to the warning sign on the stall gate, then to the huge horse with his head down, facing the wall. He glanced up and down the empty walkway. "Look," he said, taking a step toward the stall, "you and I both know that I'm not your 'dad.' And in a few days I won't even be an emergency contact. So here, knock yourself out, Frisco." Nick dropped the carrots over the gate and stepped a safe distance away. He jumped when his cell phone buzzed on his belt.

"Stathos," he said, feeling like the fool he was.

"Nicky? This is Antoinette. I need your help, darling."

He talked with her long enough to understand that Harry had wandered away from the house while she was taking a shower. He promised to be there in less than ten minutes and disconnected, watching as Frisco put his head down and moved toward the carrots.

The big horse sniffed at them for moment, then stretched his neck over the gate to gaze down the walkway. He gave a deep, insistent whinny.

There was a small, answering bray from two gates down.

Leigh leaned across the McNealys' quilt-covered bed to adjust the oxygen prongs, aware that Nick was watching her. She shouldn't be surprised that Antoinette would call him. "You were going to trim the privet hedge. Weren't you, Harry?"

"Of . . . course," her neighbor replied, his voice breathless and reedy but emphatic. There was a lipstick print on his forehead. "A man can't . . . expect his bride . . . to do that sort of work." Harry's watery eyes shifted to gaze at Nick. He waggled a finger in the air. "Right, son?"

"That's right, sir," Nick said quickly. "And I agree that the hedge needs pruning. Our . . ." He hesitated. "Our side is overgrown too. I'll get it done. Don't you worry."

"Thank you." Harry sighed and swept a tremulous hand over his snowy hair. "A little . . . at a time. That's how you do it . . . keep at it. Keep . . ." He yawned, and his lids fluttered, then closed. Leigh waited for a few moments before grasping his slender wrist very gently, checking his pulse. Much stronger now, and the rate had settled down with the two-liter flow of oxygen. No more bluish tinge to his lips. And his breathing rate . . . She nodded at his gentle snore. Far better.

She stepped away from the bedside, out of hearing range. "Poor, sweet man."

"Did you have to give him something?" Nick asked in a low whisper.

"No. The home health nurse keeps sedatives here for emergencies, but Harry settled down after Caro and I got him away from the garden shed and convinced him to put down those gigantic shears." She winced. "He could have just as easily wandered into traffic, Nick. Or set the house on fire. It could have been a horrible tragedy for both of them. I know how much Antoinette wants him here, but . . ." Her words faded at sounds in the distance. Caro and Antoinette, rattling teacups. Followed by a familiar whistle and Cha Cha's throaty call. "Forever and ever. Forever and ever."

"He's mimicking Harry," Nick said, glancing at the dresser beside the bed—dark mahogany topped with a tatted lace runner, a vintage silver hairbrush set, and at least a dozen framed photos of the couple. Including one of them dancing at their wedding. "It's what he's told Antoinette every day they've been married: 'I'll love you forever and ever.'" His eyes met Leigh's.

"Still," she said, glancing away. "These wandering episodes—nighttime agitation, 'sundowning'—tend to escalate with dementia patients. It's worsened by his emphysema; his oxygenation isn't what it should be. I should talk with Antoinette about finding a care home."

"Don't. Not yet." Nick scraped his fingers across his mouth. "Antoinette told me that their wedding anniversary is coming up. Sixty years." He met Leigh's gaze again. "They should have that. It's only a few days."

A few days. Leigh nodded, her heart hitching. "I won't say anything."

"And I'll check on them," Nick assured her. "I'll trim that hedge, too. When you're not home. I won't bother you; don't worry."

"I won't," she said, knowing it wasn't true. She would worry. About Harry and Antoinette. And she was bothered . . . about the irrational way she'd been acting lately. She'd hoped that with the divorce in its final countdown and her sister getting back on her feet after treatment, things would finally feel better. And life would move steadily toward normal. Or at least toward merciful numbness. Numb was so much better than what she'd had. But if yesterday—a miserable day that left her racing from the physicians' library to clutch a toilet bowl—was any indication, this final week was going to seem like—

"Forever," Cha Cha crooned in the distance. "Forever and ever."

+++

Kurt told himself to get out of there. He shouldn't have come back to Golden Gate Mercy so soon. There were fewer staff on evening shift, and though people had assumed he was new or that he was passing through on his way somewhere else, eventually someone might get suspicious and question him. He hunkered against the wall near the pediatrics utility room and laughed out loud. But this was so easy; some housekeeper had even offered him a piece of banana nut bread. Good thing, since he couldn't remember the last time he ate. Yesterday maybe. But then he never felt hungry or sleepy or bugged by anything when he'd scored some great crystal meth. He had done that and now he was energized. No—he *was* energy. He was pure, powerful electric current. Like one of those stinkin' heart defibrillators you saw on TV medical shows. *Yeah. Zap, zap—whoa! Look out!*

He laughed again, then clamped his hand over his mouth, fingers trembling against his dry lips like a high-tension wire. It was funny, though. To be able to jam right in here in Kristi's scrubs and keep a watch over his kids. Keep that investigator away, and dodge the old crippled security guard. Kurt laughed again, clutched at his stomach, and felt his jacket pocket sag with the cold weight of what he'd stuffed into it when he got out of the car. He shook his head, a new jolt of energy making him shiver, making him taller and smarter and completely invincible.

A heart defibrillator was nothing compared to the blast of a gun.

CHAPTER EIGHT

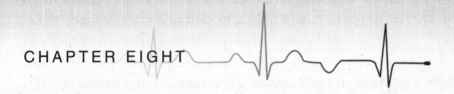

"I'm not sure you're being honest with me, sir. How did you get these wounds?"

"Just like I said. Lost my balance and fell. Yes, ma'am . . . Dr. Stathos." Freddie Barber, a wiry sixty-four-year-old, blinked as blood trickled into his eye from one of several small, perfectly round punctures on his forehead. Exactly the same shape as the dozen or more wounds that peppered his upper chest and shoulders. He looked down at his hands. "Fell down. That's the plain truth." He sighed, exuding stale alcohol fumes. "Gettin' clumsy in my old age, I guess."

"Hmm." Leigh glanced across the gurney at Riley. The chaplain wasn't buying it either. And the respite Leigh had hoped for this Sunday shift wasn't happening. In the past two days she'd dealt with Nick and Sam Gordon, then moved right on to the turmoil at the McNealys'. A roller coaster of emotion. Last night she'd been wrung out, sleepless long into the night. She wanted today to be far more routine. But most of the patients who'd streamed in since 7 a.m. had been "full moon" cases—people with needy psychological issues, complicating everything she'd tried to do. And now this guy . . .

"Maybe you want to blame this on clumsiness, Mr. Barber, but unless you fell onto a very large porcupine, I don't see how you could end up with all of these—" she grimaced—"holes." She tugged at the top of his patient gown, lifted his heavy link necklace aside, and noted the wounds there. She touched a gloved fingertip to his graying chest hair and exposed the deepest divot. Only a few needed sutures. "We'll get back to your story in a few minutes. But first, when was your last tetanus shot?"

"December. Christmas Day. Hard to forget. Had myself a little accident that day, too." Freddie smiled sheepishly, exposing gold bridgework. "So I'm good with the tetanus situation." He took a deep breath, following Leigh's instructions as she pressed her stethoscope to his chest. "Ah, man. That hurts like a . . ." He cursed, then bit his lip. "Sorry, ladies."

"Another deep breath, Mr. Barber," Leigh instructed, listening for breath sounds. Not easy with the sudden explosion of noise from the corridor: raised voices, yelling, cursing. She closed her eyes, concentrating as she pressed the disc flat against the man's chest. A wheeze. And were those breath sounds diminished? Were there crackles? Leigh pulled her stethoscope earpieces aside as Riley tapped her arm.

"I'm sorry. But his oxygen saturation's dropping and—" she pointed to the monitor, raising her voice over the continuing disturbance in the outer hallway—"his pulse is faster."

Leigh frowned. Riley was right. Oxygen 93 percent on room air, heart rate 112, BP 100 over 70. Respirations faster, skin a bit pale. She'd barely begun the man's exam, and these wounds seemed superficial, but still . . . "Mr. Barber, are you having trouble breathing?"

"Yes . . . I can't seem . . . to get . . . my breath." His eyes widened as medics stopped a stretcher outside his room. "Uh . . . oh. Oh, brother."

Leigh turned, catching sight of a plump, middle-aged woman in shorts and patterned stockings lying on the transport gurney. Her wig, berry red and shiny, rode too high on her head, and the side of her face was dotted with several puncture wounds exactly like Freddie Barber's.

The woman struggled to a sitting position on the gurney and jabbed a finger in the air, pointing into the exam room. "There you are, you lying snake! Look what she did to me. That trashy wife that you never bothered to mention!" She glared murderously and batted her hand at the paramedic trying to calm her. "No one takes a high heel to me and gets away with it. And you, you lousy . . ." The paramedics hustled the stretcher toward the next room, but the woman managed one last string of curses and a final taunt. "I hope she poked something vital with that steak knife, Freddie Barber. I hope you bleed to death!"

Knife? Leigh met Riley's eyes for a split second, checked the vital signs display, then leaned over the gurney. "You were stabbed?"

"Uh . . . I . . . My back." Perspiration glistened on his forehead.

Leigh gestured to a nurse in the hallway. "Give me a hand, would you? Help me sit him up." She dropped his gown to his waist and together they leaned him forward.

"There," Riley said, pointing below his shoulder blade.

It was a narrow wound, about a half inch long and oozing blood. Leigh palpated it gently with her fingers; the skin surrounding the stab wound felt crunchy like bubble wrap. *Air escaping into the tissues. From a lung puncture?* She pressed her stethoscope to his back, high and low, listening as he breathed in and out. Unequal sounds, likely evidence of some collapse.

"Let's get him on high-flow oxygen," Leigh told the nurse as they laid him back down. "Start an IV, normal saline. Pull labs, including a blood alcohol and a type and hold. I'll order a stat portable X-ray. And set me up for a chest tube insertion. Meanwhile . . ." She lifted the sheet from her patient. "I'm going to need to look you over stem to stern, Mr. Barber. To see if we have any more surprises here. That was quite a 'fall' you took."

Guilt flickered across his face as the nurse fitted the oxygen mask. "My wife has a troublesome temper. I knew that—" his breath fogged the green plastic—"when I married her. She's a good woman in most ways, but . . ."

Riley stepped closer as the nurse went to get the IV supplies. "She attacked you because of that woman we just saw?"

He nodded, shifting his legs to accommodate Leigh's exam. "Found us together and wouldn't listen to reason. Not even for a minute. No sir. Never does. Just goes for my throat."

"Your wife's assaulted you before?" Riley asked.

"Yeah." Freddie grasped Leigh's sleeve. "I'm sorry I lied, Doctor. But even if I've deserved it—and I'm not saying I haven't over the years—it's hard for a man to admit to being beat up by a woman, you know?"

Leigh didn't want to know. The very last thing she needed was another example of messy relationships. More lies, more excuses. "All I know right now is that I need to check you over," she said, her tone brittle even to her own ears. "And attend to that chest injury. I'm concerned about your lung. First things first."

"Will the police be called?"

"I would think they've already been notified, Mr. Barber. I'll check for sure." Riley looked toward the doorway. "I imagine your lady friend wouldn't be as protective as you were. I'll stay with you when the officers come, if you like."

Leigh glanced at Riley, wondering if her nonjudgmental kindness came from her training as a chaplain, her faith, or simply because she was naive. She was young and from a tight-knit family. Maybe she'd never been on the receiving end of betrayal.

"You're the chaplain, right?" Freddie asked Riley, extending his arm so the nurse could start his IV.

"Assistant chaplain."

"Just as good." He grimaced at the needle stick. "We used to go to church. The wife and I. But it's been a while. Almost a year. Christmas was the last time. I lied about having an accident that day, too. The truth is, she walloped me with another shoe—high heel with holly berries. Because I got drunk and stayed out all night. Christmas Eve. What was I thinking?" The mask fogged, and sudden tears shimmered in his eyes. "A year from Social Security and I'm still making a mess of my life. It's probably too late, but I've been hoping to find a way to start getting it right. Maybe I could talk with you about that."

"I'll be glad to listen," Riley said softly. "It's never too late for hope, Mr. Barber."

"Never too late"—she is naive. Leigh finished her exam quickly, checked the monitor, and left the exam room, fighting the beginning of a headache. She'd see what the X-ray showed and make a decision on the chest tube. And meanwhile, she'd have the joy of examining the other half of the shoe massacre.

She pulled up a chair at the nurses' station and sighed. The way her day was going, she'd probably end up with the knife-wielding wife on a gurney as well. She wanted to find some humor in it—even imagined for an instant threatening Nick with a riding spur—but the sad fact was that there was nothing funny about it. Somehow, without her consent, she'd joined a pathetic sisterhood. Here she was in a white coat, expected to know all the answers, but she was no different from the woman whose stomach she'd pumped on Friday or the wife who'd yanked off her holiday shoe and clobbered her husband under the mistletoe. Leigh had no answers. Except that the assistant chaplain was wrong. It did get too late for hope. She had reached that point months ago. At least she hadn't resorted to brandishing a weapon.

Her breath caught as Sam Gordon crossed the trauma room, glanced in her direction, then exited through the doors leading to the lobby. *What . . . why?* The only pediatric patient they had was a two-year-old, recovering after a febrile seizure. Doting family, no inkling of abuse. No need whatsoever for a Child Crisis investigator.

Leigh gritted her teeth. Sam had passed through the ER just to do it. Purely territorial. The old anger swirled, and in an instant she saw a flash of the dream she'd had in her few hours of sleep last night. That Samantha Gordon was dead. *No . . .* Leigh's stomach plummeted as the realization struck. *I killed her. Again.*

She stood, the headache pounding her skull like a stiletto heel. Dreams meant nothing. The reality was that she had patients to see. And from this minute forward, she was determined to approach the rest of the day as if it was nothing but routine. No matter what happened. A cup of coffee would ease the headache, and in a few hours she'd escape once again to the peaceful respite of Golden Gate Stables.

"Dr. Stathos?"

"Yes." Leigh glanced at the ward clerk.

"A woman named Patrice called a few minutes ago. She said there's a problem with your horse."

+++

Sam closed her notebook. "I was hoping to see the baby. I have his latest reports, but I always like to have personal contact." She saw, once again, the fear in Kristi Johnson's eyes. *And you wish I'd have no contact whatsoever.*

"Finn's better," the young mother said, smoothing her son's crib sheet. "He still has that cough, but he smiled at me. He knows his mama's here. And you saw Abby," she continued, "down in the playroom. She's fine. Ate all her breakfast and asked for more hash browns. She's already talking about going home." Kristi's pupils dilated, but she lifted her chin bravely and met Sam's gaze. "The power is back on in our apartment, Miss Gordon. Heat and lights. I have fifty dollars' worth of minutes on my cell phone. My boss is letting me work day shift for the next three weeks. And my girlfriend will be there to babysit. There won't be another mix-up."

Sam hesitated for a brief second, almost allowing herself to imagine someone trying to take Elisa away. Almost, then stopped herself. This was her job. Child Crisis. Emotions could play no part whatsoever. "And the baby's father? Kurt?"

"I haven't heard from him in months. I told you that. He's part of the past." Kristi's expression softened and a faint flush rose high on her cheeks. "I'm changing my life. Meeting new people through my church."

Sam raised her brows. "A new man?"

Kristi cleared her throat. "Nothing serious. But there is someone who's really nice, really *good*, you know?" Her expression showed that she regretted her words. Because Sam was the enemy who could never understand something as wonderful as hope.

"I do," Sam admitted before she could stop herself. "I do know what that feels like. Meeting a man so different from anyone you've ever known." Nick's darkly handsome face floated before her eyes. "I understand that it changes everything."

Kristi sighed. "He doesn't know the details about why I'm here. I'm not sure he'd understand. Like I said, he's different. I'm not at all like the women he's used to, and—"

"It doesn't matter!" Sam blurted. "Don't sell yourself short. Just because you've had some hard times doesn't mean you have to settle for less than a woman who's gotten all the breaks." The image of Leigh Stathos—smug in her white coat, so self-righteous with indignation at her husband's betrayal—rose in Sam's consciousness. "You deserve happiness."

"I . . . uh . . . thank you," Kristi said, confusion vying with the fear in her expression. "I guess."

Sam narrowed her eyes, fighting painful memories. A mother in prison, an absent father, a brother dead barely a year. And Nick's face at dawn, confused and so vulnerable with grief. "You go for the happy ending—hear me? Don't settle for less. There are good guys and bad guys. Get that good guy, Kristi. Make it happen. No matter what it takes. Do it for your kids. You understand what I'm saying?"

"Yes, ma'am."

Sam closed her briefcase, rose to her feet, and smoothed her pin-striped jacket. She told herself she hadn't crossed any line with the client, that she'd be back tomorrow and she'd be as tough and immovable as ever. An advocate with no skin in the game. She said good-bye to Kristi and strode down the pediatric hallway, thinking of Elisa's macaroni butterfly and remembering the anxious look on Leigh Stathos's face when she'd passed through the ER earlier. Sam smiled. Just a few more days, then things would change. Her time would come; she'd get the good guy. And that happy ending.

She slowed her pace as she approached the children's playroom and caught sight of Abby Johnson in competition with a hospital volunteer in an energetic game of Wii. She stopped and walked to the windows, glad she was doing everything to assure this child's safe future. She watched Abby wave the player's wand, then hunch over in a fit of giggles. Sam turned as a staff worker in navy scrubs joined her at the window.

"Looks like fun," he said, his voice barely above a whisper.

"That little girl deserves it, believe me."

"You know her, then?" the staffer asked.

"Professionally." Sam turned to look at him—young, shoulder-length hair, small wedge of a beard. "I'm the Child Crisis investigator handling her case."

"Ah." He nodded. "You're getting her screwed-up family all straightened out."

"Trying my best," she said, after glancing at her watch. "But now I'm officially off duty. Which means I get to go home to my own daughter."

"Well . . ." He stared at her for an awkward stretch of time. "That must be very cool."

"It is." She cleared her throat, fighting an irrational chill. "And now I'm on my way."

"Me too," he said, lifting the jacket he'd slung over his shoulder. "Have a good evening with your daughter. Who knows? I'll probably see you around sometime." A slow smile spread across his face. He slipped his arms into the gold 49ers jacket, turned, and walked toward the stairway door.

+++

"Deep breath, Mr. Barber," Leigh instructed, after tapping his shoulder to awaken him. The morphine was doing its job. And hopefully the chest tube was too. She'd sutured it into his pleural space, midaxillary line, several inches below his stab wound, with a return of air and a small amount of blood. His oxygen saturation was 100 percent and his other vital signs completely stable. "Mr. Barber?"

"Uh . . . yeah," he said, eyes fluttering open. He inhaled through his nose. "Hey, Doc."

"How's the pain? On a scale of one to ten."

He reached up to touch the oxygen prongs in his nose. "You folks are all about the numbers. I'm okay . . . I mean, three. Only hurts when I laugh."

"Good." Leigh sighed. He wasn't going to have a lot to laugh about. His wife had been arrested, his indignant girlfriend had called him "Fast Freddie"—among other ugly things—all over the afternoon news, and right now, his eighty-seven-year-old mother was waiting in the chapel. With her pastor.

He met Leigh's gaze. "I'm in a world of trouble, aren't I?"

"The lung collapse was small and the bleeding fairly minimal. I'm waiting for the radiologist's report on the second chest film, but I expect we'll see improvement. Those puncture wounds won't be a problem—"

"No," he interrupted, eyes intense. "I mean my marriage. It's over, isn't it?"

"I . . ." *can't believe you didn't think of that before.* Leigh shook her head. "I can't answer that. I only know that physically, you should do fine. You'll stay in the hospital for a few days."

"She could have killed us."

Leigh fought the memory of her disturbing dream. "Yes. She could have."

Fifteen minutes after the end of her shift, Leigh pulled into the graveled lot at Golden Gate Stables, parking beside the familiar green pickup truck, its bed crowded with lockboxes and equipment, cab door reading *Ralph Hunter, DVM.* A stainless-steel bucket sat on the open tailgate and beside it a neat coil of plastic tubing—stomach tube. Her throat tightened. *Frisco's worse?* No, she'd talked to the vet as she was leaving the hospital, and he'd only confirmed the details of Patrice's message: Her horse hadn't eaten today, and he'd seemed uncomfortable, restless, nipping at his sides a few times. Early signs of colic. Which could lead to a twisted gut, a true equine emergency, and . . . *No, he's okay.* Patrice was being cautious. And that was good.

She hurried into the barn, preparing herself for the fact that Frisco would be less alert, maybe still showing some vague signs of discomfort. She fully expected that.

What she didn't expect was Nick.

CHAPTER NINE

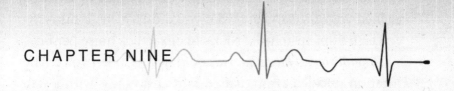

"My name's still on the card. Emergency contact." Nick pointed at the weathered phone listings posted on the stall gate. He saw Leigh frown as if she'd missed a critical diagnosis or picked up a blunt surgical instrument.

Her eyes skimmed over his uniform. "So you dropped everything to rush to the aid of my horse?" She lowered her voice. "You don't even *like* Frisco."

"I . . ." He stopped himself. *It was never about the horse or even all the hours you spent at the stable. It was about you distancing yourself from me.* "I called the house. Caroline wasn't there. And I was nearby on an arrest. Domestic dispute. A stabbing. I think Golden Gate Mercy got the victim." He gave in to familiar irritation at the skepticism on her face. The defensive parrying they'd been doing for months, like some miserable and awkward dance. "You want to see my report? I'm not following you around, Leigh."

She raised her palm. "We got the stabbing victim. I was busy with him when Patrice called. I'm sorry you were bothered." Her gaze shifted toward the stall, to her horse standing with his head down, eyes closed. "I'll fix that card, get the information current."

Erase me from your life, you mean.

They both turned as the stable owner approached.

"Ah," Patrice said, taking in Leigh's scrubs, "you came straight from the hospital. I almost called again to say we'd reached your husband and that you didn't have to hurry."

Leigh's lips twitched. "Nick's not exactly a horse person."

Or a much of a husband. He could hear it in her voice. The irritation prickled again, paired as it always was with a stab of guilt. "She's right," Nick said, shrugging. "But thank you for looking out for Leigh's horse."

"You're most welcome." Patrice smiled, looking between them. "And I appreciate what you two do every day, looking out for our community, keeping it healthy and safe. You're quite the pair."

Nick managed a smile as Leigh turned to peer into Frisco's stall.

"Dr. Hunter's done a full exam, then?" she asked.

"Yes. And gave your boy an injection of Banamine for the pain—obviously helping. Ralph's checking my broodmare right now, but I'll let him know you're here and he'll fill you in. Frisco was good—no biting—and even gifted us with a small pile of manure." She laughed at the look on Nick's face.

Leigh tossed him a tight smile. "Manure's a good sign with a horse being treated for colic. Means his gut's functioning."

"Oh."

Patrice nodded. "And now if we could only perk his appetite." She peered down the stable walkway. "Maria's walking around with her bag of carrots. She was so worried about Frisco; you could see it in her eyes. Even without saying a single word." She looked at Nick. "By the way, apparently I have you to thank for our little angel's placement here."

"Me?" he asked.

Patrice smiled. "I was talking to the county staff today, and the counselor said she'd learned about our foster care and equine therapy program from you. A Miss Gordon. I told her to come on out, I'd show her around."

Great.

Leigh's posture stiffened.

"Anyway, I thank you," she said, reaching out to touch Nick's arm. "That girl needs us, and we needed her. Now I'm going to go find our vet. And round Maria up. I swear she's going to brush the coat right off that donkey."

She disappeared, boots clomping down the walkway, and Nick turned to Leigh, prepared for the hostility he was sure he'd encounter. But all she seemed was tired. Faint shadows beneath her lower lashes, dark hair escaping her ponytail, and an expression pinched with worry. About her horse. For the first time he was glad the selfish beast had all of her attention. He didn't want to talk about Sam.

"I'll go, then," he said. When she didn't answer, he began walking away. Then stopped, remembering. "Leigh?"

"Yes?"

"I promised Harry I'd prune that hedge. Okay if I go by there and do it before it gets dark?"

"Sure. I'll be here for a couple of hours. I want to mix up a warm bran mash and see if I can get Frisco to eat it. And Caro's at work until seven. I guess you won't bother anyone."

Bother. He'd become no more than a bother. "Okay. And you know . . ." He shook his head. "Yesterday was the first time I'd seen much of Caroline since she's been back. Is she okay?" He saw Leigh's brows rise. "I mean, is she taking her meds? sleeping all right?"

"She's taking her medication. She's keeping her counseling appointments and looking for an apartment. She's fine—even gone back to teaching some Pilates classes. You don't have to be concerned." Leigh glanced toward Frisco as he shifted position in his stall.

"I'm concerned because I care."

"Don't." She pinned Nick with a look, and the hostility he'd hoped to escape slashed like a knife. "Don't say you care. Or do any of this. Don't."

"Leigh . . ."

"No. Just go prune the hedge. And while you're there, take the last of your things out of the house. Please." A tear slid down her cheek, making him ache to hold her. She swept it away, looking even angrier if possible. "The best thing you can do for Caro—for me—is leave us alone."

He turned to go.

"Nick?"

He glanced back at her.

"Don't come here again. This is my place. It's all I have. You don't belong here."

When he got to the patrol car, Maria was standing silently beside it holding her sack of carrots. And a polished wood horse brush, thick with donkey hair.

+++

Riley hunched over the sunny visitors' table and stared at the rubber ball, willing her fingers to squeeze harder, grip.

And imagining them doing so many things that had seemed ordinary less than a year ago: combing her hair, thumbing through the tabs on her study Bible, dropping a coin in a Houston parking meter, or dunking a Gulf shrimp into chipotle sauce. Starting an IV, sponging a feverish child . . . *Will I ever be a nurse again?*

She sighed, remembering an exercise she'd been given in physical therapy—reaching into a fishbowl filled with textured objects: glass marble, thumbtack, fingernail brush, feather, popcorn, square of sandpaper, penny, quarter, and seashell. And how she'd struggled to lift each very different object, touched its unique surface, then struggled even harder to identify it with her eyes closed. Completely by feel. She'd made improvement, but who would want a nurse holding a needle when she could barely tell a piece of popcorn from a thumbtack? a woman still too cowardly to walk a flight of stairs alone?

"London Olympics?"

Riley blinked up at Caroline. "Beg your pardon?"

Caroline pointed at the rubber ball, eyes teasing. "Your training. Shot put?"

Riley laughed. "In my dreams. Right now I'd settle for being able to rub my nose when it itches." She pointed at the adjacent patio chair. "Join me?"

"Sure." She glanced at the ball in Riley's fingers. "How's it going?"

"Slow enough to make me crazy. But I'm hoping that these new tingles I feel mean the nerves are regenerating. It's supposed to be one inch a month." She smiled as the lab tech's eyes traveled from Riley's shoulder to her hand. "I've measured it, believe me. Never appreciated short arms on my college tennis courts. Or thought I'd be competing in rehab Olympics. But I'm not giving up."

"How did it happen?"

Riley's breath hitched. "Took a header down a flight of stairs. Broke my neck. And a few other things." *Including my courage . . . and my trust?* She appreciated the obvious empathy in Caroline's expression. "It could have been worse. I'm grateful." *Not to be a murder statistic.*

"Now you're working as a chaplain." Caroline brushed back a length of her sun-streaked hair and glanced at Riley's notebook lying on the table. "And leading that hospital fellowship. I heard about it."

"Yes, Faith QD."

Caroline touched the cover of Riley's notebook. "You have that logo of a Florence Nightingale lamp with a cross in the handle. I saw some people wearing those T-shirts. Clever."

"I can't take credit," Riley said, thinking once again how much she'd like to see this lab tech take part. There was something fragile about her, despite her sometimes-edgy, cynical tone and shows of bravado. "The idea came from an ER nurse at Sierra Mercy Hospital. Erin Quinn. She's at Pacific Mercy now. Leigh worked with her there." She clucked her tongue. "Erin and her fiancé headed up the debriefing after that awful pesticide disaster last spring. She's worked hard to make spiritual support part of critical stress management."

Caroline nodded. "And you're taking it over here."

"I'm trying. After my injury, I knew I wouldn't be able to do ER nursing, at least for a while. So I took the Critical

Incident Stress course to become a peer counselor, then lay chaplain training through my church in Houston."

"And moved two thousand miles away." Caroline's eyes fixed on hers and Riley knew sugarcoating wasn't going to fly.

"Yes." Riley slid her arm back into its sling. "The fact is I needed to get away. My family . . . um . . ."

"Isn't easy?" Caroline studied her expression for a moment and smiled slowly. "I can relate. My mother is a piece of work. Always was." She shook her head and her hair trailed across the shoulders of her purple scrubs. "It's funny. I remember studying birds in school, maybe second grade. You know, robins, blue jays, sparrows. Crayon colors for each." She picked at the edge of the table. "That's when I found out my mother is a cowbird."

Riley kept quiet. *Listen . . . just listen.*

"The teacher said a female cowbird never builds her own nest; she flies around finding other birds' nests, then kicks their eggs out and stays long enough to lay a few of her own before taking off again. Scams those other poor birds into raising her babies." Her gaze drifted for a moment. "All the kids in the class were upset. But I sat there thinking, *That's Mom. That explains it.*" She met Riley's gaze fully again and shrugged. "On the other hand, I've had some very cool stepdads. Working on number five, as we speak."

"She's Leigh's mother, too?"

"Yes. But Leigh only got plunked in one extra nest. Because she's almost thirteen years older. She was in college by the time I got Mom pegged in the Audubon book. Still, she hasn't seen the best examples of marriage, either."

A flicker of sadness came into Caroline's eyes. "I'd hoped that she and Nick would be different. They were good for each other. But now he's gone, and she'll be moving away again. I guess I let myself believe in all that happily-ever-after stuff."

"I understand that kind of hope, and it's one of the main reasons I wanted to take this position in the chaplain service." Riley rested her hand on her notebook. "And start Faith QD here at Golden Gate. I think we all need a dose of hope, the staff as much as the patients. I'd love to have you join us."

"I don't know." The sadness filled Caroline's eyes again. "Nick goes to church—always has—and I went with him and Leigh sometimes. I liked it, actually. But my sister hasn't been back. Not since they broke up. She wouldn't want to see Nick there, I guess. Or maybe God's one of those things she wants to leave behind." Caroline glanced at her watch, then jumped up from the chair. "Oops, have to run. I need to draw blood on a patient upstairs."

Riley watched as the lab tech slipped her purse strap over her shoulder. "Please remember you're welcome at Faith QD. Anytime."

"I heard you . . . but I can't make any promises."

Riley sighed as Caroline walked away, telling herself she hadn't handled that well. Offering hope was one thing; force-feeding it was another, and—

"Hey there, chaplain lady!"

"Hi, Cappy." Riley smiled at the security guard. "How's your day going?"

"Fine as frog's hair." His grin crinkled the skin around his eyes. "And no better way to start it off this morning than by gathering with you and the other folks in the chapel. You're doing a good thing."

She could have kissed him. "You think so?"

"I know so. Folks need a good word. Especially around here—got to tip the scale against so much misery. And I'm glad to help you with anything you need to make that happen. You just let old Cappy know."

Cappy strode away, humming, and Riley gathered her things. She dropped the therapy ball into her tote, hitched the strap on her sling, and started toward the ER doors. Then stopped for a moment. She closed her eyes and raised her face, taking a slow breath and letting the autumn sunshine warm her.

She smiled at Cappy's words. He was right; people did need a good word. Caroline, Leigh, Officer Nick Stathos, that single mother upstairs, the man with the high-heel punctures on his face, and the woman with the overdose who'd been discharged home this morning. On some level, and despite their doubts, they all still wanted to believe in hope. And she wouldn't give up on trying to offer it to them.

Thank you, Lord. Thank you for knowing what I needed to hear. Help me help them.

She shifted her arm in the sling and felt the tingle in her fingers. She wouldn't give up on herself either. Maybe she wasn't ready for the Olympics, but . . .

She'd walk those stairs today.

+++

Leigh led Frisco under a canopy of trees, his feet making hollow clopping sounds against the dried clay path embossed with hoofprints. The faint sound of voices and laughter—Patrice, Gary, and their mixed class of therapy students—drifted from the riding arena in the distance. Along with Tag's lingering, plaintive bray. She'd been surprised that Frisco, even in his listless state, had to be encouraged with a cluck and tug to move past the little donkey's stall. He'd appeared content to stand there in the walkway, nose-to-nose with the poor, abused creature whose eye, sadly, was to be surgically removed. Leigh clucked as her horse slowed again. Keeping him moving, walking, was part of the treatment for colic. The worst thing that could happen was that he give in to the crampy pain. Give up. Lie down. In that position a horse was far more vulnerable to a fatal twist of the intestines.

Frisco, you've got to be okay.

He wasn't behaving normally at all. The few moments with Tag had been the only interest he'd shown in anything since she'd arrived at the barn. The mash she'd mixed for him—a huge bucket of rice bran, sweet and pungent with a trickle of molasses, steaming water, a bit of applesauce—sat in his stall untouched. She'd coaxed, lifted the heavy bucket to his nose, finally made a fool of herself by chewing some to show him. But he wasn't eating.

Leigh frowned as Nick's question about Caro came back without warning. *"Is she okay?"*

The anger rushed back, and she stopped walking. Nick had dared to question her ability to take care of her sister. After insisting that she come back from Pacific Point to do that and after she'd supported her in long months of treatment. And then he'd explained he was concerned because

. . . *"I care."* Care? She gritted her teeth. Did he care that his "concern" had his lover using Leigh's ER as a shortcut, taunting her as she passed through? Did he care how Leigh might feel about his pointing Sam in the direction of Golden Gate Stables? Would she show up here, walking the barn aisles, peering at Leigh over a bale of alfalfa? bring her child to pet the horses?

God, why are you doing this to me? She glared up through the branches overhead. She'd lost her marriage, a baby, and now this, the stable, her only sliver of peace. Was God intent on taking that from her too?

She turned, tensing, as Frisco uttered a low groan. He nipped at his side.

Leigh stepped close and tucked her fingers under his heavy jawbone, feeling for his pulse. She held her breath, counting . . . forty-eight. Strong. Still within normal limits. No labored breathing, no sweat. Just the gnawing pain . . . *that won't go away.* Leigh knew how that felt. She tried to swallow the ache that rose in her throat, but she couldn't. Her eyes filled with tears, and she flung her arms around Frisco's neck, burying her face in his mane. Listening to him breathe, feeling his warmth, but remembering Nick. The comfort of his arms, the way he'd made her feel—against a lifetime of doubts—that there was hope for happiness, for love that lasted. Really lasted. It had made her want to trust that she could have that. Finally.

But it wasn't going to happen. Praying hadn't helped. Running to Pacific Point hadn't solved anything. And now that she was back in San Francisco, it was only worse. Sam Gordon walking the floors of her ER, staking a claim on Nick for herself and her small child. Encroaching on the stable. *And invading my dreams . . .*

Leigh stepped back and swiped at the tears. She wasn't going to give in to this, even if God was stacking the deck against her. In less than a week she'd be free from the legal entanglements. She'd get the house leased, make a new start somewhere else. Even if it meant volunteering for a few months with Doctors Without Borders. She had the information; she'd consider it. Caro was doing better. She'd thrown herself back into Pilates and cycling and even picked up a schedule of spring classes from the community college—definitely better. Frisco would be too. And Leigh would go on. She'd get through it and then never let herself be this vulnerable again. Her mother had been right. Nothing lasted forever. Not love. Not marriage. And certainly not God's mercy. Good thing she'd never really trusted in any of that.

+++

Kurt took the stairs down from the second floor in a rush, enjoying the power of his descent, the echoing thud as his shoes struck the cement steps, and the brief sensation of flying as he launched down to the next. He was unstoppable, undeniable, a steely mass of energy like a locomotive tearing down the tracks, a fiery meteor sent to destroy the world, and—*whoa!*

He swore as he stumbled forward, nearly colliding with a woman leaning into the wall of the first-floor landing. A notebook and a sheaf of papers slipped from her fingers. "Whoa, lady . . . wow, didn't see you."

"Oh." She pressed a hand to her chest and stared at him, the color draining from her face. She sagged a little as if her knees had gone weak. Her other arm was in a sling, her eyes filled with terror.

The delicious sense of power surged.

"Hey, sorry," he made himself say. He caught sight of her name badge: *R. Hale. Chaplain Service.* He thought of Kristi and her new Bible-toting boyfriend, and his skin tingled like a high-tension wire. *The God squad . . . at my mercy.* "Did I scare you?"

"No." She gulped a breath and tried to smile. "I'm fine. Really. You just surprised me." Her eyes skimmed his scrub top, the fake ID badge he'd clipped on backward.

"I was just heading down for a smoke," he said quickly.

"Oh. Well, then . . ." She stooped down to reach for the things she'd dropped.

"I've got it," he said, beating her to it. He gathered the scattered papers, tucked them into the notebook, and stood. "You've got that sling on your arm. Let me carry this for you. We're walking the same way, right?"

"Right—I'm going to the ER. Thank you." She smiled, the fear in her expression replaced by something that almost looked like relief. As if his being there at that moment was a miracle from God himself.

He bit his lip to keep from howling as the dark current of power surged again. "After you, then," he said, sweeping his arm wide to let her go ahead.

This was easy. Being here, fooling these people. Too easy. What was his old man's saying? Right . . .

Like shooting fish in a barrel.

CHAPTER TEN

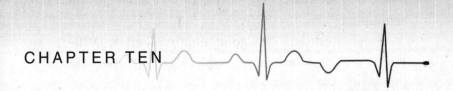

"You're still here?" Leigh crossed the shadowy lawn to the hedge, careful to avoid the scattered rakes, bundled leaf bags, and wheelbarrow piled high with clippings. Nick turned, shirtless and wearing faded Levis, holding a pair of heavy-duty pruning shears. Behind him the full moon, ember orange in the fading sunlight, climbed in the early evening sky. "I thought you'd be finished by now."

"Took longer than I figured." He swiped a hand across his perspiring forehead and laughed as Cha Cha's squawk drifted over from the McNealys' yard, followed by a resounding "Forever and ever!" "Well, not that long."

She smiled in spite of herself.

"Anyway," Nick continued, resting the shears on the wheelbarrow, "I got interrupted a few times. Antoinette brought Cha Cha outside in his cage; then she brought Harry. She thought he'd like to supervise the pruning. So we had lemonade, and I watched her trim his fingernails and listened to the story of how they met. Again . . . but it's a great story." His smile faded. "I guess Harry's been pretty agitated today. I think that's why she brought him outside.

It's funny; he can be so clear sometimes. He reminded me that he and I had planned to make an opening in the hedge. Connect the yards. With an arbor for Antoinette's climbing roses. He had those plans that showed a bench on each side, remember?"

Leigh nodded. The good neighbor arbor. Where two happy couples—one young, one older and wiser—would sit and visit.

"I could still do it for Harry. It wouldn't be hard. And—"

"He won't remember," she said, cutting him off. *And I don't want to remember. Don't make me remember. It's too late.*

Nick was quiet for a moment, his dark eyes studying her face. "How's Frisco?"

"Hanging in there," she answered, glad the subject was changed. "Dr. Hunter didn't think it was necessary to oil him." She saw Nick's forehead wrinkle and explained, "Sometimes the vet inserts a stomach tube and instills a big dose of mineral oil. A laxative to keep things moving and prevent an intestinal blockage."

Nick grimaced. "I can imagine how your horse would react to that. The vet could lose an arm."

"Frankly, I'd almost welcome Frisco's feisty temper at this point. Patrice will administer more of the pain medicine tonight, but . . ."

"But?"

"He's not eating. A horse's lack of appetite is a sure sign something's not right."

"I saw Maria with that bag of carrots. Maybe she'll get him to eat."

"Leigh? Is that you, dear?"

They both turned at the voice on the other side of the darkened hedge.

"Yes, Antoinette, I'm—" She started to walk to the hedge, stumbled over a trash bag, lurched for a few steps, then fell to her knees in the grass. In an instant Nick was there, helping her to her feet. His grasp was strong and steadying. The warmth of his touch and her immediate reaction to it stunned her.

"Are you okay?"

"Sure. I'm . . ." She breathed in the scent of him—faint trace of soap, tangy mix of sweat, autumn leaves, and masculine skin. "I'm fine," she said finally, way too conscious of his hands on her arms and the way his eyes searched hers . . . *and what a fool I am.*

"Well, my goodness." Antoinette's face appeared over the hedge, and even in the shadows, Leigh could see the delight in her expression. "You're both there. What a sight for sore eyes this is."

Leigh stepped away from Nick, rubbing at her arms as if it would erase his touch. She wanted to turn and run, even if it meant risking tripping over a rake. She needed distance. A few more days, and then . . .

"Forever and ever!" Cha Cha shrilled.

Antoinette shook her head. "That bird's a broken record, I'm afraid. But hard to teach an old bird new tricks." Her gaze darted between them. "And it's a good reminder."

"How's Harry doing?" Nick asked, his voice husky and low in the darkness.

"I've tucked him in. He's looking at the old picture

albums. I think the fresh air did him good. Thank you for trimming the hedge. Harry was so determined to get that taken care of. He'll be calmer now. He hates thinking he's left something undone."

"I understand." Nick glanced sideways at Leigh for an instant. "I'm glad I was here. You tell Harry good night for me, all right?"

"I'll do that. Good night, dear."

Antoinette's face disappeared, Cha Cha's squawks receded, and they were left standing in silence. Leigh could hear Nick breathing. He shifted beside her and cleared his throat. Her pulse quickened and she spoke before he could.

"Did you get those last boxes packed?"

"I don't want to talk about boxes."

There was another stretch of silence, filled only by the muted sounds of Geary Street traffic and faint sprinklings of childish laughter from the Chan house two doors down.

She calculated the risk of dashing through the deepening twilight.

"The lemon tree looks bad," he said, his tone remarkably similar to the one she used to inform family members of a grim prognosis. "I could take it, trim the branches back. Get it some of that citrus food."

"No." She rubbed her arms again, blaming the chill on encroaching bay fog. "It's okay where it is."

"It's dying. You're letting it die, Leigh."

"I'm what?" she asked, hearing the accusation in his tone and feeling the ruthlessly unfair barb of it strike deep. "Let me get this straight: I'm killing the lemon tree. I'm taking lousy care of my sister. What's next? I'm failing to roll out the red carpet so your girlfriend can waltz through my ER anytime she wants?" She raised a palm, saw that it was trembling. "And wait—let me guess. Next I'll be a shrew for saying that I hate it—*hate it*—that you're stuffing her down my throat at the stables."

He took a step closer and started to reach out but stopped. "C'mon. I'm not saying any of that. You know I'm not. You know me."

Tears stung her eyes. "I thought I did, once. But . . ." She shook her head. "The only thing I know now is that I'm not going to have to deal with this much longer. You can't know how good that makes me feel. And here's all you need to know." She raised her hand and touched her fingers one by one as if she were instructing a patient for aftercare. "The lemon tree doesn't matter. Caro is doing great." She took a breath and looked him full in the face as she ticked off her last point. "I need the last of your boxes out before the leasing agency—"

"They're out."

"Good."

He stared at her for a moment before retrieving his shirt and yanking it over his head. "I'll bag up what's in the wheelbarrow and put the tools away. Then I'll go."

"Good," she said again, her heart cramping as she walked back to the house.

Twenty minutes later, she heard his car start. She held her breath as it idled at the curb and pulled away. She called the stables, learned that Frisco had required another injection of Banamine, that his resting heart rate was forty-nine and his breathing was normal. Intestinal rumblings were present, but fewer than normal. He'd drunk some water. And hadn't touched his hay. Patrice, bless her, was on top of things and would check him during the night. She'd call if there was a problem. And, she'd added, Maria had drawn a picture of Frisco and Tag walking under a glittery rainbow. It was taped to his stall.

Leigh tossed her grass-stained scrubs in the hamper and took a shower. Then pulled on an old pair of olive drab riding sweats and padded downstairs to fix a sandwich. But she found there was no deli turkey and only a few slices of wheat bread, because . . . She smiled. Because her sister had eaten it all. Healthy appetite, holding down a job, making plans for college. *See, Nick? I'm right. Caro's fine.* She waited for the sense of triumph or even a small prickle of residual anger, but all that came was the memory of falling and the feel of her husband's hands as he swept her up. Warm, steady. Hands and heart, she'd wanted to believe that.

She opened a can of tomato soup, found some crackers, and had her dinner alone at the breakfast bar that had always been their substitute for a table. She spooned her Campbell's, told herself freedom was a good thing, and tried not to picture Nick in this same kitchen, laughing as he made his famous Greek soup.

"Avgolemono," he'd say slowly, accenting the *lemono* and taking her in his arms. "The secret to getting it right, Mrs. Stathos," he'd whisper against her hair, "is to add the hot broth and lemon juice to the eggs slowly and stir, stir. Stick with it; don't stop. . . . Don't ever give up."

She stared at her bowl of tomato soup. Nick had hoped that the lemon tree—a gift to remind her of their honeymoon in Capri—would provide lemons for avgolemono. Enough fruit for a family someday.

Family. Leigh spread her hands over her abdomen, imagining once again how it would have felt to have carried the baby to term. To have him or her in this house now. Three months old, beginning to smile, blinking up at her with eyes as dark as Nick's. Her throat squeezed around the ache of the what-ifs: What if she'd told him as soon as she'd suspected she was pregnant? What if planning for a baby had stopped the arguments? prevented Nick's downward spiral of grief after Toby's death—kept him from turning to Sam?

She stood, angry with herself for going down that path again. She hadn't wanted a baby; that had been one of the reasons they'd argued. The timing in her career, the danger in his; she hadn't felt ready. To imagine that telling him would have changed anything, stopped things from ending up where they were right now . . .

The image of his face came to her. His expression as he'd stood near the hedge, talking about the lemon tree. *"You're letting it die."* It had felt like he'd been talking about so much more than a tree. As if he was blaming her for all of it. *After what he did?*

The familiar anger swept back, and she welcomed the way it wrestled down the painful doubts. A baby wouldn't have changed things. Their marriage had been floundering. They'd separated; it was ending though they hadn't dared to say it aloud. Even if she'd agreed to stick with the Christian couple's counseling, it wouldn't have helped. Their marriage had been as doomed as that lemon tree.

+++

Nick stood beside his car on the hill at Alamo Square, gazing at the view that never failed to move him. San Francisco—Hayes Street to the south, Fulton Street to the north, Scott Street to the west, and Steiner to the east—lit by a full moon suspended in the night sky like a Chinatown paper lantern. It cast a golden glow over the famous panorama: the row of "painted ladies" Victorians in the foreground and a light-dotted skyline beyond, the Transamerica Pyramid, the tops of the Golden Gate and Bay bridges, city hall. And down Divisadero Street, where his restaurant had been. Still was, except that now it was a Mexican bakery, wedged between a tattoo parlor and a yoga studio.

He sighed. *Niko's.* It seemed like a lifetime ago that he'd used the skills he acquired working in his foster parents' Greek café in San Jose, waiting tables and cooking in Bay Area restaurants. Then taking out loans, first for culinary school and finally to start his own business. His vision combined with an infusion of capital by several entrepreneurial SFPD officers he'd met at the gym. An irony, considering how many times he'd scraped against the law during his adolescent years. But it had worked. He cooked; they ate. They talked; he listened—to stories of the community, action-packed tales of rescues and arrests, of kids whose lives they'd touched, saved, changed. It wasn't long before Nick started to feel a part of it. He began to want that for himself and felt a calling like he'd never experienced before. An orphan, a troubled youth . . . who wanted soul-deep to become a cop. He'd already started online courses in police science when a beautiful young doctor walked into Niko's, fell in love with his lemon soup, and . . .

And now she's walking away.

He leaned back against the BMW and closed his eyes for a moment, remembering Leigh's terse litany these past few days. *"Leave me alone. . . . Don't come here again. . . . You don't belong here. . . ."* She'd made it all too clear that their marriage was over, as dead as that lemon tree. When was he going to get that through his thick skull?

The verses about love came before he could stop them: *"It always protects, always trusts, always hopes, always perseveres. Love never fails."* First Corinthians. Words that he, like so many others before and after, had wanted to include in their wedding ceremony. But he'd let Leigh talk him out of it and into using something more "contemporary." Then, of course, their love *had* failed. His fault. And nothing he'd done since had ever fixed it, ever would. He'd be divorced on October 3, a matter of days; he'd find someplace to live, try to move forward with his life.

His cell phone buzzed on his belt. He squinted at the number, then exhaled slowly and answered. "Sam."

"Great, I caught you."

Nick stared out at the lights, trying to tell which belonged to a Greek restaurant that was now a Mexican bakery. Impossible. And pointless. "Yes," he said softly. "You did."

"Elisa still wants to give you that macaroni butterfly. I don't suppose you have time to come by? She—we—would love to see you."

"I was going to Buzz's to take a shower; I'm pretty grubby."

"There's a shower here."

"Don't come here again. . . . You don't belong here. . . ."

"But if you'd feel more comfortable at Buzz's . . ." Sam's voice trailed off.

"I'll shower, then be at your place in half an hour."

+++

"I was making one last call to check on Frisco," Leigh explained, setting the phone down as Caro walked into the kitchen.

"How is he?"

"The vet's going to check him again tomorrow." Leigh stifled a yawn. "Sorry. I'm kind of tired."

Caro picked an apple from the fruit bowl and tossed it between her hands. "You should be. How long did it take you to do all that lawn work? There must be three bags out there."

Leigh's heart cramped. "Not me. Nick. He pruned the hedge for Harry."

"Oh. That sounds like him." Something sad and vulnerable flickered in Caro's eyes. "I see that the boxes in the living room are gone." She was quiet for a long moment, tossing the apple back and forth. Then her eyes met Leigh's. "Do you think Mom was right?"

"About what?"

"Happy endings—that there's no such thing."

Leigh's stomach sank. "She actually told you that?"

"At the end of *Cinderella*, every time. Like a disclaimer."

"Wait. She read to you?"

Caro laughed and the Evers dimple appeared beside her mouth. "Are you kidding? I meant the video. I always had a suitcase full of them. *Cinderella, Sleeping Beauty, Little Mermaid*; it was the first thing I packed up whenever we moved." Her smile faded. "Did she tell you that, too? That happily ever after was so much bull; that you need to track down whatever you wanted in life, go after it, never, ever look back, and . . ." Sudden tears welled in her eyes.

"And nothing lasts forever." Leigh breathed around the lump in her throat.

"I guess, in spite of that, I wanted to believe it could. But now after you and Nick . . ."

God, please, don't do this. Not this, too.

A tear slid down Caro's face.

"Oh, sweetie . . ." Leigh moved forward and drew Caro close, wrapping her arms around her, stroking her hair. "I'm sorry," she whispered, feeling her sister's shoulders shake. "I'm so sorry."

"It's not your fault," Caro moaned. "And don't worry; I'm taking my pills, staying sober. But I can't seem to shake these feelings. . . ." She pulled away at the sound of frantic shouting in the distance. "What is that?"

Leigh rushed into the living room to find Antoinette standing in the open doorway, moonlight spilling around her.

"Thank the Lord—you're here," she gushed, staggering toward them with her snowy hair wild, glasses askew and cracked over a swollen and discolored eye. "It's Harry," she said, wringing her hands. "He's frantic and I can't get him calmed down. Please come quick!"

CHAPTER ELEVEN

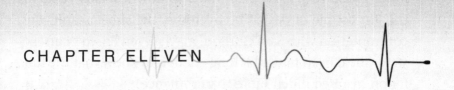

Leigh grasped her neighbor's arms, eyes scanning her bruised face and several tiny, scattered lacerations over the bridge of her nose, likely from the broken glasses. She had to ask. "Did Harry hit you?"

"Oh, my. No, dear." Antoinette shook her head and the red frames slid down her nose. "I was trying to keep him in the bedroom and he pulled on the door, and I fell down. I'm fine, but we have to hurry. I'm worried that he'll run off. He's so confused. He thinks that it's our anniversary and we're going to the Tonga Room for dinner. He pulled his oxygen off and was rummaging through the closet for his dress clothes. He got so frustrated that he started to throw things."

Caro glanced sideways at Leigh. "Do you think we should call 911?"

"No, please don't." Antoinette's chin trembled. "They'll take him away. That's what happened to the husband of one of my friends from church. And he only got more confused. He never came home. Please. The visiting nurse keeps a vial of sedatives at the house. If you could help me . . ."

"Of course," Leigh assured her. "But let me go in first. To feel things out, okay?"

Caro took their neighbor's arm, and Leigh led the way down the porch steps and across the driveways, glad for the light of the full moon. Though, she thought, this particular lunar phase very likely had much to do with the events of the last couple of days. The overdose, the shoe assault, the confrontation with Sam Gordon, maybe even Frisco's current state. She'd been in the ER long enough to know that the full moon inspired much more than romance.

They heard Harry before they saw him. His querulous voice filtered under the closed bedroom door, blending with Cha Cha's agitated squawking. "We're . . . late," he shrilled. "Can't be . . . late. Have . . . reservations."

"*Awwwk*—forever and ever!"

"Harry, poor darling." Antoinette stepped forward, but Leigh stopped her.

"Let me, Antoinette." She flinched at the sound of something striking the door, then shattering. "Caro will help you get some ice on that bruise, and I'll . . ." There was a loud thump behind the door.

"Harry?" Leigh called, close to the door, after watching Caro take Antoinette into the kitchen. "It's Leigh Stathos, your neighbor. May I come in?" She waited a few seconds, listening. "Mr. McNealy?" She opened the door cautiously.

He was sitting on the edge of the bed, naked except for a tuxedo shirt that he'd managed to put on backward like an old straitjacket. Perspiration beaded on his forehead and his face was pale, ashen. Beside him was an opened photo album, pictures strewn across the sheets, and a tangle of what appeared to be colored plastic leis, glittery party hats, grass skirts, and several dusty champagne glasses and tiki mugs.

"I . . . can't . . . manage . . . these dratted . . . buttons," he wheezed, looking up at Leigh with watery eyes as he fumbled with the backward shirt. "Can you . . . get my bride? She . . . always helps me."

"Sure, Harry." Leigh opened the door wider, and shards of broken glass scraped across the hardwood floor. She scanned the littered room and spotted the oxygen tank and tubing half-buried beneath a sequined gown. "But let's get your oxygen back on first."

"No!" he shouted, trying to rise to his feet. "No . . . time. The reservations. Tonga Room . . . won't hold them." He wobbled, then sank backward onto the bed, chest heaving and lips blue-tinged.

"There's plenty of time," Leigh reassured him, stepping into the room carefully to avoid the broken glass. She grimaced. Harry was barefoot. "Please sit back down. Let me get your oxygen."

"Don't need it!" he shouted, rising to his feet again. "Are you . . . insane, woman? Can't dance with . . . that evil contraption." He grabbed a champagne glass, hurled it at the dresser, and stumbled forward. "Antoinette! We're late!"

Leigh turned as Caro arrived at the doorway, followed by Antoinette holding a bag of frozen peas over one eye. The other was blinking back tears.

"I have that vial of medicine," Antoinette whispered. "I think if we could just give him a little shot, he'd relax. And forget all this business about our anniversary." A tear slid down her cheek. "My poor darling. I shouldn't have given him those photo albums. Harry's very sentimental. Oh, dear. He's breathing so hard. Sit down, darling, please!"

Leigh glanced from Antoinette's anxious face back to where Harry sat struggling for breath in his backward dress shirt. Harry needed oxygen. They had no choice but to call for help.

+++

"Thank you, Elisa." Nick leaned forward on the couch and touched a fingertip to a glued and glittered piece of pasta. "I've never seen such a beautiful butterfly."

The toddler, in Little Mermaid pajamas and smelling sweetly of strawberry shampoo, grinned at him. She wiggled closer and rested her palm, like a tiny starfish, on his leg. "Ith macawoni," she said with her soft lisp. "Mommy made it."

Sam's face colored. "She means we worked on it together, don't you, sweetheart?" She dropped her dish towel and walked around the breakfast bar to join them in the family room, her long skirt—sort of soft and pink and printed with flowers—fluttering as she moved. He'd never seen her dressed like that before.

She sat down beside her daughter and pressed a kiss against her downy blonde hair. "And now it's time for a certain little artist to go to bed. And maybe—" she smiled over her daughter's head—"if we ask nicely, Nick will read *Goodnight Moon*."

"I . . ." He hesitated at the intruding image of Leigh's face, rosy in the light of the rising moon. "Sure," he said, pushing the memory away. "Would you like that, Elisa?"

"Uh-huh. Pleeease." She bobbed her head, making her curls bounce.

"Good, then." Sam lifted her daughter in her arms and

stood. Her gaze moved over Nick's face. "I'll get her teeth brushed and tuck her in. It will only take a few minutes. I left the rest of the cake on the table."

"Couldn't," he said, lifting a hand in protest. "I'd have to crawl home." His eyes met hers and his stomach sank. Because he had no home and because he could see very plainly that she didn't want to him to go anywhere tonight. *Lord, what am I doing here?*

He stood after they left the room and walked toward the fireplace, careful to avoid Elisa's LEGO castle. Sam had added framed photos to the mantel since he'd been there last. Several of Elisa, and a photo of Sam and three other women standing beside a Chinatown storefront with plucked chickens dangling in the window. And one of her brother and Nick at Niko's wearing aprons, arms raised and laughing as they danced the syrto.

Toby . . . He lifted the photo from the mantel, the dull ache of grief returning.

"I found it in Toby's things," Sam said, walking toward him. "He was always talking about the good times you guys had at your restaurant. The music and the street people you fed after closing time. And what a great chef you are."

"Was," he said, looking at the photo and trying to remember exactly when it was taken. *Before Leigh? After?* He'd have to stop measuring things by her. "Not anymore."

"C'mon," she teased, stepping close enough that he could smell her perfume. "You're being modest. Talent like that doesn't go away. It's in your Greek blood." She rested her hand on his forearm and smiled at him. "And if you haven't noticed, I have a kitchen. I'd love you to cook for me."

A shower. A kitchen. A daughter waiting for a story. Was he here because he wanted this? or because he knew she did and what he needed was to be somewhere that he was wanted?

He stepped away and put the framed photo back on the mantel. "I haven't felt much like cooking since—" He stopped short, realizing that her eyes had filled with tears.

"I know," she said. "I've felt that way about so many things since we lost Toby."

I meant Leigh. Guilt washed over him and he moved close, putting his arms around her. "I'm sorry, Sam. It must be tough living in this house, with all the reminders."

She nodded, her cheek moving against his shirtfront. "It's hard sometimes, and then—" she leaned back and gazed into his eyes—"it's good too. Especially now. With you here."

He held his breath, watching her violet eyes and noticing the faint flush on her cheeks, her parted lips, the warmth of having a woman in his arms again, and thinking how easy it would be to fall into this. Too easy.

"I need you, Nick," she whispered. "I want you here with me. I'm alone; you're alone. It's crazy for you to be sleeping on that couch at Buzz's." She startled and then frowned as his cell phone rang. "Don't answer it."

"Let me check . . ." He scanned the caller ID and his throat constricted. He walked a few steps toward the dining room table. "Yes?"

"I'm sorry to bother you." Leigh's voice was rapid, breathless.

"What's wrong?"

"It's Harry. He's agitated, and I need to get him medicated

and back on his oxygen. Caro's helping, but . . . ." She was silent for a few seconds. "I need you."

"I'll be right there."

"Thank you. I didn't want to ask, but I know how much you care—" Her voice was drowned out by a deafening series of squawks and Cha Cha's imperative "Forever and ever!"

He hit the End button and turned back to Sam.

"You have to go," she said, her tone flat.

"Yes, something's come up. Thank you for the cake. I really appreciate it. Tell Elisa I'm sorry about the story."

"We'll give you a rain check."

He grabbed his jacket, then jogged toward the car, telling himself that even if Leigh hadn't called, he never would have stayed past *Goodnight Moon*.

+++

Leigh barely let Nick through the door before Antoinette rushed forward and flung herself into his arms. "Oh, Nicky . . . I knew you'd come. Thank you. I know you'll calm Harry down. He thinks of you like a son." She stepped away and raised her hand to her swollen eye. "I'm sorry; I must look a mess."

Leigh read the concern in Nick's eyes. "She fell. But—"

Harry's voice rose from behind the bedroom door. "I can't . . . find . . . my cuff links!" There was a muffled curse. Cha Cha mumbled beneath the cover on his cage.

Nick strode a few steps, then turned. "What's going on?"

Caro explained about the mistaken anniversary date, Antoinette launched into their history at the Tonga Room, and Leigh interrupted as gently as she could to give him her assessment of Harry's medical status.

"Okay. The first thing is to get him still enough to give the injection of . . ." He looked at Leigh.

"Lorazepam," she confirmed. "He hasn't had it before, so I'll start with a small dose. We can always give more. The goal is to get him calm enough to keep the oxygen on." She glanced toward the door. "With his emphysema, the low oxygen is enough to make him agitated even without the complication of Alzheimer's."

"So, meds. Oxygen." Nick looked toward Antoinette, the compassion in his expression not lost on Leigh. "Caroline, you'll keep Antoinette company?"

"Yes."

"Good." Nick gestured to Leigh. "We'll double-team him—you, me, together."

"Okay," she agreed, remembering what Patrice had said earlier at the barn: *"You're quite the pair."* For Harry's sake, she hoped that was really true. "I've got the dose drawn up and waiting on the table in the hallway."

"Let's go."

"I'll pray," Antoinette said as Caro eased her onto the couch and put the package of frozen peas back in place.

Nick led the way toward the bedroom, pausing outside the door as Leigh gathered the syringe of medication and some alcohol swabs. He listened at the door, then looked at her over his shoulder. "Good cop, bad cop."

"Huh?"

"You know, like on TV. We're partners here. And poor Harry is the perp."

"Oh. Right. So I'm the . . ."

"Bad cop."

Leigh raised her brows. "What?"

Nick smiled. "You're the one with the needle."

He waved her back a few steps and tapped on the door. "Harry? It's your friend Nick." He tapped again, waited, and opened the door a crack. "Harry?" He pushed the door a bit wider.

"Careful," Leigh whispered. "There's glass on the—"

"Uh-oh." Nick swung the door wide and grasped her arm, pulling her toward where Harry lay faceup on the floor alongside a sequined dress and the still-hissing tank of oxygen. They knelt beside him at the same instant.

"Is he . . . ?" Nick watched as Leigh pressed her fingers against their neighbor's neck.

"There's a pulse," she said, relief coursing through her. "It's strong and regular. And he's breathing. A bit fast and shallow . . ."

"So?"

"I think he wore himself out and fell asleep. I'm tempted to give him a shot right here on the floor while we've got him at our mercy." She smiled ruefully at the look on Nick's face. "But I'm not going to. Help me get the oxygen cannula back in place; we'll wait a few minutes before we ease him onto the bed. Maybe he won't be so belligerent if we get his O_2 level back up."

"And if he is?"

She reached for the discarded oxygen cannula. "Then you'll be glad you brought your bad cop."

Nick gently steadied Harry's head as Leigh checked the

flow of oxygen—two liters per minute—and placed the prongs in his nostrils, then threaded the tubing over his ears. She secured it under his chin and sat back on her heels, watching as the bluish tinge disappeared from his lips. She reached for his wrist and counted his pulse and respirations.

"Better?" Nick asked, still kneeling beside her.

"Yes. Heart rate's regular at 88. His respirations are—" she smiled as Harry inhaled with a hearty snore—"down to 28. But I'd like to take a listen to his lungs before we move him." She glanced toward the door. "Can you ask Caro for my stethoscope?"

"You brought it?"

She smirked. "Got your gun?"

His smile made her breath catch.

Five minutes later, she'd listened to Harry's lungs and done what she could to examine him for any signs of injury. She'd found none, thankfully. After sweeping aside the pile of plastic leis, grass skirts, scattered photos, and what was left of the champagne glasses, Nick grasped him under the arms, Leigh took hold of his legs, and they hefted him onto the bed. His eyes snapped open, and he immediately reached for the oxygen cannula. "What's this doggone thing doing in my nose?"

"Easy, Harry." Nick caught his hand. "It's helping you breathe."

Harry peered up at him. "You get that hedge trimmed?"

"Yes, sir."

Harry's gaze shifted to Leigh. "He do a good job?"

"He did," she said, trying not to think of all she'd said to Nick while he was doing that.

"Good." Harry sighed, then licked his lips. "Well, you two better get dressed. You can't go like that."

"Go where?" Nick lifted Harry's hand away from the cannula again.

Harry looked at Nick like he was crazy. "Tonga Room, of course. We have reservations. And they won't hold them if we're late."

"Harry—" Leigh touched his hand—"we need you to rest."

"No!" Harry shouted, struggling to sit upright. He swatted Leigh's hand away. "Don't argue with me, young lady. I always take my bride to the Fairmont. Haven't missed a year." He pointed at Nick. "Now, son, you find me my cuff links, and we'll go."

"Yes, sir." Nick glanced sideways as Leigh discreetly reached for the syringe.

+++

Nick sat on the McNealys' stiff Victorian couch next to Caroline and Antoinette—who'd switched the thawing peas for a box of brussels sprouts—and watched as Leigh tiptoed back into the room.

"How's he doing?" he asked, thinking that in the years he'd known her, this was the most he'd observed of his wife in her role as a physician. Which she absolutely was, despite the fact that she was wearing her old riding sweats and a pair of suede slippers. She'd been kind, caring, and sharp; had even managed to get the McNealys' physician on the phone for a consult. He'd agreed completely with Leigh's handling of the situation. Nick was impressed.

"Physically back to normal. And calmer. But he's still

insistent on taking Antoinette out for dinner." She smiled at her neighbor, half-visible behind the box of frozen vegetables. "He said he's the luckiest man alive to have a wife like you, and the least he can do is waltz you around the Tonga Room on your anniversary."

"We spent our honeymoon at the Fairmont," Antoinette said, setting the brussels sprouts on her lap. "And we've been back every September since. Never missed one in almost sixty years. But now that Harry's sick, we can't make it this year. And next year, well, I'm not sure if . . ." Her words faded away.

If he'll still be here. Nick swallowed, watching as Caro took Antoinette's hand. He glanced at Leigh. "There's no way?"

"That we can take him out?" She sighed. "I don't see how. Certainly not as far as the Fairmont, and he's got his heart set on the Tonga Room."

"What is that, anyway?" Caroline asked. "It sounds like something out of *The Lion King*."

Leigh laughed. "You've never been there? It's in the Fairmont, Nob Hill. Sort of a huge, subterranean tiki bar. With grass huts, a ship's mast, and—"

"Let me, dear," Antoinette said, nodding at Leigh. "I was there long before you were a twinkle in your daddy's eye." She turned to Caro. "The Tonga Room and Hurricane Bar is a grand part of San Francisco history. It began way back in 1929, when it was a seventy-five-foot swimming pool called 'The Plunge.'" She clucked her tongue. "My parents saw Helen Hayes take the first dive. But the restaurant opened in '45. It was all the rage, very Polynesian. With a floating stage and tropical thunderstorms." Her eyes glittered. "And Tony Bennett."

Caroline smiled. "So all those leis and grass skirts, paper

umbrellas, and tiki mugs that Harry pulled out of your closet . . ."

"From parties at the Tonga Room." Antoinette picked up the brussels sprouts. "We've collected them for fifty-nine years. But I guess we'll just have to tell Harry that we can't go this year."

"Don't," Nick said, mind whirling as he rose to his feet. "Just stall him a bit and give me some time. You'll have your anniversary dinner."

Leigh met his gaze. "But he can't travel all that way."

"He won't have to."

"What do you mean?"

Nick smiled, enjoying the way his wife's nose wrinkled. "We'll bring the Tonga Room to him—or rather, to our house. He'd never buy us trying to do it here." He pointed toward the bedroom. "Harry has all the props. You and Caroline can decorate our dining room, and I'll cook." He laughed. "I can cook, remember?"

Antoinette clasped her hands to chest. "I have music, too—Sinatra and Tony Bennett, all the wonderful old tunes we danced to. And home movies from those parties with our friends. I can wear one of my gowns. The blue, that's Harry's favorite. And I'll find his bow tie and cuff links."

Caroline jumped to her feet, face flushing. "Leigh can be the sous-chef. And I can be a waitress. I love this!"

Nick read doubt in Leigh's expression. "You don't like the idea?"

"It's not that," she said, discomfort flickering across her face. "Has everyone forgotten? We don't have a dining room table."

It took the three of them nearly twenty minutes to get the leaf out of the McNealys' huge mahogany table, carry it down the steep front steps, across the two driveways, and into the house next door. After they settled the elegant table in their empty dining room—and Nick loosened the chain that had shortened the chandelier all these years—they stood in awkward silence. Leigh realized, once again, that the full moon was to blame for all of this craziness. But then, the effects of lunar phases, like everything else, didn't last forever.

CHAPTER TWELVE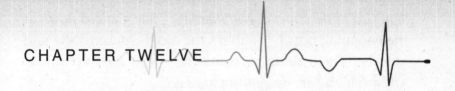

"Was that part of the hedge?" Leigh's eyes widened as Caro passed by the kitchen in a grass skirt, with yet another armful of greenery. It appeared she'd ransacked Nick's trash bags, after borrowing several of Antoinette's potted plants—including a small palm—intent on filling the darkened dining room with vegetation. Plastic leis dangled from the chandelier over a festive centerpiece comprised of a papier-mâché pineapple, a windup hula dancer doll, and an assortment of Christmas candles wedged into a half-dozen grimacing tiki mugs. Accented by a scattering of feathers that looked too much like Cha Cha's to be hygienically advisable. Frank Sinatra's voice crooned from the CD player: "Fly me to the moon . . ."

Nick nodded. "And not bad. For last-minute jungle decor."

"I can't believe we're doing this." She glanced to where Nick was grating fresh ginger, pungent and sweetly exotic. "Or that you actually found something to make a meal from. I haven't shopped for days."

He stopped grating, his dark eyes on hers. "There's

everything we need here. It's just a matter of taking the time to put it together. Building it around a central ingredient."

Central ingredient. For some crazy reason, she was reminded of something the marriage counselor had said. *"Put God in the center of your marriage."* She glanced down at the chopping board. "So that's the diced chicken," she said quickly. "Good thing we could thaw it in the microwave. And what else are we putting in here?"

"Soy sauce, honey, star anise—" he pointed toward a bundle of greens—"cilantro, green onions, and hoisin sauce."

"Hoi . . . ?"

Nick laughed and wiped his fingers on the large dish towel he'd slung over his shoulder. "Hoisin. It's a combination of soybeans, garlic, vinegar, and chili pepper. Sweet, salty, spicy."

"It was here?"

"We bought it in Chinatown," he said, capturing her gaze, "that rainy day we caught the cable car in Ghirardelli Square. And ended up helping the little kid who'd gotten separated from his grandmother." He glanced down. "Anyway, it keeps. Like I said, you had all the ingredients."

Except a table and the chef. Leigh watched as he grated a bit more of the ginger, then moved on to the next task. The forged steel knife moved expertly in his hands—*swoosh, swoosh*—as he rocked it over the cilantro, releasing the lush, earthy fragrance. She inhaled, blaming the sudden watering of her eyes on the green onions he'd completed and set aside. Even after all these months, it seemed natural to see Nick here in the kitchen, dish towel on his shoulder, sleeves rolled up, humming to himself as he worked. The look on his face was the same, as if what he was doing wasn't work at all, was much more than merely cooking. As if it were truly an act of—

"They're going to love it!" Caro gushed, popping back into the kitchen as Sinatra began belting, "Love and marriage go together like a horse and carriage." She wrinkled her nose. "Including that corny music. I've got the table all set. But I still need to get those flowers that you wanted from Antoinette's window box. So I think I'll run over there and check on them while you two are . . ." Her eyes swept between them, the look on her face the same as the one Leigh had seen earlier. Right here in this kitchen, when Caro talked about happy endings and then sobbed in her big sister's arms. "It's so good to see you together—doing this for the McNealys, I mean. It was a good idea, Nick."

"*We're* doing it. Meaning you, too, Hula Woman." Nick smiled at her. "Couldn't make this happen without you on the team." He glanced at his watch. "I'm about to slide this dish in the oven; the rice is coming right along. I'll put your sister to work on the salad." He frowned, looking down at his clothes. "And see if I can find something clean to wear in those boxes in my car."

Leigh stared at the chicken, aware of the sudden silence in the room.

"So all right," Caro said, raising her voice over Sinatra's refrain. "Let's get the Tonga Room open."

In less than hour, the house smelled of Polynesian chicken— sweet, gingery, and complete with hoisin sauce. They'd gathered around the McNealys' mahogany table, lei-festooned chandelier on a dimmer, tiki candles lit, Sinatra down low, and everyone in a vintage party hat. The McNealys' home movies, jumpy and discolored but full of obviously happy moments, flickered on the bedsheet Caro had thumbtacked to the wall behind them. Somehow, they'd done it. They'd turned their dining room into a restaurant. And a celebration.

Leigh's eyes traveled the table as Caro passed the jasmine rice. Antoinette wore a blue gown, accented by a purple eye, still visible after applications of two frozen vegetables and a thick layer of Merle Norman. The radiance of her smile, however, made it hardly noticeable. Caro had donned a sheer tunic and leggings and, in addition to the grass skirt and party hat, tucked a bright bougainvillea blossom behind her ear. She'd have no trouble walking from this room onto any fashion runway in New York City. Leigh, between salad duties, slipped away and exchanged her riding sweats for a simple black dress and her grandmother's pearls. And Nick . . . Her pulse quickened as she stole a glance at him seated next to her. White oxford shirt and Jerry Garcia tie over fresh blue jeans, all rumpled from the boxes. But in the candlelight, still so . . .

"You look handsome, Harry," Caro said, glancing down the table.

Their neighbor smiled, stifling a yawn. "Thank you, young lady." He touched his bow tie and raised an arm to show her a cuff link. "My bride gave me these for a wedding present." His eyes moved over Antoinette's face. "I'm a blessed man."

He glanced toward Leigh, sitting beside him, then at Nick. "You are too, son. Don't ever forget that."

"No, sir. I won't."

Leigh released the breath she'd been holding.

"And the food looks wonderful." Antoinette smiled across the table at Nick. "This beautiful chicken, and the way it's presented with that pretty little spray of nasturtium flowers."

"Exactly why we come to the Fairmont!" Harry boomed. "Every year. Every single . . ." His eyes glittered with sudden tears. "Forever . . . and ever." He cleared his throat. "I'm saying grace now."

He reached for Leigh's hand, then his wife's. She grasped Caro's. Caro reached across the table as Nick extended his hand. He took hold of Leigh's with his other.

"Dear Lord," Harry began, "we . . . uh . . ." Confusion flickered across his face. He looked at Nick helplessly. "I seem to have . . . forgotten. Son, would you . . . ?"

"Yes." Nick cleared his throat, and his fingers tightened around Leigh's. She could feel his wedding ring. He raised his voice just enough to be heard over the strains of Sinatra and the clicking whir of the old movie projector. "Lord, we thank you for this food and for bringing us together here, around this table. And for the many years of love that Harry and Antoinette . . ."

Leigh bowed her head, closing her eyes in the candlelight and thinking how strange it was that they were doing something Nick had always wanted. And how bittersweet that they'd finally gathered around a table in this dining room to thank God and celebrate someone else's marriage, just as they were preparing to say good-bye to their own.

+++

Sam picked up the phone for the third time, then set it down again and reached for her wineglass instead. She took a long swallow of the cabernet she could barely afford—from a Napa Valley winery where Nick said he'd once cooked for a charity event. Toby had been there too, and they'd taken a ride in a hot air balloon. Nick had teased her burly brother mercilessly for keeping a death grip on the basket, refusing to look down. Nick laughed when he'd told the story and looked genuinely happy. She'd hoped that the label, her sentimental gesture in buying the wine, would intrigue Nick enough that he wouldn't decline the offer of a glass. Or two. She'd never seen him drink. Except during those days after Toby's death, after Leigh turned him away.

You didn't want him then, and you can't have him now. Sam rested the glass against her cheek and closed her eyes, feeling the wine soften her like the frayed satin binding on Elisa's baby blanket. She told herself she couldn't know for sure that Nick was with his wife. He'd simply said, "Something's come up" and that he had to go. It could have been one of his buddies on the force or Buzz or one of the kids he mentored. But she'd seen the look on his face—in his eyes.

The truth escaped despite her efforts to swallow it down. Whenever Nick said Leigh's name, when he saw her, even thought of her, Sam always saw that look in his eyes. Something changed, something came into them. The same thing she'd wanted all her life to see in a man's eyes when he looked at her. Like she was his world. Like she held his beating heart in her hands and he wanted it that way. Like he was hers . . . forever. Leigh Stathos didn't deserve that anymore. Maybe she never did. Regardless, she'd forfeited it all by turning Nick away. She'd been selfish and cold and stupid. And Sam had been giving and warm, and very, very smart. She'd seen his need and filled it, held Nick in his sorrow, watched him rail and curse and slam his fist against a wall. Then heard his tearful prayer when he thought she was sleeping. She took him in, lay in his arms, and now . . . *he's back with her.*

"No!" She slammed the wineglass down on the counter, heard it shatter, and scrambled backward, but not before the dark liquid sluiced from the tile's edge and onto her skirt. Deep stains on delicate flowers—dark as blood. The skirt she'd chosen along with the wine to impress Nick. Part of a plan she'd put in place. Dessert, the macaroni butterfly, Elisa's bedtime story—it had been working. He'd held her, might have kissed her if he hadn't gotten that call.

Sam marched to the sink, dampened a dish towel, and rubbed at her skirt, anger sharpening edges softened by the glasses of cabernet. Nick was at Leigh's. She knew it. He wasn't answering his phone. What else could she—?

She stopped rubbing the skirt at the memory of Dr. Stathos's expression this afternoon, when she'd cut through the ER. As if she'd caught Sam trespassing on her property. Angry, threatened, bothered. Even the smallest bit fearful? Yes. So . . .

+++

"I think we can stop," Nick said, breathing into a humid layer of plastic leis. He made a grab for his grass skirt before it slid low enough to trip over, then raised his voice above the crescendo of taped drumbeats to be sure Caroline understood. "Harry's nodding off in his chair. I don't think we have to do this anymore."

"Don't be a quitter." Caroline gyrated beside him. "You've only been at it five minutes. If I'm willing to make a fool of myself, you can too. He wants Polynesian dancers. They always have them at their anniversary parties. You saw the movies. You're doing fine; just keep flailing those brawny arms and walk in place. When Antoinette comes back from the kitchen with the dessert, I want you moving. You're lucky I'm letting you keep your shirt and that we're not dancing around a fire, or—"

They both turned as Leigh's laugh snorted through her nose.

"Ummph." She crumpled in her chair beside the dozing Harry, holding her stomach. "Excuse me," she squeaked, before choking with laughter again. "It's just so . . ."

"Hey, watch it." Nick swayed in place, his fists on his skirt. "You could get recruited pretty fast." He tried to glare, but it was impossible because all he could think about was how happy she looked. It had been so long since he'd seen her laugh. Even at his expense.

"No," she said, brushing at her eyes. "I've already been recruited, remember?" Leigh glanced to where Harry dozed, chin sagging onto his tuxedo tie. She lowered her voice to a conspiratorial whisper. "Bad cop? Only the *good* cops dance." She pressed her hand to her lips, a giggle rising. "Oh, man . . ."

Antoinette walked in with a plate, then stopped and grinned. "Harry, look—our dancers!"

"Tonga time." Caroline nudged Nick and began treading her feet in earnest, swirling her arms in small circles. Harry woke up and started to applaud. Leigh crossed to the CD player and turned up the volume. So Nick danced. Sort of a half zombie walk, part Chicken Dance, and more than a little Greek syrto—he knew that one. He didn't have a clue; he felt like an idiot in the skirt, and he was completely out of sync with Caroline, but the look on Harry's face, the delight in Antoinette's eyes, and the incredible sound of Leigh's laughter made it all worth it. He'd be a fool any day for that. He whooped, raised his arms in the air, grabbed one of Caroline's hands and twirled her, joining in as she began laughing. He clapped along with the others, his gaze traveling from the jungle dining room to the home movies flickering on the wall, to the sight of Harry sliding his arm around his wife's shoulders. And then to Leigh, smiling at him. Really smiling. He watched her eyes, lost.

"You can stop now."

Nick turned to Caroline. "What?"

"The drums are over. There's new music. I think that's . . ."

"Tony Bennett." Antoinette sighed. "He's playing our song."

Nick recognized the strains of the singer's trademark song beginning to fill the room: "I left my heart in San Francisco. . . ." He watched as Harry set his oxygen tubing aside, slowly rose, and took his wife's hand. He led her to the center of the floor.

Nick and Leigh slid the chairs back to make more room,

and Caroline dimmed the lights until the glow of the full moon through the window provided the perfect illumination for their improvised dance floor. Nick pulled off the skirt and leis and tossed them on the couch. He stepped closer to Leigh. "Is he okay to do that?"

"He looks pretty okay to me. Don't you think?"

"I mean medically, without his oxygen."

"I think there isn't any better medicine for Harry right now," Leigh said, her eyes on the elderly couple moving slowly in each other's arms. She cleared her throat. "It could be their last time to dance."

"Yes," he said, watching the old man in a vintage tuxedo holding his wife of sixty years, lit by moonlight and silhouetted against a backdrop of movie scenes, their life together. "You're right. They need this dance. I'm glad we—" He stopped, seeing that Harry was beckoning to him. "Need something, sir?"

"I sure do." Harry beckoned again, waving his hand so vigorously this time that he teetered. Antoinette steadied him. "What I need . . . ," he said, pausing to take a breath, "is not to be out here on an empty dance floor. What are you waiting for, son? a personal invitation from the band leader? Bring your beautiful bride out here!"

Leigh stiffened. "I . . . we . . ." She stared at Antoinette, clearly begging the woman to bail her out. Then frowned when she didn't.

So Nick did. "Maybe next time." *Next anniversary. Which won't come for either of us, Harry.* "The song's almost over."

"No, it's not," Caroline blurted, jabbing at the buttons on the CD player. "And as your bandleader, I *am* inviting you to dance with the anniversary couple. Tonga Room rules require it." She pushed the button, released a few bars of drumbeats, hit it again, and Tony Bennett began leaving his heart in San Francisco all over again. "There. All brides on deck."

Antoinette murmured with delight, Harry grinned, and Nick glanced at Leigh. "May I have this dance?"

She stared at him, her expression unreadable. "For Harry," she said finally.

"Right." Nick released the breath he'd been holding. "For them."

He took hold of her hand and led her onto the moonlit Fairmont dance floor that had once been their living room.

+++

Leigh moved into Nick's arms, noting that her sister had adjusted the dimmer on the lighting downward again. The tiki candles and moonlight, spilling through their bay window, became the only illumination in the room. The perfect romantic ambience. *For the McNealys,* she reminded herself as her husband's palm warmed the small of her back. Her fingers, curled inside his, trembled a little as he drew her closer. He smelled of ginger and cilantro and felt . . . oh so familiar.

He cleared his throat. "Thank you." His whisper warmed her cheek. "This evening means a lot to Harry and Antoinette. And to me."

Oh, don't. Don't, Nick.

"I know you didn't want to do this." His fingers brushed lightly over the back of her hand. "But I'm glad."

"It's only a dance, Nick." Her heart thudded in her ears. "One dance. Don't make more of it, because . . ." *It won't last.* "Just don't, please."

He didn't answer, and they kept dancing. While Tony Bennett sang on. ". . . My love waits there in San Francisco, above the blue and windy sea. . . ."

She followed her husband's lead, aware of his breathing and that he'd leaned down a little, moved closer—enough that she felt the brush of his cheek against hers. She thought of pulling back, considered slipping her hand from his and ending the moment. But instead, she closed her eyes in the semidarkness, relaxed in Nick's arms, and tried to imagine that they were really in that historic hotel on Nob Hill. That he'd never gone to bed with Sam Gordon. And that she hadn't lost the baby. That they'd been married for decades, and—no matter what she knew was true—forever was possible.

"Leigh?"

"Yes?" She opened her eyes, blinking as Caro turned the lights up. Nick let go of her hand. Antoinette was standing beside Harry's chair, gesturing to her.

"I'm sorry, dear," she explained, pointing at the oxygen tank. "But I have such trouble adjusting the flow on this thing. Could you help me?"

"Of course." Leigh moved away from Nick, feeling a wave of relief. *Not regret.*

"And I think," Antoinette said as Leigh cranked open the tank's valve and adjusted the flow to two liters, "that we'll have to call it a night." She tidied her husband's sparse strands of hair. "We're tuckered out."

Leigh looked at Harry, at his off-kilter bow tie and the

maroon lipstick print at the corner of his mouth. "Did you have a good time, Harry?"

"Sure did," he said, raising his chin to gaze at his wife. "Always do. I'm a blessed man."

Antoinette's eyes shimmered with tears. "I love you, Harry."

"And I'll love you . . . forever and ever."

Nick shifted beside Leigh. "Happy anniversary," he said, stepping forward to kiss Antoinette's bruised cheek. "And you too, sir," he said, extending his hand to Harry. "Thank you for including us in your party."

"Good party—always good." His brows drew together. "Except I'll have to speak to the manager. Those Tonga dancers aren't what they used to be."

Nick pitched in and they managed to get Harry and Antoinette back to their house, where Leigh encouraged him to take a small dose of the same sedative she'd given him earlier. In pill form, this time. Which probably moved her to the rank of good cop, she thought. Nick helped Harry out of his tuxedo and into bed and set the CD player on their dresser—the Frank Sinatra disc, with no risk of sporadic drumming frenzies. Leigh switched the oxygen over to a new tank.

When they walked back through the McNealys' living room, Caro was putting sheets on the couch.

"I'm staying the night," she explained as she tied her hair back with a band. "In case Antoinette needs any help." She shook her head when Leigh tried to offer her own help. "You have to be at work early. I don't." She nodded at Nick.

"You're working too. I have your cell number on speed dial. I'll call if we need you."

"Okay." Leigh sighed. "You're pretty great, you know?"

Caro smirked, the single dimple appearing beside her mouth. "Not that great. I'm leaving you with the dishes."

Nick laughed. "Not a problem. I'm here. And I wash dishes much better than I dance."

Leigh stayed quiet for a moment, then glanced at him. "You're hired."

+++

Kurt watched Kristi from the darkness of his car, secure that even if she saw it parked down there in the moonlight, she wouldn't recognize the car. The crystal meth he'd sold in Stockton had brought in more than he'd expected, and the MINI Cooper was part of the deal. He squinted up at the apartment window. She was still washing dishes. Scraping boxed macaroni and cheese off plastic dishes probably; she'd never been a decent cook. And Abby . . .

He ground his teeth together and swore, feeling the rage pound in his temples. His daughter was probably forgetting him already or hated him after hearing Kristi spit out a string of ugly lies. Calling him a low-life druggie, a loser, a crazy person. *Not fit to be a father.* The Child Crisis woman would be selling her that and more. And the church, too—that smug jerk he'd seen walking with Kristi. Was he planning to take Kurt's place with his kids?

There wasn't much time to set things right. His son would be discharged like Abby had been. The pneumonia was better; any damage from the exposure to the propane heater would be evaluated over a period of months. Kurt shook his head, thinking again how easy it was to pull on those scrubs and sneak around the hospital, hear things.

But the scrubs and the information were nothing unless he used them. Until he stepped up as a man and put an end to this completely unfair crock of . . . He reached over to the passenger seat of the MINI Cooper and rested his palm on the cool steel surface of the new semiautomatic pistol. Another bonus included in the deal along with the car. Two guns. Twice the power. Tomorrow he'd be unstoppable. When he claimed his family again.

CHAPTER THIRTEEN

"Here," Nick offered as Leigh stood on tiptoe to hang the stainless-steel saucepan on the pot rack overhead. "I'll do that."

"No need." She pushed her palm against the countertop, grunting softly as she boosted her reach. "I'm getting it." The granite reflected her efforts in its shiny black surface as if mocking her stubbornness.

"Suit yourself." He shook his head, then let his gaze skim over her. She'd changed from the black dress into a simple white shirt, sleeves rolled up, tucked into worn jeans. But she'd kept the pearls. Then pulled on thick rag socks that bunched above her short leather paddock boots, scuffed from countless hours at the barn. For some reason the combination—classic lady and haphazard stable hand—struck him as completely irresistible. Except that he had to resist. *She's divorcing me.*

"You know," she said, turning toward him as the saucepan swung in place on the rack, "you still need to pack all your pans and knives." Her gaze moved across the kitchen. "Except for my French coffee press and my grandmother's china and maybe that dumb plastic hamburger press I bought from the infomercial, everything in this kitchen is really yours."

Yours. Mine. She couldn't have sucker punched him worse if she'd hit him in the gut with that saucepan. Nick glanced away, rubbing a dish towel over a minuscule spot on the counter.

"You know?" she repeated.

"I know."

He exhaled slowly and looked at her, wondering how she'd react if he admitted that packing up his kitchen things was going to be the hardest part of all. Moving his clothes, his toothbrush, his mother's Bible, and even his sagging pillow—lifting it from its place beside hers—hadn't been so bad. Sitting in the lawyer's office, signing the sheaf of financial documents had seemed easy, numb, nothing. Pick up the pen, initial, flip the page, initial, next page, next page. Even when she'd yanked their photos from the magnets on the refrigerator, it had inflicted only a dull ache. But the thought of packing his kitchen things, taking them from this house, it felt . . . bad. Worse than bad. Like a wound from a hand-forged German carving knife. It made him remember all the times he'd stuffed his belongings into his backpack, made one last search to see if he'd left anything behind, before moving on to the next foster home.

"The coffee's still hot," he said, hoping she wouldn't mention that the Moccamaster coffeemaker was his. And offer a packing box.

"Coffee?" Leigh tilted her head, looking at him as if he'd suggested more—that they have another dance, spread a picnic blanket on the steps of the Palace of Fine Arts . . . run off to Capri. Find each other again.

"Seems a shame to waste it."

"Well . . ."

"It's only coffee, Leigh," he said, remembering her words earlier: *"It's only a dance. . . . Don't make more of it."*

She glanced away, fingers moving to her pearls.

He dropped the dish towel onto the counter. "Okay, then. I'll—"

"Fine." She met his gaze. "I'll have some. But I need to make a quick call to the barn first. To check on Frisco."

Some things would always be the same.

She stepped away to make her call and he heard her asking questions about the animal's comfort, whether he'd eaten, was drinking, and if he'd produced any manure. Nick grimaced, opened the cupboard door, and reached for the mugs. He pushed aside the one with a handle fashioned like the hind end of a horse.

He poured the first cup, appreciating the rich aroma and wondering where they should drink it. Here in the kitchen? At the McNealys' table? Maybe shove aside the pile of grass skirts and party props on the living room couch, or . . . He stopped. Why was he making such a big deal out of this? When had a cup of coffee become so important?

He glanced toward the darkened dining room, where—for the first time in his life—he'd sat in his own dining room, held his wife's hand, and offered a blessing. First time, at their last supper. Last dance, last cup of coffee. *Last chance.* He took a slow breath and filled the other cup.

What did he have to lose?

He looked up as Leigh returned to the kitchen. "Grab a jacket. We're having our coffee out on the porch."

+++

Leigh sat on the paint-layered porch step beside Nick, watching as he tugged his tie loose and left it hanging half-mast over the open collar of his shirt. The moonlight lit his face and brushed his black hair with silvery-blue highlights. But it left his eyes in shadow, dark as the coffee. She was glad; she didn't want to read what they held. He'd done her a favor by coming to help with Harry; the least she could do was sit here for a few minutes. Drink some coffee. And hope he didn't remind her that it was the last time they'd do that. She watched the steam rise from her cup to blend with the cool air and listened to the muted sounds of evening traffic and distant foghorns.

"I appreciate your coming tonight," she said. "I thought I could handle it with Harry, but . . ."

He smiled. "But you needed a 'good cop.'"

"Yes." Her chuckle died in her throat. "And you are. You are that, Nick."

"Thank you." He looked down at his coffee. "It was something to combine it all tonight. Arrive as a cop—end the evening cooking again."

"Do you ever miss it?"

"Miss . . . ?"

"Cooking professionally—Niko's." She realized that she'd never asked him that before. Not directly. It had come up in their arguments, after she'd seen TV footage of police shoot-outs, explosions, slain officers; those times when, shaking inside, she'd remind him that people didn't shoot chefs. And of course, she'd had to grit her teeth at her mother's taunts that her doctor daughter had "fallen in love with a restaurateur and wound up married to an ordinary street cop." But after the restaurant closed, she'd never asked Nick if he missed it.

"No. I don't really miss the restaurant," he answered. "I drive by it once in a while. It's a Mexican bakery now and doing a decent business from what I can tell. The flower shop next door—you remember, Betty's Blossoms—is a tattoo place." He shook his head. "Maybe I should have stayed and offered tats and body piercing along with my lemon soup and baklava."

Nick caught her gaze and his expression sobered. "I should have told you that taking the police science classes was about more than curiosity or my friendship with Toby." He winced. "You should have known that I was thinking seriously about making the change. Before . . ."

Before I fell in love with you. "It doesn't matter now."

"It does to me. I need you to know I wasn't trying to be dishonest. I didn't think the force would even accept me after all the trouble I got into as a kid. Figured I didn't have a chance, but I kept at it anyway."

"And then business started sliding downhill."

He took a sip of his coffee. "I was relieved when Niko's closed. I never told you that, but I was." He shook his head. "I remember your mother telling everyone who'd listen that her son-in-law's restaurant had hit the skids, so he was 'settling' for being a cop."

She grimaced.

"Didn't matter. Because I'd already figured out that cooking—the business of selling food—wasn't what I was meant to do." He smiled. "Do you know the best part about owning that restaurant?"

She didn't. Her stomach sank at that truth. She'd never asked. "What? What was best?"

"After closing time. After thanking the councilman for coming, walking the *Chronicle* food critic to her car. When I put the Closed sign in the window, and . . ."

A lump rose in her throat. "Let the street people come in and eat."

He nodded. "Being a cop is like that for me, every day. It's what I do—who I am. I didn't 'settle,' Leigh. I need you to understand that."

"Okay." The word came out in a whisper and she didn't trust herself to say more. She sipped her coffee, glad Nick had stopped looking at her. Then she glanced toward the McNealys', saw a shadow on the porch. "Caro," she said, gesturing with her mug in that direction.

"She seemed better tonight," he said, "happier, I guess." He chuckled low in his throat. "I can't believe I hauled those hedge clippings twice today. A jungle in our dining room."

"The table needs to go back."

He hesitated, then exhaled slowly. "I'll do it. I'll see when Buzz is free to help me."

"Good. And tie up that chandelier."

"Right."

"Well . . ." Leigh glanced toward the McNealys' porch. Caro was gone. "I do appreciate your helping us tonight. I'm sure you had other plans."

"Nothing that couldn't wait."

"Anyway, thank you." She glanced at her watch. "We both have to work in the morning." She started to stand.

"Wait." He grasped her wrist. "Don't go. I need to say something."

+++

"Stay, please." Nick reluctantly released her arm. "Hear me out."

Leigh pulled her hand into her lap and held it with the other, lowering her head for a moment. If he didn't know better, he'd think she was praying. He wondered if she still stubbornly refused to do that. She inhaled softly and lifted her chin. "If this is about us, there's no point."

Lord, help me. He made himself wait until his heart stopped thudding in his ears. "There is—I still love you."

She pressed her fingers to her forehead. "Don't do this."

"I'm doing the only thing I can do, Leigh. I'm trying to understand. Can you really give up on our marriage so easily?" He regretted his choice of words even before he saw her reaction.

"Easily? Is that what you think this past year has been for me—easy?"

"I didn't mean that. You know I didn't mean that. C'mon." He reached out, decided against it, and drew his hand back. "I guess, what I'm really asking is . . ." The thudding in his ears started again. "Have you really stopped caring for me?"

"Our divorce is final on the third—that's Friday."

"I have the paperwork. That's not what I'm asking."

She squeezed her eyes shut again and whispered something that may have been a curse. He'd never heard her do that. Her eyes opened, and the tears surprised him. "Why are you doing this?"

Please, God . . . He grasped her hand. "I told you. I love you. I can't give up."

She shivered. "And I can't do this. I can't go through this again. It's too hard."

"Tell me what to do," he said quickly. "Anything. I'll do anything. Tell me what to do—what to say."

Her lips twisted as if she had a sudden pain. "And how would I believe you, Nick? How would I trust anything—*anything*—you had to say?"

Guilt strangled him. "It would take time; I know that. But if you give me a chance, a little more time, I'll show you. We could try the counseling again. Get a different counselor if you want. You call the shots. Just give me a chance. Leigh . . . I'm sorry."

Her eyes were huge in the moonlight. "And what about Sam?"

"What about her?"

"She's around. She's everywhere." Her body tensed.

"Sam doesn't matter. She's not part of my life. You are. Only you."

"But the court date is set, the paperwork . . ." Her eyes met his, and for the first time in months, hope seemed within his grasp. Like Leigh reaching for that pot rack.

"We can postpone it. We'll drive by the court," he told her. He lifted her hand and touched his lips to her fingers. "Please."

"I don't know," she said, her expression still wary, but softer.

"Just say you'll think about it—that we can talk again tomorrow."

"I work tomorrow, Tuesday too. Maybe Tuesday evening . . ." Her expression hinted at wariness again.

Don't push her. "Tuesday night, after work. We'll talk. And meanwhile, you'll think about what I said?"

She was quiet. Forever, it seemed, until . . . "I'll think about it," she whispered.

Relief flooded through him, choked his voice. "Thank you."

He brushed the back of his fingers gently along her cheek. It took everything he had not to pull her into his arms, cradle her close, kiss her. But anything more would overwhelm her—he knew that—and for now, he'd received the blessing he'd been praying for. A second chance to try to be the husband Leigh deserved. "Tuesday, then."

+++

Sam frowned, licked the chocolate frosting off her thumb, then leafed through another stack of papers spread out across the dining room table. Why couldn't she find it? Every other phone bill was there. She was careful, organized, paid bills on time, kept the receipts. She was responsible to a fault—had to be, she was a single mother. She frowned again, thinking of Kristi Johnson's stupid mistakes. Despite what Sam had told the young mother about finding a "good guy"—and as much as she wanted to believe in that for her own life— the truth was, Kristi's kids were very likely headed to foster care. She'd make another hospital visit tomorrow, compile reports, but it didn't look good. The kids' father was a loser and he'd show up again. Sam had no doubt about that. He'd slap Kristi around, steal her paycheck, bring friends by who would abuse her children; she'd be as guilty as he was for letting it all happen, putting her children at risk. Exactly as Sam's mother had been.

November. The receipt for the phone bill should be in that pile—no mistaking the date. The month Toby died. A month of endings and beginnings. Despair. And hope too, those few days that Nick was here with them. If she was ever going to have a chance of making that happen again, she had to—*ah, there it is.* She pulled the November phone bill from the October slot in the tabbed file, ran her finger down the list of numbers, checked the dates.

November 18, 19. Three calls. Less than a minute each. Long enough to leave messages. Nick's outgoing calls, made from her phone when his cell died. Calls to his wife that were never answered.

She reached for her wineglass and drained the last few drops of the cabernet that had almost ruined her new skirt. Then she picked up her cell phone to punch in the private number of the woman she refused to let ruin her life.

+++

Leigh sat on the porch and watched the Z4 pull away from the curb, then pulled her barn jacket close, not sure if her shivers came from the bay fog creeping in or because she was more frightened than she'd ever been in her life. More than the morning when she'd celebrated her graduation from med school by leaping from a skydiving plane thirteen thousand feet above a Lodi vineyard. Or the time, in her ER residency, when she'd opened the battered chest of a man struck by a speedboat, grasped his heart with her gloved hand, and squeezed it in her palm, forcing it to pump. Both times a life had been on the line—hers, over the vineyard; a husband and father's that day in the ER. Tonight felt the same. Could she trust Nick? Was she crazy to even consider it just days from her divorce? when only two days ago, his lover had marched into her ER and as much as claimed him?

She stared at the full moon, shrouded now in wisps of fog but still brilliant and ethereal. Was this all some cosmic lunar mishap that filled her ER with chaos, turned her house into the Fairmont Tonga Room with Tony Bennett crooning, her sister hanging plastic leis from the chandelier . . . and her soon-to-be ex-husband declaring his love?

Nick. Her heart cramped as she remembered what he'd said about his restaurant, how feeding the homeless meant the most to him, that police work made him feel that way too. Despite what his mother-in-law said, he hadn't settled for being a cop. He'd said it was who he was. She believed him; how could she not after what she'd seen him do for Harry and Antoinette tonight? And how could she not hope—when he'd looked into her eyes, pressed his lips to her hand—that he was sincerely sorry and that he wanted their marriage to work? and that Sam Gordon wasn't part of his life?

She hugged her arms around herself, remembering the conversation she'd had with Caro in the kitchen before everything had whirled into full-moon madness. About their mother. How she'd told them both that there was no such thing as happily ever after. And Leigh had grown up believing it, steeled her heart because of it, expected less, always. But what if she was wrong? What if it was okay to trust Nick, what if loving him . . . *is part of who I am?*

She closed her eyes, remembering his words: *"I still love you. . . . Only you."*

He was asking her to postpone the court date, to think about it. Was that so risky?

She stood, gazing out across the slice of cityscape. The breeze had moved the fog enough that she could see their glimpse of the Golden Gate Bridge, red-orange and lit up in the distance. *"I left my heart in San Francisco. . . ."* Maybe Mr. Bennett had a point. Maybe the worst thing she could do was call it quits and leave. Maybe it was time to start trusting.

Leigh rubbed her arms against another rush of shivers. The next few days could change a lot of things.

+++

Sam heard Leigh's phone ring for the third time and tried not to imagine why she wasn't answering; she refused to accept that Nick was making love to his wife. Her knuckles whitened as she gripped the phone, head swimming from nearly an entire bottle of cabernet.

"Hello?"

Sam waited, heart hammering as she strained to hear. Was Nick there?

"Hello?" Leigh repeated. "Is that you, Nick?"

Sam nearly groaned aloud with relief. "Dr. Stathos?" she asked, hoping the wine wouldn't sully her voice like it had her skirt. "This is Child Crisis, Samantha Gordon."

She loved the sharp intake of breath on the other side of the phone.

"Yes?" Leigh's tone was wary, curt.

"I'm sorry to bother you," she said, pressing her finger against cake crumbs on the table as her skin tingled with an intoxicating surge of control. "But I have a county meeting first thing tomorrow, and I need some information. I have another child who would benefit from the therapy program at Golden Gate Stables. I want to suggest it at our meeting but can't recall the last name of the owner. I know her name is Patrice. But I should really have the last name for the paperwork. You understand. I've left messages on the stables' voice mail, but—"

"Owen."

She smiled at the way the doctor's voice quavered as if she were the stunned and defensive victim of a home invasion. "Great. I appreciate that."

"Is that all?"

Sam licked the cake crumbs off her finger. "Yes, thank you. And again, I'm sorry for disturbing you at home. I tried to reach Nick, but no luck." She paused, the moment much more delicious than any chocolate. "I should have asked him when he was here tonight."

There was a long stretch of silence, and then the call disconnected.

Sam hit the End button. Tomorrow the ball would bounce back to her court.

CHAPTER FOURTEEN

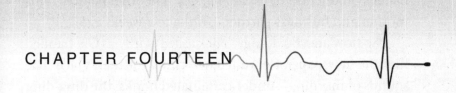

"What's this?" The flower vendor—purple beret pulled low over one brow and silhouetted in the morning light against buckets of outrageous blooms—peered into the paper sack. "Oh, my goodness, a *marranito*?" He lifted the molasses-rich pastry from the bag. "You brought me a cute little gingerbread pig?"

Nick shrugged. "Got up early to run the Panhandle and passed by this Mexican bakery next to a tattoo shop."

The middle-aged man shot him a wide-gapped, toothy grin. "That big gun doesn't fool me a bit, Officer Stathos. You are one sweet guy."

"Careful, Oly," Nick warned, pretending to scowl. "My new partner's next door getting coffee. He won't want to hear a 'sweet guy' has his back. Just sell me my *Chronicle*, same way you've been doing every morning for five long years." He winced. *No, not the same, my friend. You're alone now.*

Nick watched as the man reached toward a pile of papers stacked below a photo of himself with an elegant older woman—gracefully tall and slender next to his short and stocky, but with identical smiles—taken at the Brannan Street flower mart. Two engaging grins, a million blossoms. He'd added a second photo, a well-worn black-and-white, the same woman maybe forty years younger, in ballerina shoes, a gauzy dress, and a crown. The lead in the San Francisco Ballet's production of *Cinderella*, Oly had often boasted—his mother and business partner. Until a few weeks ago.

"So how are you doing?" Nick asked gently as Oly handed him the newspaper. He waited, watching the man's face. The sounds of morning—under-caffeinated honks, the ding-ding and brakes of cable cars, and soft cooing of pigeons—filled the short stretch of silence.

"Oh, you know . . ." Oly glanced away and broke off a bit of pastry to toss at the clutch of birds strutting, heads abob, on the damp curb. "Selling mostly mums now that fall's here. Burnt copper, lemonsota, maroon pride; thinking I'll make an adorable stack of mini pumpkins and New England leaves, pull out my kitchen witch . . ."

He met Nick's gaze and cleared his throat. "Sometimes I forget. I wake up thinking that I need to get over to the hospital, take her a fresh nightgown—she refused to wear those hideous hospital gowns. Or I'll circle a theater review in the *Chronicle*, thinking I'll read it to her so we can plan delicious revenge on those heartless critics. And sometimes I hear her setting the table for dinner . . ." Oly's eyes glistened. "She fought hard. Wouldn't quit; she thought she could hold on forever. You know?"

"Yes." Nick had hoped for that, too. Prayed for these good-hearted people. Seeing the pair together, their playful banter and unconditional love, had let him imagine the way it might have been with his own mother, if only . . .

"So I'm not going to quit either," Oly said, beginning

to smile. "I'll be okay. I have my sister, my baby niece, my friends—" he raised the pastry—"and a fresh *marranito*. What more could I ask for? Except maybe that you'd start buying flowers again."

Nick hesitated for a moment, imagining the look on Leigh's face if he showed up at the hospital with flowers. "No," he said, tucking the newspaper under his arm. "Just the paper this time."

"Think it over." Oly's smile widened. "It would support your image."

"Image?"

"Sweet guy."

Nick groaned. "One more word and I confiscate the pastry." He pointed toward someone looking at flowers on the other side of the cart. "You're ignoring your customers."

Nick paid for the paper and walked down the street to the patrol car, glancing back one more time as he reconsidered taking Leigh flowers. He was planning to drop by the hospital to see Finn Johnson, anyway. . . . He dismissed the thought for the same reason he'd resisted taking her into his arms Sunday night. Or calling her yesterday, though it had seemed as natural as morning prayer. Too much, too soon. Besides, walking into a hospital in uniform carrying a bouquet of flowers was about as obvious as you could get. There had already been enough drama at Golden Gate Mercy this week. Today was Tuesday—they'd have that talk tonight as planned.

He watched as Oly's customer, a young man wearing an oversize 49ers jacket and sunglasses, waited for a pair of bicyclists to pass before unlocking his MINI Cooper. He shifted the huge bouquet of flowers in his arms, then finally managed to get it through the car door. Nick smiled as he noticed the man's scrubs. Apparently this guy didn't care about being obvious. Someone at a San Francisco hospital was in for a surprise today. Although the guy could have chosen something better than white lilies—they always reminded Nick of funerals.

+++

"Sorry, boy." Leigh squeezed Frisco's upper lip with the nutcracker-like metal twitch and twisted it sideways. A restraint that seemed barbaric by human standards was doing the trick: distracting her horse from the fact that Dr. Hunter had threaded a large plastic tube through his nostril and into his stomach.

"I feel like I should be doing more," she said, watching in pale morning light as the veterinarian instilled the last two liters of viscous fluid into Frisco's stomach. She glanced around the saddling area, where they'd secured him by lengths of chain attached to his halter. "Beyond holding a twitch."

She grimaced, thinking that the 5 a.m. call from the stables had been her own twitch, distracting her from sleepless brooding about that call from Sam. And Nick's lie. *"She's not part of my life."* According to Sam, they'd been together Sunday night. Maybe even again, since then.

Dr. Hunter peered at her. "You've kept this big fella from kicking and striking. I consider that the best kind of assistance. I'm sorry we had to get you out of bed, Leigh. But when Patrice says one of her horses isn't coming along, I believe her. And as you can see, he's been uncomfortable."

She nodded, running her other hand gently along Frisco's neck, feeling the dried nervous sweat in his hair. "Will we need to trailer him to your clinic? or to UC Davis?"

"Not sure yet. I'm giving a couple of liters of mineral oil and a gallon of water—maybe a bit more; he's dry. But there's no gastric reflux; he's still got bowel sounds. And his vital signs aren't alarming. Still . . ."

"You don't like it," Leigh said, relieved to see Frisco's eyelid drooping. The pain medication was working, thank goodness. She leaned closer, feeling his comforting warmth.

"No," the vet agreed. "I don't like it." He turned his head, peering toward the stalls as a series of plaintive brays sounded. "Your horse has a concerned friend, it seems."

"The rescue donkey. I'm surprised. Frisco's never been a social animal."

"Don't kid yourself; horses aren't that different from humans." He smiled, tapping the stomach tube. "Beyond the hundred feet of intestines, of course. All God's creatures need fellowship. Donkeys, children, even this stubborn horse of yours."

"I guess that's true. But every time we move, it takes Frisco weeks to settle down. And then I have to worry about him biting or kicking someone." She sighed. "That's why I pay for the empty stall. To give him a cushion of space. It seemed safer that way, less complicated, and . . ." She let her words trail off, suddenly uncomfortable for no reason she could identify. The image of Caro's tear-filled eyes rose, unbidden.

Dr. Hunter shrugged his shoulders. "I've seen some unusual equine friendships. Horses and goats, horses and pigs. I once had a huge Clydesdale that thought the sun rose and set in a homely little banty hen. You never saw such a devoted pair. Amazing who the good Lord brings together as family." He clucked his tongue. "Anyway, hang on to that twitch until I get this tube out and draw a couple of vials of blood. Then I'll write some instructions. You have to get back to the hospital, don't you?"

"I've got coverage for another hour or so." She moved slightly as Frisco shifted beside her. "And I can be reached by phone if needed. Patrice can call me. I'm off tomorrow, all day. I'll be here."

Twenty minutes later Leigh walked Frisco to his stall and secured the gate, fortified with instructions, but not completely reassured that her beautiful horse wouldn't end up in a University of California surgery suite due to a twisted gut. And she could lose the best friend she'd ever . . .

A plaintive bray swept down the stable aisle, and Frisco—sweat-crusted and medicated—answered with a low, exhausted whinny. Leigh walked past the empty space to Tag's stall, and her throat tightened at the sight of him. His eye, ruptured by the pellet gun, was gone, the eyelid dark and sunken.

"Hello, Tag," she whispered, extending her fingers through the wooden slats. "Where on earth did you come from?" Her mother's voice rose without mercy: *"Who are his people, Leigh?"* She flinched, shoving the memory away, and amended her question. "How could you have ended up where someone would do this to you?" Her gaze swept his tidy body. The gang graffiti had been clipped away in raggedy fashion. His hooves shone with oily polish, and his wispy forelock was secured by a glittery pink clip-on bow. By horse show standards, he looked like the butt of a snide, tittering joke. As the object of girlish love, he was unabashedly beautiful. Leigh glanced up as Maria arrived at her side, one side of her hair in a tidy braid and the other still hanging loose.

"Hi, sweetie," she said, offering a smile. "Did you come to say good-bye to Tag before you go to school?"

The little girl watched her silently, dark eyes unblinking as her fingers played with her necklace, a silver chain and small cross. Leigh tried not to focus on the circular scars on her forearms. *Why shouldn't she be silent? What on earth could she say about what she's endured? Why should she even try?*

She watched as Maria walked down to Frisco's stall, reached her hand through the slats.

"Be careful, he . . ." Leigh's warning faded away as Frisco moved to rest his muzzle in the little girl's hand without a hint of malice.

Patrice called from the doorway to the stable. "Maria? I have to finish your hair. The school bus will be here in a few minutes." She acknowledged Leigh with a wave. "I'll talk with you as soon as I get her off to school," she promised.

Leigh looked down as Maria appeared beside her again. She gazed at Leigh before pulling a clip out her hair. She handed it over, smiling faintly, then turned and scurried down the stall aisle toward her foster mother.

Leigh closed her fingers around the hair clip and walked back to the empty stall beside Frisco's. She opened the latch, walked inside, and sank down into the soft, untouched mound of pine shavings. She leaned back against the heavy oak planks at the back of the stall, closed her eyes, and listened to the always-soothing blend of sounds: Frisco's breathing, deep and steady, to one side, Tag's snuffles and chewing noises on the other. She heard the high *chit-chit* of barn swallows swooping through the rafters, a wheelbarrow laden with feed squeaking down the barn's aisles accompanied by the steady thud of work boots, nickers of horses, and faraway strains of a radio playing something in Spanish laced with guitar and trumpet. All so different from the chaos and turmoil of her hours in the ER. It was peaceful here, bone-level peace. No, it was the soul-level peace she craved. She wondered, idly, what it would be like to sleep here, to bed down in the stables. She opened her eyes. Maybe Nick hadn't been so far off when he'd chided her about living at the barn.

His words drifted back: *"I still love you."*

After all that happened, had she wanted to believe him? Had she really been close to letting herself trust him again? Because of one evening that began with her sister's tears, brought the McNealys' dinner table to their dining room, and—for a few minutes—put her back in her husband's arms. One crazy, disconnected evening, and she'd almost started to believe.

Leigh glanced at the hair clip in her hands, noticing that it matched the one she'd seen in Tag's forelock. Pink, glittery, with a plastic picture in the center—*Cinderella*. Tears sprang to her eyes as she remembered Caro's little suitcase of fairy tales and how she'd said they were the first thing she'd pack every time their mother pulled up stakes and moved on. Even though Caro, like Leigh, had been told that there was no such thing as forever. And now this little girl, mute after such unimaginable abuse . . . *Oh, how can it be?*

"How, Lord?" Leigh whispered, staring up at shafts of light filtering through the stable's roof. "How can she have faith in happy endings? And how can you expect that of her after all she's been through, all she's seen? You're supposed to be a loving God and you take that child's mother, a poor donkey's eye, and . . ." She closed her eyes, struggling against a sob. *My husband. Our baby.* She wrapped her arms around herself and a moan escaped her lips. "How am I supposed to trust you, Lord? How can I believe you're really there?"

She turned the Cinderella barrette over and over in her hands and listened for the barn sounds, wanting the soul-deep peace to soothe her again. What she heard was Frisco's slow, deep breathing in perfect rhythm with that of the donkey. She thought once again of what it would be like to sleep in a stable. But then, sleep wasn't an option—she was going back to the ER. And with Finn Johnson still in the hospital, Nick would likely make a visit. He'd probably stop by the ER, want to see Leigh, too.

A metal twitch sounded like a much better prospect.

+++

"Will you be taking Finn home today?" Riley asked, watching as Abby Johnson leaned over the arm of the rocking chair to press a kiss on her brother's curls. He giggled around his bottle, dribbling milk from the corner of his mouth. His eyes were bright, face chubby and pink. Such a relief to see Kristi's children looking healthy again. Even if their mother still seemed so troubled.

"I think so. I hope." Kristi's gaze darted toward the door.

"He'll still have to be checked regularly for several months. Miss Gordon's talking with the doctors right now, and then she'll come tell me what Child Crisis wants me to do. . . . Has she said anything to you?"

"No, not at all," Riley said quickly. "But I'd imagine that all your good efforts would factor in. Along with the support you have from friends. Like the friend who babysits for you and the people at church." She pointed to the vase of white lilies on the table. "Did someone from church send those?"

"No. I mean . . ." The young mother's eyes shone, and color rose to her cheeks. "I'm not sure. There wasn't a card." She watched as her daughter moved across the room and settled down in front of the DVD player. "It could be that Officer Nick sent them; he's been so good to us. I'm hoping he'll stop by today."

Leigh in the ER, Sam Gordon up here on the second floor, Nick Stathos coming in. Riley took a slow breath, thinking about how this little family's near tragedy had drawn the three of them together. And how hard that must be for Leigh. Probably for all of them. Riley had to trust that God had a plan in the works. The same way she trusted that he had one for her life as well. She rubbed her fingers over her sling and smiled at Kristi. "Officer Stathos sounds like a good friend. I'm glad he's been there for you and your children."

"He loves kids. He never says much about his personal life, but I think he wants children. I can see it. I hope someday he and Dr. Stathos—"

"Good morning, Johnson family."

Sam Gordon smiled from the doorway, then shifted her

briefcase to her other hand. "If you'll excuse us, Chaplain, Kristi and I need to get our plan on target."

+++

Kurt waited outside the hospital's loading dock doors beside an idling linen truck. He pretended to smoke, well within smelling distance of a huge metal compactor stinking of medical waste, melted plastic, and every other kind of gangrenous garbage, probably. It looked like some surreal graphic novel character. A Transformer belching fumes from burning body parts, boiling germicides, and radiation waste. He bit back a laugh, picturing how cool that would be. Then he took a deep breath, filling his lungs and imagining the compactor's spewed molecules—toxic to anyone but him—combining with his own DNA. Feeding his awesome and destructive power. He trembled with excitement, ran his tongue over his dry lips. Then glanced down casually as a worker from the linen truck off-loaded another cart.

Caution was important. Even if he'd walked right through the front doors of this stinking hospital a half-dozen times before, today had to be different. Today was his last chance to make things right. He couldn't risk that someone would finally question his identity. The scrubs helped, but today his jacket barely closed over the rumpled navy top. Even walking was awkward. But he'd still have to take the stairs. Get up to the second floor. His timing was perfect. Kristi and Abby were there, and the Gordon woman had arrived. He'd asked a volunteer to deliver the lilies—they'd be in the room when he arrived. Kristi would be wondering who sent them. Then he'd sweep in, and . . .

He took one more deep breath, then followed the linen cart through Golden Gate Mercy's back doors. Walking as casually as he could with his mind whirling. And a 9mm Glock and a second semiautomatic pistol under his jacket.

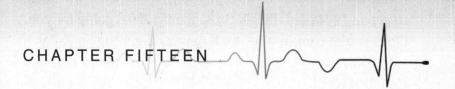

CHAPTER FIFTEEN

"Let's give ketorolac," Leigh ordered, "thirty milligrams, IV. If that doesn't get it, we'll titrate some morphine. And I'll get something on board for nausea, to stay ahead of that. Promethazine 12.5." She turned back to her patient, a thirty-year-old construction worker, pasty-pale despite his deep tan. He writhed on the gurney. "There's blood in your urine, Mr. Phelps."

He groaned and sat up. "I can't lie down. What do you mean, blood?"

"I mean you have a kidney stone," she said, wanting to thank him for having a straightforward malady completely unrelated to any full-moon lunacy. She'd needed that this morning. "About the size of a grain of sand, most likely." Leigh patted his shoulder with empathy. "That feels as big as the Rock of Gibraltar when your body tries to pass it. I know you're miserable."

"Ahh . . . tell me about it. Gotta get up, gotta walk around. Sorry, Doc." He swiped at the sweat beading on his fore-head, then slid from the gurney to pace in circles, holding a calloused hand to his flank. "Oh, man, now I know what my wife felt like when she was in labor with our daughter.

Women are tough." His eyes, pupils widened with pain, connected with hers. "You have babies, Doc?"

"No . . . no babies." She glanced down at her clipboard. "Now if you can try to hold still long enough for the nurse to get an IV started, I'll get those medications going for you. Once you're comfortable, we'll see about getting an X-ray."

"You mean the pain will go away?" he asked through clenched teeth.

"Yes."

"Thank you, Jesus," he breathed, glancing toward the ceiling. "I thought it was going to be like this forever."

"Nothing lasts forever." Leigh was glad that this time her mother's wisdom was merciful.

"I promise you'll be fine." She looked toward the door to the waiting room, where she knew there were a minimum of eight laborers in steel-toed work boots pacing the floor. "Shall we get a message out to your coworkers? I think they're planning to storm the door if they don't hear something soon."

Her patient's lips stretched in a wan smile. "Probably will. Last month Denny nailed his kneecap pretty bad. Before that, Grubber had heatstroke. And Ben's dad passed away this spring. Always somethin' we need to help each other with. We're sort of like a family, you know?"

"Sure," she said, reminded, ridiculously, of Dr. Hunter's story of the Clydesdale and the banty hen. "I'll see that your men get a heads-up."

"Thank you." He sat on the edge of the gurney as the nurse wheeled the IV pole toward him. "And I'm betting they called my wife. She'll be easy to spot. She travels with a fairy-tale princess."

Another Cinderella . . . Do you have to rub it in, Lord?

Leigh told the nurse which labs she'd be ordering, then walked back toward the nurses' desk wondering again about this new, grumpy monologue she seemed to be having with God lately. She hadn't prayed to him in almost a year—wasn't sure he even listened—and now she was grumbling at him. She wondered exactly how risky that was. But then, he'd taken all he could away, hadn't he? Except . . . She caught the clerk's gaze.

"No calls, Dr. Stathos. I've been here the whole time." The heavyset young redhead's lips pursed together as if she wanted to say something else but didn't dare. "But if you want me to, I'll call the stables right now."

"No need," Leigh said with a wave of her hand. "Thank you," she added, after seeing the look that passed between the two nurses at the desk. *Watch out for Stathos,* it warned, as clear as a flaming red allergy band around the wrist of a patient.

Guilt washed over her; she hated that this foreign and uncomfortable edginess was affecting her team. Worry about Frisco on top of skimpy sleep was making her . . . No, that wasn't the truth. She'd had things under control until Sam Gordon walked through the middle of the ER about twenty minutes ago. Again. Invading Leigh's space the same way she'd done before. The way she had Sunday night with that idiotic phone call. But this time she'd seemed even more confident. Strolling through, dressed in a tailored blazer paired with a pink flowered skirt that seemed completely inappropriate for business—sheer, feminine, with a modest slit that showed her leg when she walked. *Like a woman dressing for a date. With my husband.* She'd hesitated as she came close to Leigh, looked her directly in the eyes, and mouthed, "Thank you." Before continuing on and exiting through the door to the lobby.

"Thank you"? For what? Answering that bogus question on the phone? Or for handing Nick over? Leigh snatched her coffee cup from the counter and walked back to the doctors' desk. She sat and scanned the nurses' assignment board on the far wall: the kidney stone, a woman with mild congestive heart failure, a rule-out appendicitis waiting for a consult with the surgeon, someone new in room seven with a fever and headache. No overdoses, no adulterous husband bludgeoned with a shoe—she should be grateful. She should be ordering dim sum for her staff or calling her friend Erin Quinn about her upcoming engagement party. Checking on Harry McNealy again. Not grumbling at the God she hadn't spoken to in nearly a year. Or wondering how the dying lemon tree had managed to go missing Sunday night and if Nick had taken it with him. To bring it back to life. . . . She took a quick sip of her lukewarm coffee, appalled at the sudden threat of tears. She wasn't going to do that. No way.

And she wouldn't—absolutely *would not*—do any more second-guessing of how she was going to handle things if Nick did show up here today. That is, if he hadn't already changed his mind about everything he'd said to her. *If he didn't go back to Sam after he left me.* Leigh had work to do, patients to see. Everything else could wait.

"Dr. Stathos?"

"Yes?" Leigh looked up at the nurse and reminded herself to smile. "Does Mr. Phelps need some morphine, Jess?"

"No," the nurse said, wariness flickering across her face. "Your husband's here. I let him wait in your office. I hope that's okay."

+++

"I want you to understand that while my primary duty is to advocate for children, I do my best to consider the feelings of parents."

"I need my children with me." Kristi wrapped her arms tighter around her baby and stared at Sam. "And they need me. *That's* how I feel."

Sam sighed, thinking once again how she'd react if anyone threatened to take Elisa. "I understand that."

"Then why did you say that the decision to let me take Abby and Finn home is 'temporary'? Does that mean that the county can just show up someday and steal them away while I'm at work?" Her gaze drifted to the door, expression showing observable anxiety.

"Abby's there. In the playroom," Sam reassured her. "No one's taken her—no one will. All I'm saying is that the doctors need to examine Finn regularly for any delayed effects of carbon monoxide poisoning. Child Crisis will make certain that happens and schedule home visits over the next several months. To see how you're getting along."

"You mean, to see if I'm doing drugs, bringing dangerous felons to the apartment, or forgetting to feed my kids."

"Putting them at risk, like you absolutely did when you made the decision to run that propane stove. And didn't check to see if your babysitter had arrived. Those are facts, Kristi." Sam saw tears gather in the young mother's eyes.

"The plan we're putting in place is for their safety and yours. Very much like that new carbon monoxide detector the fire department installed in your apartment. Try thinking of it that way. We're helping you to be the best parent you can be. All right?"

"Could Officer Nick be the one who checks on us?"

"Well . . ." Sam smiled at the intriguing possibilities. "Maybe we could do the visits together. I'll be glad to talk with him about that." She pulled some papers from her briefcase. "Meanwhile, let me go over some of the services the county can make available to you. Like day care and coupons for groceries." She tapped a stapled document. "I also have information on the program for tracking down deadbeat dads. Even with a restraining order in place, there's no excuse for your children's father not to contribute money."

"No." Kristi's face went deathly pale. "I don't need Kurt's help. I don't know where he is, and I want it to stay that way. I can't—"

"Mommy!" Abby called from the doorway, tugging on a man's hand. "Look, it's Daddy! He's who sent us the pretty flowers!"

Sam stood so quickly that her skirt caught, tugging the plastic chair forward until it smacked into the back of her knees. "You can't be here, Mr. Denton."

"Says who?"

"A police restraining order." She kept her tone as calmly authoritative as she could, despite her confusion. He was wearing scrub pants under a jacket; he looked familiar somehow. Had she seen him here before?

"And you?" he asked, his mouth twisting into a vicious

smirk. "You're saying I don't have the right to be with my family?"

"Kurt . . ." Kristi beckoned to Abby, then gasped as he gripped the child's shoulder, holding her back. "Don't do this. Please."

"Shut up!" He glared at her, jaw muscles twitching as his teeth ground together.

"Mr. Denton, easy there," Sam said, dread rising as she noted the man's dilated pupils, the fine tremor in his hands. And the way he kept nervously patting the front of his jacket. She tried to see around him, locate staff.

"Don't even think about calling someone," he growled, lurching within inches of her. Abby scurried to her mother's side.

"I wasn't," Sam said quickly, trying not to tremble as she met his gaze. His eyes were wild and bloodshot, lips cracked, breath fetid and sour. Her heart rose to her throat as he patted the front of his jacket again. *Oh no . . . not a weapon.* "I realize now," she said, as calmly as she could, "that this is a perfect opportunity to include you in our plan."

"Plan?" His lips twisted in a sneer. "To put me in jail?" He swore, then whirled to face Kristi, still perched on the edge of the rocker and holding her children close. "You know that's what they want, right? To throw me in jail!"

Abby whimpered and Kurt stepped toward them. Sam stared out the door again, pulse hammering. She didn't dare leave the kids alone with this man. She had to get someone's attention. She nearly groaned with relief as she caught sight of Riley Hale.

Kurt stooped down, talking to his daughter. "You don't

want your daddy to go to jail, do you, princess? We won't let this mean lady do that, will we?"

Finn coughed and started to wail.

Sam saw the chaplain begin to walk toward them and shook her head quickly, bringing confusion to Riley's face. She raised her hand, gesturing as best she could to indicate a phone call. *Call security; get help.*

"What are you doing?" Kurt shouted, yanking Sam's arm down. "I told you to stay away from that door." He shoved her aside, strode to the door and slammed it, then pinned Sam with a glare that made her throat close.

"Now," he said, "you're going to listen to *my* plan."

+++

"I don't have time to talk," Leigh said from the doorway of her office.

Nick was leaning against her desk, dressed in his SFPD blues, the body armor adding angular bulk to his torso. He straightened, his leather Sam Browne belt creaking with the movement. "Good morning to you, too," he said, offering her a smile that hinted of holding her in his arms Sunday night. And proved that he hadn't a clue Sam called her after he left.

"I have a surgeon coming in for a consult—we're busy, Nick."

His radio crackled. "Yeah, I saw the hard hat battalion out in your waiting room. I came by to see if the Johnson baby's being released. But . . ." He swallowed. "I thought I'd stop by for a minute. And maybe arrange a time for tonight. I thought we could take a drive out to Pier 39, get some dinner. And do some more talking about—"

"I don't think that's a good idea."

A muscle along his jaw tensed. "What are you saying? That tonight's a bad time to talk—tomorrow would be better?" He stepped toward her. "Or . . . that it wasn't a good idea for me to tell you that I love you? and that I want to postpone the court date?" He took hold of her hand.

She closed her eyes for moment, feeling the warmth of his touch, wanting to feel that tiny glimmer of hope she'd had sitting on the porch steps with him. But . . .

"Leigh?"

"I'm saying," she said, pulling away, "that I think it isn't a good idea to expect me to believe that Sam Gordon doesn't matter and isn't part of your life when that's obviously not the case."

"What do you mean?"

"She called me after you left the other night. She said you'd been there with her."

Leigh watched Nick's expression, holding her breath.

"I was," he admitted. "But nothing really happened. Not what you think, anyway, and—"

"What I think," she said, cutting him off, "is that I have patients to see. And you're wanted upstairs—Sam's there, too." She grimaced as the PA system screeched overhead.

The operator's nasal voice began to page: "Mr. Strong, second floor. Mr. Strong, Pediatrics floor. Mr. Strong, please."

Nick squared his shoulders. "Isn't that a distress call?"

"Hospital code for assistance with a combative patient or disgruntled visitor. Usually doesn't amount to much." Leigh shook her head. "Somebody's probably complaining about their child's breakfast. Security will handle it."

+++

"Down there, Cappy." Riley pointed toward the Johnson baby's room. "Some of the staff is already trying to help, but that guy's not listening to anybody from what I can see."

"Who is he?"

"I don't know. Someone said he's in scrubs, which doesn't make sense. If he works here, why would he shut himself in the room and create a scene?" She grimaced, seeing the young man's arms flailing even from a distance. "I just wish he'd let the kids out or someone in. Maybe I should try."

"No." Cappy stretched tall and shifted his work belt on his hips, making his heavy collection of keys jingle. "You send a prayer up from a safe distance away, little lady. I'll see if I can get a handle on things. Most times these guys see a uniform and simmer down; but if that doesn't happen, I won't hesitate to call law enforcement. Done it before. Keepin' my hospital folks safe is what matters."

Riley nodded, realizing her mouth had gone dry. Violence, even the threat of it, brought back too many memories. *Father, please* . . . "Be careful."

"I will." He winked. "Got to stay in one piece if I'm going to take my best girl out to the movies tonight."

She watched from the desk as he joined a small group of staff outside the patient room, saw him knock on the door. The man inside responded with an obscene gesture. She wondered if she should go ahead and ask the staff to call the police, then noticed that the ward clerk had wandered down the hallway. The desk was empty.

Riley tried to remember if protocol dictated that she first call the hospital operator or if she could directly dial 911.

Then she told herself she was being ridiculously paranoid. From what she could see, Sam Gordon was remaining calm. Cappy had managed to get a foot in the door, and—

Riley froze as the young man burst from the room, shoving Kristi Johnson ahead of him and shouting.

"Get back! All of you—out of my way!"

A male nurse tried to intervene, and the man kicked him in the chest, knocking him to the floor. "Get away!" He pointed at Cappy. "You too, old man. Don't be stupid."

Kristi cried out and stumbled, and he yanked her to her feet by her hair, herding her along the hallway toward the desk. Sam Gordon followed, staying close to Cappy. One of the staff slipped into the room with the crying children and closed the door.

No. Oh, please . . . Riley scrambled, heart pounding, to get around the expanse of desk to a phone. Then she heard someone scream.

"A gun—he's a got a gun!"

She froze. Then dropped down beside the desk and out of sight, as the man shouted again.

"Everybody get back in their rooms. Stay away from the elevators; touch a phone and I start killing people!"

The guard's voice, low and calm, filled the terrified wake of silence. "Son . . . please, you don't want to do that. Listen to old Cappy. Life is short. Nothing's worth—"

There was a single deafening blast, followed by a chorus of screams.

Riley hunched low and ran, heart hammering in her ears, seeing nothing but the door to the stairs. She threw it open, fighting a dizzying wave of nausea, and ran down the steps.

There was a phone outside the door onto the first floor. If she could only get there . . . *Stay with me, Lord.*

+++

Leigh stepped out of the treatment room and stared at the speaker on the ceiling. She couldn't have heard it right. It had almost sounded like—

"Code Silver," the operator repeated, her voice audibly anxious. "Code Silver, second floor."

Silver meant . . . Leigh's breath caught. *Person with a weapon.*

CHAPTER SIXTEEN

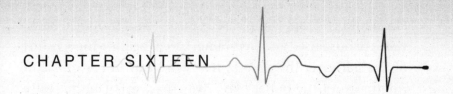

Nick slid behind the wheel of the patrol car and nodded to his partner, busy writing a report. "Let's get out of here."

"That was fast—thought you were going to check on that Child Crisis case."

"It's complicated. We'll come back later." Nick frowned. *After Sam's gone. She called Leigh?*

"Fine by me."

Nick updated their status with dispatch, pulled out into traffic, and made it two blocks before a call came in: "All units in the vicinity of Fulton and Stanyan . . ."

Stanyan? What—?

"Be advised: You have a 417, Golden Gate Mercy Hospital. Man with gun. Shots fired."

Pulse quickening, Nick pressed the car forward in traffic, searching for an opening; his partner grabbed the radio mike and hit the lights and siren as dispatch continued.

"Suspect described as white male, midtwenties, shoulder-length brown hair. Wearing dark hospital scrubs, gold jacket . . . Witness reports one shooting victim."

One victim. Nick cranked the wheel, whipped the car

around, and, tires squealing, raced back to the hospital. *Lord . . . don't let it be Leigh.*

+++

"Don't, Kurt. Stop! Oh, please . . . no. " Sam stumbled backward, hands raised and trembling, barely hearing the screams of the staff over the thud of her own heart in her ears, still ringing from the bullet blast. Was that real? Did he really shoot? She stared, horrified, down at the floor—at the guard's crumpled body near her feet, the widening expanse of pooling blood. *Run, run!*

"No one move!" Kurt shouted, tightening his arm around Kristi's throat until she gagged, eyes rolling back. "And you—" he took a step toward Sam, eyes wild—"you even breathe and I blast you clear to the gates of hell. You hear me, witch?"

Sam tried to nod, then startled as the wounded guard grabbed desperately for the hem of her skirt but sank back down, his hand sliding down her leg.

"Help," he groaned, gargling a mouthful of blood.

"Please." A nurse, crouched beside the desk, rose to her feet. "Please," she begged again between sobs, "let me help Cappy. Let me just go to him."

"Yes, Kurt," Sam whispered, hearing her voice quaver. "Let us call for help. You don't want him to die. You—"

"Don't tell me what I want!" Kurt bellowed, throwing Kristi to the floor. He clawed at the zipper of his jacket, pulled out a second gun, and bit his lip so hard that blood welled. He sputtered, spit, and glared at Sam. "I'll tell you what I want." He whirled around, the muzzles of the guns sweeping over the terrified staff. "I want all of you to stop trying to keep me away from my kids. Stop calling the cops, writing reports. Stop saying I'm not man enough to—" He halted, eyes jerking toward the overhead speakers as they crackled to life again.

"Code Triage, Internal. All departments prepare for general lockdown. Code Triage, Internal. Prepare for hospital-wide lockdown."

The fire doors slammed shut at the end of the corridor, and Kurt jumped, aimed both guns in that direction. His gaze darted around the area as he stepped up to where Kristi crouched. He kicked her hip. She whimpered, and he kicked her again. "You had a chance—but that's over. I don't care what you do anymore. I'm taking my kids. You'll never see them again."

"No. Please . . ."

He glared at her and whirled away, jogging toward the baby's room.

"No!" Sam yelled after him, fear for the children over-riding all else. "You can't—"

There was a sharp explosion and her body jerked backward. She shook her head, confused.

What's happening? She heard a barrage of sounds: *crack, crack*, endless, like a long string of firecrackers. Then screams, keening wails followed by frantic footfalls and shouts. She staggered forward and gasped for breath, fighting a sudden, incapacitating wave of weakness, but lost the struggle and fell to her knees. She tried to stand again and finally felt the pain. Searing, bursting like a grenade, exploding across her belly.

She sat back and stared down in a daze, seeing the blood,

a river of red soaking through her blouse, her skirt, and pooling in her lap, warm and sticky. She clutched her stomach, grabbed a fistful of the flimsy flowered fabric, tried to stanch the flow even as she realized everything around her was going gray and fading away.

She stretched out on the floor, curled up on her side, and found herself looking into Cappy's face—eyes open, glazed, lifeless. She thought of Elisa, of Toby, and of Nick. Then wondered if it was too late to pray.

+++

Kurt shoved his shoulder against the door leading to the loading dock, dropped the Glock, grabbed it up, and rammed the door again. *Lockdown. Did that mean every stupid door was*— He shoved again, cursing, and almost fell through as it opened into the morning light. Sirens. They were coming. He had to make it to the car.

He hefted the guns, one in each fist, and ran toward the parking lot, heart pounding, muscles twitching, his mind beginning to stagger into prickly confusion. The thrill ride that had swept him into the hospital was gone. In its wake was something hollow and brittle, lonely. He pushed his legs faster, sucked in a breath, and smelled blood: acrid, coppery— condemning. He'd shot people. Watched them fall. Heard his children crying, screaming. Abby begging him. *My little girl.* Looking at him like she didn't know him. Like he was monster, not a hero. How did that happen? That's not what he'd wanted.

He heard a shout, then saw people standing around the MINI Cooper. Security guards. They pointed his way and crouched for cover. He stopped, guns dangling in his hands, mind staggering again. The steady drone of helicopter blades made him blink skyward. Cops. The sirens growing closer. If he shot the guards, got his car . . . Abby's face filled his mind. Would she understand?

He gagged, remembering Kristi on the floor. He'd kicked her. Had Abby seen that, too? And Finn—was he too young to remember? Kurt froze at the sound of a car squealing to a stop. A patrol car, with officers exiting to hunch low behind the opened doors—guns pointed. *How did things get this far?*

"Drop your weapons."

He hesitated, watching the nearest officer's dark eyes and knowing in a glance that the man was deadly serious. Would kill him without blinking.

"Drop them, now," the cop repeated, raising his voice as more patrol cars surged in. "Don't make us shoot. Let's settle this peacefully."

Peacefully. Kurt thought of Finn's face. Smiling in Kristi's arms until his father stormed in and . . . *What have I done?*

Kurt held the officers' gaze as he took a step forward. He hesitated, held his breath . . . and pointed the guns. In eerie slow motion he saw the officers thrust theirs forward, heard a spray of gunfire—then felt a bullet hit hard against the top of his chest, jerking him sideways. Another grazed his side as his knees began to buckle. A third bullet blasted through his skull.

+++

"Suction!" Leigh ordered, straining to see through a frothy red tide of blood at the back of Cappy's throat. "I can't see the cords without . . ." She grabbed for the offered Yankauer tube and buried it deep in the pooling fluid, hearing it suck as it tried to clear the guard's airway. She needed to see well enough to find the vocal cords, slide the endotracheal tube in place.

"Bag him," she told the respiratory therapist holding an Ambu bag. "Continue cardiac compressions, give another round of epi, and then I'll try again." *Try to get him to the OR . . . not let him die here. Don't die on me, Cappy.* The surreal sense of horror struck her as she glanced at the unconscious man on her gurney. Gunshot wound to left chest, massive blood loss, no heart activity. She fought against a sinking wave of dizziness, taking a deep breath. *Stay focused.*

"Keep pumping the Ringer's lactate—someone make sure the lab's getting those blood products to the OR stat. The OR, not here." She signaled the charge nurse. "When can surgery take him?"

"Any minute," the nurse answered, expression stoic despite soot-dark tear smudges. "They're taking Cappy first while the other team sets up for Samantha Gordon."

Leigh's throat constricted, the disbelief swirling again. She glanced toward the other trauma cubicle. "How's she doing?"

"Conscious, but still really shocky. Dr. Bartle wants to explore her belly as soon as they can get her into the OR." The charge nurse's brows scrunched. "She's worried about her little girl. Sounds like she has no one else."

No one. Leigh glanced toward the group of officers standing near the nurses' desk, then shook the thought away.

She turned to watch as the ER tech performed cardiac compressions. Cappy's wife was at the beauty shop when they'd reached her; their pastor would drive her to the hospital. Leigh would talk with her, tell her that they'd done all they could to get him to the operating room as fast as they could. But . . .

"Halt compressions," she ordered, watching the monitor as the tech stepped back.

"Looks the same, Dr. Stathos," the nurse told her. "Wide complexes, slow rate."

Leigh pressed her fingers deep into the flesh beneath Cappy's pale jaw. *But no pulse.*

"I'm ready," she said, returning to the head of the gurney. "Let's do this."

She tilted Cappy's head, positioned the laryngoscope and tube, and asked the therapist to apply gentle pressure on the Adam's apple. Leigh peered down the lighted blade and got an adequate view of the cords. She slid the endotracheal tube in place, inflated its balloon, and checked the placement.

"Okay," she instructed. "Continue compressions, one more round of epi, and get ready to roll him down to the OR." She swallowed around the growing ache in her throat. "Let's give this good man the only chance he has."

Even before the next dose of epinephrine was due, the surgical crew, including anesthesiologist, arrived to wheel Cappy down the hallway to surgery. Leigh didn't realize she was holding her breath until Riley appeared beside her. She exhaled, grateful for company that didn't require her to give orders. Or bad news.

"How are you holding up, Leigh?"

"I'm not sure I'm holding up as much as holding on. Or trying to. I hear you were our Paul Revere. Got the word to the operator?"

Discomfort flickered across Riley's face. "I was close to the stairs. Thank God." She glanced toward the door of an exam area across the room. "Is Mr. Denton . . . ?"

"Alive. In a coma. The chest wound was high—no lung or vascular injury, looks like. The wound in the torso was superficial. But the head wound . . ." She shook her head. "He's gone down for a brain CT with a fleet of officers in tow. And the neurosurgeon's on his way in. But I'm fairly certain the injury is devastating." She frowned, uncomfortable with the mix of feelings his prognosis stirred. *He's killed Cappy.*

"It was your husband who made that shot."

"Or maybe his partner," Leigh answered, then realized it had been a statement, not a question. "You've seen Nick since the shooting?"

"Yes . . ." Riley paused, as if considering her words. "He was in with Sam Gordon."

Leigh began stripping off her gloves, wishing her emotions were as easy to shed. *If I ever doubted that you've given up on me, God . . .*

"I'm going to meet with social services this afternoon," Riley said, glancing around the littered ER and toward the nurses gathered at the desk. "We'll need to start doing some individual peer counseling and set up a full hospital debriefing for the affected staff, probably a few days from now."

Leigh thought of last spring's pesticide disaster in Pacific

Point. Her friend, nurse Erin Quinn, had done the peer counseling then.

"Unfortunately," Riley continued, "this incident today made Golden Gate Mercy the poster child for Critical Incident Stress. And it's not over. We've got Cappy in surgery with an uncertain outcome." She winced at the prognosis on Leigh's face. "There's a Child Crisis investigator going to surgery as well, a pregnant pediatrics nurse with a bullet in her calf, Kristi upstairs in a state of emotional shock, staff trying to keep it all together in the face of their own trauma. And then we have the man responsible for it all. Somehow we're going to have to find a way to care for him. To the best of our ability."

Leigh brushed her hair back, sighing. "I've never had this happen. In all my experience in the ER, I've never been required to treat an assailant whose victims I know. And—" the shock of it struck her again—"who was shot by my husband. How can this be happening?"

She scanned the emergency department, strangely vacant in the wake of Cappy's departure because the patients being treated prior to the incident had been moved to the adjacent clinic. "I'm just grateful I had a surgeon here, a cardiothoracic surgeon on call, and that two of our other docs were close by." She nodded at Riley. "We're handling it. We'll get through it." She heard a deep groan in the distance and knew it was Sam. *I'll get through all of this, somehow.*

"Yes," Riley agreed. "We'll survive. Although—" she glanced toward the ambulance bay doors—"things will get pretty crazy when we're officially off lockdown. It seems calm right now, but that's because we're in the eye of the storm. The operators are fielding hundreds of calls; the media is chomping at the bit to converge on us. And the officers are already scrambling to identify visitors trying to get in to check on family members."

"One of those will be my sister." Leigh fought a shiver. "Caro will be frantic to get in. I'm going to try to get a message to her, but I've got to use this temporary lull now to reassess where we stand with the patients I have here."

"Meaning Sam Gordon?"

"Yes. Although Dr. Bartle's directing her treatment." Leigh glanced toward the other trauma cubicle. "I was busy with Cappy, and her wounds required a surgeon."

"Would you like me to go with you? to see Sam?"

"No," Leigh said quickly, telling herself Riley's offer was part of the job, proof of her kindness. *Not because she can read my mind. How do I do this? How do I shut off all these awful feelings?*

"Page me if you need me," Riley said gently. "For anything. I'm going back upstairs to check on Kristi Johnson and the staff. Then I'm going to set up the chapel as a respite area, have the cafeteria prepare a small table with some snacks, make it comfortable and welcoming for anyone who needs support. Or prayer." She smiled. "Doctors too."

"I'll let people know."

"I meant you. You're welcome there, Leigh."

She bit back a response. How could she explain to this chaplain that she was the last person on God's comfort list?

"I'm good—no problem." Leigh glanced up as the PA speaker crackled.

"Chaplain Hale, call social services, please. Public Information officer, report to main lobby. Nursing supervisor, report to main lobby. . . ."

Riley sighed. "It seems our lull is already ending."

Leigh watched Riley walk back through the ER, then glanced around the trauma room at the clutter and debris remaining from the resuscitation. Crash cart drawers open, empty epinephrine syringes lying on top, dangling cardiac electrodes, the laryngoscope, and suction tubing, filled with frothy blood and still making futile, soft sucking noises. She crossed to the machine and turned the knob, silencing it. Her eyes caught on Cappy's cutaway clothing lying in the corner. Bloodstained shirt, trousers with his belt, a cluster of keys with the worn, plastic charm holding photos of his grandchildren. Her throat squeezed and the thought came again—just as she'd asked Riley. *How can this be happening?*

"Dr. Stathos?"

Leigh glanced at the nurse. "Need me?"

"Dr. Bartle's gone ahead to the OR. Can you peek in on Miss Gordon? We're just about to hang the first unit of blood."

"Sure. I'm on my way." Out of the lull, back into the storm. *That God wants me to battle alone.*

+++

Sam closed her eyes, swallowing around the rigid tube threaded through her nostril and down the back of her throat. She tried not to gag or think about how much of the dark fluid siphoning back was blood. Then she shuddered at something so much worse—the terrifying image of Kurt Denton aiming the gun. *How did this happen?*

Through a floating haze of morphine that kept the pain in her belly barely below screaming level, she heard a voice at the doorway. "Nick?"

"No. It's Leigh Stathos."

CHAPTER SEVENTEEN

Leigh scanned the monitor's display of vital signs: BP 92 over 48, pulse 104, respirations 22, pulse oximetry 98 percent. Then she glanced down at Sam's face. She was pale, deathly pale, making the incredible lilac eyes shocking in contrast. Her lips were sallow, nasal folds as white as a fish belly, all signs of critical blood loss. She'd suffered a penetrating wound to the lower abdomen—intestinal most likely. Beneath an oxygen cannula, a nasogastric tube emerged from her nostril, dark as an eel with blood and bile. Three IVs and a unit of fresh frozen plasma hung from metal hooks overhead. Sam's flowered skirt, stained and cut to shreds, was draped over the garbage bin. "How are you feeling?"

"Like I've been shot in the gut."

Leigh wrestled a bitter urge to say she knew how that felt. "On a scale of one to ten, how's the pain? I can order something for you."

Sam's eyes drifted upward, and Leigh glanced quickly at the monitor. No change. "Sam?"

"Where's Dr. Bartle?"

"He's in the OR; we'll be moving you there in a few minutes. He's really the one directing your care."

"Because you don't want to."

Leigh made herself take a slow breath. "You needed a surgeon. I had a patient under CPR."

"The guard. How is he?"

"In surgery."

"I saw his eyes . . . all that blood." Sam's fingers fluttered to her throat, IV tubing dangling from her wrist.

Leigh thought of Riley's words, that Golden Gate Mercy was the "poster child for Critical Incident Stress." Sam Gordon looked stressed as well as gut shot.

Her bloodless lips pressed together. "Kurt Denton's still alive?"

"Yes." Leigh glanced toward his assigned room. He hadn't returned from CT. "I can't really discuss his condition."

"I'm not asking you to," Sam said, gasping against an apparent stab of pain. "Nick will tell me what I want to know."

Don't, Leigh. Let it go.

"Where is he?" Sam asked, glancing toward the door.

"I don't know. And I'm leaving," Leigh said, catching sight of the nurse outside the door. "I have to see my other patients. If you want anything, have the nurse call me."

"The only thing I want is . . ." Sam smiled weakly, her gaze focusing beyond Leigh. "There he is."

Leigh turned to see Nick standing against the wall outside the trauma room. He lifted his hand and it took her a few seconds to realize that he was gesturing to her, not Sam. But it took less than an instant to realize the truth. His critically injured lover had nailed it: Leigh hadn't wanted to treat her. The truth was that she'd asked Bartle to take over because, in the confusing and chaotic moment that Sam was rushed, bleeding and helpless, into the ER, Leigh had remembered: *I killed her in my dreams again last night.* The memory had horrified her. A doctor dreaming of murder— how could that be?

She walked over to her husband, wondering when God would stop playing with her like a dead mouse in the paws of a barn cat.

+++

Nick looked at Leigh and wondered if his appearance was as bad: sleepless, exhausted, and shell-shocked. He cleared his throat.

"How are you doing?" he asked, wishing he'd pulled Leigh away somewhere out of Sam's sight.

"I should ask you the same thing."

He wanted to believe she cared. He wanted to go back to Sunday night, a year ago, do it all over again. Do it right. "I'm okay." His gut twisted, proving it wasn't true. "I want to go up to talk with Kristi Johnson, but it's against regulations."

"Our side or yours?"

"Mine. They've exchanged my weapon, taken an initial statement. Then there's the post-shooting debriefing, and I have to meet with the department psychologist." He met Leigh's eyes. "Any word on Denton's condition?"

"No. But the head wound looked devastating."

"And Cappy?"

"In the OR." Sadness filled her eyes. "I couldn't get a pulse."

He glanced toward the door to Sam's room, saw her watching. "And . . . ?"

"Sam?"

"Will she be okay?"

"Dr. Bartle's handling her case—because he's a surgeon and I had my hands full with Cappy."

Nick caught the inflection in her voice. She was defending herself, felt the need to do that. *Help us, Lord. Please. This is such a mess.*

"She's lost a lot of blood," Leigh continued, "but we're replacing it. And her vital signs are encouraging. They'll know more when they get her opened up, and . . ." She hesitated at his obvious discomfort. "Once she stabilizes, controlling infection will be the real battle. She . . . You . . . It will be a long haul for everyone." Leigh glanced away.

Guilt jabbed again as he remembered less than two hours ago, when he'd had nothing on his mind, in his heart, but Leigh.

"The nurse said she was asking for her daughter," Leigh added. "There's no other family?"

Nick checked his watch. "Elisa gets out of preschool at two. I told Sam I'd pick her up. She knows me." He saw the reaction in Leigh's eyes and felt sick. "Her babysitter doesn't drive. I'll get her there. And then I'll try to contact Elisa's aunt Tina, Toby's ex, in Sunnyvale. She and Sam are still friendly. That's really all the family there is."

"I'm sure you'll do your best for them."

God, please. He reached for her hand. "Leigh, listen. It's complicated right now—it's ungodly complicated—but it doesn't change things. Not really. It doesn't mean—"

"It means," she said, pulling her hand away, "that Sam needs you. And things are going to stay very complicated. It's good we didn't make the mistake of fooling ourselves into something that can never be."

Mistake. He started to say something, anything, but halted as a nurse stepped up beside them. Her eyes were red-rimmed.

"Surgery called. Cappy died on the table. His wife and pastor are waiting in the lounge. Riley's with them. The surgeon asked if you could be there when he breaks the news."

Leigh squeezed her eyes closed for a moment, then squared her shoulders and walked toward the nurses' station. Nick knew she'd handle whatever happened. She always did. Even if she was hurting on the inside—and he knew she was; he could see it in her eyes. Still, she'd do what had to be done and move on. The way she'd loaded Frisco into a trailer and driven off to Pacific Point last December. Leaving him behind. And the way she'd tossed out their lemon tree; he'd seen that it was missing Sunday night. Now she was just as determined to pull the plug on any chance they had to reclaim their future. He had no doubt she'd done the same with God. Given up on him, too.

But then Nick knew something the very sharp and very determined Dr. Stathos didn't. God would never give up on her.

+++

Riley held the Kleenex box, wishing it were more. She was glad that Esther Thomas's pastor had driven her to the hospital. The stunned new widow leaned heavily on his arm, her mouth sagging in despair, the back of her hair still wrapped in rollers.

"You couldn't sew up the bullet hole?" she asked, tears

ready to spill over. "Do some kind of a graft? I've seen such miracles on TV."

"No." The surgeon, balding and with eyes as dark and kind as a cocker spaniel's, folded his hands across his chest. "I'm sorry. But the injury was very extensive, disrupting the ventricles. And the blood loss . . ." He glanced at Leigh.

"The second-floor staff raced to get your husband to us as fast as possible, Mrs. Thomas. Even so, he lost his pulse right after he arrived. We did CPR, gave him a breathing tube and IV fluids, drugs to stimulate his heart. We got him to the operating room very quickly."

Mrs. Thomas pressed her hand against her chest. "Was he awake? Did he say anything?"

"Not in the ER, but . . ."

Riley's throat tightened. "I talked with Cappy upstairs when he responded to our call for help. He said he wanted to keep his hospital staff safe. But that he'd be careful because he had plans with you." Mrs. Thomas's tears began to spill over. Riley walked closer, touched her arm. "Your husband told me more than once that you are a blessing from God, Mrs. Thomas."

Cappy's wife nodded mutely over and over. Then she lifted her chin and smiled. "Yes. That's my husband. That would be what my dear man would say." She looked between the surgeon and Leigh Stathos. "I know you did everything you could. And I'm so grateful. I am. It's just . . ." Her voice shuddered. "I wanted to have him with me a little longer. Not forever. That's what heaven is for—only the Creator can promise that. But I wanted a little . . . longer." She closed her eyes, swaying, and Riley and the pastor eased her into a chair.

Riley sat down beside her, and the pastor took the chair on the other side.

He opened his Bible. "Shall we have a prayer, Esther?"

"Yes," she whispered, her shoulders shaking, "before I go to see him. Yes, please. Cappy would want that. He would want all of you included. He loved you like family."

The surgeon stepped forward, folded his hands, and bowed his head. Leigh sighed and closed her eyes.

"Merciful God," the pastor began, "look with compassion on all who are bound by sorrow and pain. . . ."

+++

"Wait." Sam peered up at the technician pushing her gurney toward the doors to the OR. "Please, stop for a minute."

"They need to get you in there," Nick said, hustling alongside.

"And I need . . . to talk with you, just for minute." She blinked up into the fluorescent hallway lighting, seeing Nick in a blur of motion, his dark blue uniform and badge beyond a tangle of swaying IV bottles and plastic bags of blood the color of spilled cabernet. The portable monitor beeped close to her ear as her surgeon's name was paged overhead.

"I need to tell you something, Nick. I need to . . ." The gurney jolted to a rattling stop, and the tech's head, topped by a blue surgical cap, loomed over her.

"Miss Gordon, we're here. I'm going to step aside for just a minute and let you talk to this officer. But I'll have to ask you to make it short, okay? There's no time."

"Okay," she breathed, wincing as the nasogastric tube tugged against her nostril. The tech adjusted the slack and stepped aside. "Thank you."

Nick stepped close and bent down, his dark eyes clouded with concern. "If you're worrying about Elisa, don't. I talked with your babysitter and the woman at the preschool; she'll keep her busy until I get there. She said something about the neighbor's cat having a new litter of kittens." He tried to smile. "Don't cry, Sam. She'll be fine. I've already left a message in Sunnyvale, and—"

"I love you," she blurted. "I wasn't going to tell you yet, but in case something goes wrong . . ." Her heart sank at the immediate discomfort in his eyes.

"It won't," he said, glancing toward the technician, then taking hold of her hand. "You're going to be fine. But you've got to let them get you in there." He gave her hand a small squeeze.

"I always wished I'd had a chance to tell Toby that I loved him. One more time. You know?"

"I know," he said, his voice a thick whisper.

"I love you, Nick. I need you to know that."

He shut his eyes, swallowed, and nodded.

She tightened her fingers against his, told herself she shouldn't expect him to say anything. . . . *Tell me you love me. Say it, please.*

"We're rolling, Miss Gordon." The tech hit the button on automatic doors to the surgical suite. "Let's get you well."

Nick stepped back as the gurney started to move. Sam held on to his hand for as long as she could, then felt his fingers slip away. She craned her head to peer back at him as they rolled forward, saw his lips forming words. Not "I love you." Maybe "Don't worry" or . . .

Sam closed her eyes against the bright overhead lights inside the surgery suite and flinched with a cruel snarl of pain that had nothing to do with the bullet wound in her abdomen.

She refused to accept that Nick had whispered, "I'm sorry."

+++

Nick hunched forward on the chapel chair, aware suddenly in the empty stillness of the room that he was bone tired. Barely noon and he wasn't sure if he'd have the strength to walk out to the parking lot, get into the lieutenant's car for the drive back to the station—to a debriefing and required psych evaluation. *I shot those kids' father.* It had been his shot, not his partner's, that caused the massive brain injury. Kurt Denton would probably die. Nick's first time to fire his weapon on duty, and he'd killed a man. He'd had no choice; Denton shot three people, refused to put down his weapons. Then took deadly aim at officers. *Looked me in the eyes. He looked me right in the eyes. Almost like he wanted me to shoot.* He'd done the only thing he could do and expected the investigators would agree. It was just that . . . how had everything turned into such a mess so fast? when today had started out filled with more promise than he'd felt in months?

Nick shook his head, remembering how he'd lain awake again last night thinking of Leigh's willingness to give him another chance, how they'd planned to meet tonight. And then he'd decided to jog the park just after dawn, found himself on Divisadero Street at the bakery that was once Niko's. It had felt unexpectedly good to see that new beginning, those hopeful shopkeepers. Full circle, part of a bigger plan, maybe. Then he'd brought the gingerbread pig to Oly at the flower stand, even toyed with the idea of buying a bouquet for—

Nick leaped to his feet, mind racing. The man at the flower stand this morning, in sunglasses and scrubs and the 49ers jacket . . . *with the flowers*. Was that Kurt Denton? Could he really have been there, already setting his deadly plan in motion? Nick had met him before. If only he hadn't had that glimpse from such a distance; if he hadn't been wearing those sunglasses. Maybe Nick would have recognized him, stopped him, ended the ugly chain of events that unfolded just hours ago. He groaned, knowing he was being an idiot. Arrest a guy for buying flowers? Guess, somehow, that he was headed to Golden Gate Mercy? The fact was, it was too late now, regardless.

Cappy Thomas was dead. Kristi's children might soon be fatherless. A future with Leigh was more of an impossibility than ever before. And Sam . . . *"I love you."* He shut his eyes against the memory of her words.

Nick walked around the table someone had prepared with juice and crackers and boxes of Kleenex and toward the chapel's modest altar. He stared up at the window, a contemporary stained-glass nativity: kneeling parents, blessed child, sheep, donkey, and a radiant star—lemon yellow from the light streaming through.

"I've made a mess of things, Lord. I can't seem to get it right. But I'm not giving up. I can't. You know I can't. Help me, please. Help me to make things right."

"Leigh—oh, thank heaven!"

Leigh stepped away from the doorway at the sound of Caro's voice, then nearly stumbled backward as her sister threw her arms around her. "Easy there," she said against the thick tumble of Caro's hair. "I'm fine. It's okay."

"Are you sure?" Caro leaned away, searching Leigh's face. "Your message was so short, and the officers at the door wouldn't tell me who the victims were. The TV news is barely catching up. The radio reported that there was a second incident out in the employee parking lot. That the shooter had taken aim at two patrol officers, and—" Her hand flew to her mouth. "Oh no, Nick!"

Leigh grasped Caro's hand, drew her a few steps forward. She pointed through the doors of the chapel to where Nick sat, head bowed, in the chair closest to the altar. "There," she whispered. She felt tears threaten and cleared her throat. "I asked you to meet me here because Riley set it up as a respite area with food and things. But now with him sitting there . . ."

"It doesn't matter," Caro said, watching Nick. She turned to Leigh, her eyes shining with tears. "I only needed to know that my family is okay. That's all I need."

CHAPTER EIGHTEEN

The ICU charge nurse slid the suction catheter from the corner of her patient's mouth, inspected the display of vital signs on the monitor overhead, then pulled off her gloves. She turned to Riley. "I'll be honest with you. I'm not sure I can do this." Her voice was barely audible over the insistent, sucking hiss of the rigid plastic tube in her hand.

Riley nodded, knowing full well that the fiftysomething nurse didn't doubt her ability. Her name badge was studded with Mercy Hospital service pins; Barbara had been at the helm of this particular unit for more than a decade. Her whispered honesty had nothing to do with clinical skills and everything to do with the identity of the patient lying comatose on the bed.

Kurt Denton, scalp bandaged in Elastoplast, eyes purple and swollen shut, lay with the head of the bed elevated and an endotracheal tube protruding from between his lips. A ventilator expanded his chest, filling his lungs in a monotonous rhythm of hollow clicks and raspy, phlegmatic whooshes. IV fluids, one with a potent diuretic, infused into his arms via tubes attached to metering pumps. His wrists were secured to the bed by soft, protective restraints to prevent him from reaching up and dislodging the breathing tube, endangering his life—a precaution as unnecessary as the handcuffs that tethered him to the bed. And the armed police officer standing watch outside the ICU door. This young man wouldn't be causing anybody any more trouble. Nick Stathos's bullet had traversed two lobes of his brain.

Barbara's fingers moved to the stethoscope around her neck. "I worked eight years on the p.m. shift before I became charge nurse and moved to days. Sometimes it was past midnight when I got out of here. I'm scared of the dark, even with the new parking lot lights." Her forehead furrowed. "You never know if someone's hiding somewhere."

Riley fought a shiver. *This isn't about Houston. . . .*

The charge nurse continued. "Cappy worked nights then; he'd stop by the desk around eleven thirty. He'd say something like, 'I've got to check that parking lot out yonder. Old Cappy's a big chicken and I'd be grateful if you'd walk my way, ma'am. Keep me safe.'" She blinked against tears. "He was there, every night, walking me to my car. Insisting I was doing him the favor. He always had a story about his grandkids or a silly fishing adventure. His wife, Esther, was in my Bible study class last spring."

"It must be hard to think of all that while you're caring for Mr. Denton," Riley said, hearing the ventilator give its patient a long, programmed sigh.

"Pia was assigned to him, but her cousin is the nurse who was shot in the leg." The charge nurse winced. "Pregnant. What if she'd been shot in the abdomen, like that Child Crisis investigator?"

Riley watched as Barbara twisted her hands together. She

had no doubt that a long list of terrifying what-if scenarios was running through the minds of most of the staff, patients, and family members. She thought of Caroline, of how anxious she'd looked hurrying to meet her sister at the chapel. All of this was part of the initial stress reaction to a critical incident. "Did I understand that you'll be receiving help from some outside staff?"

"Yes, even with the lockdown still in effect. I was told I'd be able to relieve all my nurses who feel they need that. And—" she reached for her gloves as saliva gathered at the corner of Kurt Denton's mouth—"I'll keep reminding myself that no matter how I feel about what this man's done . . ." She looked at Riley, discomfort and confusion flickering across her face. "In all my years, I've never felt this way. I'm asking God to help me see him only as a human being in need of help, but I keep remembering the photos those visitors sent to the TV news station from their phones. Cappy lying there and this man aiming guns at our staff. How do I do this?"

"How do I do this?" For some reason, Riley thought of the stairs.

"One step at a time," she said gently. "Keep praying; remind yourself that it's normal to feel this way. As caregivers, we sometimes hold ourselves to impossibly high standards." She caught Barbara's gaze, made sure she understood. "If you need respite, ask for it. There's no weakness in accepting help. Okay?"

"Okay."

"I'll be working with chaplain services and social services—probably the police chaplain as well—to offer individual counseling. Then we'll plan a Critical Incident debriefing.

To help bolster coping skills, bring some closure." She reached out and touched the nurse's shoulder. "I'm here for whatever you need. We'll get through this, Barbara. I promise."

Riley stopped by the nurses' station and got a list of the day's staff from the ward clerk, then headed toward the ICU's exit. When she reached for the door, she saw that she was trembling. She thought of the charge nurse's words: *I keep remembering the photos . . .*" Riley understood. Right now, she was seeing her own frightening collage of images: Cappy marching toward the Johnson baby's room. Kurt Denton, eyes wild, shoving Kristi from the room. The gun . . . and the shadowy image of the man on those parking lot stairs in Houston.

She fought a wave of nausea. She'd told Barbara she'd be getting help for the staff; she promised. But now she wasn't sure how she'd do that because suddenly she felt like a victim all over again. Not like someone who should be offering help, but a woman with a paralyzed arm . . . who'd had to suck up all the courage she had left just to open the door to that stairwell.

Lord, are you there? Can I do this?

Riley took a deep breath and opened the door. Nick Stathos was talking to the police officer guarding the exit. He looked as undone as Riley felt.

+++

Sam dragged her tongue across her lips, tasting the lemony residue of the swab the SICU nurse had used to moisten her mouth. She cleared her throat, wincing at a grating stab of pain from the breathing tube they'd removed in the recovery room. It made the stomach tube, still in place, even more aggravating. She pressed the button on her medication pump and felt an instantaneous sensation of floating as the analgesic infused into her veins.

"Thank you for coming," she whispered, glancing at the young chaplain. "I was thinking about the Johnsons. Kristi and her children. No one here knew for sure what's happening with them." She swallowed and winced again, then adjusted the oxygen prongs in her overly crowded nostrils.

"They've gone home," Riley told her. "The doctors decided to go ahead and discharge Finn. Kristi was badly shaken up, but not physically hurt. She was given a mild sedative, and a friend will let them all stay at her house for tonight at least. One of your fellow counselors will be checking on them. The police released the paperwork you left in the pediatrics room."

"Good. But then I guess my chief concern isn't a problem anymore." She shivered uncontrollably and told herself it was the aftereffects of anesthesia. Or medication the pump just administered. "I mean the children's father. The nurses said he's in a coma. That he's here . . ." She turned her head toward the dimly lit row of patient rooms.

"Not in this unit," the chaplain said quickly. "And the police have him under guard."

"I wasn't worried," Sam told her, wondering only vaguely if it was a lie. No. The only thing she was concerned about was . . . "Have you seen Nick?"

"Officer Stathos?"

"Yes." *Leigh's husband. Is that how you think of him?* She saw no clue in the chaplain's expression. "Is he still here in the hospital?"

"I'm not sure."

Irritation prickled despite the floating effect of the morphine. "Not sure or don't want to tell me?"

Riley's forehead wrinkled. "What do you mean?"

The blood pressure cuff inflated with a hum. "I know you're a friend of Leigh Stathos, and I'm sure you're aware of our situation."

"I'm sorry, but I don't see how that—"

"Don't," Sam interrupted, raising her shoulders from the pillow. Pain seared her abdomen, but she didn't care. "Don't stand there and pretend that everyone doesn't look at me and see one thing: the tramp who broke up Dr. Stathos's marriage."

The chaplain was silent, her eyes mirroring the truth. Sam wondered how it would translate.

"Look," Riley said, rubbing her fingers across her sling. "I do consider Leigh a friend. I am sad for her situation. But I'm here as a chaplain—I see you as a patient. And a victim of an awful crime." Her expression was sympathetic, almost as if she understood how that felt. "That's the only way I see you. I'm offering help, not judgment. I'm new at being a chaplain and I'm trying my best. I'm honestly not sure where Nick Stathos is. I saw him about half an hour ago. But I didn't talk with him."

"Was he still in the ER?"

"No. It was at the ICU." Riley raised her brows. "But wasn't he going to pick up your daughter?"

"Yes," Sam whispered, the relief of Riley's words making her head swim as effectively as the morphine. Nick wasn't still down there with his wife, and soon he'd be with Elisa. "He's picking her up from preschool, bringing her here."

"Here?" Riley glanced around the room. "Do you think she'll be okay with all this? the equipment and noises and—" Riley touched her own nose—"your NG tube? You don't think she'll be—?"

"She'll be fine," Sam said, cutting her off. "She's tough. Like her mother. Nick's good with her." *And she's our bond.*

"Well . . ." Riley glanced at the clock. "I'm supposed to meet with social services. Is there anything I can do for you before I leave? A prayer?"

Prayers—right. "No."

She watched Riley Hale leave, then lay still, listening to the distant beeps and whirs of medical machinery and the soft footfalls of the nursing staff. She thought about the chaplain's offer of prayer. And wondered idly, brain fuzzy with medication, what God would think of a mother using her child as a means of drawing a man close, keeping him there—if he was really any more forgiving than Leigh Stathos's cohorts down in the ER. And if, after denying her so many things all her life, God was finally ready to accept that Sam was willing to do anything to grab her own happy ending. That she wasn't about to let him stand in the way.

Sam turned toward the sound of footsteps outside her doorway, hope rising in her chest. *Nick . . .*

Then she was sure she could hear God's cruel laughter as Leigh Stathos walked in.

+++

"I thought I'd come by to . . ." Leigh hesitated, realizing suddenly that she had no clue why she'd come to Sam Gordon's room.

"To see if Nick is here?" Sam asked, the hoarseness of her voice deepening the obviously intentional barb.

"No, of course not," Leigh said quickly, hating that this woman was probably right. Was that why she came? *Get out of here. Don't be a fool.* She crossed her arms, glanced at the monitor display. "Dr. Bartle told me the bullet did far less damage than they'd expected. And he was able to make repairs without having to resect a lot of bowel."

"Well . . ." Sam's lips twisted. "No one ever said Toby Gordon's kid sister didn't have plenty of guts."

Leigh forced a smile. "I'm sure."

They stared at each other for a few seconds in awkward silence, and Leigh was certain she felt the curious eyes of the staff at the desk beyond.

Sam glanced toward the door. "They think you're here to pinch off my oxygen tubing."

Leigh's mouth sagged open. "Oh, come on. Don't—"

"Tell the truth?" Sam grimaced as she hiked a few inches higher on the pillow. "Why? That wouldn't be professional? ladylike?" She shook her head, pinning Leigh with those startling lilac eyes. "No one's ever said I was a lady, either. Go ahead and blame it on the fact that I'm chock-full of drugs. Or that I've recently had someone try to make a gruesome donut out of me with a handgun. But I think the time for pretense is past, Dr. Stathos. Why are you here?"

Leigh took a slow breath, refused to tremble. "Never mind. I'm going."

"No, you're not. You came here to find out something. And it has nothing to do with my medical condition—Dr. Bartle already disappointed you with the news that I didn't die on his table." She exhaled, watching Leigh's face. "What did you want to know?"

"Forget it. This was a mistake. I'm—"

"A coward? Afraid of the truth?" Sam shook her head. "I don't understand how a passionate man like Nick could have settled for such a spineless coward."

"Sunday night," Leigh hissed through clenched teeth, "why did you really call me?"

"That's better. Now we're getting somewhere." Sam glanced toward the doorway. "But be a lady and close the door, would you? We don't want to disturb anyone."

+++

Nick peered through the window at the patient in the hospital bed. He turned to the chaplain's assistant. "Why does he look so swollen?"

"It's the bleeding from the bullet's damage." Riley Hale looked at him, concern in her eyes. Nick had the feeling it was for him. "Should you be here? I don't know your department policy, but we did have a call from Buzz Chumbley. And he said he'd be talking with you at the station."

"I asked the officer in the hallway to cut me a little slack—I had to see Denton. I won't try to go in there, but I had to see for myself." Nick's eyes scanned the blipping monitors, ventilator, suspended bags of IV fluids, handcuffs—all lit eerily by fluorescent lighting shining down on the still body in the bed. Thin, pale, bruised, bandaged . . . Kurt Denton looked dead already. Nick swallowed and tried to remember that this was the ruthless perpetrator who'd aimed weapons at his partner and him after shooting three people.

"He could have killed more," the chaplain said quietly, as if she'd read his mind. "There are medical offices across the parking lots with patients and staff coming and going. And there's Bay City Elementary on the corner." She waited, and when he didn't respond, she cleared her throat. He thought he saw her tremble.

"I was there," she whispered. "Upstairs, just before he pulled out that gun and started to shoot. I saw the look in his eyes. Cappy tried, but there was no way to talk him down. He seemed pumped up on drugs, crazed, and so desperate to take Kristi with him. I think he'd have done anything to make that happen." She rested her hand lightly on Nick's uniform sleeve. "I'm thanking God you were here."

"I . . . I've got to go," Nick said, avoiding her eyes. He shifted his weight and his holster creaked, strangely ominous against the soft background whir of lifesaving equipment. "If anyone asks, I'll say you questioned my showing up here. Don't worry."

"Not worried. And I'm glad you'll be talking with your chaplain. I think that's a good idea, Nick."

He nodded and walked toward the hallway door without looking back at the mortally wounded man on the bed. He'd seen what he came to see. But he was leaving with more than he wanted to deal with. It wasn't so much the way Kurt Denton had looked—bloated, bruised, hooked to machines. Nick had seen critically injured people before, at highway accidents and assault scenes. Even Toby, hours before he died. He'd been as prepared as he could have been to see the man he'd shot a few hours ago. And told himself—like he'd be telling the SFPD shooting investigators—that what Riley

Hale just said was true: Nick had dropped a killer before he could kill again.

What he hadn't expected was what he'd felt when she'd said those things about Denton's motive, his desperation. Nick's stomach churned as he exited the ICU. He tried to stop a rush of memories of those days after Leigh threw him out. His calls, pleading, frustration. Then the panic and fear of losing her that finally left him sleeping in a car outside their house. Caused her to threaten him with a restraining order, put his job at risk. Because he wanted her back so badly, was desperate for that, and would have done anything to make it happen.

He wouldn't believe he was anything like the man he'd shot.

CHAPTER NINETEEN

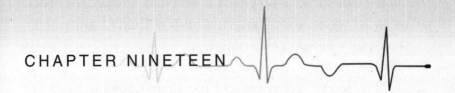

"Why did you call me that night?" Leigh repeated. She scraped a visitor's chair across the floor and perched on its edge. "And don't give me that line about needing to know Patrice's last name—it's in the phone book."

Sam smiled, lips still pale despite the infusing unit of blood. "Not my best work, I admit. I called to see if Nick was there."

"And to let me know he'd been with you." Leigh's stomach sank, remembering his words of defense this morning. *"Nothing really happened."*

"He came for dessert," Sam said, reaching for the cord to her medication pump. "And to see my daughter. In fact, we'd tucked Elisa into bed, and he was just about to read *Goodnight Moon* when . . ." She pressed the button. "It was you who called, right?"

Leigh nodded, her heart cramping at the image of Nick reading a bedtime story to this woman's child. It was worse—so much more intimate—than imagining him in Sam's bed.

"Why?" Sam asked, her lids dipping noticeably from the effects of the medication.

"Our elderly neighbor was having some problems."

"No." Sam's eyes narrowed. "I mean, why are you so self-ish? You didn't want him, but now—"

"You went after him." Leigh gripped the arms of the chair, felt her face sting. "Don't deny it. You took advantage of Nick when he was in shock, grieving his best friend." She caught the change in Sam's expression.

"His friend . . . my brother."

"I'm sorry." Leigh pressed her fingers against her forehead. "Really. That wasn't fair."

"What's unfair is what you're doing to Nick. Intruding in his life—jerking him around—when he finally has the chance to have what he wants."

"Meaning you?"

Sam lifted her chin in a show of strength, surprisingly undiluted by the tubing cluttering her face. "Yes. And all the things I can give him that you never would."

Leigh held her breath, feeling all at once like they'd traded places and she was about to be shot in the gut. She told herself not to ask, that it didn't matter. *Things I never would . . .* "Like what?"

Sam opened her mouth to answer, then stopped. Her pale face lit. "Oh, there you are. Come here, both of you!"

Leigh turned.

Nick stood in the doorway holding a blonde toddler, her arms wrapped tightly around his neck.

+++

Ten minutes later, Sam blew a kiss as a volunteer carried Elisa off to find a coloring book. She felt a twinge of guilt. *I needed you here, baby girl. Because we need him.*

"I don't think it was a good idea to let her see you yet," Nick said. "She seemed scared by all this." His dark eyes swept the equipment crowding her bed. "And you look . . . beat."

"Thanks," she said, still trying to forget the look on his face when he'd seen Leigh. "You know just what to say to a girl."

"You know what I meant."

"I did. I do," she said, her heart warming at the concern in his eyes. Almost worth a bullet. "I always know what you mean. We think alike." *Except you haven't realized that you love me, yet.*

Nick glanced down at his hands. "Tina said she'd be here around five, give or take with traffic. She'll stop by and see you, then pick Elisa up at the babysitter's. She said she's happy to keep her for as long as you need." He shifted in the chair, and Sam caught a whiff of shampoo—he'd showered, changed into khakis and a blue striped dress shirt.

"She's a good aunt. A good person," Sam added. "Even though her marriage to Toby didn't last, she's happy now. It all worked out."

Nick looked up, his expression saying she'd laid it on too thick. She knew it and she hated feeling like she had to. Like she was scrambling against time to get her world upright again, helpless as a turtle flipped over on its back.

"Why was Leigh here?"

Sam thought about lying but was too tired. "She wanted to know why I called her Sunday night."

Nick's eyes were maddeningly unreadable. "And what did you tell her?"

She sighed, grateful she hadn't denied it. *He knows.* "I said

I was curious if you'd gone to see her. If she was the person who'd called your cell at my house."

He was quiet for several seconds. "Her number isn't listed."

She told herself he wasn't defending Leigh, reminded herself that he'd just shot someone in defense of her. And decided there wasn't enough time for anything but the truth. Why had she fallen in love with a cop? Their minds were too incisive and suspicious. "I found it in those old phone records from back in November. When you were staying with me and tried to reach her." *And she wouldn't call you back. Remember? She wasn't there for you—I was.*

He looked back down at his hands, and she could hear the beeping of her heart monitor pick up speed.

"I drank too much wine," she admitted. "I hated it that she called and you jumped, and—"

"Our neighbors had an emergency," he interrupted.

"That's what she said."

"It's the truth." His eyes were intense. Almost as if he were instructing a gunman to lay down a lethal weapon. "Leigh doesn't lie."

+++

Leigh climbed the last flight of stairs to the second floor, feeling her pulse throb in her neck and her breath quicken. She wasn't surprised; it had been days since she'd been able to exercise. Days since she'd had more than a few hours' sleep. And months since she'd slept well . . . since Nick. No wonder the events of the last few days had knocked her off-kilter, why today seemed so surreal.

She grasped the doorknob and stepped out onto the pediatrics floor. She was met by eerie silence. And a police officer.

"Ma'am." The officer—young, with a barely sprouting mustache—glanced at her scrubs and white coat. "Doctor . . . ?"

"Stathos," she said and saw immediate recognition of the name. She glanced down the corridor, empty except for a pair of investigators in police coveralls.

"We're still on lockdown, Dr. Stathos. I'll have to see your identification."

"I've been treating the victims," she said, handing him her badge, "and I wondered if I could have a look. Get a feel of it, because . . ." Her words trailed off as she realized that she wasn't sure why she'd come to this evacuated floor. It made no more sense than showing up in Sam Gordon's room.

"No problem," he said, returning her badge. "We're almost finished. I can walk you down there, but I'll have to ask you not to touch anything or go beyond any of the perimeter tape."

"Of course," she said, noticing that she'd dropped her voice to a near whisper. Her mouth had gone dry.

They walked past the shut-down elevators to the nurses' desk, littered with charts and abandoned coffee mugs; past rooms with open doors and empty cribs, a cafeteria cart still loaded with breakfast trays, the children's playroom with its mural of Seuss creatures, and—

"Oh!" Leigh jumped sideways, heart hammering in her chest.

"Sorry," the officer said, snatching at the string of the bobbing happy face balloon. "I've been trying to get it; the air ducts keep sailing it around the ceiling." He glanced at her. "Are you all right?"

She pulled her hand away from her chest and sucked in a breath. "Sure. It surprised me, that's all. I'm a little tired, I guess." She smiled weakly. "Long day."

He continued down the corridor and she followed, aware of the unnatural echo of their footsteps and of the distant sound of a patient's TV left on during the haste of evacuation.

"Golden Gate Mercy Hospital remains on lockdown after a shooting spree that ended when two Mission District police officers . . ."

"Here," the officer said, stopping to point at the floor, "is where the security guard was shot, and there—" he pointed to a second stain nearby—"is where the Child Crisis investigator fell. And you can see . . ."

How Sam struggled. Oh, dear God . . . Leigh held her breath, eyes moving over the side-by-side pools of blood, dark purple, larger than seemed possible. One with smeared palm prints, like some macabre finger painting. Her knees weakened.

"And down here," he continued, walking a few more steps, "is the Johnson baby's room, where it all started."

Leigh inched forward, then stopped, her gaze moving past the yellow crime scene tape into the room beyond: crib, an IV pump, diaper bag, and an overturned vase of flowers. White lilies, at least a dozen, strewn all over the floor. And next to them, Abby Johnson's stuffed pony. Tears sprang to her eyes. "I've seen enough," she said, turning away. "I can get back by myself, thank you."

She jogged down the empty corridor, eyes on the stairwell door. She passed the room with the TV and tried not to listen.

"*. . . according to hospital sources, remains in critical condition. Per department policy, the two SFPD officers will remain on administrative leave pending investigation. . . .*"

She yanked open the door to the stairs, lurched through to the landing, and leaned back against the cold wall, fighting a vicious wave of nausea. She'd been a fool to come up here; she was a doctor, not a forensic scientist. She dealt with living beings, did what she could to save them. She performed the skills she'd been taught, made diagnoses, wielded instruments, applied joules of electricity to dying hearts, did everything she'd spent years learning to do. And then walked away. That was how it was supposed to go. But this . . . this aftermath was horrible. Too much like standing there with Cappy's widow, listening to prayers, when all Leigh wanted to do was get away. Distance herself—leave the pain of it behind.

She retched, closed her eyes, and inhaled slowly through her nostrils, pushing down the images of drying blood she could do nothing about. She'd nearly panicked over a helium balloon. A balloon. She raised her hand to her mouth. How awful had it been for Cappy? Sam? . . . And Nick, out there in the parking lot? Risking his life for all of them.

She took another deep breath, then pushed away from the wall. There were a few patients to finish with in the ER, but no new ones because of the lockdown. Her cell phone buzzed in the pocket of her lab coat.

"Yes?"

"Sorry, Dr. Stathos," the charge nurse said, "but looks like we have one more victim from the incident. One of the peds nurses is here. Apparently he was kicked in the chest."

"I'll be right there."

Leigh hustled downstairs, telling herself she was hurrying toward what she was trained to do, not running away from things she didn't have the stomach to face.

+++

"What's the first thing I thought of?" Nick looked over the rim of his coffee cup at the police chaplain sitting behind his cluttered desk. The man's ever-present electrical fan whirred over the distant sounds of afternoon traffic and fluttered the sheet of paper in his hands.

Buzz smiled. "It's a question straight off my critical incident stress algorithm." He tapped the paper. "Actually, it suggests we ask, 'What was the first thing that you thought of once you stopped functioning on automatic?'" He set the paper aside.

"I know. The department psychologist already asked me." Nick studied Buzz's face for a moment. "You want the same answer?"

"I'm here for whatever you need to say."

Nick forced a laugh. "Why is this easier over a slice of cold pizza on your lumpy couch?" He sighed and met his roommate's gaze. "Not official?"

"And completely confidential. You know that."

Nick scraped his thumbnail across the SFPD logo on his cup. "When we got the call for a 417 at Golden Gate with shots fired, the first thing I thought of was Leigh. That someone had hurt her. We were wedged into traffic just two lousy blocks away, and I couldn't get clear. I thought my head would explode. I almost jumped out of the car and started running for that hospital." He stared into Buzz's eyes. "Truth? Looking down the barrels of Denton's guns was nothing compared to thinking that I could lose Leigh. That I'd never have the chance to make things right between us."

Buzz was quiet for moment. "And now you know it was Sam Gordon who was shot."

"Right."

The chaplain leaned forward slightly. "So how are you doing with that?"

"How much time do you have?"

+++

"It's not that bad, is it?" the male nurse asked, looking at Riley. He flinched as Leigh's fingers palpated the bruised area over his lower chest.

Riley noticed that the middle-aged and bearded man wore a surgical cap printed with Care Bears.

He tried to chuckle and flinched again. "I mean when a guy's on an ER gurney and sees the chaplain show up, it makes him wonder if he's going to need last rites." His smile faded, and sadness flooded his eyes. He swallowed.

Riley watched as Leigh pressed her stethoscope against the man's chest and asked him to breathe in and out. She repeated it on his uninjured side and then asked him to lie flat on the gurney.

"I didn't want to come down here. The kids are still pretty

shook up, and there's no playroom on the third floor, where we moved them." He inhaled deeply at the doctor's request and grimaced very slightly as she palpated his abdominal wall below the bruised ribs. He looked at Riley, his pupils widening. "I didn't think he kicked me that hard. All I could think was I had to stop him from hurting those kids. My wife and I can't have any children of our own. She's a volunteer up there on weekends. I guess sometimes we think of those little guys as . . ." He glanced away. "I'm glad they caught him."

Leigh checked the display of vital signs, then stepped away from the gurney. "I'm ordering a chest X-ray with rib detail," she said, draping her stethoscope around her neck. "And a blood count and urinalysis—just to be safe. You're not tender over your spleen or your kidney, but that's a bad bruise. And I won't be surprised if you have a rib fracture. Or two."

The nurse was silent for a few seconds. "We all know how hard you worked to save Cappy. And I hope you'll tell your husband that I'm grateful he stopped that guy before more people were hurt."

"Thank you." Leigh looked away. "Now let me order your X-ray. Get you all set up."

Riley followed as Leigh strode out, then caught up with her at the doorway to her office.

"Leigh?"

She turned, and there was no mistaking the fatigue etched on her face.

"I have fresh coffee in the chapel and some of that nut bread from the cafeteria." *And I'll listen, my friend.*

"Chapel?" Leigh shook her head. "I'll give you credit, you don't give up. But no thanks, I'll pass. As soon as I see our big Care Bear's films, I'm out of here. I'm going to sleep until noon tomorrow, then spend my day off someplace even God can't track me down."

CHAPTER TWENTY

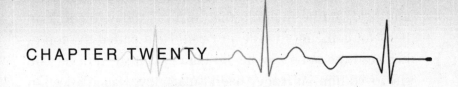

Sam jerked awake, confused for a moment, then caught sight of the date on the room's message board below the wall clock: Wednesday, October 1—5 p.m. She'd slept the day away. She groaned at the familiar wave of pain spreading across her lower abdomen. Dr. Bartle's "fortunately less serious than we'd feared" description of her injury belied the vicious reality: it felt like someone had detonated explosives in her navel. She reached for the cord to the pain-med pump and squinted at her IVs. No more blood transfusions, but such an endless nightmare. Still, none of it, not the pain or indignity or sense of helplessness, was as bad as . . .

Nick hadn't stayed more than twenty minutes yesterday. He'd said she looked tired, that he needed to drive Elisa to the babysitter and get back to the department for his officer-involved-shooting interviews. All true, of course. But she'd hoped that he'd come back, imagined him sitting here all night. Holding her hand. And that sometime, in the wee hours this morning, he'd mention what she'd told him before they wheeled her into surgery. Say that he'd been surprised, of course, but that he was glad she'd told him she loved him. That the only reason he hadn't been able to express those same feelings to her was that he wasn't free yet. He had to put things on hold until the divorce was final. She jabbed the button on the medication pump.

The truth was, she'd asked him to come back last night and he'd said he couldn't, that he'd call today to check on her. Not come by to visit, just call. He'd patted the top of her head the same way he did Elisa's. As if she'd never said she loved him. As if they hadn't made love, fallen asleep in each other's arms in those long, gray days after Toby died. It would be different now, all so different, if Leigh Stathos hadn't called the night he'd come for dessert. Sam had seen it in his eyes when he held her; he'd been ready to give up on his marriage. And now, after all Leigh had done to hurt him these past months—all Sam had done to help him through it—he was defending her. *"Leigh doesn't lie."*

She shut her eyes, letting the medicine's floating effect compete with the fresh sting of anger. Strangely the anger made things clearer, helped her understand what she had to do. The divorce had to happen. She couldn't let anything— even a bullet in her belly—stop her from getting the happy ending she'd been cheated of her whole life.

"Miss Gordon?"

Sam turned to see the evening nurse in the doorway, holding a small IV pouch.

"I have the antibiotic your surgeon ordered." She checked Sam's patient identity band, questioned her about medication allergies, then connected the tubing to an infusion pump. "There," the nurse said, smiling at her. "You're all set. Need anything else while I'm here?"

"Yes. How do I get in touch with a doctor?"

"Dr. Bartle's still in the house," the nurse answered. "I could have him stop by."

"No. Dr. Stathos in the ER."

"She's not on duty today. And I'm sorry, but the ER doctors don't take calls."

"I think she'll take mine," Sam said, noticing a mild burning sensation as the antibiotic began to flow. "Tell her I need to talk with her."

+++

Leigh pressed her heel against the mare's side, signaling the big red horse to move into a canter, and then urged her forward, faster. She rose from the saddle in a half seat and stood in the stirrup irons, squeezing her calves until they were in a brisk gallop—hooves flinging clods from the soft, moist dirt of the coastal trail. *Yes, better . . . but more.* She gathered the reins in one hand, tapped her crop against the mare's hip, and felt her spring forward in response, stretching out, mane flying. Leigh followed the horse's head with her hands, letting the wind whip through her hair and bring tears to her eyes, seeing the park's knee-high grasses and trees blur like an impressionist painting. Feeling only the wind, the mare's muscles bunching beneath her; hearing the rhythm of hooves against earth, the horse's breathing, and her own heart singing in her ears. Finally singing, in sweet escape. She sucked in a deep breath of bay air, tasted the brine in it—kept riding, kept breathing. Felt alive again. She didn't want it to ever, ever stop. She wanted it to go on forever.

Forever. Oh, God, no. Don't do this to me. Not here. Not now.

Leigh shortened the reins, easing the mare back from

the gallop with a half halt. She settled into the saddle as the horse returned to a canter and finally broke to a big, up-and-down trot, breath heaving. She posted the trot for several strides, then sat deep in the saddle and drew back on the reins again, patting the horse's neck as they finally slowed to a brisk walk. Leigh sighed. For a few minutes, she'd escaped. She'd forgotten it wasn't Frisco beneath her, that Cappy Thomas was dead, that her mother had left that message on her phone.

"Leigh-Leigh, darling, Mom. Only have a minute—ship to shore costs like murder. Heard the news. I told you that hospital was in a bad area. If Nick Stathos wants to live like that forever, let him. But you don't have to. Nor does Caroline. I've been discussing it with my new beau, Phillip. He's a plastic surgeon, remember? With a lovely practice in Palm Beach. And modeling connections, too—oh, I have to go. We'll be late for dinner. E-mail me. I'll try and check it tomorrow sometime. After our shore excursion. Hope you're okay."

Leigh slipped her boots from the stirrups and turned the mare around, her legs hanging along the animal's warm sides as they followed the trail back to the barn. She let the small of her back relax, feeling her hip joints stretch forward and back alternately with the horse's movement, legs free, body free. *Free.* Leigh closed her eyes, tipped her head back, and raised her arms, palms up. She breathed in slowly, let it out, and searched for peace. For that connection, that balanced center, she'd lost somehow. In the last year, these quiet moments in the saddle had been the closest she came to . . . *prayer.*

Leigh thought of what she'd told Riley yesterday, that

even God couldn't track her down here. Then she opened her eyes, searched the clouds, and asked the question that was whispering inside her head more and more these past few weeks. "Do you want to? Do you want to find me, Lord?"

+++

Nick dribbled the basketball, whirled, dodged the gangly ten-year-old in braces and headgear, then found a break and drove forward—took his shot and missed. The kids howled and hooted among themselves.

"Gettin' old and slow, Officer Nick!"

"My grammy can aim better than that with a can of SpaghettiOs!"

"Yeah, at the back of your ugly head, Addison!"

Nick laughed, threw his hands up, then yanked at a handful of his tank top and wiped it across his face. Sweat burned his eyes and his legs had turned to rubber. He leaned over, hands on his thighs. "Okay . . . I'm done. You win. All I'm good for now is saying, 'Thank you for the food, Lord,' and chewing. Pepperoni or sausage pizza? Shoot your baskets and make up your mind—this old man's starving."

He walked to the bleachers, sank down, and watched the boys take turns from the free throw line, wishing the rest of life could be like this. Work hard, give it all you got, play by the rules . . . He winced. But he hadn't, of course. He hadn't played by the rules and Leigh would never forgive that. No matter how hard he tried to make up for it, no matter how long he kept at it. Even if he'd been so close to seeing it happen just two days ago. But now . . . She hadn't responded to his text message, and—

"Officer Nick?"

Nick looked into the huge brown eyes of his littlest player. Edwin, barely seven, had cheeks like a chipmunk and wore his hair in dozens of fuzzy twists and his thrift-store sneakers two sizes too big. He walked like one of Oly's pigeons but—perched on Nick's shoulders—shot hoops like Kobe Bryant. "Yeah, Ed-winner. What can I do you for?"

"Is it true, what folks are sayin'?"

Nick's chest tightened. "What are they saying?"

"That you shot somebody."

Father God . . . "Yes, it's true."

Edwin's eyes held Nick's, unblinking. "He was a bad guy?"

"He did a bad thing. I couldn't let him do it again."

The boy's brows puckered. "How did it feel—to shoot somebody?"

Nick took a slow breath. "Bad. Real bad."

Edwin rested his small palm on Nick's knee. "I'm going to ask my Jesus to look after you. Even though you're big."

Nick smiled over the lump in his throat. "I'd appreciate that."

+++

Riley slipped through the door of the ICU, blinked against the dim lighting, then crossed the short stretch of maroon carpeting to Kurt Denton's room. She held the staff list in her hand and told herself she'd come to be certain she hadn't missed anyone who might need stress counseling, but she knew that wasn't the truth. She needed to see this man, the vicious assailant who'd killed without mercy, because he put a face on her nightmares. She glanced toward the nurses' desk, took a slow breath, and stepped into the room, struggling against the memory of plunging headfirst down a flight of stairs. *Father, I'm afraid. . . . I'm afraid.*

Her gaze moved first, irrationally, to the handcuffs that secured him to the bed. As if that precaution were the only thing that kept this young killer's eyes from popping open, stopped him from leaping over the bed rails, snatching a gun from under the pillow, and grabbing her around the neck like he'd done to Kristi Johnson. It wasn't handcuffs that tethered Kurt Denton to the bed; it was a bullet to the brain.

She startled, feeling immediately foolish as the blood pressure cuff inflated on his arm, Velcro crackling. She watched the digital display as the machine searched for his systolic pressure. The device hummed and inflated further, and then numbers appeared: 260, 240, 220 . . . Her eyes moved to his heart rhythm, sinus bradycardia, slower than normal at barely 50 beats per minute. High blood pressure, slow pulse, signs of intracranial pressure—ominous. He'd been given a death sentence. Kurt Denton would pay for his crime.

The memory intruded before Riley could stop it. Houston, her father. At her hospital bedside.

"I'll see that there's justice, baby girl. We'll find this guy if I have to do it myself. What I'd give to feel my hands around his throat. As God is my witness, I'll make him pay. He could have killed you!"

But they hadn't found him. And worse—what still left Riley with nightmares—was that they'd never discovered any motive for her attack in the medical center parking lot. A hooded man in the shadows of the stairwell, hands around her throat; then the ruthless shove that sent her hurtling down the steps. *Why? Why?* Her purse had been found on the landing, cash and credit cards in place; not a kidnapping, no attempt at sexual assault. Riley's stomach roiled and she wrapped her free arm around her sling. "A random act of violence," the Houston papers had reported, as if that would make it feel less personal somehow, bring peaceful closure.

Riley jumped as the monitor alarm sounded.

"His pressure isn't responding to the medications," the nurse said, stepping to the bedside to reset the alarm. "Any luck reaching family?"

"No. According to the mother of his children, he's been estranged from them for years." Riley glanced at the nurse's ID badge, saw she was from a local staffing registry. "We appreciate your coming in to relieve our nurses."

"Not a problem," she said, smoothing the sheet over Denton's chest. "I'm a 'traveler,' new to the area, so I don't know the staff that were shot." Her brows scrunched. "Maybe I'd feel different if he were awake, staring at me. But at least we know why he did what he did: some really messed-up attempt to keep his family together. In my mind, that feels easier to accept, safer, than some random act of violence."

Riley hugged her sling close. "Yes."

The nurse pressed a button, raising the head of her patient's bed a few inches. "I saw the critical stress information you left at the nurses' station. Those tips about eating right, exercising, and listening to music." She glanced up and smiled. "I was working at Sierra Mercy during that day care explosion last year. When Claire Avery—she's Claire Caldwell now—did CISM peer counseling and a staff debriefing. It was a good thing, made me feel like someone cared. I'm glad you're doing it for these folks. If I can help you in some way, I'd be happy to."

Riley felt a rush of warmth. "Thank you. I'll be working with the senior chaplain and social services to get that going. And I have a small hospital ministry in place that I hope will help, too. We meet in the chapel before our shifts."

"Faith QD. Erin Quinn started that at Sierra Mercy. I still have my T-shirt with that stenciled nurse's lamp." The traveler nurse's smile broadened. "It looks like you've got it covered, Chaplain."

Riley glanced at the comatose patient and exhaled softly. "I'm trying."

+++

"Is this all the water he's taken today?" Leigh asked, staring down at the large rubber bucket the stable staff installed in a corner of Frisco's stall.

"I'm afraid so." Patrice sighed. "I turned off the automatic waterer and filled the bucket myself so I could keep an accurate record. Dr. Hunter's up-to-date. He said the water he gave through the stomach tube helped, but if this keeps up, he'll need to give some IV fluids." She reached out and brushed Frisco's dark forelock aside. "But his vital signs are normal. And he isn't in pain; you can see that."

Leigh's throat tightened at the dull look in her horse's eye, his depressed posture. She glanced around the stall thickly bedded with pine shavings. "No manure?"

"Not yet. But I still hear bowel sounds."

"So we wait." Leigh thought of Sam lying in a hospital bed with her own belly problems.

"You're off duty tomorrow too, aren't you?" Patrice asked. "That awful incident yesterday hasn't changed things for you?"

If you only knew. She'd tossed and turned half the night. Then had that text from Nick this morning: *"Call me?"* "It's still my day off. Although I promised to work a couple of hours as a favor to one of the doctors. His wife has an OB appointment. Otherwise, I'll be out here, walking Frisco and trying to coax him to eat."

"Good." Patrice turned as Maria approached, leading Tag at the end of a pink rope. The donkey's big ears pricked forward as Frisco nickered. "I'm glad you'll be available," the stable owner continued. "Gary and I have to make a visit to the family of a former foster child. We'll be gone until tomorrow night." She patted Maria's head. "My sister, Glenna, will be here to watch Maria and generally oversee things. She's not an experienced horsewoman. But she'll have the stable hands and access to all the emergency numbers, of course."

Maria stepped up to Frisco's gate and traced her finger along Nick's name on the contact card.

Leigh turned to Patrice. "You'd have her call me," she said quickly. "If anything happens, be sure your sister calls Dr. Hunter and me."

"Absolutely," Patrice said with a reassuring smile. "Your very nice husband 'isn't a horse person.'" She chuckled. "I'll never forget the look on his face when I called him Frisco's dad."

Maria smiled, silently tracing her finger along the final digits in Nick's cell number.

"Well, I'll be available," Leigh said. "Nothing will keep me away."

"Great." Patrice smiled at Maria. "And Maria will keep an eye on her pal Frisco, too, won't you?"

Maria nodded enthusiastically and blinked at Leigh, her shining eyes saying everything her voice couldn't. Sam's intrusive meddling had done one good thing, anyway. Whatever the motive, she'd placed this child here, and Maria's sweet presence seemed evident in every corner of this stable.

Leigh smiled at her. "I know he can count on you, sweetie."

She thanked Patrice again for loaning her the chestnut mare, then led Frisco back out to the same trail she'd galloped along earlier. They walked—heavy, dragging clops and light, booted footfalls—toward the gold-pink glow of the setting sun. Leigh thought about how many times she'd sought this kind of escape during her life.

Somehow horses had always figured in. In books she'd lugged home from the library as a child—*My Friend Flicka*, *Black Beauty*, and *The Black Stallion*. And in movies. She smiled, remembering how she'd watched *National Velvet* over and over, copying child star Elizabeth Taylor by tying string to her toes like reins, clucking and racing her imaginary thoroughbred over jumps at the Grand National steeplechase. And those other times, when she'd close the door of her bedroom against her mother's shrewish rants at her gentle father, gather her plastic horses close, imagine galloping away to someplace peaceful and happy.

When Alton Evers paid for riding lessons—even before

he'd become her stepfather—and leased Leigh's first horse, it helped to fill the emptiness of leaving her own father behind, then buffered the pain when he succumbed to a heart attack only five years later. It taught her that while nothing good lasted forever, a means of escape made the worst of things tolerable. When life crowded in, she'd seek out the quiet solitude of the stables, breathe it in, pull on her boots, climb in the saddle, and gallop, gallop, gallop. Trying to make the moment, the finite escape, feel as wonderful as a promise of forever. But now . . .

Leigh stopped and Frisco halted behind her. Then she walked, boots sinking into the soft earth, to a scrubby tree and looped the lead rope over a branch. She watched, encouraged, as he nipped halfheartedly at a few wisps of grass, then sank down beside him and stared at the deepening sun. She traced a circle in the dirt with her finger and tried to remember the phases of the moon. What came after the full moon? Waning, she thought. A slow slicing away of the full moon's bright surface, finally snuffing its light. Her soul had felt that way this past year—her spirit. Fading away, slice by slice, month by month since she and Nick separated. Worse than any loneliness she'd felt before, an inescapable hollow, a painful hole. Nothing had helped this time. Not work, not distance—she'd tried that at Pacific Point—not this new stable.

She stood, moved close to Frisco, and buried her face against his neck, stretching her arms up and weaving her fingers into his mane. She listened to him breathe, felt his solid warmth, drew in the musky scent of him. Finally she let the tears she'd held back for two days gather and spill over. "Get well, boy, please," she whispered. "I can't bear it if I lose you." Her tears splashed onto her horse, soaking into his soft coat like rain on a velvet skirt. "I can't lose anything more. I can't."

She squeezed her eyes tight against a cruel barrage of images: Harry McNealy in his backward tux shirt, Caro crying in the kitchen, the dying lemon tree, Cappy Thomas's widow . . . Nick with someone else's child in his arms. "Lord," she murmured, her lips brushing against Frisco's neck, "why can't you make one good thing be forever?"

+++

Riley grimaced as Leigh's voice came on the line.

"It's Riley," she said, wishing the doctor hadn't answered. "I'm sorry to bother you at home."

"I'm at the stable. Is something wrong?"

"Not really." Riley looked toward the SICU room in the distance. "Only that Sam Gordon insists she needs to see you."

"I'm not her doctor. She knows that—you know that, Riley."

She flinched against the mild rebuke. "I know, I'm sorry, and I'm fully prepared to argue that again with her. But the fact is she's been harassing the nursing staff, the hospital operators, the evening crew down in ER . . ."

"Is it a medical problem?"

"Um . . . apparently not."

There was a long silence. Riley thought she heard the low braying of a donkey. She forged ahead. "I'll say I couldn't reach you, or—"

"Tell her I need to wash away some horse sweat first and pull off my boots and spurs." There was a grim chuckle. "Scratch that; I'll keep the spurs. Tell Miss Gordon I'll be right there."

CHAPTER TWENTY-ONE

Leigh passed through the darkened SICU and saw the staff's eyes widen—maybe because of her riding attire, but more likely because she'd actually responded to Sam's belligerent summons. Frankly, she didn't care. It was time to deal with this woman, put things to rest, and move on. She'd left her spurs in the car, but . . . *I'm in control; you can't get to me this time.* She squared her shoulders and crossed the last stretch of carpeting to the room—to find Sam dozing, face pale against the pillowcase and one hand curled on her chest with IV tubing trailing.

Guilt stabbed as she reminded herself of the obvious: this woman, regardless of her sinister role in Leigh's private life, was a trauma patient. Injured, helpless—

Sam's eyes opened. "I knew you'd come." She ran her tongue over her lips, glanced toward the nurses' station, then back at Leigh. "Pull up a chair. We need to finish that conversation we were having earlier."

"You had me paged to finish a conversation?"

"We were talking about Nick. What I can give him that you can't. And I got the feeling you wanted to know."

"You're wrong."

"You're here."

Leigh thought of the metal twitch on her horse's lip and brushed her hand across her mouth.

Sam smiled. "And I'd want to know if I were in your place. I'd *need* to know what it was that the other woman offered that I didn't. If that was something as simple as good conversation, a sympathetic ear, or something as important as great, steamy—"

Leigh slammed the door closed, then perched stiffly on the chair beside the bed. "Let's get this straight: I'm here because Riley Hale asked me to come to keep you from pestering the staff."

"Even if we both know better, I'll let you have that—but not Nick. You can't have him."

"I don't think I need to remind you that I'm divorcing him."

"No. You're the one who needs reminding." Sam shook her head. "And don't give me that business about needing his help with your neighbors. You called Nick because you can't stand the idea of him wanting me. And you can't deal with the reality that your failed marriage has nothing to do with me, and everything to do with—"

"With me?" Leigh hunched forward, gripping the edge of the chair so hard her fingers cramped. "Are you actually saying that it's my fault? You slept with my husband, and now it's my fault?"

Sam's eyes swept over Leigh. "If the boot fits." She touched her oxygen cannula. "I suppose now I'll really need to worry about this tubing."

"What?"

Sam smiled grimly. "That you'll pinch it off."

Leigh thought about denying the temptation but didn't see the point. She glanced toward the monitor, watching the blips on the darkened screen, hearing this woman's very viable heartbeat, and struggling against the sudden threat of tears. She told herself it was because she was tired, because the last few days had been horrific and she was sick with worry over Frisco, and . . . "What?" she whispered finally. Her eyes connected with Sam's. "What do you think you can give Nick that I didn't?"

"Respect, for one thing. For his career. I know how much it means to him to be a police officer, how much it meant to my brother. And I can accept the inherent risks without whining at him night and day about the dangers."

"I was worried." Leigh's stomach tensed the way it had all those times she'd listened to the police scanner. "I couldn't stand the idea of his being hurt or . . ."

"Killed? Like Toby?"

Leigh swallowed, the memory flooding back. "When I heard about the squad car rollover—an officer being pinned in the car—I thought it was Nick. I made calls trying to find out. I was frantic."

"You kicked him out. Weeks before that."

"We agreed that we needed time . . . space."

"It sounds to me like you always had space—you liked it that way. The more space the better." Sam's laugh was short, sharp. "How many miles is it to that stable?" She shook her head. "You should know Nick resents that nag as much as you resent me."

Leigh doubted it was possible.

"But I'll be there for him," Sam continued. "He'll know he's my first priority—the center of my whole life. Any 'space' will be our space together. Nick and me and Elisa."

Leigh flinched at the memory of the child in Nick's arms, hers around his neck. She began to tremble inside.

"He's crazy about my baby girl," Sam said. "And that's what I'll give Nick that you can't. That you *wouldn't*." Her frosty eyes pinned Leigh. "A family. Children. You know how much he wants that."

Leigh fought the memory of pain so much deeper than the relentless cramping that had kept her curled up in bed last December. *God, don't do this to me.*

"I'll give that to him," Sam repeated. "The family he's never had. And would never have if he stayed with you." Her lips twisted into a sneer. "Because having Nick's baby would crowd Dr. Stathos's all-important 'space,' and—"

"Stop it!" Leigh growled. "Don't you dare say another word. You know nothing about me, nothing about what I've been through." She pressed her fist against her belly, hunching against the memory, but stared into Sam's eyes. "And everything I suffered because of you. What your ugly intrusion into my life cost me." She squeezed her eyes shut for a moment, knowing she was about to say words she'd never spoken aloud before. "I was pregnant. . . . I was carrying Nick's baby. I miscarried after I found out about you, and—" She stood up so quickly that the chair tipped over. She tried to breathe, felt it stick in her chest as a wave of anger and pain rose with suffocating ferocity. *I hate her, hate her. It's all her fault.*

"Nick never said you'd been pregnant." Sam's eyes widened. "Wait a minute. . . . You didn't tell him?"

Leigh bolted for the door, her mind a blur as she flung it open and strode—then began jogging—toward the hallway door. The faster she moved, the slower it felt. Almost as if her words, her unexpected revelation to Sam Gordon, had turned her escape route to quicksand. And at any moment she'd be swallowed up completely.

+++

Sam watched as the nurse checked the bags of IV fluids and confirmed the settings of the sequential pressure sleeves on her legs. Then she made a point of thanking the woman, knowing this nurse had likely gotten an earful in report about the "difficult" patient who'd insisted on paging an ER doctor at home.

But it had been more than worth it to see the arrogant Leigh Stathos stomp in here in those knee-high boots like she'd come to correct an unruly horse. Then run out like the coward she really was—after handing Sam a gift better than any bouquet of flowers or get-well card: a weak spot, as vulnerable as an exposed nerve under a dental instrument. Leigh had been pregnant and kept it a secret from Nick. Sam could use that; she could . . .

Sam battled a wave of guilt remembering the pain on Leigh's face. *She lost a child*; Sam was a mother too. Still . . .

She shook her head, remembering Nick's words, his continued defense of a woman who had never deserved him. *"Leigh doesn't lie."*

What would he do if he knew the truth?

Riley expected to see Leigh at the hospital but was surprised to find her sitting alone in the chapel. She was at the respite table, tall leather riding boots crossed at the ankles and dark hair spilling around her shoulders. She hadn't turned on the lights and the soft glow of candles—dozens offered in memory of Cappy Thomas—lit her features just enough to hint that she'd been crying. The Kleenex box, pulled close, proved it like forensic evidence.

"Hi," Riley said as Leigh raised her head. *Oh, you look ragged, my friend.* "I don't want to disturb you, but I saw you in here, so . . ."

"No problem. You'll save me from being struck by lightning. God probably knows I'm only here for the juice and crackers." She smiled ruefully. "And that if I'd stayed another minute in Sam Gordon's room, I *would* have tied her oxygen tubing in a knot. That alone buys me a jillion heavenly volts."

"Was it that bad?" Riley took the seat beside her.

"Worse. You don't want to know."

"I do . . . if you want me to."

Leigh picked at the seeds on a cracker, then snapped it in half. "She summoned me there to tell me how I'd failed as a wife."

Riley's mouth sagged open. "As chaplain, I'm supposed to ask something like 'And how does that make you feel?'" She grimaced. "But as your friend, I want to say . . . I got a badge for knot tying in the San Jacinto Council of Girl Scouts. Where's that oxygen tubing?"

Leigh's quick laugh was accompanied by a heartbreaking rush of tears. "I'm sorry. Oh, why did I go see her?"

"Because I asked you to." Riley handed her a fresh Kleenex. "I'm the one who's sorry."

"You and the nursing staff shouldn't have had to put up with her badgering. It wouldn't have stopped." Leigh sighed. "I'm usually so much tougher, but . . ."

Riley waited, sensing more.

Leigh's shoulders rose and fell, and she glanced toward Cappy's candles. "She said that I wasn't willing to give Nick what he wants most—a family. But . . ." Her voice choked. "The truth is that I was pregnant when we separated. Almost too early to confirm with a test, and I'll admit I waited to take one. We were having trouble. I asked him to move out." Leigh looked up at Riley, her dark eyes huge and shiny in the dim light. "I didn't know how I felt about being pregnant. I hadn't planned to have a baby. I didn't want it to be the only reason to try to work things out. I didn't trust that we could make it." A tear slid down her cheek. "Before I could come to grips with it, Nick's best friend was killed and then Sam was in the picture." Leigh shredded the Kleenex. "While I was struggling to deal with that, I had a miscarriage."

"So many losses, so fast."

"I never told him," Leigh whispered, staring at her hands. "I didn't see the point of it. Afterward, I mean. But this past year, during all of this, I'd lie awake at night wondering if it would have changed things. If I should have told him, even after I lost the baby. I finally stopped thinking about that. Put all those doubts behind me. Or at least that's what I thought. Until tonight. When Sam accused me of refusing to give Nick what he wanted most in this world, it made me so angry, and it stirred it all up again." She swallowed, shaking her head. "Like I said, I'm usually so much tougher."

Riley touched her hand. "But it's been a couple of miserable days. And you're human. You're an incredibly skilled doctor, but you're still human. None of us should expect to function business-as-usual in the face of what's happened here. We're all feeling it. That's why I've been talking with the staff. To get a feel for who might need a little extra support and who might benefit from a staff debriefing."

"Are you saying I've just been counseled?"

Riley squeezed her hand. "I'm saying you have an offer of help from a friend, if you should need it."

Leigh's lips hinted at a smile. "Beyond knot tying."

"Yes." Riley smiled back. "And I'm going to remind you that God's here for you too. With love and understanding, not lightning bolts. When you're ready. And when you are, I'd be happy to . . ." She stopped midsentence as Leigh stiffened in her chair and peered at the chapel doorway.

"It's Nick," Leigh said, voice just above a whisper. "He must be going up to see Sam."

"I'm not so sure about that. He called me a little while ago to say that he was meeting Kristi Johnson at the ICU." Riley glanced at her watch. "The doctors took Kurt Denton off life support about an hour ago."

+++

"Heather is watching Abby and Finn," Kristi told Nick, glancing toward the door of the ICU. "Abby knows I went to see her daddy, but not why. She's so confused by everything that happened." She swallowed. "I am too. When the chaplain called to tell me they'd turned off the machines, I didn't think I wanted to come. But . . ."

He nodded, still reeling from the news of Denton's death and Kristi's request that he accompany her to the hospital. Riley had said that seeing Denton might help her with "closure." He wondered if it would feel that way to him, too. He watched as the young mother searched through her tote bag. She lifted out the bedraggled toy pony and her eyes filled with tears.

"Abby wants him to have this. The new Child Crisis investigator returned it after the police finished with the hospital room. But Abby told me that she wanted her daddy to have it. She thought it would make him feel better, make him remember happy things." She brushed a finger over the pony's frayed yarn mane. "Kurt bought it for her at Disneyland." A tear slid down her cheek. "It did seem like a fairy tale back then. Like one of those happily-ever-after moments. I guess I wanted to believe it could stay that way forever. You know?"

Nick cleared his throat. "I do."

He held the door for her and they walked into the darkened ICU toward the curtained room where Kurt Denton lay. As they got closer, Kristi's breath shuddered and her hand rose to her mouth.

Nick watched Kristi's face, remembering how shocked he'd been at the sight of Kurt earlier, wanting to spare her that. Wishing he could go back, do it all differently somehow. Give them that fairy-tale ending, instead of—

"Oh no," Kristi murmured between her fingers. She swayed and Nick slid an arm around her. "He's really gone."

The staff had done the best they could to soften the shock: turned the lights down low, removed the tubes—and the handcuffs. They'd freshened the linens and moved the equipment away. But the deceased patient lying against the pillow, bandaged and bruised, in no way resembled the young man who'd walked into the hospital Tuesday morning, high on drugs and determined to claim his family. The killer who, in his last conscious moments, stared straight into Nick's eyes.

Kristi stepped to the bed, hugged the stuffed pony close for a brief moment, and then laid it on the sheet over Denton's chest.

"Your daughter wanted you to have it," she whispered. "I . . . won't . . . say bad things about you, Kurt. I promise. We'll give our babies that much." A sob escaped and she stepped away.

Riley appeared in the doorway. "Is there anything I can do?"

Kristi folded her hands across her chest and watched Kurt's face for a moment. "Would it be okay to say a prayer? He wasn't much on church. But I think I'd feel better if . . . maybe we could say the Lord's Prayer? Abby would like that. We say it together at bedtime. Every night."

"Of course."

They stood there beside the bed: chaplain, mother of the deceased man's children, and the cop who'd killed him. A moment of silence framed by the distant sounds of ventilators and whispers of caregivers; then three voices saying the words Jesus had offered so long ago.

Nick closed his eyes, whispering around the ache in his

throat for Kristi, her children, and for the happy ending that would never be. ". . . for thine is the kingdom, the power, and the glory. Forever and ever . . ."

Nick waited in the dark parking lot while Kristi unlocked her car door, knowing that only yesterday morning and mere yards from where they now stood, he'd aimed his gun. "Are you sure you're okay? I could drive you home."

"I'm fine. And I want to thank you . . ."

"No," he said. "Don't thank me. I should be telling you how sorry I am. That I wish it hadn't happened like this. It's true. I wish—"

"It's okay," she said, peering at him. "It's okay. You did what you had to do. I know that. He would have killed you. Look what he did to Miss Gordon and Cappy and . . ." Her voice broke as she touched Nick's sleeve. "You're a good, decent man. I wish Kurt had had someone like you to show him how to be that way. I'm glad you're here for all of us in the neighborhood. You make us feel that someone cares, that at least one person really wants us to have a happy life."

"I do."

"I know." Kristi opened the car door. "And I want that for you and Dr. Stathos. You be happy too. Promise me that."

"Sure," he murmured, glancing away.

He watched her drive off before walking to his car. He unlocked the door, then leaned against it, listening to the sounds of traffic in the distance and staring at the moon. Thinking about Kristi and Finn and Abby—the little girl who'd sent her favorite toy to the man who dragged her mother down a hospital corridor. She wanted him to remember

Disneyland; she wanted to believe in happy endings. Nick did too . . . or used to. Now he wasn't sure anymore. That chance was waning like the moon, and—

"Nick?"

He looked down to see Leigh standing in the moonlight.

CHAPTER TWENTY-TWO

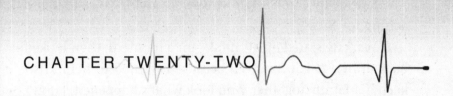

Leigh had never seen Nick look so awful, even in those days he'd slept in his car outside their house trying to convince her to talk with him. He'd been both scattered and intense then, desperate. Even so, there'd been a flicker of hope in his eyes. But now . . . Her heart squeezed. He'd killed someone. Why hadn't she considered how he'd feel about that?

"I saw you out here," she said, looking at him. "Are you okay?"

His smile was forced, grim. "On a scale of one to ten, I'd say a strong two and holding. Maybe."

"Riley said you met Kristi Johnson here."

"Yeah." He scraped his hand across his mouth in gesture she'd seen him do a hundred times before. "They took Denton off life support. He's dead."

Leigh nodded. Only five days ago he'd rescued the man's baby.

"His little girl," Nick said, his voice hollow and low, "sent her favorite stuffed toy to him—a pony she carried everywhere with her."

Leigh remembered it, could still see it lying on the floor next to the overturned lilies.

"When I told Denton to drop his weapons, he stood there for a few seconds. Looked right into my eyes. As if he knew I'd use deadly force, and it was okay with him. Like . . ."

"Suicide by cop," Leigh whispered, giving voice to it and aching for Nick.

"Yes." He stared up at the sky for a moment, then looked back at her. "I got involved because I wanted to help Kristi keep her family together. And look what's happened. I don't know, Leigh. I don't know. . . ."

She reached for his hand without thinking. "You've talked with the investigators at the department?"

"Right on down the line, ending with Buzz." He shook his head. "Something strange about being expected to officially spill your guts to the guy who's been letting you sleep on his couch. And now I'm on administrative leave. Through Friday, and . . ." He stopped, brows furrowing.

Friday. The same day the divorce was final. Leigh felt his fingers move against hers, knew he was thinking the same thing.

"Thank you," he said. "For coming out here. I didn't expect—"

What she didn't expect was to step forward and wrap her arms around him and for tears to come. "I'm sorry," she whispered, her face burrowed against his shirtfront. "I hate it that this happened to you, Nick. I know—*oh, I know*—how much you try to help these people."

She felt his arms move tentatively around her. His heart thudded beneath her ear.

"And you," he said gently, "worked hard to save Cappy. You didn't give up; you kept going. I saw that, even from a distance." His arms tightened and he drew her close, his palm cradling the back of her head as her tears continued.

"I did . . . I did try," she whispered. "But it was too late." She started to tremble and Nick stooped down, touching his lips to her temple and caressing her hair gently as if she were a child in need of comfort. She closed her eyes and breathed in the familiar scent of him, letting it soothe her like a balm. Pretending, just for a moment, that nothing else mattered, that she hadn't come here tonight because she'd been rudely summoned by—

"You're in your riding clothes," Nick said, his breath warm against her hair. "It's your day off. Did you get called in for an emergency?"

"I . . ." She stepped away from him, felt his arms slide from her. "Caro," she hedged, "is working p.m.'s, so . . ." She hugged her arms around herself, missing the comfort of his arms and feeling a lonely vacuum in the space between them. Sam's sharp laugh, her words, swept back: *It sounds to me like you always had space—you liked it that way. The more space the better.*

"You stopped by on your way home from the stables to see her," Nick finished.

She glanced away, knowing she'd skirted the truth and trying not to wonder if Sam was right about Leigh's need for space. Then told herself it didn't matter anymore. "And now I guess I should go home and pull off these boots."

"Don't," he said, taking hold of her hand. "Come with me . . . just for a while."

"Where?"

"I don't know. All I know is that I don't want go back to

Buzz's right now. And I don't want to be alone. I thought I did, but now . . ." His thumb brushed across the back of her hand.

"I'm in riding clothes and probably have hay in my hair."

"I know a place. Coffee and pastry—barn casual."

+++

He took the long way though he knew all the shortcuts from chasing suspects, with lights and sirens, in his squad car. And long before that, from the days when he'd hopped fences as a kid, trundled his suitcases up and down the steps of foster homes. But tonight he wanted to take the long way because it might be the last time he drove through his favorite city with his wife.

She was onto his plan way too soon.

"You're kidding, right? Lombard Street? What do you think I am, a tourist?"

"I think you'd better hang on tight."

He steered the Z4 downward into the first of eight hairpin turns on the one-way section on Russian Hill, between Hyde and Leavenworth, known as "the crookedest street in the world." A steep redbrick-paved road on a 27 percent grade with a posted speed limit of five miles per hour. "No sweat," he said. "We took these turns during training. I could do this at a raging six miles an hour . . . chewing gum." Her grin made his chest warm.

"And wipe out an entire bank of hydrangeas," she said, pointing across the lush hedges and leaning back—way back—in her seat. "Don't be a maniac, Nick."

He nosed the car into the next switchback and hit the button on his CD player, filling the car with blues, then thought of Antoinette and Harry dancing to Tony Bennett. And remembered holding Leigh only minutes ago. Maybe he'd drive slower; 5 mph was too fast for a last ride.

He left Lombard and drove southeast toward Mission, then onto the Embarcadero, weaving in and out of traffic under the jumble of electric bus wires, passing a double-decker sight-seeing bus and a group of helmeted tourists navigating the crowded sidewalk on Segways. Then drove downhill toward Beach Street, Fisherman's Wharf, and the view of the bay beyond the marina that always made his breath catch.

He skirted Golden Gate Park on the loop back, breath-ing in the familiar scent from the huge, peeling, and silvery green stands of eucalyptus that lined it—sweet, clean, sharp . . . a hint of camphor. The same scent, in subtle traces, was in Leigh's favorite herbal shampoo, and he'd teased her more than once that she smelled like his favorite city. *Like home* . . . He sneaked a glimpse of her, noticing that she'd closed her eyes and relaxed against the headrest. Almost as if she were sleeping. He tried not to think that he'd never see her that way again.

When he finally pulled the car to the curb, miraculously finding a space, Leigh opened her eyes. Her brows drew together and he wondered if he'd made a mistake.

"It's Niko's," she said, turning to look at him.

"Reynaldo's." He pointed to the sign. "See? Macaroons, conchas, quesadilla cake."

"Quesadilla cake?"

"And Mexican hot chocolate." He waited, holding his breath.

"Okay—you got me with the hot chocolate."

Sam left a third message, knowing that he'd turned his phone off. When she called Buzz's apartment, the chaplain had said only that he had no idea when to expect Nick back. He'd offered nothing more, though he'd politely inquired about how she was feeling. Sam frowned. What she was feeling was frustrated. She'd dozed off not long after checking on Elisa—she was playing hide-and-seek with her cousins and giggling her head off. The nurses hadn't awakened Sam for Nick's call. She'd been hoping to at least talk with him, find out what time he was coming in the morning. He was on administrative leave, so no excuses about time. She'd suggest that he pick up Elisa at Tina's, take her for the day—the zoo again or the Discovery Museum. Then come back here, so they could all be together. *Nick, me, and Elisa.* Just the way she'd told Leigh.

Except she couldn't make any of that happen until she talked with Nick.

Sam picked up the phone and punched in his cell number again. She listened to the message, feeling the blood pressure cuff inflate on her arm, then spoke—keeping her tone soft, fragile, bruised.

"Nick, I talked with Elisa just now. She's frightened, crying—it's breaking my heart. I tried to tell her I was okay, that Mommy wouldn't die . . . like her uncle Toby did. She asked for you."

That should do it.

+++

Leigh pointed to Nick's face, brushing at her own. "You have a little flake of churro, right . . . You got it." She watched him over the rim of her cup—rich Mexican chocolate with cream, eggs, vanilla, and a dash of cinnamon. She almost never indulged in something so decadent, but today . . . "This is perfect," she said, noticing that Nick still had a faint sprinkling of sugar in the dark beard growth on his chin. "The chocolate, I mean," she added quickly.

"I knew what you meant." He glanced around the pastry shop, and she could tell by his expression that he was remembering the few years this space had been his. The lemon soup he made, the street folks he'd fed after hours, his friends clowning. Toby.

"You stood right there," he said, pointing to where a Mexican flag was draped along the wall by the cash register, "that first time you walked in here. You were wearing your riding boots that day too, with a scrub top over your breeches. Sort of Dr. Cowgirl." He turned back to look at her. "You planted yourself right there and complained that nothing on my menu was takeout."

"I had a two-hour reprieve from the ER. I wanted to ride, but I was starving." She exhaled, remembering the moment she'd first seen him. Even in sturdy boots, her knees had gone weak.

"I came out from the kitchen and tried to explain that good food takes time to prepare, and eating it—enjoying it— should take at least as long."

"You said, 'Fast is for racehorses.'"

"And you—" she saw a flicker of sadness in his eyes— "you said you'd come for food, not a commitment."

I said that?

The stretch of silence between them was filled by strains

of mariachi music from a radio behind the counter. Leigh noticed for the first time that the other patrons had gone and the staff was wiping down the tables. The faint odor of bleach mingled with the scents of chocolate and fried pastries.

"I think they're getting ready to close," she said, still thinking of the moment she'd met him. She in riding clothes, he with a dish towel draped over his shoulder; their discussion about the takeout, her tour of the kitchen, and her first taste of his lemon soup. There had been scents of mint, garlic, and roasting lamb, and it had begun to rain. *I stayed, Nick. I stayed that day.* "I suppose we should go."

"Right," he said. "I'll drop you back at the hospital, and then I'll . . ." That foreign, hopeless look she'd seen in the parking lot earlier came back into his eyes.

"And you'll do what?"

"I don't know," he said with a shrug. "I'll drive around. I'm not sure yet. But I'm just not ready to face Buzz's couch. I'll drive for a while and think." He caught the look on her face and gave a short laugh. "Don't worry; I won't sleep in my car outside your house."

"Our house," she heard herself say. "It's still ours—together. Regardless."

"Okay. I won't sleep in the car outside our house. Regardless."

Their eyes met and they were silent again.

They drove back to the hospital, saying very little. Nick pulled up to her car and got out, leaving the engine running while she unlocked it. She stood for a moment with her back to him, thinking. Trying not to think. Feeling, despite every red flag, that—

"Don't drive around," she said, turning to him. "I don't want you to wander around with no place to go. Not after what happened in the ICU tonight with Kristi, and . . ."

"What are you saying?"

"That you should come to our house. I'll make coffee." She smiled. "Wait—you can do it. It's your coffeemaker."

He was quiet for a few seconds, then exhaled. "Deal."

She sat in her car, pretending to warm the engine, and waited for her hands to stop shaking. Then drove out of the parking lot with Nick following. She hoped he wouldn't mention that he'd taken the lemon tree—rescued it from her. The past two days had been tough enough and she didn't need another reminder of her failures.

+++

Nick opened the door for Leigh and made a point of not looking at the empty spot where their potted lemon tree had always stood. He didn't want to think about how she'd tossed it out—too much of a reminder that he was on the same course, even with this unexpected reprieve. He wasn't sure why tonight was happening, but he'd take it.

They stood in the foyer in awkward silence, Leigh wiping her boots a few more times than necessary on the throw rug, Nick making a production of putting his keys back in his pocket and then inspecting the weather stripping around the doorframe. A homeowner concerned about his investment, nothing deeper than that.

"Well," she said after clearing her throat, "you know where the coffee is." She flexed the toe of her riding boot and grimaced. "I need to get out of these boots and breeches, maybe pull on a sweater; it's kind of chilly. It won't take but a few minutes." She pointed to the staircase. "I'll just be right up—"

"I know where," he said, wondering for a strange moment whether or not the "our house" she'd insisted upon earlier extended as far as "our bedroom," "our shower." He thought not, then felt a quick stab of guilt as he recalled Sam's invitation a few nights before: *"There's a shower here."* Going there that night had been a mistake. And a reminder—like picking at a scab—of the far bigger one he'd made almost a year ago.

"Okay," she said, hand on the banister. "Make yourself at—" She grimaced and hurried up the stairs without looking back, her riding boots thumping against the sisal carpeting.

Make yourself at home. He groaned at the irony of her swallowed words as he walked toward the kitchen, catching a glimpse of the dining room as he passed. The McNealys' table still sat there, under a chandelier no longer choked short. The elegant vintage fixture hung freely as it was meant to, ready to cast sparkling prisms of light over a family gathered below. After all his attempts to put a table in that room, it was finally there—days before his wife divorced him. He shook his head, thinking of how they'd carried the old table across the driveways, he and Leigh and Caroline. Everything had seemed hopeful—so like an answer to his prayers—until Sam had placed that phone call to Leigh. The first in an ugly roll of events that ended in his raising a weapon to take a man's life.

He crossed the kitchen to the refrigerator and reached for the door handle, his gaze moving over the haphazard grouping of papers held by magnets. He glanced quickly toward the stairway, feeling oddly like a Peeping Tom in his own home. Their photos, of course, had long since been taken down. And now there was only a list of community college classes, the business card for Frisco's vet, a scribbled telephone number for a Holland America cruise ship—Leigh's mother, most likely. And an invitation to an engagement party. *Erin Quinn, Scott McKenna.* He'd met the red-haired charge nurse at Pacific Mercy very briefly, the day he'd driven there to tell Leigh about Caroline's DUI arrest . . . and to ask her to come home. He'd told Leigh that her sister needed her; that was the truth. And that he'd move out of the house so she could stay with Caroline until she got back on even ground and could live by herself; he'd done that. What he hadn't said was that he'd hoped—prayed—that having Leigh back in San Francisco would give them one last chance to save their marriage. That, he hadn't accomplished.

Nick pulled the refrigerator door open, found the coffee, and got it brewing, the gurgle and hiss of the Moccamaster mingling with the distant sound of the upstairs shower. He grabbed cups and tried to ignore the heaviness weighing in on him, the sense of finality and ending as real as Kurt Denton's body lying in that ICU. His gaze fell on a brochure lying on the counter beside the refrigerator. *Doctors Without Borders?* He picked up the tri-folded paper, its cover showing a heavily robed woman holding an infant, above a list of sites urgently needing physicians: Somalia, Pakistan, Sri Lanka. And a featured book, written by a participating doctor: *Six Months in Sudan.* His throat closed. He knew Leigh had been pursuing job opportunities outside San Francisco, but he'd never dreamed she would go that far.

He gritted his teeth. This could *not* happen. He wouldn't let her go to Somalia or Sudan. Go . . . anywhere. This time he wasn't sitting outside in a car. Tonight he'd been invited in. He had an advantage; he had a shot—Nick winced, then took a slow breath. In truth, it wasn't all that different. Though he wished it hadn't happened, he'd done what he had to do yesterday in that hospital parking lot. And now, tonight, he was prepared to aim just as carefully to save his marriage.

CHAPTER TWENTY-THREE

"You made a fire," Leigh said, surprised. She stepped into the living room, breathing in the scents of coffee and earthy-rich burning oak. Nick sat on the couch, holding a coffee mug.

"You said you were cold." His brows scrunched together. "You're limping."

Leigh shrugged. "New boots. The left one must have been laced too tightly—my foot's aching. I should have changed my clothes before I went to the hospital." *Except I was so angry about Sam.* She hugged her soft shawl cardigan close, noticing how the firelight, orange as the Golden Gate Bridge, played off Nick's features and cast a warm glow around the room. He'd shed his jacket and laid his holster on the tall mantel, the same way he'd done a thousand times before. Except tonight was so very different. "Coffee smells good."

She started to sit and saw that he'd moved her yarn and needles from the couch to the end table. He caught her gaze.

"I didn't know you learned to knit," he said, pointing at the pile of soft wool. "What is that?"

"Something to relax with, that's all. I'm knitting caps for an African ministry, Knit One, Save One."

"Caps?"

"For newborns. At-risk babies. To keep their heads warm."

The look that came into his eyes shouldn't have. Babies. *Don't do that, Nick.*

She lifted her cup from the table and settled onto the far end of the couch, watching the flames, listening to the crackle, and wondering if inviting Nick in was a huge mistake. *Why did I ask him here?* She glanced toward him. "I didn't know there was any firewood."

"It's from that pile stacked out back by the fence. The fallen tree Toby and I cut down out on his property last September." A look of sadness crossed his face. "Anyway, it had to dry and season. Oak takes a while, and now . . . it's ready."

"Oh." She glanced away and took a sip of her coffee. "Does administrative leave mean you don't go into work at all?" She noticed for the first time that the McNealys' Tony Bennett CD was playing in the background.

"I can work at a desk, but—" he smiled—"you know me."

She smiled back. "I do. If you're not out with the people, you're not doing your job. I guess I'd feel the same way. If I couldn't be treating patients . . ."

"You'd be at the stables. I know you, too. I forgot to ask— how is Frisco?"

"I called a few minutes ago. Patrice said he drank some water, but not as much as we'd like." Leigh sighed. "I won't bore you."

"I'm not bored. I know how concerned you are."

Leigh wondered, with a bittersweet twinge, if he really meant it. Or if this newfound truce—his acceptance of her interests, her new empathy for his career—was simply a sign that they'd finally surrendered, given up. And that their parting would be far gentler than their years together. There was something unfair about it. "If Frisco doesn't drink and if his digestive system doesn't show signs of recovery, he could end up in surgery. I could lose him. I know how that sounds after everything that's happened with Cappy and—" she glanced down—"Sam, Kurt Denton, and the others. An animal doesn't compare, but I love him." A rush of tears filled her eyes. "I'm sorry. I'm tired."

"Hey, don't apologize. There's no need." He set his coffee down next to hers. "You're shivering."

"I'm okay," she said, feeling her chin tremble as Nick reached for the down-filled throw draped over the back of the couch.

"Hush," he said, sliding closer. "I've seen homeless people huddled under newspapers shivering less than you are. Don't argue with the officer."

She smiled feebly and closed her eyes, feeling the feather-soft weight of the blanket and Nick's warmth as he tucked it around her. His scent—soap, oak bark, coffee, and a faint trace of leather—filled her senses. She struggled against another shiver and a frisson of regret as he slid back to his spot on the couch.

"Now, let me have that foot," he said as she opened her eyes.

"What?"

"Your aching foot," he said, snapping his fingers. "Let's have it. You know I'm good."

Her face warmed. "I . . ."

"It's only a foot. And this is your last chance. I won't offer again."

Last chance.

"That's more like it," he said, settling her stocking foot across his thighs. "Where does it hurt?"

She wrinkled her nose. "That's my line; I'm still paying student loans for the privilege of asking it."

He smiled, gently taking her foot in his hands. "I'm the doctor now. Where's the pain?"

My heart—my whole life.

"The arch and instep," she said as his warm fingers began to knead. "Ah . . . ouch, that's the place."

She shook her head as Tony Bennett started to croon, "I left my heart in San Francisco. . . ."

"Does it seem as impossible to you as it does to me, that it was just three nights ago that the McNealys were here for dinner?" As soon as the words left her lips, she knew it was a mistake. She saw it in his eyes.

Nick was quiet for several seconds. "What seems impossible is that we sat on our porch that night and talked about delaying the divorce. And by Tuesday we were back at square one." His thumbs moved over her instep and his eyes held hers, unwavering.

"Nick, don't start this. I'm exhausted." She started to pull her foot back and pressed her lips together when he stopped her. "You were at her house."

"I was. I admitted that. I also told you that nothing happened between us." His forehead creased. "But you didn't give me a chance to say that I went there because Elisa made a gift for me. A macaroni butterfly. You didn't let me tell you that I haven't been there, to that house, for more than a few minutes since that time in November. I swear."

The shivers returned. "And if I hadn't called you this time, interrupted you?"

"What are you asking?"

"For the truth, Nick. Would you have slept with her again?"

He was silent long enough to make her want to throw Tony Bennett against the wall.

"The truth is," he said, his voice low and halting, "I think Sam wants that. I know she does. But I don't. I don't love her—I never loved her. I can't even imagine that, because . . ." He took a breath. "I love my wife."

Tears threatened again. "Nick, please—"

"I'm not finished," he said, letting go of her foot. "I'm not even started. You said you want the truth. Okay. You're getting it. The truth is that I screwed up last November; I made the biggest mistake of my life. I hurt you—it still makes me sick to know that. But I've tried, Leigh. I've tried everything I know to get you to listen to me. I know I did it wrong sometimes, wrong enough for you to start talking about a restraining order. Then pack up and leave. I don't know how to do this. I've never done it before and, God knows, I don't want to ever do it again. But I want us to have another chance. I can't give up on us. I can't lose you."

He cleared his throat and took a slow breath. "When I got that call from dispatch yesterday, all I could think about was you, someone hurting you. I thought I'd never see you again. I shot someone; I killed those children's father, and my best friend's sister is lying in that hospital, but all I can think about is you. You, Leigh. You're what matters to me." The look in his eyes made her heart ache.

She didn't know who moved first, but somehow she was in Nick's arms. They were in each other's arms, her face burrowed against his neck and his hands in her hair. She was crying and he was rocking her.

"I love you," he whispered against her hair. "You have to believe me—say you believe me." He held her away to stare into her face. "Do you?"

A tear slid down her face. "I think I do, but I'm afraid that . . ." Her voice choked.

"There's nothing to be afraid of," Nick whispered. "I promise." He cradled her face in his hands. "I love you. I'm going to make this work." He brushed his lips across her forehead before leaning close and kissing her. Gently at first, more insistently as her arms slid around his neck and she responded. Then more deeply . . . as if he never intended to stop.

She moved away finally, her senses swirling. "Nick, wait. I don't know how to handle this. I'm not sure what I want, or . . ." She smiled, completely confused as her pulse thrummed in her ears. "I'm trying to be honest."

"Good." He brushed her hair away from her face. "That's the way it's going to be from now on. Completely honest. The truth, always." He smiled, then groaned painfully.

"What?"

"The truth is that right now all I can think about is carrying you upstairs and making love to you until dawn. Maybe noon tomorrow. And waking up with you in my arms, begging me for an omelet."

She raised her brows. "I don't beg."

"You have . . . you will." He smiled at her. "But I don't want those things to happen because you're tired and confused or because the last two days have been a nightmare. I want them to happen because you know you love me and that you can trust me and because you want our marriage to work." He glanced toward the stairs, honest regret on his face. "So all I need right now is for you to say there's a chance for all of that." His dark eyes searched hers. "Is there?"

Leigh reached up and rested her palm against his face. "Yes. I do know that much. I want us to have a chance."

He pulled her close, hugging her tightly, and kissed her again. And again. She chuckled against his lips.

"What?"

"If Tony leaves his heart in San Francisco one more time, I'm calling the transplant team. And—" she yawned—"I'm so tired I can't focus my eyes."

Nick nuzzled her neck. "So shut them." He scooted back against the armrest, pulled her into his arms, and arranged the down blanket over them. "Comfortable now?"

Leigh nodded, lulled by the feel of his chest rising and falling and the soft thudding of his heart. She wanted to say she'd never been more comfortable in her life, that she loved him, that with all her heart she wished that she could believe in forever. She couldn't help but think it would feel a lot like this.

+++

Nick's eyes flicked open at the clicking sound, and he tensed for moment, pulse quickening. His gaze darted toward his duty weapon on the mantel; then he blinked, realizing that the sound was from a key in the front door. He lifted his arm to glance at his watch, careful not to disturb Leigh. Midnight—Caroline, coming home from her evening shift at the hospital. He waited for the inevitable.

She stepped into the foyer, switched on the light, and walked toward the kitchen, then did a double take as she caught sight of the still-glowing embers in the fireplace—and of him on the couch. Her eyes widened. She walked a few steps closer, her mouth dropping open as she saw Leigh asleep in his arms, her dark hair tumbled over his chest. He smiled sheepishly in the darkness.

She shook her head, a grin spreading slowly across her face. Then lifted her hand in a thumbs-up before quietly retracing her steps, switching off the hallway light, and tiptoeing toward the stairs.

Nick could have hugged her. *Thank you, sis.*

He listened to Leigh breathe for a while and then glanced toward the bleached pine bookshelves framing the fireplace. Second shelf on the right, fifth book, the gold lettering on its spine lit by the fading fire—the study Bible he'd bought Leigh when they'd started attending church together. He had no doubt it needed dusting; he was fairly certain she hadn't picked it up since November. He was sure, too, that the bookmark was still on the same page it had been months before that: 1 Corinthians 13. The verses he'd read aloud to her in those last tumultuous weeks before they'd separated. The ones he'd wanted to say at their wedding. About love: *"It always protects, always trusts, always hopes, always perseveres. Love never fails."*

He rested his palm against Leigh's hair, felt her warm

weight lying against him, smelled the faint trace of eucalyptus from her shampoo. *"Love never fails."* His heart tugged. He had failed her, but he wouldn't do it again. He'd spend the rest of his life proving that to her, protecting her, loving her . . . showing her she could trust him. She was giving him a chance. And that was what he'd been praying for all these months. God was giving them a second chance to get it right. Nick would make good on that. When he'd told Leigh he'd wait to make love to her, it hadn't only been because she was tired and because he wanted her to say she loved him, to feel committed to their marriage. It was also because he knew that in order to finally get it right, God had to be part of it—at its center, exactly as the marriage counselor had said. If they had a chance for survival, it had to be that way. God's blessing was their hope. *"Love always hopes . . ."*

He needed time to talk with her about that. And he would. Because now he had the luxury of time. He'd call the court and get the divorce put on hold. They'd already agreed to honesty and a second chance. Add God to that, and they'd have it all. He tightened his arms as Leigh murmured in her sleep and remembered the tiny infant caps she'd been knitting. Warmth filled his chest. Tonight he'd sleep with his wife in his arms. The first night of forever. His home, his family . . . *Thank you, Lord. Thank you for your grace.*

He glanced toward the ceiling at the sound of soft footfalls. Caroline. In a few hours, he'd be fixing omelets for three.

+++

Sam shivered, teeth chattering, and batted at the air around her head. The snowball had gone right down her wool sweater. She shivered again, racked by a chill so forceful she bit her tongue. "Stop it, Toby! It's c-c-c-old; you're gonna freeze me! Try that again and I swear I'll pop you one!" She batted again, and strong fingers grabbed her arm.

"Miss Gordon. Samantha, relax. There's no snow here. It's a cooling blanket. You have a fever; you're in the hospital. Open your eyes and look around."

"What?" Sam blinked against the light. "What the . . . ?" She grimaced and grabbed at something hanging from her nose. Then glared at a heavyset woman with crooked teeth and unplucked brows leaning over the bed. "Get this off my face!"

"Can't," the woman explained gently, reaching for Sam's arm again. "It's oxygen tubing. You've had surgery, dear. On Tuesday morning."

Sam lifted her head and felt a stab of pain in her abdomen. Surgery? She squinted, surveying the room and shivering as the puzzle pieces started to lock together. *Surgery, because I was . . .* She closed her eyes as the ugly truth settled in around her. The nurse's voice continued.

"That's better. You spiked a temp of 104. That's far too high. Sometimes it happens as a reaction to anesthesia; we're not sure yet. You've had a Tylenol suppository."

Sam grimaced at the indignity and shivered again—this time with fear. *What will happen to Elisa if I don't make it?*

"And we've drawn a CBC and blood cultures. You'll have a portable chest X-ray, and I've taken a urine sample from your catheter. Dr. Bartle is on top of things; don't worry." The nurse glanced at a small IV bottle hanging from a hook overhead. "You've got a second dose of broad-spectrum antibiotic hanging, but if the fever continues, there will likely be a new one ordered on day shift. We'll know which kind to use after the blood cultures." She leveled a no-nonsense look that Sam hadn't seen since grammar school. "I'm sorry about the cooling blanket. But it's necessary." She raised a warning finger. "If you pull at your oxygen or get any more agitated, I'll have to ask the doctor for permission to use soft restraints on your wrists. For your safety." She smiled and showed several more equally crooked teeth. "All righty then. Are you on board?"

"I'm sorry. I'll behave." Sam glanced toward the phone on her bedside table. "I was expecting a call."

"I heard how upset you were earlier about missing a call, Miss Gordon. And I promise you that I'm being very watch-ful. There haven't been any calls. But it's 4 a.m. Most folks are still snuggled down, of course." She sighed. "I must say, I'm envious; I usually work evenings."

Sam promised once again to be cooperative, lay quietly as the toothy nurse checked her temperature—103.1—and watched as she waddled back toward the nurses' station. Sam stared at the antibiotic bag, carefully metering curative solu-tion drop by drop, then glanced back at the phone. Nick hadn't called even after she'd left the pathetic, fabricated message about Elisa. And two other calls. Was she right that he'd turned his phone off? Why would he do that? She shiv-ered. Was he with Leigh?

She leaned back against the cooling blanket, submitting to its merciless and teeth-chattering chill, and hoped that the Tylenol and antibiotic would do their magic. She had to get well. And she needed a clear head, all the strength she could muster. If Nick was with Leigh, she would have to do everything she could to stop things from going any further. Her whole future depended on it.

CHAPTER TWENTY-FOUR

Leigh opened her eyes to pale morning light, confused for a moment. Then she realized she was on the couch in Nick's arms. Last night's sense of amazement mixed with nervous uncertainty flooded back. She lifted her head from where it rested against his chest and looked at him. He was asleep, hair mussed, arm flung over his head. Pale sunlight spilled through the windows, glinted on his platinum wedding band, and played over black lashes nestled in the hollows of his eyes. His mouth sagged softly open as he breathed. He looked, somehow, boyish and solidly heroic all at the same time.

Heroic. She glanced toward his gun on the mantel, remembering how he'd talked of the shooting. How hard it had been and how he'd raced to the hospital, afraid of losing Leigh. And then his sensitivity last night, when he'd understood her confusion; he hadn't pressured her to go to bed with him. She smiled, remembering the expression on his face when he'd looked at the stairs. But then he'd told her he didn't want that to happen until she knew she loved him, could trust him, *wanted* their marriage to work. Leigh's stomach quivered as the nervous confusion returned. Could she do that? put all that had happened behind, trust that things would be better between them? look him in the eyes and promise that she'd love him . . . forever?

The doubts swirled. She'd insisted that Nick tell her the truth, but was she being as honest? with him . . . with herself? She'd tried last night. The truth was, it wasn't the idea of making love that had stalled her; that intimacy had always been wonderful for them. It was everything else that came with it. How could she tell her husband that she'd never believed in forever when she saw it so plainly in his eyes?

Nick stirred, and his arms found her. "Good morning." He lifted his head and smiled, warmth filling his eyes. "I thought I'd dreamed it all. But—" he stroked her hair—"here you are."

She pushed herself up to a sitting position. "And you must be completely cramped—you're too big to sleep on a couch."

His chuckle was part yawn. "Yeah, well, don't tell Buzz."

There was a stretch of silence as awkward, she imagined, as the aftermath of a reckless one-night stand. She could feel the question hanging in the air between them: *What happens next?*

"You're off work today?" he asked, groaning a little as he dropped his legs over the edge of the couch.

"I'm going in for a few hours as a favor for one of the docs. And I need to check on Frisco; Patrice is away for the day and her sister's not that experienced with horses. Other than that, I'm not sure what—" She stopped midsentence as he took her hand.

"I meant what I said last night. Everything I said." His gaze moved over her face. "I'm not going to pressure you. I can stay with Buzz." His thumb brushed over her hand. "We'll . . . go on dates. Yeah." His eyes lit. "I'll take you to the places we've always liked, and we'll find new ones, too. Places we never got around to, like hiking at Yosemite—the fall colors should be incredible—and up to Lake Tahoe for the first snowfall; down the coast, too. You always wanted to see Big Sur; we'll pack a lunch and climb in the BMW, hit the coast highway . . ." He took a breath, watching her. "We'll take it slow, Leigh; I promise. We'll do it right. It's too important."

Her throat constricted. "I'll . . . try," she whispered, knowing—and hating—that her vow of honesty wouldn't let her say more. "I do want a chance."

"That's all I need to hear." He cupped her face in his hands, thumbs gently brushing her skin, and bent close, kissing her tenderly. Then touched his lips to her forehead, the tip of her nose, her chin, and—

Caro cleared her throat dramatically, and they turned.

"So," she said, arms crossed and sleep-tumbled hair trailing across the shoulders of her long pink nightshirt, "I have one burning question for you two."

Leigh held her breath.

"Give it to us," Nick said, sliding his arm around Leigh's shoulders.

Caro grinned, the single dimple appearing beside her mouth. "Does this mean omelets?"

+++

Riley hadn't counted heads, but she was certain that this was the highest attendance she'd ever had at a Faith QD meeting.

Evening shift staff had come from several departments: nurses from pediatrics, ICU, surgical intensive care; kitchen workers; and security, of course. She glanced toward the table by the altar. There must have been fifty candles burning for Cappy. It would be the first time he'd missed a gathering since she'd begun them. Even a few of the victims had filed quietly into the chapel: the pregnant nurse—on crutches because of the wound in her calf—and her coworker, the bearded man with the Care Bears scrub cap Leigh had treated for bruised ribs. His wife, the volunteer, stood by his side.

Riley had expected—prayed—that the Golden Gate medical staff would find some measure of comfort here. What she hadn't expected was to see Leigh Stathos walk in. Riley glanced at her, standing between the pregnant nurse and a female security guard, and thought once again that she looked different today. Something had changed. She had a feeling it was for the better.

Riley spoke to the gathered group. "Are there other special concerns today? for patients or for yourselves as care-givers and support staff?"

The nurse on crutches shifted her weight and winced against obvious pain. "I'd like us to offer a prayer for the parents of our peds patients. One of the fathers called me this morning. He . . ." Her voice cracked. "That poor man actually apologized for not coming to my aid that day. He said he'd been awake all night thinking that he should have done something. He'd gathered his little boy up after the shooting started and hid in the bathroom. He sang songs to keep his son distracted from the sounds of screaming. He feels guilty. And I feel awful for him."

A gray-haired cafeteria worker spoke up, her eyes tear-filled behind her glasses. "My staff is having a hard time." She reached up and tucked a stray hair into her elastic-edged cap. "Cappy was on that special diet, and even though his wife brought his lunch, he'd come in and load up a tray—sometimes ten or fifteen dollars' worth. And he'd take it out to those homeless folks down on the corner across from the Laundromat; you know where I mean." She sniffed and glanced down. "It's going to be hard."

Riley waited, hearing a few other sniffles.

"Those officers, too," a guard said. "We should pray for them. I was at the other end of the parking lot by the gunman's car when it all went down." He swallowed. "They had a lot of guts, and sometimes police officers get a bad rap. I'm grateful they were there."

Riley saw Leigh nod.

"I want to remind you," Riley said, when no one offered more, "that the social service and chaplaincy departments will be holding debriefings starting today. Your individual department heads will be giving you more information. Meanwhile—" she looked from face to face around the circle—"I'm available anytime if anyone needs to talk. I'll do anything I can to help. I thank you all, so much, for being here today to support one another. And now . . ." She bowed her head.

"Heavenly Father," Riley began, "we're grateful for . . ."

+++

"You're surprised," Leigh said once the others had gone and she and Riley were alone in the chapel. "Admit it."

Riley smiled. "The last time I saw you here, you were expecting a lightning strike. 'A jillion heavenly volts,' I think you said."

"I still wouldn't stand too close to me, but . . ." Leigh's stomach dipped and she realized that what she was feeling—what had compelled her to come to Faith QD, seek Riley out right now—could very well be hope. She pressed her fingers to her lips, felt tears gather.

"What?" Riley asked, her voice gentle, interested. "What's happened?"

"Nick," she said simply, feeling it again . . . *hope.* "We've been talking. And I think it's possible that we might have another chance together."

"Oh, Leigh! That's wonderful." Riley wrapped an arm around Leigh, hugging her. "Tell me more. You're stopping the legal proceedings?"

Leigh leaned away and smiled at Riley. "Nick and I are going to the court this afternoon, when I'm finished with work. But first he's going to talk with Sam. Make sure she understands." Something that looked like concern flickered across Riley's face. "Is something wrong?"

"Not really. It's just that I stopped by the SICU this morning, and the nurses were saying she had a rough night," Riley explained. "An unexpected fever. They had her on the cooling pad. It sounds like she was delirious for a while."

"And she gave the staff a hard time, I'd bet."

"You'd win that bet." Riley grimaced. "She accused them of withholding calls from your husband."

"He didn't call. He was with me." Leigh nodded. "He'll tell her. She needs to hear the truth. Nick will see to that."

"And meanwhile, you came here."

"Yes." Leigh glanced toward the altar, lit by the glow of Cappy's candles. "There was a lull in the ER. And I wanted to be here for the staff, but I also . . ."

Riley stayed silent.

Leigh swallowed and her voice emerged in a whisper. "I'm meeting Nick in a few minutes. But right now I think I'd like to just sit here for a little while. Is that okay?"

"Very okay."

Leigh hugged Riley once more, watched her leave, then walked slowly toward the front of the chapel. She pulled her stethoscope from around her neck, tucked it into the pocket of her white coat, and took a seat in the front row. Her gaze moved from the candles to the simple cross affixed to the wall above, illuminated now by light streaming through the narrow pane of yellow glass. She thought of how she'd waited for Caro outside these doors after the shooting and how Nick had been here. Seated right where she was now. She thought of Cappy and his wife, Antoinette and Harry, the Owens, and how they all had more in common than a solid, happy marriage. She thought about her friend Erin and her upcoming wedding to Scott McKenna and of how many times Erin had invited Leigh into the chapel at Pacific Mercy. The common denominator in all those success stories was faith. Undeniably.

Then she remembered running to seek the comfort of the stables yesterday and how she'd flung her arms around Frisco, wound her fingers in his mane, and cried. How lonely she'd felt. And how, after telling Riley she was going where even God couldn't find her, she'd still raised her eyes to the sky and demanded to know, "Do you want to find me, Lord?"

Why had she done that? Why was she here now? She thought of Nick in the kitchen just hours ago, singing with that dish towel tossed over his shoulder as he made omelets. Laughing with Caro. Slipping his arms around Leigh's waist as she did the dishes, nuzzling her neck, and whispering, "Bless you for this chance."

She folded her hands and stared at her lap. Then cleared her throat. "If it's not too late, maybe I should give you another chance too, Lord."

+++

"I didn't get your messages until a few minutes ago," Nick said, alarmed by the flush on Sam's cheeks and the shiny, glazed look in her eyes. Her hair was damp with sweat, lips pale. The nurses had said only that she had a fever, but it looked worse than that. He glanced at her IVs, saw a red medication label. "I'm on leave, and I was beat. I turned my phone off." He saw her frown and quickly amended his words. "I called you—the nurses said you were sleeping and doing well."

Sam licked her lips, drew in a breath, her eyes riveted to his. "When?"

"When . . . what?"

"When did you call?"

"I don't know. Early evening. I'm not sure."

She tried to lift her head and groaned with pain.

Nick stepped closer. "Sam, should I call the nurse? Do you need—"

"I need to know if you heard what I told you before I went into surgery."

His stomach twisted. "I heard. And I know how frightened you were. So—"

"I love you," she said, cutting him off again. "I didn't say it because I was scared or because I'd been shot or because I was out of my head from blood loss." She stared at him hard, the flush on her face deepening. "I said it because it's true. I'm in love with you."

Guilt stabbed. "Sam . . . I'm sorry. Look . . ." He dragged his hand across his mouth. "You're Toby's sister. I care about you and Elisa. I was wrong to let what happened between us happen. There's no excuse. I'm to blame. Only me. I've told you that before and I'm telling you again. I was wrong. I'm sorry. But there's no way—"

"She's no good for you, Nick. She's not like you or me. She doesn't want the same things we do. She doesn't want you."

"I love her. I've never stopped loving her. You know that." Nick drew in a breath. *Please, Lord. Help me know what to say.* "Leigh and I talked last night, Sam. We're going to give our marriage another chance."

"No!" Sam hauled herself onto her elbows, eyes wild. "No, no, no! You can't do it; you can't go back to her."

"I am. It's what I want and what she wants. I've tried to be honest with you."

"Honest?" Sam's lips twisted into an ugly sneer.

"I never lied," he said, realizing it was futile and knowing he should just leave. He had no right to defend himself.

"I'm not talking about you," she said, her voice suddenly cold, steely. "I'm talking about that holier-than-thou wife of yours. That virtuous woman in a pure white coat that you say never lies." Her lips twisted again and she made a sound that seemed part sob, part cruel laugh. "You said that, right? that your beloved *wife* never lies?"

"I'm leaving. I don't have anything more to say. You need your rest."

"And you need to hear the truth."

"Good-bye, Sam." He took a step back and she grabbed his arm.

"She told me she was pregnant. Before Toby. Before . . . us."

Nick's stomach lurched. "I don't believe that."

"Believe it. She never told you because she didn't want it. She was carrying your baby, and she didn't want to have it." She gripped his arm so hard that her nails bit into his flesh. "She's not like us. She doesn't want a family. She'll never love you the way I can."

He yanked his arm from her grasp, his pulse hammering so hard in his ears that he couldn't hear. Shock, fury at Sam . . . fear that it could somehow be true. It couldn't be true. Leigh would have told him if she were pregnant. She would never . . .

He turned and bolted from the room, seeing nothing as he jogged toward the stairwell. Sam was delirious, sick. And this was a vicious lie, a desperate act. Desperate people did desperate things. His law enforcement career had taught him that over and over. He yanked at the door to the stairs, the last look in Kurt Denton's eyes flashing into his memory.

He and Leigh had promised last night that they'd be honest. That their whole future would be built on that. She was going to meet him outside the ER. He'd find her and ask. There was no way this could be true.

+++

Leigh shifted on the bench of the hospital gazebo, watching as Nick crossed the parking lot and thinking how many things had changed since they'd talked outside the hospital only a week before. The first time she'd seen him in months, the day he'd saved Finn Johnson's life, and the day she'd met Sam Gordon. It had all led to that breath-stealing moment last night when she'd stopped thinking about divorce and started trying to believe—for the first time in her life—that the forever kind of happiness was possible. It had made her hope, against all odds, that it could really be hers. And it was what she'd asked God for, only a few minutes ago in the chapel. *Please, Lord. Show me that it's possible. . . . Give me my forever.*

She raised her hand and smiled as Nick caught sight of her and broke into a jog. She'd have to tell him that she had to stay and work another hour. He'd be disappointed, but he'd wait for her. She had no doubt about that now—he'd waited almost a year, after all. . . . Her heart filled her chest. *I love him, God. I do. I love him.* Her smile faded at the look on his face. Serious, troubled . . .

"What's wrong?" she asked as he reached the gazebo. Dread made her mouth go dry. "Is it Sam? Is she worse? Did she—"

"She said this crazy thing," he said, catching his breath. "That you were . . . pregnant last year."

Her breath stuck in her throat.

"It's not true, is it?"

A siren wailed in the distance. She raised her hands to her mouth, thoughts staggering.

"Leigh?"

"I . . . had a miscarriage."

His face paled and he shut his eyes for a heart-stopping moment. "When?"

"December," she whispered. "I miscarried the first week in December."

His jaw clenched. "I meant, when did you know? When did you know you were carrying our baby?"

Our baby. Her knees weakened and she reached for the gazebo railing. "Around the first of October."

He groaned. "You knew you were pregnant when you asked me to move out?"

Tears filled her eyes. "I was confused. I didn't how I felt about things. I didn't know—"

"If you wanted to keep my baby?"

"I . . ." The implication of his question—the look in his eyes—hit her like a fist in the gut. "No. Nick, please. Don't even think that." She reached for his hand, and he pulled it away.

"What am I supposed to think?"

"I told you," she said, beginning to tremble. "I was confused. We were having problems. I didn't even know I was pregnant for a while."

"You're a doctor."

"I'm human, too. Please, listen." She took a step forward, willing him to understand. "You know how stressed we were back then. We couldn't seem to agree about anything. My work, yours . . . counseling. By the time I suspected I was pregnant . . ." She spread her palms. "I didn't want a baby to be the only reason we stayed together."

"You didn't want a baby at all. It was one of those 'things' we didn't agree about, remember?"

"I needed time," she struggled to explain. "I needed to trust that it would all work out. Then all of a sudden Sam was in the picture. And while I was trying to deal with that . . . the baby was gone."

"And you still didn't tell me."

"I was hurting, Nick."

He stared at her, his expression incredulous. "And I was sleeping in my car outside the house, begging you to talk with me! Do you think for one minute that didn't hurt? that it didn't rip my heart out when you moved away without telling me?"

The tears in his eyes made it impossible for her to speak.

"I thought," he said, his voice hollow and raw, "that if I prayed hard enough, if I kept trying . . . if I didn't quit, that I'd finally make it all right again. That I could make it even better between us." He shook his head. "I tried to forget that I had to talk you into marrying me in the first place. I told myself that you were fussy about tables, that eventually we'd find the right one. And someday we'd sit there with our children . . ."

"Please, don't—"

"I have to go. I need to think."

"Nick, let's go somewhere and talk."

He raised his hands. "I can't do this now."

She watched, helpless, as he strode away. Then she sank onto the bench, wrapping her arms tightly around her stomach, feeling emptier than she had even last December.

Where did you go, God?

CHAPTER TWENTY-FIVE

Nick raced across the court, slamming the basketball against the lacquered wooden floor, pulse hammering in his neck and sweat stinging his eyes. He lurched to a stop at the free throw line and gulped for air as he raised the ball for at least the hundredth shot in the last hour, then hurled the ball toward the empty bleachers. He bit back a curse, wanting instead to shout it at the top of his lungs and hear it echo against the cement walls, despite all the times he'd forbidden that very same thing with his ragtag team of youthful players. *My kids . . .*

He stripped off his T-shirt, swiping at the sweat on his face and neck as he walked to the bleachers and sat. The hour's workout had done nothing to ease the soul-sick feelings he'd been battling since he left the hospital. He could slam that ball against the floor of every gym in San Francisco—every hospital wall, pastry shop, all down the twisting red bricks of Lombard Street—and it wouldn't obliterate the sound of Leigh's voice in his head: *"Around the first of October."* While he'd been reading Scripture, making counseling appointments, and trying to find some truth that would save their marriage, she'd been withholding the one thing she knew he wanted most in the world. She'd sent him away knowing she was carrying his child.

He tried to push away the memory of Sam's face, the look in her eyes, when she'd spat those words at him. *"She never told you because . . . she didn't want to have it."* No matter what she'd implied, Leigh would never have terminated the pregnancy. He knew how she felt about that. But would she have packed up and moved away without telling him he was going to be a father? Was she really capable of cheating him of that joy?

Leigh had railed against him for betraying her, had been furious and unforgiving to the point of threatening a restraining order, while she was cheating him out of his rights as a father. If only he'd known, things could have been so different. Maybe with the hope of a child, Toby's death wouldn't have rocked him so hard. And then nothing would have happened with Sam, and . . . He swallowed against the bitter taste of bile. Everything would have been different if Leigh had trusted him, believed in their marriage enough to be honest about the baby.

He squeezed his eyes shut, but it did nothing to stop the memory of holding Leigh last night. Asking her to give him a second chance, promising her that their relationship would be based on truth. He'd told her he loved her, but she hadn't said the same to him. Maybe she didn't love him—not enough, anyway. He'd have to accept that. His heart gave a dull thud.

He stared up, past the top of the basketball standard . . . beyond the ceiling. He thought of little Edwin comforting him about the shooting and offering, *"I'm going to ask my Jesus to look after you."*

Loneliness crowded in, worse than any time he'd said good-bye to a foster family. "Where are you, Lord? I can't find you in this."

He sat there for a while—long enough to determine there would be no answer to his question—then climbed the bleachers and grabbed his basketball.

He'd shot a couple dozen baskets, worked up another sweat, when his cell phone buzzed against his waist. Nick quit dribbling, stopped the ball with his foot, and frowned at the caller ID: *Golden Gate Stables*.

"Mr. . . . Stathos?" Male voice. Thick accent.

"Yes."

"Senor . . . the girl . . . she ask me to call. Your horse is—"

"No," Nick insisted, irritated. "Not my horse. Call the other number. I'm not involved anymore. Do you understand? Tell Patrice to call—"

"Mr. Nick?"

He hesitated, confused by a new voice. A child's. "Who is this?"

"Maria. You know me. I gave you carrots."

And you don't talk. "What's wrong?"

"You need to come. Frisco's sick again. I'm scared he'll die. Please . . ." A sob swallowed her words.

Leigh had said Patrice Owen was away, that her sister would take over. "Did someone call Leigh?" he asked gently, wondering about the courage it had taken for this little girl to break her trauma-induced silence.

"Only messages. The other lady, Glenna, said she didn't call back." There was plaintive braying in the background. "Please come."

"Tell Glenna that I give permission to call the vet and that I'm on my way. I'm coming. Don't worry."

He punched in Leigh's number, and when it went to voice mail, he left a brief message. Then left a similar one on Caroline's phone. He grabbed his shirt and jogged out to the car, telling himself he couldn't let the little girl down. He'd stick around long enough to give whatever authorizations were necessary for the horse's treatment. He gunned the engine and headed for the shortest route to Golden Gate Stables, trying not to think of how darkly ironic it was that Patrice Owen had once called him "Frisco's dad."

+++

Leigh patted her face dry with a paper towel and stared in the mirror, wondering if it was becoming a habit to have emotional meltdowns in the doctors' library bathroom. The last time she'd been here was the day she'd met Sam. And the first time she'd raced in sick and emotionally ragged was . . . *when I took that pregnancy test last fall.* Her heart cramped, thinking again of the look on Nick's face out in the gazebo. She leaned on the sink and stared at herself. "Why? Why didn't you tell him?" She watched a fresh tear slide down her face. "And why didn't you say last night that you love him?"

He was right. About their wedding, the subject of having children, even the dining room table. She'd needed time. That's all. Why couldn't he understand that? Why did he have to keep pressuring her? She needed him to give her the time and space to trust that their relationship could work, that their marriage could be solid. It was irresponsible to bring a child into . . .

She grimaced and pressed her palms low against her scrub top. He'd said it out loud. *"My baby."* His baby. She hadn't just had a miscarriage; she'd lost Nick's baby. The baby they'd conceived together. He'd had the right to know. Maybe it wouldn't have changed anything at the time, but it might have made things different now. Telling him the truth could have given them that chance. And kept Sam from having the ammunition to blow it all to bits.

Leigh wadded the paper towel into a ball and hurled it into the wastebasket, anger snuffing her last vestige of tears. It had been stupid to let it slip that she'd had a miscarriage, but that awful woman had such a uncanny sense of how to push Leigh's buttons, and . . . *If I'd been honest with Nick, she couldn't have done that.* She and Nick would be making plans for the future. When he came to the gazebo, she intended to tell him that she'd thought about a lot of things while she'd sat in the chapel. That she thought maybe the Christian marriage counseling might be a good thing after all. But now she wasn't sure any of it was possible.

Nick had said, "I can't do this now." She'd never seen him quit anything in all the years she'd known him, but it sounded like he was giving up on her. On them. That he wasn't willing to give her the time, the *space*, to be sure about things. And Nick wasn't the only one who was unwilling. God was treating her the same way. She'd asked him, finally, to help her—talked with him after such a lonely dry spell— and look what had happened.

She ran a comb through her hair, took a deep breath, and headed back to the ER. The other doc had arrived to work the rest of his shift. She was finished for the day. Now all that was left was to grab her things and get out of here. Go to the stables, check on Frisco. Pull on her riding boots, saddle that chestnut mare, and ride and ride and ride. To anywhere that didn't hurt.

"Dr. Stathos?" The ward clerk caught her as she stepped outside the ambulance bay door and was about to turn her cell phone back on. "Medical records is asking if you could sign that ER record from the other day. The man who got beaten with the high-heel shoe."

Leigh groaned. "I knew that. They've asked twice. Tell them I'm sorry. I'll run up and do it right now. Telemetry unit, right?"

"SICU bed 6. There wasn't a bed in the ICU, so they moved him this morning." She wrinkled her nose. "Alcohol withdrawal symptoms complicated things, I guess."

Leigh jogged the stairs, signed the chart, and even peeked in on Freddie Barber—asleep with an open Bible on his bed-side table. She'd almost escaped the intensive care unit when she heard the shout. Strong, harassing, way too familiar.

"Don't tell me I'm imagining things! I saw her walk by the desk. Tell her I need to see her."

It occurred to Leigh to bolt and escape—she was, after all, an accused runner—but she wasn't about to give Sam the satisfaction. The woman might be winning the war . . . *but this last skirmish is mine.*

+++

Nick might not be a horse person, but he knew the moment he set eyes on the big bay gelding that the animal was in trouble.

"He's dripping with sweat," he said, turning to Glenna. "I didn't think horses did that, except under their saddles. Even that white stripe on his face is soaked."

"It's the pain," the woman explained, her expression anxious. "Patrice said to watch for that or pawing and turning in circles." She grimaced as the big horse turned his head to nip at his flank. "And that. That's a sign of colic pain too, the way he's biting himself. I don't like how he's holding his head. Hanging it down like—" she glanced at Maria, then lowered her voice to a whisper—"like he's giving up."

Nick's stomach sank. "No word from Leigh?"

"I've left several messages, but she hasn't called back." Glenna's lips pressed together. "I'm sorry I didn't call you, but Patrice said Dr. Stathos left specific instructions that only she and the vet were to be called in an emergency. I had no idea that Maria had even started to talk, let alone phoned you. It's a day of miracles and disasters, I'm afraid."

Nick nodded. He couldn't argue with that.

Glenna rested her hand on the slats of the stall next to Frisco's, now filled with the one-eyed donkey. "Maria moved Tag in there. She said they're brothers." She smiled. "I wasn't going to touch that one. But I do think that donkey's been a comfort to your horse."

Your horse. "The vet's on his way?"

"Dr. Hunter will be here as soon as he can. He was in surgery; a rancher's dog was hit by a car. He said to do what we could to keep Frisco from lying down and rolling. Walk him slowly around; keep him moving without wearing him out. The stable hands have gone for the day and I'm not very experienced." Maria appeared and peered out from under

Glenna's arm, holding a halter much too large for the donkey. "Maria wants to walk him, but I don't think that's wise. He's so big, and if he tried to lie down all of a sudden—"

"I'll do it," Nick heard himself say. "If Maria can show me how to put that halter on Frisco and find us a rope, we'll do it together." He smiled at her. "Won't we?"

"You betcha, Mr. Nick."

+++

Sam wondered if Leigh knew there were smudges of mascara under her eyes—not enough to spoil her looks, but proof she'd been crying. *I know the feeling.*

"I don't want to play games," Leigh said, crossing her arms. "If you called me in here to rub my nose in the fact that you told Nick about the miscarriage . . ."

"I thought you'd want to know why."

"I'm not going to bite this time, Sam. The only reason I came in here is to tell you I'm through with this. It's a waste of time for all of us, and it's inappropriate. I should never have engaged in personal conversation with you. You're a patient, a fairly sick one, and I'm—"

"The woman Nick thinks he wants. Or wanted. I'm guessing that's past tense now from the way you look." She shivered, felt a strange wave of dizziness, and glanced toward the new IV antibiotic they'd started minutes earlier. She hoped this one would work. "Nick was upset?"

"I'm not discussing that with you."

"I don't blame you for hating me." Sam scratched at her ear. "I can't count the number of times over the past year that I've wished you'd break your neck on that horse or fall in love with a brain surgeon." She was surprised by a rush of tears. "I . . . I only wanted a chance. It sounds idiotic . . . pathetically corny, but I wanted what everyone else has—a happy ending." She thought of Elisa and her LEGO castle and her throat tightened. "Nick understands that feeling. But I don't think someone like you can."

"Someone like me?"

Sam cleared her throat, rubbed her tongue over the tingling roof of her mouth. "You've had it good all your life. Parents, great schools, nice clothes . . . people who protected you, cared about you. Nick didn't have that. Neither did Toby and I." She closed her eyes for moment and felt her lids scratch oddly over the surfaces, as if her eyeballs had been roughened by sandpaper. "Let me tell you how it was at my house when your father was helping you with your math, and your mother was wearing pearls to bake sugar cookies for the PTA." She stared hard at Leigh. "No dad at the Gordons'. Plenty of men, though. And the ziplock bags hidden under the lid of our toilet weren't filled with sugar cookies. No one helped Toby and me with our homework. But if we kept quiet while Mom thrashed around in her bedroom, we'd get a candy bar. If Toby tried to interfere, he'd get a split lip." She narrowed her eyes, fighting a wave of nausea she thought she'd left behind two decades ago. "And if I was really nice to those men and didn't tell anyone what they did to me after Mom passed out . . ." She saw Leigh flinch and knew she'd hit her mark.

Sam scratched her forehead and grimaced against a wave of itching. "I'm not trying to get pity. I'm tough. Tougher than that punk who shot me." She smiled grimly. "Only not so fast on my feet anymore. All I'm trying to tell you is that

I've only met two men in my entire life that I think are worth something. Toby was one. Nick is the other. I'm not kidding myself that your husband climbed into my bed because he loved me, but I swear I won't give up . . . trying . . . to . . ." Her voice choked and she struggled to swallow. "Something's . . . wrong."

Leigh stepped to the bedside. Her eyes widened and then her gaze darted to the IV fluids. "Sam, you've got hives. All over you. Give me your arm." She grasped Sam's arm, slid the clamp on the IV closed. "Are you itching?"

"Yes . . . I'm on fire." Sam scraped her fingernails against the side of her neck. "My throat itches, too. I think my lips are swelling." She gasped for a breath and wheezed.

Leigh crossed to the door and shouted, "I need a nurse! Bring IV Benadryl and epinephrine. Grab the crash cart and get respiratory therapy here. We've got an allergic reaction. A bad one."

Sam struggled to sit upright, felt searing pain in her incision but didn't care. She had to get up, stop what was happening. The blood pressure cuff inflated on her arm, making the itching turn to unbearable burning. Tighter, tighter. She thrashed, tried to pull it off, tried to—

"Hold still, Sam. Let us put this oxygen mask on. The nurse is going to get your IVs pumping faster. Hold still. Don't fight us."

Acrid plastic covered her face and Leigh's voice sounded farther away, like it was coming from a tunnel. "Fifty of Benadryl, IV. Pull out some Solu-Medrol. Is that the BP reading—72 over 40? Check it again. Saline wide open, pour it in. She's anaphylactic."

Alarms buzzed above her, persistent as bees. The stinging and itching worsened until she wanted to scratch her skin bloody. She was smothering to death.

She tried to focus, couldn't see through the fog, then struggled again to sit up so that she could suck air, barely, past her swollen throat. Her voice emerged like the last gasp of a strangler's victim.

"I . . . can't . . . breathe."

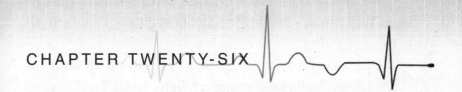

CHAPTER TWENTY-SIX

Leigh bent close, trying to reassure her—Sam was panicked.

"Sam, listen to me. The epinephrine's making your heart race and causing your shakiness, but that's okay. Hang in there. We've got to stop this reaction. You're allergic to the antibiotic. I know this is frightening, but—"

Sam gagged and Leigh snatched the misting treatment mask away as she began vomiting, each retch followed by a shrill, whistling wheeze when she struggled to get a breath. Sam's lips had gone gray. "Suction!" Leigh ordered. "Clear her airway!"

Leigh's gaze darted toward the monitor display as the nurses and respiratory therapist worked: BP 78 over 38, pulse 146, oxygen saturation . . . 81 percent? She gestured to one of the nurses. "Set me up for intubation. Is that steroid on board?"

"Yes, Doctor. Plus the diphenhydramine and a second dose of epi. The saline's running wide open, but—"

"I see the blood pressure," Leigh interjected, her mouth going dry. *And I know she's getting worse instead of better.* She leaned over the bed again, very aware of Sam's stridor and wheezes, despite the medication infusing through the mask. There was terror in her eyes.

"I'm . . . going . . . to die." Her hand, grasping Leigh's, was cold, clammy with sweat—her face, lips, and eyelids were rapidly swelling.

"No. We've informed Dr. Bartle, but there isn't time to wait. Your throat's swelling inside. I need to put a tube in to help you breathe."

"Oh . . . God, help . . . me." Sam's eyes swam upward and then she focused again, gripped Leigh's hand even harder. "Elisa . . . tell Nick . . ." Tears filled her eyes, spilled over, but her gaze stayed riveted to Leigh's. The anguish in them made Leigh's heart ache.

Lord, please help me help her.

"I'm . . . going . . . to die," Sam repeated as the monitor alarms shrilled.

The nurse stepped close. "Your intubation tray is ready, Doctor."

"I'm . . . sorry . . . ," Sam whispered. "I only . . . wanted . . ." Her eyes rolled back and her head sank against the pillow.

Leigh grasped Sam's hand, leaned close. "I won't let you die. Do you hear me? Nick can't lose you too. You stay with me—fight, Sam!"

She whirled, nodded to the respiratory therapist. "Let's hyperventilate her so I can get this tube in."

In less than two minutes, she slid the laryngoscope blade over Sam's swollen tongue and saw with dread that the entire back of her throat was massively edematous. It was impossible to visualize the necessary landmarks—epiglottis, vocal cords . . . "Suction!"

Leigh suctioned the saliva away and held her breath as she tried to slide the tube past . . . "Too big—give me a cuffed number five," she ordered, seeing with dismay that her patient's face had gone grayer. "Bag her, please!"

Heart pounding nearly as fast as her patient's, Leigh tried again with the child-sized tube, but the swelling had progressed. "Did the OR call back? Is anesthesia—"

"The anesthesiologists are all in surgery. I could call downstairs and see if they can pull the ER doctor away, or—"

"No. No time. Bag her again," Leigh said, pulling the tube away. "Give me a number four tube. I'll try to insert it nasally." *It won't work. She is going to die. Unless . . .* "Never mind. Get me a number fifteen scalpel, some hemostats, and prep her neck fast. I'm doing a cricothyrotomy."

In minutes the staff had Sam, mercifully unconscious from shock, positioned with a rolled towel under her shoulders, head lolled back and throat exposed. Leigh said a prayer under her breath and touched a gloved finger to Sam's Adam's apple—the thyroid cartilage. She identified the cricothyroid membrane beneath, reminding herself of the underlying anatomy location of associated blood vessels. *Don't let me hit a vessel . . .* She lifted the scalpel, held her breath, and quickly made a two-centimeter vertical slice, sponged away the blood and widened the opening with the hemostat, then inserted a number six endotracheal tube.

"Inflate the cuff, please," she whispered to the technician, relief making her weak as Sam inhaled and she heard the first sweet rush of air through the tube—like a child playing with a soda straw. "We'll get it secured in place, bag assist her for a few minutes, then continue those albuterol treatments."

And you'll live, Sam. You'll live. Thank you, God.

Nick felt a tug on the rope and looked back over his shoulder to see that Frisco, flanked by Tag and Maria, had stopped walking again. He couldn't blame the horse; forty minutes of plodding in circles around the sandy riding arena felt way too long.

"He's resting for a minute," Maria said, surprising him again with her voice—angelic, sweet, and confident. Why he imagined that it would be different, he wasn't sure. Except he knew the abuse and heartache she'd survived and expected, perhaps, to hear it in her voice. "Tag won't let him lie down and roll; don't worry," she assured him. The donkey, as if on cue, nudged the big horse gently with his nose.

Nick smiled. "I see that."

He walked back to Frisco, raised a hand . . . hesitated.

"It's okay. He won't bite you."

Nick stroked his fingers along the gelding's white blaze, relieved to see that the sweat was drying. Although the look in the animal's dark eyes . . . *He's still hurting. The order of the day. All around.* He touched Frisco's soft nose, then turned to Maria. "It was your idea to call me?"

She nodded. "I knew you'd come."

He raised his brows.

"You're a policeman. You help people." She stepped close to Frisco, and the horse turned his head toward her and sighed. "Animals too. Besides, he's part of your family. And families—" she reached up to pet Frisco's nose and Nick caught sight of the scars on her arm—"should always, always help each other. No matter what."

Nick struggled to answer. "I think you're right, princess."

She smiled. "We'd better walk."

He clucked to Frisco and the big horse moved to follow him. Tag and Maria stepped alongside, and they started another slow circuit of the sandy arena. They passed the wooden mounting block Gary had built so that the smaller riders would have an easier time climbing onto their horses. They walked by neat rows of protective riding helmets—some as big as NFL gear, for brain-injured children—hanging on pegs by the gate. The late afternoon sunlight glinted on a cluster of chrome wheelchairs and aluminum crutches. Frisco plodded quietly behind, head hanging low, and Nick led, his thoughts tumbling.

So much had happened in the past few days, things he'd never anticipated, like being here now, leading Leigh's horse in circles with a near-blind donkey and a little girl. A child who'd been mute until today, when she'd called him to help this horse he'd never really liked. Because "*. . . he's part of your family. And families should always, always help each other. . . .*"

"*No matter what.*" His heart cramped at the image of Leigh's face in the gazebo today, when she'd try to explain. "*I was hurting.*" She still was; he saw that in her eyes every time he looked at her. Even last night, when she'd told him she wanted them to give their marriage another chance. She was frightened and confused. Maybe she had been all along. Had he really considered that? tried to understand why? Or had he always just moved ahead with what he thought was best—get married, start a family . . . buy that table? It had seemed right, solid, secure. He'd done it all because he loved Leigh; she had to know that. But if that was true, why had things ended up the way they had?

Nick clucked to Frisco, heard Maria echo it, then walked on, waiting for the vet and thinking how strange it was that he'd prodded Leigh for the truth, when maybe a much bigger truth was waiting for him right here in this dirt arena. Prompted by a little girl with cruel scars and the voice of an angel.

I'm listening, Lord. Show me, please.

+++

Sam drew a breath, grateful for its freedom despite the fact that it was flowing through a tube emerging from a gaping hole in her neck. She groaned, but no sound came because the tube bypassed her vocal cords. It was surreal. Especially the fact that it was Leigh Stathos who'd performed the emergency procedure. And saved her life, more than one nurse had told her in the past hour. Dr. Bartle had confirmed it. If Leigh hadn't been there at the bedside, made the split-second decision to insert the breathing tube . . . *Elisa would be motherless right now.* Tears filled her eyes.

She hadn't told the nurses or Dr. Bartle that the only reason Leigh had been here was that Sam had summoned her so she could enjoy the fact that she'd ruined her chances for reconciliation with Nick. If Sam were inclined to believe such things, she'd think that God had masterminded their bedside meeting. She caught sight of Leigh in the hallway and reached for the pad and pencil the nurse had provided. They'd be taking the tube out in a few hours, but Sam couldn't wait that long. Her heart thudded. *I have to do this.*

"Hello," Leigh said, stepping through the doorway. Her gaze swept the monitor displays. "Dr. Bartle says you're doing well." She stepped to the bedside. "No more hives, itching?"

Sam started to speak, remembered she couldn't, and shook her head.

"Good." Leigh rubbed her hand across the back of her neck, looking obviously fatigued. "I think I'm going to go, then. The tube will be out in a few hours—Band-Aid, very little scar—and you'll stay on steroids and antihistamines. You'll be fine. I'm . . ." She cleared her throat. "I'm glad I was here."

Sam raised her hand, beckoned to Leigh before she could leave. She lifted the clipboard and tapped the pencil against it, feeling a knot gather in her throat that had nothing to do with allergic hives.

"Question?" Leigh asked. She stepped close again as Sam wrote.

You saved my life.

Leigh started to speak and Sam shook her head, pressed the pencil to the paper again.

I was awful to you and you still helped me.

"I'm a doctor." Leigh swallowed. "And I meant what I said; I didn't want Nick to lose you. I wasn't there for him when Toby died. You were. I can't bear the thought of him losing someone else."

Sam felt a tear slide alongside her nose as she wrote again.

He never cooked for me. I think cooking is like love for him. He loves you. Always has.

Leigh's eyes glistened.

I'm so sorry.

"Sam, I don't know what to say. . . ."

She looked at Leigh for a long moment and inhaled slowly through the lifesaving tube.

Love him back. He's one of the good guys.

Sam returned the warm squeeze of Leigh's hand, watched her walk away, then punched the button on the morphine pump. She sank back against the cool pillow and felt the effects of the medication swirl, thinking of Elisa and her play castle. She hoped someday her little girl would find that prince. Because of Nick, Sam knew they existed. She hoped he would have his happy ending too.

But if his wife was ever foolish enough to turn him away again . . .

+++

Leigh pulled into the stables' parking area, heart pounding. When she'd finally turned her cell phone back on, there had been half a dozen messages: Patrice's sister Glenna, Dr. Hunter's technician, several from Caro, and one from Nick. His voice had been flat, unemotional, and he'd simply said, "I don't know why they called me. But no one can find you. So I'm going to the stables to check on your horse. Call them." *Them. Not him.*

She slid out of the car thinking of the information she'd learned about Frisco. The colic symptoms were back; he'd been trying to lie down, and he didn't look right, according to the distraught message from Glenna. The veterinary office assured her that while Dr. Hunter was in surgery, he'd be there as soon as possible. If things worsened, one of his associates out on a ranch call could probably stop by. She jogged through the doorway of the barn and nearly ran into Caro.

Leigh's gaze swept Frisco's empty stall and her stomach lurched. "Where is he? Did he—"

"It's okay. Dr. Hunter brought the equine ambulance and they just pulled out. They're taking Frisco to the UC Davis vet school. If he needs surgery, that's where Dr. Hunter wants him. He already has an IV and they gave him something for pain. Dr. Hunter said Nick did a great job."

"Nick?"

"He and Maria and that funny little donkey walked Frisco for an hour; Nick sponged him down, kept him from rolling. I got here about half an hour ago, long enough to see that your horse-shy husband looked like a pro. I think Frisco's in good hands. Don't look so worried—it'll be okay."

Leigh swiped at a rush of tears. "It's not only that. It's so much else. When did they leave?"

"Less than ten minutes ago. It took a while to load Frisco in the trailer, but then Nick and Maria thought of sending Tag in first."

"Tag went?"

"And Maria and Nick; the front section of that rig is huge. Patrice thought it would be good for Maria to follow through, since she was the one who first saw that Frisco was in trouble and phoned Nick. So—"

"Wait. Phoned? She doesn't talk."

Caro smiled. "She does now."

Leigh shook her head. "I'm so confused. But I need to get there. UC Davis?"

"Right." Caro reached into her pocket and pulled out a set of keys. "And I've got the Z4. I was going to follow, but if we can intercept them . . ."

"I can ride along with Frisco, too."

"And Maria—and Nick." Caro tipped her head, her expression concerned. "He didn't tell me any details, but I got the feeling things aren't quite where they left off this morning?"

"No. Something happened." Tears gathered again. "It's something I should probably tell you about too." *I should have told you before. . . . Lord, I've made such a mess of things.*

"Okay, then," Caro said, wrapping her in a quick hug. "Do that on the road; we have a horse ambulance to catch." She started down the barn aisle, then stopped. "Where were you, by the way?"

"You won't believe this. I was at the hospital saving Sam Gordon's life." Leigh expected the look on her sister's face. "Yes. I never dreamed I'd be doing that either."

Never dreamed . . . The impact of it hit as she followed her sister to Nick's car. She'd just saved the life of the woman she'd killed over and over in all those awful, troubling nightmares. Her throat tightened and goose bumps rose. *Lord, you are there. You have found me. Can you stick with me now? Will you stay?*

+++

"We're here already?" Maria stood on a bale of straw to peer through the small window in the front section of the large trailer serving as an equine ambulance.

"Couldn't be." Nick glanced at his watch. "We haven't been on the road long enough. Maybe we've pulled off so the tech can come back and check Frisco." He glanced through metal bars at the horse tethered in the slant-load trailer, roomy enough that if the worst happened, the big horse could lie down on the thick rubber mats. Securely tied with a quick-release rope, Frisco's head hung low, dark eyes half-lidded from the sedative given via the IV. Tag rode in the third space, completely unflappable and pulling wisps of leafy, fragrant alfalfa from a hay net. Nick wondered for the umpteenth time why Leigh hadn't answered her calls. *Where are you?*

He reached for the intercom button that connected to the truck's cab. "I'll ask why we're stopping."

Before he could do it, the trailer door opened. He squinted into the glare of sunlight and saw blue scrubs . . . and Leigh's face.

CHAPTER TWENTY-SEVEN

"I'd like to ride along," Leigh said, putting one foot into the trailer. Frisco nickered softly at the sound of her voice and Nick saw her eyes fill with worry. "Caro has your car out there. She was planning to follow. But if you'd rather drive back with her . . ."

"Frisco wants you both here," Maria said quickly, closing the Bible storybook in her lap. "All of us. There's room. See?" She swept her little arm wide, indicating the space thickly bedded in fresh straw where she and Nick sat. "It's all comfy because they were going to take some baby lambs to the hospital. But Frisco needed it more. Come in. It's okay."

Leigh glanced over her shoulder. "I could tell Caro—"

"I'll stay here," Nick said and heard her breath escape in a sigh. She waved to Caro and climbed in. The faint trace of her shampoo mingled with the scent of straw as she moved toward the metal divider and reached through to gently stroke Frisco's nose. For some reason, Nick thought of her knitting bag—the baby caps—and his painful confusion returned. He wondered if he should go with Caroline after all, then heard the BMW's engine as she pulled away.

The trailer started forward and Leigh sank down in the

straw beside him. "Thank you," she said, smiling at Maria before turning to Nick. "Dr. Hunter said that you walked Frisco and sponged him down."

"I'm not responsible for the Cinderella bow."

"I figured that. But . . ." Her eyes held his. "I mean it, Nick. Thank you."

"Where were you?" he asked, seeing the fatigue etched on her face.

"At the hospital."

"I thought you were only working two hours today." *Then we'd planned to go to court together, stop the divorce . . .*

"I had to work a little longer. But then there was something else . . ."

Her expression made his pulse quicken. "What is it? What happened?"

"Sam."

Nick groaned. "She has no right to harass you."

"No. I mean she had a medical problem. A severe allergic reaction to a new antibiotic. I was there when it happened."

"Is she okay?"

"Yes. But it was life threatening. I had to do an emergency crike."

"You mean . . . ?"

"Her throat swelled so fast that I couldn't get a tube in through her mouth. Or nose. An anesthesiologist wasn't available. She went into shock and lost consciousnesses. I had no choice—it was her only chance. I made an incision and inserted the tube through her neck."

He struggled to understand. "When did this happen?"

"Not long after you left. I was in the unit seeing another

patient, and . . ." She nodded quickly. "Anyway, she's okay. She's conscious and stable now. The reaction is under control. Dr. Bartle ought to be taking the tube out soon. There shouldn't be any complications."

"You saved her life," he said, trying to wrap his mind around it.

"That's what she does." Maria set her book down and peered at him. "She's a doctor. And you're a policeman. You both help people." She shook her head like she shouldn't have to explain such things. Then she yawned and returned to her book.

When he turned back to Leigh, there were tears in her eyes.

"It's strange," she said, glancing toward the partition that separated the trailer. Tag's munching filled the short stretch of silence. "You went to help my horse, and I was there with . . ."

"Toby's sister." He met her eyes, the enormity of it still too much to take in. "Does she understand what you did for her?"

A look he couldn't read passed across her face. She glanced away. "You should call her. She probably can't talk on the phone yet, but you could leave a message with the nurses. I'm sure she'd want to know you're thinking of her. She's had a lot to deal with . . . for a long time."

"Okay," he whispered, thinking mostly of Leigh. *Lord, help me. Help me understand all of this.*

They were quiet for a long while, the absence of words filled by the rumble of the trailer moving over the road, Tag's chewing, and Maria's soft snoring. The storybook slid from her hands and Nick set it on a bale of straw. The book's cover showed Jesus surrounded by children.

"She called you?" Leigh asked.

"I'm still shocked. She said she knew I'd come because Frisco's part of my family. And families should always help each other." He smiled at Leigh. "That's pretty incredible after all she's been through. She's an amazing kid."

"You're pretty amazing yourself. Caro told me how she saw the four of you walking out there. She said you looked like a pro." Leigh pointed to the shoulder of his black polo shirt. "I think the dried slobber proves it. I hope Frisco didn't bite you."

"No. I think you might say we bonded." He grimaced. "But don't expect me to be applauding for manure."

Leigh laughed. "I won't. That's above and beyond the call of duty."

He shook his head. "This is weird, you know. Here you are running off with your horse again, but I'm here too this time." He glanced at her and saw her smile fade, knew he'd said the wrong thing. "I'm sorry, Leigh—I didn't mean that the way it sounded."

"It's okay. I understand."

He wondered if she did. If she ever could.

+++

Riley walked toward the SICU, telling herself that the TV news clip—a national item flashed between continuing coverage of the hospital shooting—had nothing to do with her. Houston police were investigating the case of a twenty-three-year-old woman, found strangled . . . *in a vacant condo, not a hospital parking garage. A Realtor, not a nurse.* She gritted her teeth, refusing to smell the concrete of that hospital stairwell, feel the suffocation of those hands squeezing her throat. The Houston police had arrested a suspect, the nephew of a U.S. senator, the only reason the story had gone national. There was no reason for Riley to think it was in any way related to her assault. But she was certain it had prompted her parents' e-mail: *"Sweetheart: Missing you, as always, but thankful you're there doing work you enjoy, making new friends, continuing your physical therapy. Your father and I know, more than ever before, that it's what's best for now."*

But was it really?

She drew in a slow breath and pushed open the door to the SICU, then crossed to Sam Gordon's room. She was sitting upright, oxygen in place and a large Band-Aid on her neck.

"They say I can talk, if I promise to whisper," she said, her voice hoarse and hushed. "I'm not sure how much of that is medical and how much is nurses' revenge. They're pretty sick of my tirades." A grim smile did nothing to hide the sadness in her eyes.

"You had rough afternoon, I hear."

"In spades."

Riley stepped closer. Sam's eyes were swollen, red, her lashes wet; less to do with the allergic reaction, more to do with . . . *She's been crying.*

Sam glanced down at a small photograph she held in her lap. "Leigh Stathos saved my life. Did you know that?"

"I heard," Riley said, remembering the shell-shocked look on Leigh's face as she told her the story.

"I keep thinking—" her finger brushed over the photograph—"that if I'd died, my little girl would have been alone. Right now some overworked county staffer could be making decisions to put her in temporary foster care." Sam shook her head. "Like I've done so many times for other women's children."

Riley nodded silently. *Praise God Leigh was here.*

Sam's lips pressed together. "I called her here to gloat over something I'd done to destroy her marriage—stick it to her one last time." She gave a short, raspy laugh. "I suppose you thought God sent her."

Riley smiled.

"I've never been good with the idea of God. But I believed in Nick." The Band-Aid bobbed as she swallowed. "He was going to be everything for us. And I would have done anything to have him. Leigh knew that. But now . . ."

"You feel differently?"

"I'm . . ." Sam's eyes shone with sudden tears. "I'm confused, I guess. Grateful and empty at the same time. I miss my brother more than I ever have. My sister-in-law is watching Elisa; she wants me to move to Sunnyvale when I'm released. I think I'll do that. She and her children are the only family we have and we need one right now. You know?"

Riley exhaled. "I do. I miss my family too."

Sam was quiet for several seconds, brushed at a tear. "Thank you for listening." She shook her head. "And for not bringing God into all of this."

Riley rested her hand over Sam's. "I'm glad to help," she said, thinking how fortunate it was that the true Healer didn't always wait for an invitation.

And that maybe he was telling Riley it was time for her to go home.

+++

Leigh shifted on the straw to rest her head against the wall of the trailer, feeling the vibration of the road beneath them and thinking of what Nick had said about her running away with her horse. Running away, period. She knew he wasn't just referring to her move to Pacific Point last December; he'd meant the space Leigh had always required in their relationship. Like this last week, when life—and death—crowded in around her and she escaped to the stables. She'd sat there and wondered what it would be like to sleep there, to lie in that peaceful place. Leigh glanced at Nick and Maria. They were both asleep now, the little girl leaning against him, her braid trailing along his shoulder. Dozing in the straw, lulled by the soft sounds of the animals, the scent of hay, warm horseflesh, gentle breathing. A moving stables.

Nick was here. And wasn't that what she'd wanted, what she'd agreed to when she'd said she wanted to give their marriage a second chance? Wasn't that what she'd be doing right now if Sam hadn't told him about the miscarriage?

"Dr. Leigh?" Maria lifted her head from Nick's shoulder.

"Yes, sweetie?"

"Do you and Mr. Nick have kids?"

"No."

"Oh." Maria reached for her book and pulled it into her lap. Her fingertips, sparkling with glitter polish, brushed over the drawing of the children gathered around Jesus. *"Let the little children come to me . . ."* Leigh glanced at the scars on Maria's arms.

"He was there," Maria whispered. "Jesus."

"Where?"

"At my house. That night the man hurt my mother. He kept me safe . . . and he took Mama to heaven."

Leigh's heart cramped.

"Jesus is always here," Maria continued. "We're his family and he loves us. We don't have to be afraid, because he'll always be here, no matter what." She smiled, dark lashes blinking. "Forever and ever."

Forever . . .

Maria yawned and nestled her head back against Nick's shoulder. She closed her eyes and folded her arms over the storybook. "Don't worry. He's watching after you and Mr. Nick. And Tag . . . Frisco, too."

Leigh closed her eyes and leaned back against the trailer wall, surrounded by straw, a donkey, a horse, a man, a child . . . and by truths she'd never considered. Never seen until right this minute. Even though she'd heard them from Nick today: *"I had to talk you into marrying me . . ."* And, bitterly, from Sam Gordon, a woman who'd lied about so many things but was so right about Leigh: *"It sounds to me like you always had space—you liked it that way. The more space the better."* She remembered how Nick reminded her of the words she'd spoken to him the first day she met him at Niko's. *"I came for food—not a commitment."*

She'd blamed her mother all these years for stealing her belief in happily ever after, in forever. But that wasn't the truth. Leigh had been afraid of marriage, children, a home, even a long-term career because she didn't trust herself. She'd been afraid she'd fail as badly as her mother. She thought—in some sad but completely arrogant way—that forever was something required of her. A burden she couldn't carry. When all the while . . .

Her heart ached at the memory of Maria's words: *"We don't have to be afraid, because he'll always be here, no matter what. Forever and ever."*

God's love was forever. The hope and comfort of that had been there all along, and she hadn't seen it. She'd let Nick's affair make it easier to run; she'd kept the miracle of Nick's baby a secret from him, called the miscarriage a blessing in disguise while knitting caps for dozens of babies thousands of miles away . . . and let her marriage die, the same as that lemon tree. She'd used the excuse of "space" to do exactly what her mother had done—abandon her husband. And Caro, too, by believing that getting her on medication, into counseling, and on to college would substitute for having her big sister close enough to hug. *All because I thought forever began and ended with . . . with me.*

Leigh hiked up her knees, buried her head in her arms, and felt tears slide down her cheeks, certain her heart would break. "Father," she whispered, her voice blending with the road sounds, "I've been such a fool. So wrong. Please forgive me. I should have trusted you. I should have asked for your help. I am now. I need forever . . . to start with you."

+++

The sounds awoke Nick with a jolt—hooves against flooring loud as thunder, a screaming donkey bray. And Maria's cry.

"What's happening?" he asked, moving to his feet.

"Quick, oh, hurry!" Leigh shouted, scrambling forward across the slippery straw. "Use the intercom; tell them Frisco's panicking. I've got to get his head loose before he hangs himself. And I have to keep his IV from being pulled out. Oh, please, Frisco . . . Easy, boy, easy. I'm here. I won't leave you." She fumbled with the latch in the feed door of the partition and grabbed hold of the quick release rope attached to horse's halter.

Nick bent low and spoke into the intercom, then grasped Maria's shoulder to keep her back. The truck's brakes grabbed, eased, grabbed again, and the trailer began to turn. Tag's bray sounded again, Frisco grunted, and there was a horrible sound of impact against metal—horse against metal railing—then a larger groan and a thud that shook the entire trailer. Frisco sat down hard on his hindquarters, his breath coming in painful heaves, front legs extended.

"Don't lie down, boy. Stay up; stay up," Leigh begged, her voice rising.

Nick held Maria as the trailer's small side escape door opened. Sunlight streamed in, along with Dr. Hunter's calm voice. "We're less than a mile from the hospital. I'll give another dose of sedative and call to have the staff standing by. Everyone hang on tight. We'll get there."

CHAPTER TWENTY-EIGHT

Nick stepped back into the veterinary exam room after leaving a message with Sam's nurse. He immediately saw the worry in Leigh's expression.

"An enterolith?" she asked, crossing her arms.

"That's right, Dr. Stathos. Look right here." The veterinary surgical resident in dark green scrubs slid a film onto the viewer and peered through wire-rimmed glasses. "Sometimes they're not visible on film. But this one's as big as a softball. You'll notice that it isn't possible to identify individual loops of gut on an equine X-ray—just a mush of opacities—but the way Frisco's presenting clinically, we're suspicious that the stone's wedged tight. It's good you got him here—these things can cause intestinal rupture. With a high incidence of mortality."

"Did he swallow something?" Maria squinted at the film.

"It happens sort of the way pearls are made," Caroline explained. "Minerals from water and food—the alfalfa hay— form a little ball in his stomach. Then it grows bigger and bigger until it causes problems."

"Surgery's the only solution?" Nick asked, stepping up beside Leigh.

"Yes—he's already being prepped. We should have him ready in a few minutes. He's young, in good shape, and hasn't been obstructed long, so the outlook is encouraging." The resident glanced at Maria. "It's going to be several hours, though. And then he'll be in recovery after that. Your horse won't be up for visitors, I'm afraid."

"That's okay." Caroline slipped her arm around Maria's shoulders. "We're going to ride home in the front of the ambulance." She smiled at Dr. Hunter's assistant. "And we'll find a place we can park that big rig while we get a hamburger. And a milkshake."

Maria tugged at the hem of the resident's scrub top. Nick smiled; the little girl was making up for lost time with her questions. She blinked at the doctor. "Can Tag stay? He's Frisco's brother."

The resident's brows rose and he grinned. "I guessed that right away. Dr. Hunter already asked us to fix up a stall next to Frisco's."

"That's right," the vet assistant added. "And it's not far from where a very famous cow lives. The fistulated cow—she has a sort of 'window' in her side. So students can learn about her stomach compartments." He smiled at Maria's incredulous expression. "Would you like to see?"

The assistant led Caro and Maria out the doorway, and the surgical resident pulled the film from the viewer. "I'm going to get scrubbed for the OR." He turned to Nick and Leigh. "Unless you have any more questions?"

"How long will Frisco be here?" Nick asked.

"Hard to tell until we see how he does. I'd plan on at least three days. Maybe up to five. We'll know more after he's out of surgery. Are you folks going back with the others?"

Nick spoke first. "No. We have a car. We'll be staying." He felt Leigh's eyes on him, heard her exhale.

She hugged her arms around herself. "I know he's already sedated, but is it possible to see Frisco for a minute, before . . ." Her voice caught. "Would that be okay?"

"Absolutely. Follow me."

They walked through a corridor to one of the surgery suites. Through the window, they saw a team of people in green scrubs attaching monitors, adjusting IVs, and preparing instruments. Frisco, obviously sedated, was tied head and tail to what appeared to be a huge . . . "What is that?" Nick asked, his gaze moving over large bands supporting the horse's belly.

"A hydraulic table," the resident explained. "It's sort of like a car lift—can't put a thousand-pound patient on a table very easily. After Frisco is anesthetized, he'll be intubated. Then the table moves into a horizontal position and we'll slide him onto the surgery table."

Leigh nodded, her teeth sinking into her lower lip. "I never thought he could look small, but . . ."

Nick slid his arm around her shoulders. "Where can we wait?"

In fifteen minutes, they'd found the picnic table in a grove of oak trees. And only moments later Nick was straddling the bench, holding Leigh as she cried. From the heartbreaking sound of her sobs and the way she clung to him, he guessed it was about far more than her horse.

"I think . . . ," Leigh said, finally moving away, "I'm finished now."

He brushed a strand of hair from the side of her face, letting his fingers linger there for a few seconds. His tenderness almost hurt. "I'd like to offer you a tissue, but all I have is this shirt covered in dried horse slobber—and some from his donkey brother."

She tried to smile and her eyes filled again. "What I need right now is for you to listen." Her expression grew serious. "Will you do that?"

"I'm right here."

And you're there, God. I know it now. Help me find the words. She took a slow breath. "Remember how Maria told you families should always help each other?"

Nick nodded.

"Well, she told me something, too. While you were asleep. She said . . ." Leigh's throat tightened and she swallowed. "She talked about the night her mother died. She said that Jesus was there with her. That he's always with us. Because we're his family. And that we don't have to be afraid. He'll always be here, no matter what. Forever and ever."

Nick took her hand.

"I've never believed in forever. I never trusted it. I told myself it was because of my mother, her failures at marriage and the way she left Caro and me over and over again." Leigh shook her head and swiped at a tear. "I convinced myself I didn't trust marriage, that staying at one job—in one place— for too long was stifling. Children were confining, and . . . that even God was the fair-weather type. I learned to protect myself, land on my feet, keep things as skin-deep as I could." She clucked her tongue. "I think that was even the draw of emergency medicine at first. A career without a long-term commitment. All of my relationships had been like that. But then I met you." She laid her palm along his jaw. "And you threatened all my rules."

Nick winced. "Leigh, I—"

"Wait. Please. What I'm trying to say is that I fell in love with you. And I didn't know how to handle it. You wanted everything. A wedding. A table. A family. And then you insisted that the God of Creation be smack in the center of all that. And I—" She stopped as he grasped her hands.

"It's true," he said, his eyes suddenly shiny with tears. "I pushed you. I was wrong to do that, Leigh. I made it about what I wanted, the things I'd never had. I shouldn't have done that. But I loved you so much; I wanted to make it all right. And instead I made a huge mess of things. You were alone . . . after having a miscarriage. You were in pain. And when I found out about it today, I was so involved in myself that I didn't even think how awful that was for you. I was selfish." He grimaced. "In some ways no better than Kurt Dent—"

"No," she said, cutting him off. "Don't say that. You were right about so many things, Nick. But it scared me because . . ." Her voice broke. "I thought 'forever' was up to me. And I knew I couldn't make it happen. I held myself apart from you because I didn't think *I* would last. I didn't think *I* had what it takes to make a marriage work, to be a mother. That's why I pushed you away. Because of me, not you. I used everything as an excuse, my worries about the risks of your work . . . and finally, your affair with Sam."

She saw the guilt on his face and shook her head. "I wasn't there for you when Toby died. I didn't tell you about the baby. I'd convinced myself our marriage could never work because we were too different. I'm not saying that what happened between you and Sam wasn't wrong." She searched his eyes. "I'm saying that I knew you were truly sorry, and I still didn't give us a chance. That wasn't fair. But the worst—the very worst—is that I never saw God in forever. I made it about me, and it can't work that way. This past year has been hollow, horrible . . . lonely. I miss you. And I miss a baby I never thought I wanted. It's like there's been a hole in me that I can't fill." She blinked back tears. "You tried to tell me so many times that God needed to be at the center of our lives, but I wouldn't listen. I guess I had to hear it in the back of a stock trailer. Running away with my horse . . . and you." She smiled despite the tears streaming down her face. "I love you, Nick. With all my heart. I don't want to lose you."

"You won't," he whispered. "Ever."

He cupped her face in his hands, kissed her closed eyelids, her cheek, and then tenderly covered her mouth with his own. He drew her into his arms and their kiss deepened. Her heart crowded her chest as she twined her arms around him, kissing him back, feeling his solid warmth, aching with the familiar dearness of him. When at last she broke away, she was breathless, giddy. She reached up to brush her fingers through Nick's hair. "You have some little pieces of straw . . ."

He ran his thumb over her lips. "I probably smell like a stable."

She kissed his fingertip. "Be careful. You have no idea how enticing that is to a horsewoman."

"Good. I may never shower." His brows scrunched.

"What?"

"What's today?"

"Thursday, the second." She heard him sigh with obvious relief, and warmth flooded through her as she read his thoughts. "Oh."

Nick smiled. "We're still married. For at least twenty-four hours." He glanced at his watch. "It's too late to call the court tonight. But tomorrow . . ."

She met his gaze, loving the look in his eyes, as if all his dreams had just come true. "Tomorrow we'll wake up in a bed-and-breakfast as near to this hospital as we can find. I'll kiss you good morning; you'll graciously pretend I'm not wearing hospital scrubs to breakfast, and I'll ignore your horse-bonding shirt. Then we'll buy carrots for Tag and check on Frisco." She melted as he bent close, his lips finding the hollow of her neck. "And after that we'll be at our home in the city and you'll make omelets for me. Every morning for the rest of our lives—with a dish towel over your shoulder."

"Are you begging, Mrs. Stathos?"

She shook head. "No. I'm counting my blessings."

"Me too," he whispered before touching his lips to hers again. In a kiss that tasted like forever.

EPILOGUE

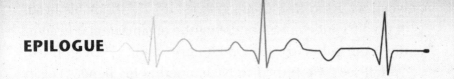

April

"The . . . um, the Chihuahua is wearing a bow tie." Nick gestured toward the silver-haired gentleman standing in the sand beside an elegant, redheaded woman about his age. The bride's grandmother—was that what Leigh had said? He was playing catch-up as fast as he could but was still confused. The groom, a tall firefighter in a gray cutaway jacket, laughed beside him, his low rumble blending with the sound of the ocean waves.

"Jonah's less formal at work," Scott explained, the salty breeze lifting his short hair. "He's a pet therapy dog." The corners of his eyes crinkled. "We're just hoping he doesn't start yodeling when they play the wedding march, right, Cody?"

"Could happen." The best man, a blond boy of about eleven, grinned and a dimple appeared beside his mouth. "Better than you forgetting those verses. You should look at them one more time. Got your cheat sheet?"

"Right here." Scott patted his breast pocket and his brows pinched together "Oh no—"

"Don't panic, pal; I have it." A tall man with dark hair joined them and clapped Scott on the back. He shifted a sleeping, cherub-lipped baby onto his shoulder and pulled a printed index card from his pocket. "You left it up at Arlo's when we got coffee. Claire grabbed it." He shook his head. "I used to pride myself on being the organizational head of my team, but marry a sharp ER nurse, and . . ." He grinned. "You'll see." He turned to Nick, offering his hand. "Logan Caldwell. You're Leigh's husband, right?"

"Nick," he said, returning the firm handshake. "You're from Sierra Mercy." He shook his head. "I feel like I'm rolling to a call without a street map. Pacific Mercy, Sierra Mercy, Golden Gate . . ."

"So many Mercys," Cody agreed, peering across the wood planking toward a makeshift altar at the edge of the seawall. Its driftwood arch was strung with shells and tinkling glass mobiles and flanked by buckets sunk into the sand and over-flowing with white flowers and sea grasses. An elderly couple, the man's wild white curls moving in the breeze, gestured toward them.

"Uncle Scotty, the Popps are waving at us. It's almost sun-set and I saw the bridesmaids lining up. There's Pastor Mark. I think we're ready to get married." The small ensemble of musi-cians began anew with strains of Vivaldi's *Four Seasons*, cello and violins mingling with tinkling glass and calls of gulls.

Scott glanced down at the card and started to walk, read-ing aloud. "'. . . always protects, always trusts, always hopes, always perseveres. Love never fails.'"

Always perseveres. Nick smiled.

Logan cupped his palm protectively against the baby's

head. "We'd better get to our seats. I want to be sure Hope is settled. Erin insisted we bring her, but if she fusses . . ." His smile was conspiratorial. "I'm blaming it on the Chihuahua. You back me up. Who's going to argue with a cop?"

"Deal."

They sat behind the groom's grandfather, his dog, and Erin's grandmother and mother, on wooden chairs wrapped in white fabric that seated what was likely half of the city's fire department and most of the staff in the Pacific Mercy ER. Probably a few police officers, too. Nick glanced up the cliff at the small building that overlooked the beach wedding, Arlo's Bait & Moor. He shook his head; he'd never understand how that incredible wedding cake came out of a bait shop, but he agreed that Annie Popp served the best coffee he'd ever tasted. And even if he hadn't learned who was who yet, put names to the faces, he absolutely understood how these friends—teammates—could come to feel like a family. They worked side by side in scenarios of unbelievable stress, matters of life and death; they struggled together, fought against each other, laughed, cried, prayed . . . loved, lost.

He'd seen all of that this last year. Felt everything from grief and despair to the most amazing . . . He turned to look as the music swelled and the matron of honor and bridesmaids, dressed in gowns he'd been told were "sea-foam green," walked slowly forward on a wooden walkway laid over the sand.

The bride's sister came first, then Sandy from Pacific Mercy, and—Nick's heart wedged toward his throat as Leigh's eyes met his. Her shiny hair was lifted high off her neck, shoulders bare, cheeks flushed. She carried her bouquet—shells, lavender sea fans, beach grasses—considerably lower than all the other bridesmaids. She'd practiced it in the mirror all morning, shifting the bouquet over the front of her gown, up, down, sideways, then turned to Nick. "Can you tell how tight this waist is? There's no way to let it out. Truth now: do I look fat?"

"You look gorgeous," he'd said, wrapping his arms around her from behind and smiling into the mirror. "More beautiful than any woman I've ever seen. And like you're carrying our child."

My family. His heart crowded his chest.

"There's Mommy," Logan whispered against his daughter's tiny ear as Claire moved into step behind Leigh. He watched for a moment, then turned toward Nick, his blue eyes saying it all. Though Cody, the best man, had unwittingly given it voice: *"So many mercies."* He'd meant hospitals of course—Sierra, Pacific, Golden Gate—but Nick and Logan knew better. And now Scott McKenna would too.

Mercy and grace and a love that endures. God promised it all, and they were blessed to receive it in their marriages to these three amazing women.

The wedding march began and the stunning redhead appeared, gliding forward on her proud father's arm and smiling like it was the first day of a glorious forever.

Nick's thoughts were already on the reception: he wanted his family back in his arms.

+++

Leigh clutched Erin's hand and laughed again. "I can't believe your grandmother caught your bouquet. She leaped like an L.A. Laker—isn't Iris seventy-seven?"

"Seventy-eight now." The bride smiled, her gaze on the couple in the distance, her grandmother and Scott's grandfather holding the Chihuahua—now wearing Erin's lace garter around his neck. "And after that double score, I'd say we'll be seeing another McKenna wedding before too long."

Leigh shook her head and sighed, then turned to Erin and Claire. "It's something, isn't it? How we've all come to feel like family?"

Claire brushed her lips against her daughter's hair. "And become that, literally. I never dreamed that first day I walked into Sierra Mercy ER and butted heads with 'Dr. McSnarly' that I'd be here today as his wife—and a bridesmaid for his charge nurse." She smiled at Erin. "Back then you were far more comfortable in boxing gloves."

Leigh nodded. "I was always a little nervous she'd show up at Pacific Mercy wearing them. I think Scott was too, not that he'd have admitted it." She gazed to where their husbands stood talking, fast becoming tall silhouettes in a dusk dotted with white paper lanterns. "The two of you were pretty stubborn." She heard Erin laugh and turned to see the bride's green eyes light with amusement.

"You're talking stubborn, Dr. Stathos? I seem to remember screening your calls in the ER: Yes to any contact from the horse stables. No to all messages from a very determined police officer in San Francisco. And now . . ." She stepped close and touched her palm gently to the rounded front of Leigh's gown. "Now look at you. Look how beautiful, happy—" she grinned—"and how great it's turned out for all of us. A miracle, considering the disasters we've dealt with these past couple of years."

"Explosion, pesticide spill, the shooting at Golden Gate. So much tragedy and chaos. You're right; it could have done the same thing to all of our lives." Claire glanced toward the tables. "We've seen God's blessings. All of us."

Leigh smiled, warmth filling her heart as she caught sight of Nick walking toward them. "And here comes one of mine, right now."

"Amen." Erin chuckled. "I hope that gorgeous example of San Francisco's finest can sing. Karaoke starts after dinner. I'm telling you right now, the little dog's a ringer."

+++

Easter fell the weekend after the wedding and Nick made good on his promise to have the yard spruced in time for their dinner guests, which included Cha Cha. The irascible cockatiel was already settled in his cage under a shade tree. Antoinette said he would pull his feathers out if they left him at home and that she frankly didn't know who was more trying these days, Harry or the bird. But she loved them both and intended to keep on doing that—

"Forever and ever!" Cha Cha shrilled, making Leigh laugh as she walked down the back steps from the house and into the yard.

"The kitchen smells like heaven. You're a miracle worker."

"I aim to please," Nick said, smiling at the sight of her in blue jeans tucked into barn boots with an old scrub top she'd discovered worked well as maternity stable wear. She'd let her hair grow longer and it trailed past her shoulders, making her look like an amazing combination of schoolgirl and mother-to-be. His throat tightened. "How's my pal Frisco?"

"Fat." She wrinkled her nose, then spread her palms over her stomach as she walked closer. "And he can't blame it on omelets or little . . . Jacob? Ethan?"

He laughed and kissed the top of her head as she hugged him. "Keep trying."

"Anyway," Leigh continued, "I've found someone to exercise him now that I'm out until September. But to tell you the truth, I think my show horse is completely content being petted and brushed and fussed over by dozens of therapy kids. Tag's spoiled him for the blue ribbon circuit. By the way, you and I are both on Patrice's volunteer schedule for next weekend. I signed you up for donkey golf." She chuckled against his shirtfront. "Don't worry; I'll ask two of the kids from church to caddy for you."

Leigh stepped away, gazing across the small yard to survey his handiwork. "It looks great. I'm so glad you got the opening in the hedge finished in time. And with the McNealys' table added, we should have plenty of seating.

"Let's see . . ." She dipped her finger toward the chairs, reciting the guests aloud: "The McNealys. His nurse will be bringing him in a wheelchair for the visit, so we'll need extra room. Kristi and her boyfriend. Abby, Finn in his high chair with plenty of space around him—he's a wild man these days. The Owens and Maria, Caro, and—" She turned to Nick. "Oh, I forgot to tell you that I invited Caro's roommate. She's not going home for Easter after all. They want to study together for midterms. I said no problem, we have plenty of room."

"And I added Edwin and Althea Bower. She made a pecan pie. And a Waldorf salad." Nick smiled as his wife's brows scrunched with confusion. "Edwin and his grandmother. My littlest basketball star. You remember. I should warn you, he told me yesterday he planned to be 'hungry enough to eat a horse.'"

Leigh peered at him, her expression incredulous. "Anybody else, Mr. Stathos?"

He shrugged and gave her a sheepish grin. "Just Oly. The vendor down on Divisadero. And he's bringing—"

"Let me guess: flowers." She smiled slowly. "Buy a table, and they will come."

"Yes," he said, slipping his arms around her. "Isn't it great?"

Leigh was quiet for a moment and the look in her eyes melted his heart.

"It is," she said, reaching up to rest her hand along his jaw. "It's better than anything I could have imagined. Our table. You . . . our baby. I'm so happy, Nick."

He bent low and she slid her arms around his neck, standing on tiptoe and lifting her face so that he could kiss her, slow and sweet and—

"Oh, wait!" She twisted in his arms to look back at the yard. "I forgot. Did she bring it? Is it here?"

"What?" he asked, feigning innocence. Then bit back a smile.

"Our lemon tree," she said, peering around the yard.

Nick took her hand and led her to the other side of the porch. He watched her smile, her eyes shiny with tears.

"It's blooming." She pressed her hand to her chest. "I can smell the blossoms from here. And it's covered in new leaves and—" she turned to him, raising her brows—"little Easter eggs?"

"Harry's idea." Nick shook his head. "He wanted to string plastic leis from the Tonga Room on it, but Antoinette steered him toward these."

Leigh sighed. "I was so sure you sneaked the lemon tree away to rescue it. And you thought I threw it out. But Caro gave it to Antoinette."

Nick nodded. "And she wasn't about to let us see it until she was good and ready. She walked through the hedge about an hour ago, pulling it in a gardening wagon. Told me she knew all along that it would bloom, even back when it looked half-dead. She wagged her finger and said, 'You can't give up on things, Nicky. God doesn't. You have to have faith.'"

Leigh leaned against him, resting her head against his chest. "I believe that now. About faith. Because . . . that's exactly where forever starts."

Nick couldn't agree more. He wrapped his arms around her, his palm cradling the soft swell that was his growing son. His family in his arms. A blessing he'd prayed for all his life.

Thank you, Lord. I'm home.

ABOUT THE AUTHOR

Candace Calvert is a former ER nurse who believes love, laughter, and faith are the best medicines. A multipublished author of humorous mysteries, she invites readers to "scrub in" on the dramatic, pulse-pounding world of emergency medicine via her new Mercy Hospital series. Wife, mother, and very proud grandmother, Candace makes her home in northern California. Visit her Web site at www.candacecalvert.com.

BOOK DISCUSSION GUIDE

Use these questions for individual reflection or for discussion within your book club or small group.

Note: Book clubs that choose to read *Code Triage* and would like me to "attend" your get-together, please e-mail me at Candace@candacecalvert.com. I'll try to arrange a speakerphone conversation to join your discussion.

1. In the opening scene of *Code Triage*, off-duty police officer Nick Stathos faces danger to aid a young mother at risk of losing her children. He stubbornly insists, "I don't give up. Ever." What does this scene say about his character? his background? values? Considering those things, were you surprised to learn that Nick's marriage was ending because of his infidelity? Discuss.

2. The reader first meets ER physician Leigh Stathos as she's attempting to pump the stomach of an overdose patient, a woman despondent over her husband's affair. Leigh's manner is firm, professional, and emotionally neutral. How does this differ from her "gut-level" internal reaction to the woman's situation? What does that—and

Leigh's eagerness to complete the divorce and move away from San Francisco—tell you about her character? Did you see a conflict in the personalities of Nick and Leigh Stathos?

3. What was your initial reaction to Samantha Gordon? Were the scenes from the point of view of "the other woman" effective for you as a reader? Why do you think they were included?

4. Secondary characters played significant roles in *Code Triage*. Who is your favorite? Cappy Thomas? Harry or Antoinette McNealy? Maria? Caroline? What did that character add to the story?

5. What impact did her sister's impending divorce have on Caroline? Do you think it's true that there is a "ripple effect" of divorce? How so?

6. How did the unlikely friendship of Tag and Frisco add to the story? Did you see a parallel between Leigh's need to give her horse "a cushion of space" (an empty stall beside his) and her own approach to relationships? Discuss.

7. Leigh knew she was pregnant when she and Nick separated, but she never told him. If she had, do you think it would it have changed things? If so, how?

8. In the scene where they prepare an anniversary dinner for the McNealys, former chef Nick tells Leigh that recipes are built around a "central ingredient." His statement reminds Leigh of their Christian counselor's advice regarding a successful marriage: to have God at its center. What importance do you place on shared faith in a

marriage? Have you seen wounded relationships heal as a result of "putting God at the center"?

9. After the ER shift that included a hospital shooting, Leigh tells Riley that she intends to go someplace where "even God can't track me down." Golden Gate Stables has become her comfort and refuge when troubles crowd in. Do you have a place like that? Do you feel God's presence there?

10. A nurse struggling with her ability to set aside personal feelings to care for Kurt Denton, the man who killed a coworker, asks chaplain Riley Hale, "How do I do this?" Riley's answer is "One step at a time." How does that answer relate to Riley's own struggle as a victim of crime? What do you imagine the future holds for this character?

11. A lemon tree and a dining room table become important motifs in the story. In your opinion, what the does the tree symbolize? Can you compare the significance of a table in Nick's life to the significance in Leigh's? How important was a family table in your childhood? Is that different now?

12. When abused orphan Maria finally breaks her silence, she tells Leigh that "we don't have to be afraid," because God will "always be here . . . forever and ever." Why did that statement affect Leigh so deeply?

13. How did you feel about Sam Gordon at the story's end? Are you hopeful for her future? Why or why not?

14. The epilogue brings together characters from all three Mercy Hospital books, reunited at a beach wedding. Did

that make for a satisfying ending? Were there any questions that you felt were left unanswered at the story's end? Discuss.

Thank you for reading *Code Triage*. Send me a note; I'd love to hear from you.

Warmly,
Candace Calvert

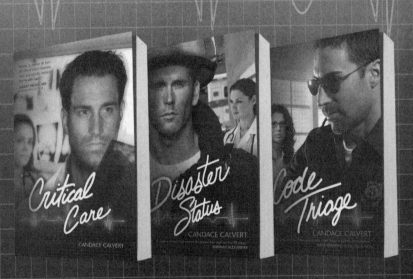